WELCOM

TIME OF

The Warhammer world i
of brave heroes, and th
enemies. Now for the
mythical events have been brought to the
range of books. Divided into a series of trilogies, each
brings you hitherto untold details of the lives and
times of the most legendary of all Warhammer heroes
and villains. Combined together, they will reveal
some of the hidden connections that underpin the
history of the Warhammer world.

THE BLACK PLAGUE

The tale of an Empire divided, its heroic defenders
and the enemies who endeavour to destroy it with
the deadliest plague ever loosed upon the world of
man. This series begins with *Dead Winter* and *Blighted
Empire* and culminates in *Wolf of Sigmar*.

THE WAR OF VENGEANCE

The ancient races of elf and dwarf clash in a devastating
war that will decide not only their fates, but that of the
entire Old World. The first novel in this series is *The
Great Betrayal*, and is followed by *Master of Dragons*.

BLOOD OF NAGASH

The first vampires, tainted children of Nagash, spread
across the world and plot to gain power over the kingdoms of men. This series starts in *Neferata*, and carries
on with *Master of Death*.

Keep up to date with the latest information from the
Time of Legends at *www.blacklibrary.com*

· THE LEGEND OF SIGMAR ·
Graham McNeill

Available as an omnibus edition, containing the novels
Heldenhammer, Empire and *God King*

· THE SUNDERING ·
Gav Thorpe

Available as an omnibus edition, containing the novels *Malekith,
Shadow King* and *Caledor* and the novella *The Bloody-Handed*

· THE RISE OF NAGASH ·
Mike Lee

Available as an omnibus edition, containing the novels *Nagash
the Sorcerer, Nagash the Unbroken* and *Nagash Immortal*

· THE BLACK PLAGUE ·
C L Werner

Book 1 – DEAD WINTER
Book 2 – BLIGHTED EMPIRE
Book 3 – WOLF OF SIGMAR

· THE WAR OF VENGEANCE ·
Nick Kyme and Chris Wraight

Book 1 – THE GREAT BETRAYAL
Book 2 – MASTER OF DRAGONS
Book 3 – ELFDOOM (2014)

· THE BLOOD OF NAGASH ·
Josh Reynolds

Book 1 – NEFERATA
Book 2 – MASTER OF DEATH
Book 3 – BLOOD DRAGON (2014)

AGE OF LEGEND
Edited by Christian Dunn
A Time of Legends short story anthology

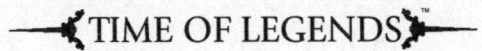

TIME OF LEGENDS

Book Three of the Black Plague

WOLF OF SIGMAR

The Black Plague

C L Werner

BLACK LIBRARY

For Robert – Something to read in hopefully much nicer surroundings than a foxhole or PX

A BLACK LIBRARY PUBLICATION

First published in Great Britain in 2014 by
Black Library,
Games Workshop Ltd.,
Willow Road, Nottingham,
NG7 2WS, UK

10 9 8 7 6 5 4 3 2 1

Cover illustration by Fares Maese.
Map by Nuala Kennedy.

© Games Workshop Limited 2014. All rights reserved.

Black Library, the Black Library logo, Warhammer, the Warhammer logo, Time of Legends, the Time of Legends logo, Games Workshop, the Games Workshop logo and all associated brands, names, characters, illustrations and images from the Warhammer universe are either ®, ™ and/or © Games Workshop Ltd 2000-2014, variably registered in the UK and other countries around the world. All rights reserved.

A CIP record for this book is available from the British Library.

UK ISBN: 978 1 84970 578 3
US ISBN: 978 1 84970 579 0

No part of this publication may be reproduced, stored in a retrieval system, or transmitted in any form or by any means, electronic, mechanical, photocopying, recording or otherwise, without the prior permission of the publishers.

This is a work of fiction. All the characters and events portrayed in this book are fictional, and any resemblance to real people or incidents is purely coincidental.

See Black Library on the internet at
www.blacklibrary.com

Find out more about Games Workshop
and the world of Warhammer at
www.games-workshop.com

Printed and bound by CPI Group (UK) Ltd, Croydon, CR0 4YY

It is an age of legend.

It is a dark age, a bloody age, an age of unspeakable pacts and powerful magic. It is an age of war and of death, and of apocalyptic terror. But amidst all of the flames and fury it is a time, too, of mighty heroes, of bold deeds and great courage...

At the heart of the Old World lies Sigmar's Empire. Over a thousand years after the god-king's passing, it is a land in turmoil. The corrupt and incompetent Emperor, Boris Goldgather, has bled the common folk of the Empire to keep himself in comfort, leaving his people to starve. The border forts, the Empire's first line of defence against the many foes that threaten Sigmar's lands, lie unmanned and the Imperial armies struggle to repel the barbarous northmen, savage greenskins and monstrous beastmen that rampage through the provinces.

None know that the gravest threat to the realm lies not in the darkness of the forests or the mountain passes, but beneath the feet of men. The sinister, ratlike skaven, long believed to be a myth, plot to destroy the Empire. Untold armies lurk in dank caverns deep below the earth, unnumbered skaven from the warrior clans ready to spread across the lands of men and wipe them out. And in the deepest vaults, the demented plague priests of Clan Pestilens brew a noxious contagion that will bring the men of the Empire to their knees.

The Black Plague.

GEOGRAPHICAL MAP OF THE EMPIRE

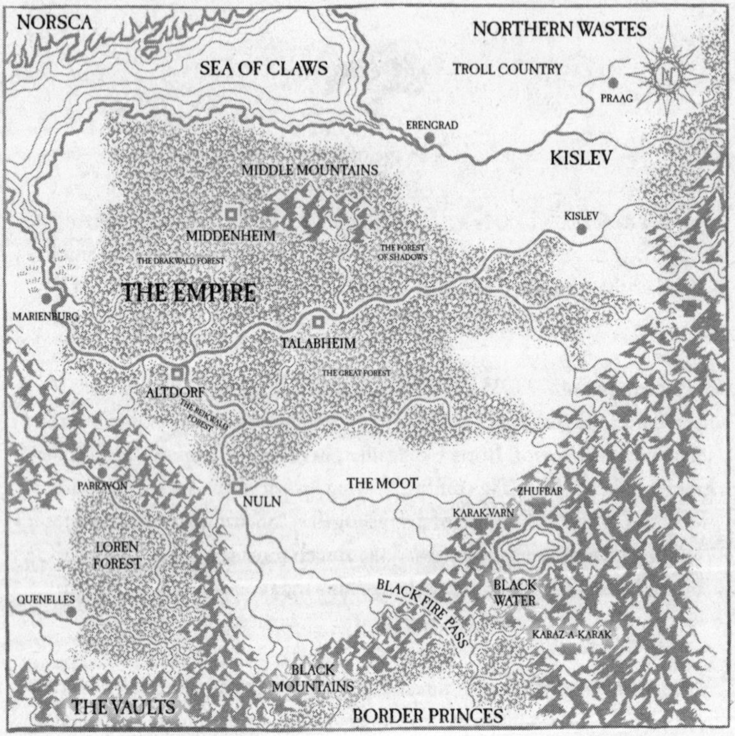

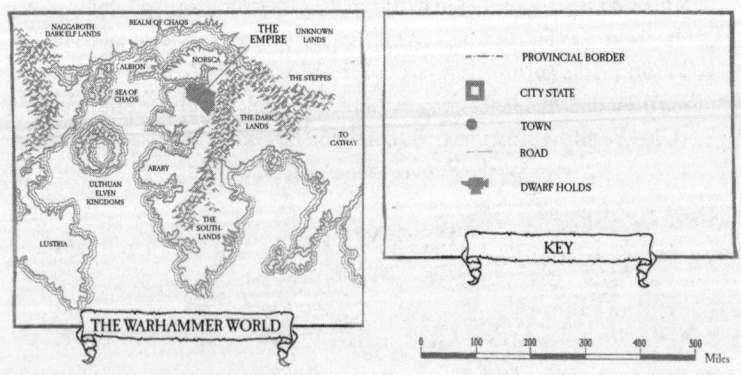

NORSCA

SEA OF CLAWS

NORTHERN WASTES

TROLL COUNTRY

PRAAG

ERENGRAD

MIDDLE MOUNTAINS

KISLEV

KISLEV

MIDDENHEIM

THE FOREST OF SHADOWS

THE DRAKWALD FOREST

THE EMPIRE

MARIENBURG

TALABHEIM

THE GREAT FOREST

ALTDORF

THE REIKWALD FOREST

ZHUFBAR

PARRAVON

NULN

THE MOOT

KARAK-VARN

LOREN FOREST

BLACK FIRE PASS

BLACK WATER

QUENELLES

KARAZ-A-KARAK

BLACK MOUNTAINS

THE VAULTS

BORDER PRINCES

THE WARHAMMER WORLD

NAGGAROTH DARK ELF LANDS

REALM OF CHAOS

THE EMPIRE

UNKNOWN LANDS

ALBION

NORSCA

THE STEPPES

SEA OF CHAOS

THE DARK LANDS

TO CATHAY

ARABY

ULTHUAN ELVEN KINGDOMS

THE SOUTH LANDS

LUSTRIA

	PROVINCIAL BORDER
	CITY STATE
	TOWN
	ROAD
	DWARF HOLDS

KEY

0   100   200   300   400   500
Miles

⤙ PREFACE ⤚

In this third and final volume of *A Folkloric History of the Black Plague and the Wolf of Sigmar*, I have striven to retain the same attitude of credulity that has been characteristic of previous volumes. It is difficult for the learned reader in this more enlightened age to imagine the Empire as it was in the early 1100s. Myth and superstition were the governing forces of men in the darker days of the Black Plague. The disease had struck particularly hard among the cultured and the lettered; the clergy and physicians with the knowledge to combat the contagion frequently became its victims due to their heightened exposure to it. Under such conditions, it was the common and unlettered who survived in disproportionate numbers. In many cases, feeling that religion and the gods had failed them, these simple people reverted to traditional legends to explain the catastrophe afflicting their land. When a traveller told them that distant Pfeildorf had been overrun by verminous underfolk, he was well and sincerely believed.

The previous volume of this work recounted the horrific rise of the necromancer Vanhal, an all too historic monster whose existence is ratified in the records of both the Sigmarite and Morrite temples as well as the *Doomsday Canticle* kept in the Waldenhof Museum. From his tragic fall from serving Morr as one of his priests, Vanhal embraced the black arts to become the most fearsome necromancer of his age. With an army of the undead, he ravaged the county of Sylvania, driving the Voivode Malbork von Drak into the southern areas of that region. Seeking to emulate Vanhal, the perverse Mordheim nobleman Baron Lothar von Diehl likewise became a follower of the profane rites of necromancy, eventually accepting service with Vanhal as his apprentice. Together these human fiends raised the cursed tower of Vanhaldenschlosse through magics both eldritch and obscene, creating a sorcerous fortress whose ruins even to this day are shunned and considered haunted.

Here established history gives way to mythic fancy as Vanhal and von Diehl find themselves beset by the skaven armies of Seerlord Skrittar and Bonelord Nekrot. In contest are the poisonous rocks that have rained down upon Sylvania in the Starfall. Useful to the necromancers in their unspeakable sorceries, the rocks are held sacred by the chittering ratmen. A war between the shambling undead and the skittering skaven rages about Vanhaldenschlosse, ending with the destruction of Skrittar and the retreat of Nekrot.

Adolf Kreyssig, the ruthless commander of the Kaiserjaeger, the secret police of Emperor Boris, is appointed Protector of the Empire when Boris flees plague-ridden Altdorf for the seclusion of Schloss Hohenbach. With the help of the witch Baroness Kirstina von den Linden, Kreyssig secures his power, removing from the Imperial council those who oppose his rule. Kreyssig gains control over Lector Stefan Schoppe by capturing his daughter and has him appointed Grand Theogonist.

Kreyssig's power, however, comes under attack when his skaven allies prove duplicitous, seeking to weaken the city by playing different factions against one another. Realising their peril, Kreyssig musters the city's forces and leads the effort to drive the skaven back when the hordes of Warplord Sythar Doom erupt from beneath the streets. The glory of defeating the ratmen, however, has to be shared with Baroness von den Linden and Stefan, who had taken the dwarfish name Gazulgrund as Grand Theogonist. Worried about the witch's ambitions, Kreyssig colludes with Gazulgrund to eliminate her, treacherously sealing her alive in a chamber filled with enraged bees – one of the most eccentric murders attributed to the Imperial palace.

Emperor Boris, fleeing to escape the Black Plague, makes Schloss Hohenbach outside Carroburg his refuge. Surrounding himself with all the noble leaders of the Empire, Boris intends to sit out the plague in decadent opulence. His intentions are thwarted, however, when the skaven strike. Plague monks visit disease and destruction upon Carroburg, then turn their attentions to the castle where Boris has hidden himself. The Emperor is the final victim of the disease unleashed by the ratmen. Only Princess Erna of Middenheim and the Emperor's physician, Doktor Moschner, survive.

Although spared the first attacks of the plague in 1111, seven years later Middenheim finds itself experiencing the slow creep of the disease into its midst. The dwarf community deep inside the mountain experiences attacks by the ratmen and is compelled to accept the offer of aid from their human neighbours. Prince Mandred, whose heroic exploits include the rescue of Lady Mirella and Arch-Lector Hartwich from beastmen, is particularly zealous in his offer to help Kurgaz Smallhammer against the skaven, having lost his lover Sofia to the blades of the ratkin.

Warmonger Vecteek, however, is playing a treacherous game of deceit, intending to lure the human armies into the tunnels within the mountain while he conquers the city on top of it. He employs the brutal Warlord Vrrmik to bait his trap, while the plagues of Poxmaster Puskab Foulfur weaken the city. He hasn't planned on the treachery of his minions, however. When Vecteek attacks Middenheim, he finds far less of the population stricken by the plague than Puskab had promised. Down below, Vrrmik withdraws his warriors early enough that Mandred is able to lead his army back up to the surface and relieve his embattled father Graf Gunthar.

Though Gunthar and Mandred are able to destroy Vecteek and vanquish the skaven army, their victory turns bitter when Gunthar is shot down by Deathmaster Silke. Desperate to save his dying father, Mandred takes Gunthar to the Temple of Ulric to beg his god for divine aid. Silke strikes again while the prince is in the temple, intending to kill both son and father. In the ensuing struggle, Mandred and Silke pitch into the Eternal Flame of Ulric. While the skaven disintegrates into ash, Mandred emerges from the flame completely healed of his wounds. The miracle amazes those watching and Arch-Lector Hartwich proclaims Mandred 'the Wolf of Sigmar', a man who is blessed by the gods.

With his father's death, Prince Mandred becomes Graf Mandred. Now lord of his realm, he musters his army. He is determined to scourge the land of the skaven infesting it. And in so doing he earns the title Mandred Skavenslayer.

Delving into these curious admixtures of myth and

history, one almost regrets that this heroic character has become more commonly known as 'Mandred Ratcatcher' in modern historical texts.

– Reikhard Mattiasson,
A Folkloric History of the Black Plague and the Wolf of Sigmar Vol. III
Altdorf Press, Nachexen 2514
Suppressed by order of Lord Thaddeus Gamow, Jahrdrung 2514

⫷ PROLOGUE ⫸

Skavenblight
Geheimnisnacht, 1120

Reeking of decay and corruption, Poxmaster Puskab Foul-fur climbed the steps of the raised dais, his scabby hand clenched about the gnarled wooden staff he bore. The plaguelord's tattered robes befouled the ancient stone steps, leaving behind a glistening trail like the slime of a slug. As he made his ascent, the ratman lifted his rotten snout and drew in the perfidious atmosphere of what had been the Grand Observatory of the grey seers.

A liquid, glottal chuckle shook the skaven as he reflected upon how far the once-mighty grey seers had fallen. Their order was archaic, a relic that had endured past its time. Soon it would be swept away into the gutter, cast off into an oblivion that was long overdue. As the plague monks had supplanted the atavistic horned prophets in the halls of the Shattered Tower, so they would soon expunge them from all Skavenblight. From all skavendom!

Puskab settled his scrawny body into the throne of bone

and sinew that rested atop the dais. Briefly he gazed up at the great gaping hole in the wall of the chamber, the place where the grey seers had housed their villainous star-eye. A creation of the equally abhorrent heretics of Clan Skryre, the construction of warpstone lenses and crystal plates, bronze pipes and copper tubes, had allowed the Seerlords to gaze upon the stars themselves. In their heresy, the grey seers had believed they could sniff portents and omens from the alignment of stars, as though the Horned One would consign His wisdom to such a frivolous pursuit.

The Poxmaster stroked the long tuft of fur sprouting from the side of his chin, a lone wisp of white fur on his otherwise wrinkled and furless face. He took a vain pride in that sickly patch of fur. It resembled nothing so much as some mouldy growth, and it exuded a wondrously wretched smell. Many among the acolytes of Clan Pestilens took it as a mark of the Horned One's favour, a divine reward for the conquest Puskab had made possible. Fabricator of the plague, engineer of the decimation of the man-things, destroyer of their surface realm!

Puskab bruxed his fangs as he pondered his accomplishments. From a minor plague priest he had risen to assume a seat on the Council of Thirteen, to join the insidious ranks of the Grey Lords. He had risen to become second only to Arch-Plaguelord Nurglitch within the hierarchy of Clan Pestilens.

The Poxmaster's beady eyes became embers of hate as he reflected upon his position and how his own authority had been usurped. His great rival had always been Vrask Bilebroth. For a time, Puskab had been certain in his supremacy, sure that the merest twitch of his whisker would be enough to destroy his rival. But Vrask had proven too cunning to eliminate. He'd sought protection from Seerlord

Skrittar, joining the Seerlord's mysterious expedition into the east. Skrittar had perished in that journey, betrayed by Vrask. Through his poisoned counsel, Vrask claimed to have arranged the death of the Seerlord. More, he had stolen the great treasure that had caused Skrittar to stir from the Shattered Tower: enough warpstone to bribe the Horned One Himself! Vrask had even brought the once-mighty Clan Fester with him as a gift for Nurglitch. Their bodies wracked with contagion, Fester had sworn allegiance to the plague monks in a desperate bid for survival. Clan Fester had joined the circle of thrall clans known as the Pestilent Brotherhood, their autonomy crushed between the claws of the Arch-Plaguelord.

Always keen to scent an opportunity, Nurglitch had installed Vrask on the Council, placing him in the seat vacated by Warlord Manglrr Baneburrow of Fester. Vrask had been given honours and power equal to those enjoyed by Puskab. It was a manoeuvre to ensure Nurglitch's own position, once again raising the two enemies to equal standing, setting them against each other and ensuring that each was too busy protecting the position they already possessed to allow them time to consider loftier ambitions. Nurglitch was already a hoary old monster, but with the cocktail of elixirs and arcane rituals he employed, he might endure for another century and more before age and infirmity claimed him. He was taking pains to protect against any early diminishment.

The clamour of slaves breaking apart the heretical warp-scope of Clan Skryre brought Puskab's attention back to the great hall before him. Packs of emaciated skaven, their fur mangy with disease, laboured with sledgehammers to break apart the mammoth construction. Green-robed plague monks scrabbled at the floor with their claws, pulling up the intricate mosaic that had depicted the star charts and constellations of the grey seers' astrology. Other plague monks assaulted the walls, tearing down elaborate frescoes and murals. Censer bearers circled the hall, the toxic fumes emanating from the baskets of their staves billowing across the room, blotting out the lingering stink of a millennium's incense. Great banners flayed from the hides of especially diseased skaven hung from poles scattered about the chamber, each daubed with the insignia of the fly-scratch and adorned with the formulae for the most potent plagues.

Puskab caught the distinctive smell of one plague banner, the twisted wreck of his tail twitching happily as the scent blazed through his memories. It was the hide of Wormlord Blight Tenscratch, despot of Clan Verms, the Grey Lord Puskab had defeated in single combat to secure his position on the Council. But that was only part of his achievements. Scratched into the preserved hide was his true power: the formula for the Black Plague, the Horned One's gift to His favoured son!

The Poxmaster nodded his antlered head. Yes, it was his destiny to lead Clan Pestilens to complete domination of skavendom, to usher in a new age of glory and decay! He would fulfil the role the Horned One had given him, despite the obstructions of his fellow skaven and even the short-sighted interference of Arch-Plaguelord Nurglitch.

Nurglitch did well to fear his Poxmaster! From the moment when he had colluded with Warlord Vrrmik of Mors to depose and destroy Warmonger Vecteek of Rictus, Puskab had been laying the foundation for his master's downfall. Vrrmik wasn't more powerful than Vecteek, but he was equally cunning. He had stirred the imaginations of the other clans, driving them into campaigns not merely of conquest but also occupation of the surface world. Each warlord was spending the strength of his clan to secure his own kingdom on the surface, vying with the scattered man-things for control of their land. It was such a vast expenditure of resources that it could only be likened to a rich warpstone strike and the resultant rush of ratmen to stake their claim.

Through it all, Clan Pestilens would keep to the shadows, conserving its own power. Let the warlords squabble over the ruins of the man-things, the plague monks would be secure in their service to the Horned One. If the rush to the surface was allowed to take its natural course, the plague monks would be able to overwhelm a skavendom engaged in hundreds of petty wars. That would secure Nurglitch's legacy.

Puskab would never allow it to go so far, however. When he judged the moment to be right, he would use Vrrmik to steer the warlord clans against Nurglitch's acolytes and Vrask's minions. The other skaven would rally to the cause, refighting the civil war in the belief that they were throwing off the shackles of domination.

In truth, they would be casting their own chains. Nurglitch's pride and arrogance blinded him to the true pinnacle of power. It wasn't the ratman who called himself Supreme Grand Warlord, the skaven who was first among equals on the Council. No, the true power was with the faceless, unknown figure that stood behind the thrones, who ruled the rulers from the shadows. True power did not announce itself with thunder and steel. True power was the whispered threat, the unspoken fear that could set even the mightiest empire trembling.

Puskab Foulfur would have such power.

It was his destiny.

⭰ CHAPTER I ⭲

Carroburg, 1119

The ratman's sharp fangs snapped about the steel bill of the helmet, worrying at the metal as the creature thrashed about in a paroxysm of viciousness. Froth mixed with the putrid black blood of the skaven streamed from the monster's mouth. The filthy drool dripped into the warrior's face, burning against his cheeks and nose, discolouring his beard. The sick stink of the vermin's spittle threatened to choke the man. Only a determination born of the mightiest resolve kept him from reeling, from disengaging with the loathsome brute.

Instead of recoiling in disgust, the armoured warrior ripped the dagger from his belt and brought its edge sawing against the ratman's neck. The creature squealed and flailed, skewering itself still deeper on the sword thrust into its gut. The beast's violence threatened to spill both fighters from the back of the stomping warhorse. The man pressed his legs tighter against the barrel of his steed, refusing to loose his hold on either dagger or sword.

Animalistic panic shone in the eyes of the skaven as the dagger sawed through the rotten flaps of its leather helm and into the matted fur beneath. The man it had attacked glared back at it, raw hatred blazing in his gaze. Neither pity nor mercy stayed him as his blade chewed into the vermin's throat and sent a spray of blood jetting from its arteries. As strength drained from the beast, the armoured warrior tried to fling it to the ground. The creature's fangs clenched tight to his helm, the final death agony causing them to punch through the metal. It took repeated blows from the pommel of his dagger to break the ratman's jaw and dislodge its tenacious grip.

The rider glared down at the quivering carcass strewn across the cobblestones. It was an unseemly thing, but he brought his rearing warhorse around to stamp its hooves against the skaven's skull and splatter its head into gory ruin. One tiny grain of satisfaction in an ocean of hatred.

Other ratmen swarmed around the lone rider, scuttling out from the shattered debris that had once been a great city. They snarled and snapped, squealed and chittered, thrusting at him with jagged spears and crooked swords. Watching their leader being butchered had curbed some of their taste for battle. Their verminous courage hung by the merest thread. The rider scowled at them from beneath the bill of his helm. He didn't want them running.

The warrior straightened in his saddle, waving his sword and sending drops of black blood spattering across the ground. 'I am Mandred von Zelt,' he called out in a bitter tone. 'Graf of Middenheim. Lord of Middenland. Defender of the Eternal Flame.' His eyes narrowed into slivers of rage. 'Scourge of the Skaven,' he declared in a low snarl, baring his teeth at the ring of monsters.

The boldest of the skaven lunged at him, swarming

towards Mandred in a burst of animalistic fury. A spear snapped against his horse's barding, another broke against his pauldron as he leaned down to receive his attackers. The blade of Legbiter, fabled Runefang of the Teutogens, burned with magical brilliance as it sheered through the shoulder of the spear-rat and sawed across the beast's ribs. Mandred was already turning away from the mutilated monster, striking out at a ratman thrusting at him from the other side of his horse. The edge of the runefang raked across the skaven's face, leaving a gory slash where its eyes had been.

Voices rang out above the shrill squeaks and screams of the skaven, hard voices that bellowed jubilantly. 'The graf! It is the graf!' they shouted. 'Rally to Graf Mandred! Strike down the ratkin!'

Mandred dug his spurs into the flanks of his warhorse, urging the beast forwards, charging it full into the pack of ratmen before they could slink back into their burrows and escape. Stamping hooves pulverised rodent bones, flashing steel split verminous flesh. Like some vengeful god of the forsaken north, Mandred pursued his foes, strewing the ruined street with butchered heaps of skaven. As his warriors came charging forwards to join him, to relieve their leader and join him in his battle, a sense of resentment filled his heart. Who were these men to share in his revenge?

Resentment collapsed into shame. Mandred drew back on his steed's reins, allowing the knights and soldiers to pursue the routed skaven through the rubble of Carroburg. He felt guilty as he watched the warriors cut down the ratkin, many of them shouting the cry that had poured fire back into the hearts of a defeated people.

'For the Wolf!' the fighters shouted as they wrought havoc among the monsters. 'For the Wolf of Sigmar!'

A tear slowly crawled through the skaven filth caking

Mandred's face. Who was he to command such loyalty? Who was he to inspire such hope when he had none inside his own heart?

'We nearly lost you in this maze,' a knight declared as he rode up beside Mandred. Beck's face was haggard, drawn with concern for his liege and sovereign. Despite the gore coating his own armour and the leaking wound across his own scalp, the knight reached into his belt and handed a cloth to Mandred that he might wipe his face. 'You must be more careful, your highness.' Beck forced a laugh from his exhausted body. 'I can't protect you if I can't find you.'

Mandred clapped the knight's shoulder in a display of appreciation. His mind retreated to years before, when his assigned protector had been Franz. How often he had delighted in slipping out from under Franz's watchfulness. How often he had obliviously made a mockery of the knight's sense of duty.

Beck smiled at his lord, a new vigour blotting out the weariness of only a moment before. The regard of his leader was a greater tonic than any elixir conjured from an alchemist's cauldron. It didn't matter who Mandred believed himself to be. What mattered was who his people thought him to be.

'See to yourself,' Mandred ordered, handing Beck's cloth back to him. The graf raised an armoured finger to his eye. Beck followed his example, frowning when he found that his eyepatch had been lost somewhere during the battle. A skaven blade had taken that eye, leaving Beck mutilated for life. Just another tiny reminder of how much mankind owed the vermin. Mandred looked away from Beck, looked out across the desolation of Carroburg.

How dare he believe himself special, that his pain was somehow unique. He had lost his father to these monsters, but how many other men had lost entire families to the slinking fiends? His city had been ransacked and devastated by the ratkin, his home defiled. What was that beside the horrors endured by Carroburg, once the jewel of Drakwald, now reduced to a stinking mire of rubble and filth? For almost four years the ratmen had ruled the city, herding captives here to slave in muddy fields and squalid mills for their inhuman masters. Could he, for a moment, even imagine the terrors the people of Carroburg had endured?

'We will drive the ratmen out,' Beck swore, beating his fist against his breastplate to signify the gravity of his vow. 'Most of the streets are already clear. The only real concentration of ratkin left is up in the castle.'

Mandred raised his eyes, staring up at the hill and the sombre battlements of Schloss Hohenbach. The castle had been the final refuge of Emperor Boris in his vain attempt to flee the Black Plague. Boris had sought to escape his doom by hiding in the fortress. Instead the castle had become his tomb. Now the tattered banners of the ratmen fluttered from its walls, the noxious sigils of the vile skaven.

'Kurgaz said the dwarfs have a plan to breech the castle,' Mandred mused as he studied those imposing walls.

Beck frowned and shook his head. 'Their plan would undermine the foundations and send the whole fortress toppling into the river,' he reminded the graf. 'The castle will be an important asset if your highness is to administer this region once the skaven have been driven out.'

It was the old argument again. The Council of Middenheim had been unanimous in their support when Mandred told them of his intention to relieve Carroburg. Their motives, however, had been anything but united. Some could look no farther than political opportunism, seeing in Carroburg's distress an opportunity to claim the whole of the Drakwald as their own. Some, like the Sigmarite Arch-Lector Wolfgang Hartwich and old Ar-Ulric urged the more humanist ambition of freeing those enslaved by the ratmen.

And his part? What was it that moved him to send men into battle? Mandred felt a chill settle around his heart as he stared at the castle and imagined all the men who would be lost taking it back.

'Tell Kurgaz I approve the dwarf plan,' Mandred declared. He fixed Beck with a stony gaze. 'Don't tell anyone except the dwarfs,' he warned. He wasn't in the mood for another debate with the blue-blooded scavengers who could only see profit where others found tragedy.

Beck stared uneasily at his master, making no move to turn his horse about. Slowly, Mandred returned Legbiter to its scabbard. 'Even if I wanted to go looking for another fight, my horse has earned a rest,' he told the knight. Satisfied, Beck bowed his head and rode off down the street towards the fields where the Middenheimers had formed their encampment.

Mandred watched Beck until he vanished around a rubble-strewn corner. Then he lifted his gaze back to the grim mass of Schloss Hohenbach. If what Kurgaz had told him was true, the dwarfs would send the top of the rock sliding into the Reik. It was sobering to think that the dwarfs had such power at their command. But a more important concern gripped the graf's mind. It was the thought of how many lives would be saved by avoiding a siege.

Sending men to die that Carroburg might be liberated had been no easy thing, but at least it was a noble cause. To waste men in a pointless battle was something else. Deep down inside, Mandred wanted to break open Schloss Hohenbach, to cut down the slinking ratmen with his runefang, to hurl their shrieking bodies from the highest tower.

That wasn't war, however. That was nothing more than revenge.

As Graf of Middenheim and Lord of Middenland, he could command his people to do many things, but he wouldn't order them to die for his own revenge.

Skavenblight, 1120

The stink of fear musk released by the clenched glands of a hundred skaven overwhelmed the thousand other smells in the air. It was a scent that spoke louder than fawning words and empty flattery. The tongue of a ratman was duplicitous and born to treachery. It was only in his scent that truth could be found.

Scorned, derided and mocked, the ancient Order of Grey Seers was a waning power in the vicious hierarchy of Skavenblight. The heretical plague monks had seized dominance through a blend of terror and greed. The lesser clans flocked to their diseased, abominable corruption of the Horned Rat's dogma, some hoping to protect themselves from the might of Clan Pestilens, others trying to ingratiate themselves with the plaguelords and share in their vast power. The plague monks had often been openly antagonistic towards the grey seers, but now their sentiments were echoed in the chittering tones of dozens of warrior clans both within and without the noxious Pestilent Brotherhood. It was the way of skaven from time immemorial to sniff out any sign of weakness and pounce on it.

Let them squeak, Seerlord Queekual thought as he marched through the grimy tunnels beneath the streets of Skavenblight. His gleaming eyes prowled the darkness, watching the slinking shapes that cowered in the shadows cast by worm-oil lamps. Let the vermin hiss and howl all they wanted, in their craven hearts they knew better. Their souls still belonged to the Horned Rat – the true Horned Rat! They knew that the only ones who could intercede with their terrible god were the grey seers. For all the lies told by the plaguelords, the teeming hordes of skavendom recognised the truth!

Queekual paused as a yellow-robed slaveherder of Clan Moulder came scurrying towards him. The ratman was grotesquely proportioned, his obesity compelling him to scurry sidewise in a shuffling fashion. A string of dirty goblins, their necks shackled together, came trooping along behind him.

The Seerlord glared at the slaveherder, waiting for the fat creature to bow his head in obeisance. Instead, the slaveherder's lip peeled back in a gleam of fangs. 'You are Queekual?' he asked, his tone and posture insolent.

'Seerlord Queekual,' the grey prophet corrected him. He raised his paw, spreading his claws in one of the thirteen gestures of destruction. Before the slaveherder could even blink, Queekual's talons blazed with an unholy glow. Malefic energy leapt from the Seerlord's fingers, striking out at the insolent ratman. In the silence that filled the tunnel, the sound of rending flesh was like the roar of ocean waves. For an instant, Queekual held his claw poised, before the glow faded from his fingers. Absently he discarded the windpipe his spell had torn from the slaveherder's body, wiping the ratman's black blood on his cloak. The heavy charcoal-grey robe seemed to drink in the gore, absorbing it with hungry rapacity.

The string of goblins shrieked as the slaveherder fell dead. The wizened green monsters struggled to pull free, to flee down the tunnel. In the shadows, lurking skaven pressed themselves closer to the walls and emptied their glands.

Queekual hefted the horned staff he bore, pointing it at one of the cowering ratmen. When he spoke, his voice was like a blade of ice. 'You will go and announce me to Slave-master Skuzzyl. Tell him to send an escort worthy of a Grey Lord.' Queekual allowed the ratman a heartbeat to overcome his fear and do as he was commanded. When he found the wretch still frozen with fear, the Seerlord stretched forth his hand and again made one of the thirteen gestures.

Wiping the gore from his talons, Queekual fixed his burning gaze on another cowering ratman. 'You will go and announce me to Slavemaster Skuzzyl...'

The skaven didn't need to hear anything more. With a squeak of fright, he leapt into the middle of the passageway and hurried to carry out the Seerlord's command. He made a wide detour as he passed the carcass of the slaveherder and the string of goblins sadistically mutilating it with a jagged piece of stone.

Seerlord Queekual hissed with satisfaction. Let the lies of Pestilens fare where they would, the hordes of skavendom would not forget the power of the grey seers. When the time came, they would flock once more to the true faith of the Horned Rat, would seek the salvation only Seerlord Queekual could deliver to them.

Yes, he thought as he watched a pack of rats scurry out of the darkness and begin feeding on the skaven he had slain. Yes, skavendom would once again grovel before the grey seers. They would grovel, or they would all die!

The network of burrows was dank and slimy even by the loose standards of Skavenblight. The walls were caked in mud and black water dripped from the ceiling. Slime seemed to coat everything, almost growing before an observer's eye. The smells were those of sweat and blood and fear. Not the scent of ratkin, but the stink of lower creatures. The stench of man.

Queekual's escort of grizzled stormvermin marched alongside him in enforced silence. The flesh-shapers of Clan Moulder were careful about their elite guard, taking no chance that they might betray the secrets of their masters. About the neck of each guard-rat a thick iron collar had been locked, but they weren't so extensive as to completely obscure the jagged scar along each throat where the slave-masters had slashed the vocal cords of their minions. The Seerlord's eyes strayed to the twisted, bestial claws of each stormvermin. Even if the brutes were able to understand written Queekish, they'd have a hard time scratching out a message with such disfigured claws.

It mattered little. Let Clan Moulder cling to their petty secrets. It was only by some caprice of the Horned Rat that such a lowly and insignificant clan had weaselled their way onto the Council. What were they but semi-clever animal breeders? They might be capable enough to create larger varieties of rat, encourage certain cosmetically appealing turns of scent and pelt, nurture a particularly delectable sort of taste, but were such activities essential to the teeming hordes of skavendom? Their more audacious creations, the art of their vaunted flesh-moulding, were vicious horrors no ratman could control. The image of an entire mob of Clan Moulder skaven being torn apart by the wolf-rats they were exhibiting for the Grey Lords was vivid in Queekual's mind. So was the savagely impressive performance of their new ogre-rat against one of the deathwalkers of Clan Verms in Skavenblight's Abattoir many years ago. He could still see that enormous brute standing, bloodied and poisoned, perched atop the dismembered carcass of Blight Tenscratch's gigantic scorpion.

Maybe it was a bit hasty to dismiss the peculiar art of Clan Moulder out of paw.

The Seerlord shook aside any thought about Clan Moulder's potential. It was too soon to consider the value of any lesser clan. The exploitation of under-vermin would have to wait until the threat posed by Clan Pestilens had been eliminated. It would be a shame to hatch plans for a new pawn before knowing if they would be survivor or victim of what Queekual intended to unleash.

For now, it was enough that the slave-herders of Moulder could help Queekual further those plans. Even if they didn't know it yet.

The slimy tunnel opened into a great cavern, its floor littered with cages of iron, wicker, wood and bone. More cages swung from the ceiling, suspended by a deranged network of rope and chain. The walls themselves were pockmarked with the barred doorways of cells and pens. The stink of man was even thicker here, the reek of subjugation and slavery. Queekual could hear the miserable creatures whimpering and moaning in their cages, cowering before the supremacy of their masters.

The ratkin of Moulder were everywhere, crawling about the cages, forcing fodder onto their charges, checking them for obvious signs of disease. The dead, the sick and the insane were dragged from their cages and hauled to a great pit yawning in the centre of the floor. Queekual could smell the butcher-stink rising from the hole. He applauded the practicality of Slavemaster Skuzzyl. Feed the useless to the useful. A commendable disposition of resources.

Skuzzyl leered down at Queekual from atop a heap of man-thing bones. He was a grotesquely obese ratman, his pelt greasy with animal fat, his ears notched with a confusion of jewellery, his fingers swollen with a multitude of rings. Even more than his belly's appetite, Skuzzyl had a consuming hunger for shiny trinkets. As a favoured underling of High Vivisectionist Rattnak Vile, Skuzzyl had plenty of opportunity to indulge all his gluttony. Few dared call him 'Packrat of Hellpit' within his hearing.

Queekual stared back at Skuzzyl on his bony perch. The Seerlord let just a slight edge of sorcerous light shine from his narrowed eyes, a reminder to the slaveherder that he wasn't dealing with some ten-flea warlord or fungus-licking adept. The display pierced Skuzzyl's arrogance, the pile of bones teetering as he recoiled from the Horned Rat's prophet.

'We are honour-pleased by your visit, most great-mighty Queekual…' Skuzzyl addressed his guest with a nasal paean of flattery.

A dull rumble throbbed through the cavern as Queekual brought the butt of his staff slamming against the floor. Bottles bounced from the tables, crashing against the floor. Clods of earth crumbled from the walls. Dirt rained down from the roof. Humans in their cages cried out in terror as they felt the ground shudder. Skaven vented their glands as the tremor of Queekual's magic throbbed through their bodies. A small, even petty display, but it spoke louder than any words the Seerlord might have used. He was in no mood for empty praise or mercenary squabbling. He had a purpose, one that would brook no interference.

'Your flea-fondlers have what I want, yes-yes?' Queekual asked, his hiss sharper than the crack of a slavemaster's whip.

Skuzzyl shifted uncomfortably, knocking a skull and a femur from his perch. 'Yes-yes, Most Horrible One!' he tried to reassure the Seerlord, ears laid back in an expression of sincere submission. A flick of his claws sent a pack of skaven scrambling about the barred door to one of the pens. With a viciousness that bordered on panic, the slavers forced a tangle of humans stumbling into the cavern.

Queekual sniffed at the captured humans, watching them with his beady eyes. 'These?' he snarled, his tail twitching with annoyance.

The wattle of flesh that hung from Skuzzyl's lower jaw flopped as he swallowed the horror that rose up in his throat. 'We do best-good!' Skuzzyl protested. 'Not find-catch many man-things clever-learned! Many die-sick from Black Plague! Many die-sick when bring to Skavenblight!'

The Seerlord didn't look at the simpering Skuzzyl, but continued to study the humans the slaveherder's minions had brought. They were a pathetic sight, scrawny and wrinkled, their hides blotched with age, their fur pale and matted. Under ordinary circumstances such slaves would have been chopped up weeks ago and fed to the stronger specimens. But these weren't ordinary circumstances and, if Moulder had done what was expected of them, these weren't ordinary slaves.

'That breeder-thing,' Skuzzyl wheezed, pointing a claw at a wizened old woman who had caught Queekual's eye. 'It think-know way to eat-chew plant-herb. Heal sick-things.' Finding he had the Seerlord's attention, Skuzzyl pointed at another slave, a dusky specimen with a great patch of fur under his nose. 'That one find-catch in sand-land. It think-know way to stab flesh-body. Make pain leave.'

Skuzzyl felt confidence seeping back into him as he noted the keenness with which Queekual responded to his descriptions of the special slaves. The slaveherder snapped his claws and had his minions push one particular slave to the fore. He bruxed his fangs when he saw the scrawny, elderly human stumble and fall at the Seerlord's feet.

'Best of all!' Skuzzyl chortled, his laughter dislodging a few more bones from his perch. 'Just what Seerlord Queekual ask-want! That was-is doktor-thing of old king-man!'

Queekual felt a surge of excitement pulse through him as he heard Skuzzyl's speech. Eagerly, almost half-afraid it was simply the empty boast of a slave-seller, Queekual seized the human's jaw in his paw and forced the man to stare up at him.

'You, doktor? Know-serve Boris-man?' the Seerlord snapped in faltering Reikspiel. 'Say-speak, quick-quick! Lie-die slow-slow!'

The half-starved human cringed beneath Queekual's terrifying scrutiny. 'Yes! Yes! I ministered to the Emperor! I am Doktor Moschner, personal physician to Emperor Boris Hohenbach!'

Queekual's lips pulled back to expose his long fangs. The audacity of the man-thing, trying to intimidate him by evoking the name of his king! Even if the Boris-man were still alive, the temerity of the animal to think Queekual would be impressed.

The slavemasters of Clan Moulder had impressed upon their chattel the consequences of displeasing a skaven. Moaning in horror, Moschner abased himself before Queekual, wrapping his hands about the ratman's foot. 'Please, don't send me back! Don't leave me here! I'll serve you, I'll be loyal! Don't leave me here!'

The Seerlord kicked the begging human away. Slavemasters pounced on Moschner, lashing him back into line with the other slaves.

'They please you, yes-yes?' Skuzzyl asked, one paw preening the fur covering his fat throat. 'Much-hard to find-catch.

Cost much-much!' Queekual glared up at him. How easy it would be to tear that greedy gizzard from the slaveherder's corrupt bulk.

'Do not think to cheat-lie,' Queekual hissed. This time his eyes fairly burned with an unholy green light. 'The Horned Rat listens,' he snarled. 'The Horned Rat knows.'

Skuzzyl grinned down from his perch. 'Does the Horned Rat care?' he challenged. 'Does the Horned Rat love Clan Pestilens more?' The slaveherder chittered with a peal of mockery. 'Why do grey seers need-want healer-things? Why not ask the Horned Rat to protect-save from Black Plague?'

A bolt of green lightning licked out from Queekual's paw. The base of Skuzzyl's perch exploded in a burst of black smoke and bone fragments. The fat ratman squealed as he came crashing down, slamming into the cavern floor and rolling nearly to the lip of the pit. Skuzzyl's minions blinked in shocked horror, both at the violence of Queekual's magic and its startling abruptness.

'The price stays as agreed,' Queekual growled at the prostrate Skuzzyl. He pointed his staff at the slaveherder. 'You ask many questions of the Horned Rat. Would you like-want to see Him and get answers?'

Bobbing his head, crawling along the floor in an expression of grovelling contrition, Skuzzyl made every assurance his conniving mind could conceive to placate the ire of his customer. Seerlord Queekual barely heard him. It was all he could do to keep the amusement from escaping his body in a peal of laughter.

So, Skuzzyl thought the grey seers needed these slaves to help protect themselves from the Black Plague and the heretical sorcery of Clan Pestilens? Such a misconception fitted Queekual's plans more perfectly than he could have hoped. When Skuzzyl inevitably informed the plague monks of what Queekual was doing, it would deceive those vile heretics completely. It was a small thing to suffer the contempt of mouse-sniffers like Puskab and Vrask for a season or three, a minor burden to be carried on the road to victory.

If the plaguelords deceived themselves with Skuzzyl's report they would be oblivious to Queekual's true purpose.

At least until it was too late to be stopped.

—< CHAPTER II >—

Carroburg, 1119

The blast shook the whole of Carroburg, spilling rubble into the desolate streets and sending a black cloud wafting over the city. The wretched survivors of the city, those who had endured plague, starvation and the bestial tyranny of skaven masters, lifted their faces and watched as the forbidding battlements of Schloss Hohenbach collapsed. A ragged cheer rose from the huddled masses of dejected humanity. The castle had become the symbol of their verminous overlords. Watching it crumble into the river was something that spoke to their very souls. Graf Mandred's army had liberated them, but it was only as they watched the castle topple into the river that the people understood.

It was over. The years of cruel captivity and slavery were finished. They were free.

Within the marble sanctuary of what had been Carroburg's Cathedral of Verena, the sound of the cheering Drakwalders almost drowned out the rumbling echoes of the explosion. Trickles of dust fell from the ruined ceiling, a charred beam crashed to the floor in some forlorn corner of the temple. The defiled altar, scarred and chipped by ska- ven axes and hammers, vibrated in sympathy to the tremor emanating from the Otwinsstein, the great rock upon which the Hohenbachs had raised their fortress. The noble lords assembled within the cathedral, the only major building to survive the skaven occupation, and brushed dirt from the long table about which they were assembled.

'That is that then,' grumbled Margraf Udo von Ulmann. The forest baron had been the most vocal critic of demol- ishing the castle. Now he was trying his best to accept Mandred's decision with a show of good grace. He wasn't quite succeeding.

'There is more to ruling a land than seizing a castle,' observed Duke Schneidereit. 'Indeed, it may be better destroying the castle in such remarkable fashion. It dem- onstrates to the Drakwalders that the old order won't be coming back. Impresses on them where the power now resides.'

Mandred listened to his councillors discuss the adminis- tration of Drakwald, how they would partition the province and carve new fiefdoms for Middenland nobles and those of the old Drakwald order who proved sufficiently amenable to the purposes of their new lords. Some of the noblemen argued for outright annexation of Drakwald while others urged the more prudent course of installing a puppet ruler to administer the region for them. Such a gesture would ease any misgivings in neighbouring provinces.

As he listened, Mandred felt his stomach turn. The people of Drakwald had welcomed his army as liberators. Some of the same men he now heard speaking of exploitation and annexation had fought the hardest to free those people.

In the midst of battle they hadn't thought of profit and plunder. They'd been driven by nobler purpose and loftier ambition. How then, when the fight was won, could they bring themselves so low?

'The heart of man is a fickle thing.' The words were spoken almost at Mandred's shoulder. He looked away from the callous debate of his nobles, attending to the priest seated beside him. Arch-Lector Wolfgang Hartwich still affected the simple monk's robe he had worn when he'd arrived in Middenheim disguised as the erudite Brother Richter. The only change to his raiment was the large silver hammer that hung about his neck on a jewelled chain of jade and gold.

The Sigmarite shook his head sadly as he continued the thought. 'In turmoil, men seek only brotherhood, a comrade to share their struggle. In peace, men lust after dominance. Tragedy reveals the best in men. Prosperity exposes the worst in men.' Wolfgang fingered the talisman he wore. 'Only the wisdom and beneficence of the gods can protect us from ourselves, can keep us from destroying the gifts they have bestowed upon us.'

'A bleak sentiment,' Mandred remarked.

'A harsh lesson,' the priest corrected him. He gestured at the ruin in which they sat. 'A building, a city, even an Empire can be rebuilt. Anything raised by mortal hands may be torn down, but so too can it be restored. Only the profanation of the soul is eternal. Only a defiled spirit is lost forever.'

Mandred was familiar enough with Wolfgang to recognise that the priest was leading him into some philosophical trap. It was far safer to debate morality and theology with Ar-Ulric, his wisdom was pragmatic and straightforward. Wolfgang's was more esoteric, filled with nuances of meaning that bore two questions for every answer. The Sigmarite also possessed an uncanny facility for judging Mandred's moods and the thoughts behind them.

'Men did not destroy this city,' Mandred said. 'Or would Sigmar absolve the skaven of their outrages?' The graf at once repented the anger he allowed to creep into his voice. The priest didn't fail to notice the emotion and its source.

'Perhaps they are sent to test us, to find what strength is left in an Empire brought low by corruption and greed,' Wolfgang said. 'In every catastrophe, the seeds of great things are sown. It is up to men to let them grow.'

'What can grow from such wholesale misery?' Mandred scoffed. 'First the plague, then the skaven! How many thousands have perished because of the indifference of the gods?' His gaze became a bitter stare, boring hatefully into the priest's countenance. 'If the gods have any power at all, why do they not ease the suffering of their people?' He waved in disgust at his councillors. 'Listen to them! Like vultures picking at a carcass.'

Some of the nearest of the nobles cast an anxious look towards their sovereign when they heard his outburst. The intensity on Mandred's face caused them to discreetly pretend they had heard nothing.

Wolfgang smiled benignly. 'Ar-Ulric told me a curious parable before we marched from Middenheim. He said that there are two wolves living in each man's heart. The name of one wolf is Life. He provides sustenance for his pups and comfort to his mate. The other wolf is Death. He defends his territory from intruders and brings destruction to his enemies. A man who acknowledges only Life will wither; he will fade into a cowardly shadow. The man who feeds only Death becomes a monster, existing only to kill. To be strong, a man must nurture both the wolves in his heart equally. He must never favour one above the other.'

'That sounds like a warning,' Mandred accused.

'Wisdom, even Ulrican wisdom, only sounds threatening to those who already know the truth but refuse to accept it,' the priest returned. 'Every man is keeper of his own soul. The gods may show us the road, but it is left to each man whether he will walk the path.' Wolfgang looked across the squabbling nobles. 'Sometimes men need a leader to walk the road ahead of them.'

Mandred rose from his seat, ignoring the bows and genuflections of his subjects as he stalked away from the meeting. 'My path is my own,' he told Wolfgang. 'I ask no one to walk it with me.'

As he marched from the ruined sanctuary, the arguing voices of the nobles echoed in Mandred's ears. Each word, each syllable, stirred the anger in his heart. He hadn't brought his army to Carroburg so his barons could loot the rubble. He'd marched his troops here to liberate an enslaved province.

His steps faltered as he found the shattered image of Verena staring down accusingly at him in stony silence from the wall. There was no deceiving the God of Truth and Learning. Mandred hastened his step, putting the image behind him as quickly as he could. The lies a man might tell himself fell empty when he tried to justify them to a god.

Footsteps pursued Mandred as he quickened his pace. For a few steps, the irrational fear that Verena had jumped down from his wall and was pursuing him filled the graf's mind. Reason beat down superstitious fright, however. When he stopped and turned around he was greeted not by a judgemental stone god, but by the sympathetic softness of a lovely woman.

'I was told you stormed out of the council meeting,' the woman said. When she added a demure smile, a crimson flush rose into Mandred's face. However rich her clothes, however luxurious her surroundings, whenever Lady Mirella smiled at him like that he could only picture the beautiful damsel he'd rescued from the Kineater... and the distress of her wardrobe when he'd first met her.

'They wanted to make me Count of Drakwald,' Mandred said. 'I told them no.' He sighed and shook his head. 'What these people need is help, not a new set of rulers telling them what to do.'

Mirella was pensive for a moment. 'Maybe they just need the right ruler telling them what to do,' she said, stepping forward to embrace the man she loved. She drew back when she felt the tension in Mandred's body, found him unwilling to take comfort in her arms.

'I'm not the one,' Mandred stated, a terrible weariness in his voice. 'Everyone thinks I am, everyone looks up to me for something I don't know how to give them. Thanks to Wolfgang, they all think I've been chosen by the gods to lead them gods know where.'

'You walked from the Sacred Flame of Ulric, unharmed and unscathed, every wound and scar on your body healed,' Mirella reminded him. 'That speaks louder than any sermon Wolfgang or Ar-Ulric could ever preach.' She lifted a hand to Mandred's cheek. 'The people believe in you. I believe in you.'

Mandred pulled away. 'Beware what you trust. It could betray you.'

'You would never betray your people,' Mirella assured him. Mandred turned from her and marched away.

'Perhaps I already have,' he said. As he continued down the ruined corridor, he dreaded to hear Mirella's footsteps in pursuit of him. It was easier to disappoint a god than a woman.

* * *

The darkness of the forest folded itself around the lone rider, seeming to conspire with him against his pursuers. He could hear their voices calling to him as they thundered down the trail. The panic in their tones stabbed at his heart. He wasn't deserving of such concern. They looked to him as a leader, but he was so much less than that. A leader forgot about himself, set aside his own needs and desires so that he might do what was best for his subjects.

That was how Graf Gunthar had ruled Middenheim. Only once in his father's long reign had he seen Gunthar allow selfishness to threaten his subjects. That was when he had ordered an idealistic, reckless youth back into the city after being exposed to the plague-ridden squalor of Warrenburg. For his son, Gunthar had betrayed his people.

Mandred watched from the shadows while Beck and a squadron of knights galloped past. They were good vassals, stalwart warriors, but poor woodsmen. If Beck hoped to pick up his master's trail then he would be well-advised to fetch Mad Albrecht or one of the rangers. Left to his own devices, Beck would have a hard time tracking a mammoth across a mud flat.

As the shouting voices faded into the distance, Mandred wheeled his horse around. He'd ridden into the forest hoping to run down some skaven stragglers. The reports from the quartermasters who maintained the army's supplies made it clear that small bands of ratmen were creeping into Carroburg to steal food. A few of the vermin had even been caught, but the persistence of the thieving made it clear that there were still more of them out there.

The prospect of killing ratmen was a lure Mandred couldn't resist. The skaven wouldn't risk a fair fight, but if they thought they held the upper hand they might show themselves. The fewer the hunters, the greater the chance of drawing the cowardly creatures from hiding. One was the smallest number Mandred knew of.

He smiled bitterly. The example of Beck and his knights following him into the forest epitomised the turmoil in Mandred's heart. Because of who he was, everyone wanted him to lead them. They didn't seem to care where he took them.

Mandred cared, however. That was why he felt only disgust for himself. He'd led this great army to liberate Carroburg, but he hadn't done it to save the people or enrich his domains. He hadn't even done it for the gods. He'd done it for himself and no one else. He'd brought his army against Carroburg for one purpose: to kill skaven.

Vengeance. It was the meat with which Mandred was feeding the wolf in his heart. Revenge for the father the ratmen had taken from him. How could he offer his subjects hope when all that was inside him was hatred? How could he ask men to die for something that belonged to him and him alone?

The baseness of his motives disgusted him, made him recognise himself as a traitor to the expectations of thousands. Yet how could he bring about the great things they saw in him when he couldn't see them?

Mandred's horse suddenly reared, neighing in alarm. He reached one hand over to pat the animal's neck and quiet it. His other hand reached for Legbiter. If there were skaven near, the horse would smell them long before its rider was aware of them.

The graf froze, his fingers just touching the sword's hilt. Ahead of him, sitting beside a berry bush, was an enormous white wolf. The beast was watching him with piercing eyes. Though it had been over a year, the image of the white wolf that had led him to the Kineater's camp, that had intervened when the monster was about to kill him, was vivid in his memory. It was impossible for him to doubt that this was the same animal.

The wolf seemed to wait until it was certain Mandred had recognised it. Then it rose to its feet and curled back its lips in a snarl. The predator's sudden show of ferocity threw the horse into greater panic. Mandred fought to keep the bucking steed under control, but soon found himself hurtling from the saddle.

Mandred slammed into the ground, the impact driving the wind from his body. More than the physical impact, however, it was the sound of his horse galloping off through the brush that elicited a pained groan from him. It would be a long walk back to Carroburg.

A low growl reminded him of the cause of his predicament. Again his hand snatched at Legbiter. He had regarded the white wolf as some kind of omen, a divine benefactor, but it seemed the creature was only a hungry animal after all.

Drawing his sword even as he scrambled to his feet, he looked about for the beast. He found it seated once more on its haunches beside the berry bush. Somehow, it seemed to exude a sense of amusement as it watched him.

Mandred lowered his sword. The wolf confused, annoyed and puzzled him, but strangely he felt no fear of it. He was certain that it had deliberately scared his horse, yet it made no move to menace him.

'What do you want?' he demanded, feeling more than a little foolish shouting at a wolf.

The animal rose to its feet and turned its back to him. Before loping off into the brush, it looked back at him over its shoulder, seeming to beckon him.

Mandred returned his runefang to its scabbard. As he had a year before, he accepted the strange animal's unspoken invitation.

Alone, he followed the white wolf into the dark of the forest.

Sylvania, 1120

Under the merciless lashes of the Nachtsheer, the grim battlements of Castle Drakenhof began to take shape once more. Hundreds of peasant slaves toiled to drag the heavy blocks of stone up earthen ramps to the towering castle walls. Indentured artisans, masons and architects culled from every settlement within reach of the Nachtsheer, both within and without the county of Sylvania, laboured with hammer and chisel to give form to those blocks. Day and night they chipped away until the blocks were reduced to jagged, fang-like crescents. Only then were they hoisted onto the parapets and made fast with staples of steel.

From the windows of the Red Spire, Malbork von Drak watched his fortress being reborn, restored after the devastation wrought by the terrifying Starfall seven years ago. The largest of the noxious black stones was still embedded deep beneath the castle dungeons, lodged too securely for even a thousand slaves to remove. Even if the Sylvanian voivode had been prepared to accept the loss of workers due to the sickening miasma the so-called Jewel of Morrslieb exuded, his best architects had assured him removing the stone would compromise the foundations of the castle. Malbork trusted the judgement of his engineers, especially when, after executing three of them for possessing a defeatist bearing, the fourth engineer told him the exact same thing. He'd rewarded the man's honesty with a purse of gold.

The Voivode of Sylvania prided himself on his impeccable sense of justice.

'Your excellency must understand that the transition in Wurtbad does not change the duties incumbent upon the county whose governance you have been entrusted with.' The words were those of Baron von Waldberg-Raabs, envoy from the Grand Count of Stirland. Sylvania had enjoyed five years without interference from their liege lord. Already decimated by plague, Stirland had further suffered in the aftermath of the former grand count's death. Along with most of the electors of the Empire, Grand Count von Boeselager had perished in Carroburg when plague struck the fortified refuge of the late Emperor Boris. No direct heir had been left behind by von Boeselager, and for four years the streets of Wurtbad and the countryside of Stirland had witnessed vicious battles between half a dozen claimants. Only in the last spring had Karl von Oberreuth prevailed over his rivals and established himself as the new Grand Count.

Malbork stroked the thick moustache that drooped from his upper lip. It was so terribly tempting simply to push the irritating Stirlander out of the tower window. Rising far above the rooftop of Drakenhof's central keep, the Red Spire offered more than simply a stunning view of the construction below. Immediately to the west of the tower yawned a great pit, a natural fissure that tradition held had once been the home of a dragon. Tradition also held that the pit was without a bottom. Certainly it was deep enough that no body had ever been recovered from it. For generations, the von Draks had used the Wyrm's Gizzard to dispose of people they didn't want to see again.

The voivode smiled when he saw the look of horror on the face of Clucer Scarlat when the courtier saw his lord gazing at the tall window overlooking the pit. For the moment, the heavy shutters with their engraved dragons were closed, but it would only take a word from von Drak and his soldiers would fling them open... and fling the envoy to his doom. The ramifications of such an incident made the foppish Scarlat sick with horror. Some men had no stomach for war.

Malbork turned away from the window and scrutinised his noble visitor. Von Waldberg-Raabs was a middle-aged man, the prime of health slowly draining from what had once been a robust physique. There was a strength of character about the man's features that Malbork always found suspicious in his minions and frustrating in his peers. It denoted a propensity for defiance in the former and a decided lack of corruptibility in the latter. Any thoughts of offering the envoy a bribe would be as inadvisable as putting the Wyrm's Gizzard to use.

'It pains me, but these lands have been harder hit than most,' Malbork told the baron. 'Sylvania was among the first to suffer the misery of plague...'

Von Waldberg-Raabs offered the voivode a thin and utterly insincere smile. 'As the first to suffer the plague, you must also be the first to emerge from its shadow.' The envoy pointed to the battlements far below and the construction gangs labouring to restore the castle. 'Forgive me for observing, but there seems no shortage of peasants in your *fiefdom*.'

Malbork glared murder at the Stirlander for his insulting turn of phrase. 'Get out,' he hissed in a low, vicious tone.

Baron von Waldberg-Raabs blinked in confusion, unable to process the voivode's abandonment of protocol. 'Excuse me, your excellency?'

The voivode turned about, stroking his moustache as he looked to the shuttered window. 'Get out or you will be shown out.'

Clucer Scarlat, all colour drained from his face, hooked

an arm around that of the envoy and began a hasty retreat from the Red Spire. 'His excellency needs time to consider the logistics of your request,' the courtier explained. Soon, the two men were out in the corridor descending the spiral stairs leading down into the keep. Malbork von Drak was alone in the ancient execution chamber.

Or so the voivode's reason told him. His senses told him otherwise. As soon as the sound of Scarlat's conversation grew distant enough that the clucer's voice was nothing but an indistinct murmur, there came a new sound just at the edge of Malbork's hearing. It was a strange, eerie noise that defied all efforts to determine its source. He could liken it only to the prolonged tearing of some old and rotten cloth, thin and porous with age. From everywhere and nowhere the noise came, until it seemed the Red Spire was saturated with the clamour.

It was then, when the noise had grown to its most antagonistic, that Malbork saw the shadow. Rising from the corner of the room closest to the shuttered window and the Wyrm's Gizzard, the shade was indistinct at first, merely a blot on the join between floor and wall. But with each passing breath, the shadow grew, becoming both denser and more distinct. It began to take on man-like shape, a manikin of darkness, robed in a veil of black.

An awful fascination imprisoned Malbork. He could neither move nor speak, only watch as the spectre assumed form. The tyrant of Sylvania, the despot who lorded over thousands of lives, was as helpless as a sparrow caught in the serpent's gaze.

Ice crackled on the tower's stone floor as the shadow stepped out from the wall and became three-dimensional: a lean, withered body draped in a cloak ribbed like the wing of some monstrous bat. Against the folds of a high, crimson-hued collar, a vulturine face regarded the voivode with malignant intensity. Malbork felt his skin crawl under the scrutiny of those blood-shot eyes.

'Vanhal,' the count gasped. Malbork was reckoned a fierce, formidable warrior by those who had met him on the battle-field, yet the spectral visitation had sapped even his courage. Tales of the necromancer's terrifying sorceries were never far from the thoughts of any Sylvanian, far less the man who nominally reigned over them all. That the dreadful warlock should be able to violate the defences of Castle Drakenhof so easily was a horror he had never dared imagine.

The cadaverous face pulled back in a thin, sneering smile. 'If I were *him*, you would be dead right now,' the morbid intruder declared in a scratchy, withered voice. 'I am the Baron Lothar von Diehl of Mordheim. I tell you this in order that you might understand it is an equal and not some unwashed peasant who treats with you.'

Malbork stepped back, one hand closing about the dagger hanging from his belt. 'I have heard of you,' he said. 'You are Vanhal's creature, his minion. You too have despoiled my lands and stolen my people from their graves!'

'Graves you so obligingly filled,' Lothar said, bowing his shrivelled head in acknowledgement. 'But I did not come so far to dwell upon the past, excellency. I came here to discuss the future.'

'What demands does Vanhal make of me?' Malbork asked, managing to keep the fear he felt from his voice. With the skaven sniffing at the borders of his lands, with Stirland growing increasingly onerous in their demands for past duties and tithes, now was the worst time for the necroman-cer's deathless legions to stir from Vanhaldenschlosse.

Lothar blinked, surprised by the voivode's question. 'Van-hal makes no demands,' he laughed. 'Were he able, he would simply take what he wanted.' He raised an almost skeletal finger to indicate the significance of the point he was making. 'Were he able,' Lothar repeated. 'But I fear my mentor still recovers from his exertions. Decimating the skaven, annihilating their sorcerer-priest, violating the governance of time-space, these have extracted their toll from my master.'

Malbork's hand eased away from the dagger, his brows knotted in keen interest. 'What is it that Lothar von Diehl wants? And why?'

The Mordheimer gave Malbork another of his ghoulish smiles. 'I have come to offer you my services. In return, you will agree to show me certain considerations.'

'What considerations?'

A theatrical flourish of his emaciated hand brought a streamer of shadow expanding from Lothar's hand. In a few breaths, the darkness became a tiny yet precise miniature of Vanhaldenschlosse's crooked battlements. 'I want Vanhaldenschlosse,' he said. 'The tower and a promise of non-interference as I pursue my studies.' A grisly chuckle wracked the scrawny necromancer. 'I can afford to procure any materials I might require on my own.'

The voivode eyed his visitant with hostile suspicion. He could guess what kind of materials the necromancer referred to and the sort of obscenities that would be conducted within Vanhaldenschlosse. 'What services do I buy for such considerations?'

Lothar snapped his fingers, dispelling the shadowy miniature. 'As I have said, Vanhal has been recuperating from his exertions. His power is diminished. After the battle, he could maintain but a scant thousand of his legion, only a handful of his zombie dragons. Have you not wondered why he doesn't stir from his castle? Why his undead do not threaten your towns and villages?'

'So you are telling me now is the time to strike?' Malbork curled his lip in contempt. 'If it is so easy, why do you not dispose of him yourself?'

'You misunderstand me. I said that Vanhal *was* recuperating. He has already regained a formidable degree of his power.'

Anger coloured Malbork's face, overwhelming the fear Lothar's eerie entrance had provoked. 'Then you are saying it is already too late to strike!' He shook his fist in frustration.

Lothar merely smiled. 'Too late now. But I have studied my master's recovery most carefully. I have a better understanding of his abilities now. Of what he can do and what may again drain him to the point of vulnerability. The proper crisis, a conflict to draw him from his lair...'

'I will not risk my army on some fool's venture,' Malbork growled.

'Then we will not use your army, excellency,' Lothar said, a cunning gleam in his eye. 'Surely, between us, we could turn Vanhal's ire towards another antagonist. Say, for instance, your liege lord, Grand Count von Oberreuth?'

Malbork marvelled at the perfidy of the necromancer. Pit one enemy against the other? Whichever emerged victor, the true winner would be Sylvania. 'You seem certain of your influence over your master.'

Lothar shrugged. 'As he recovers, he depends upon me for the little, mundane matters. Attending to invaders for instance. I can tell him such foes are from Stirland as easily as Sylvania.'

The light of suspicion crept back into the count's gaze. 'And all you want is the tower?'

'The tower, freedom to conduct my researches and the protection of your soldiers against those who might take a dim view of my researches.' Lothar paused, looking at the ceiling for an instant. When he continued it was as though remembering a minor detail that had almost slipped his memory. 'I will also require a slight bauble, a bit of bric-a-brac recovered from the Inquisitorium of Verena in Mordheim. Certain... shall we say inimical concentrations of ideology make it difficult for me to get it myself.'

'A sorcerer can't trespass on holy ground,' Malbork scoffed.

'Something of the sort,' Lothar admitted nonchalantly. 'But I think it would be wise to act upon my request. Just in case Vanhal should prevail over your other enemies. Neither of us wants him coming back. This trinket will ensure he doesn't.'

Malbork nodded as he carefully considered the necromancer's claims. 'Discuss your plans in more detail, sorcerer. It may be that we can form a compact.'

In sober tones the two noblemen made their plans of treachery and slaughter, secure in the isolation of the Red Spire. Unaware of the verminous ears lurking behind the walls, sharp to catch every nuance of their intrigues. Lips peeled away from inhuman fangs as the ratkin listened and plotted their own revenge.

⊰ CHAPTER III ⊱

Drakwald, 1119

For what felt like hours, Mandred followed the white wolf through the forest. Whenever he felt foolish, whenever doubt crept into his mind, the beast ahead of him would pause and look back at him. There was such an aura of expectancy in those piercing blue eyes that the nobleman would feel a surge of determination swell up inside him. Wherever the wolf was leading him, he was resolved to see the end of the trail.

The sun was sinking from the sky, the pale sliver of Mannslieb just beginning to cast its silvery rays into the shadowy forest. A cool, crisp wind moaned through the trees, sending dead leaves rustling across the ground. The white wolf trotted on, its pale pelt stark as a beacon in the gloom. A sudden increase in its pace left Mandred well behind. A flicker of alarm coursed through the noble. He sensed he was near wherever it was the animal was leading him. If he lost it now, he feared he would never learn the wolf's secret.

One hand closed about his sword's scabbard to keep the weapon from jouncing against his leg, Mandred rushed after the wolf. The animal broke into a steady run, weaving between the trees with an incredible grace. It wasn't long before Mandred lost sight of the beast entirely. For an instant, he ran onwards, thinking he might pick up the animal's trail again. Then reason asserted itself and he stopped running. He was alone in the twilit wood, chasing after a beast that was clearly anything but natural. An idiot could see the foolishness of pressing on.

Frustrated, angry at himself for allowing the wolf to lead him so far from the trails he knew, Mandred took stock of his surroundings. The trees and bushes around him looked much like any other in the Drakwald, but he recalled an old bit of woodcraft that claimed moss would grow only on the northern side of a tree. Or perhaps it was the southern side. Either way, unless some divine perversity caused the sun to set in the east, he'd be able to get his bearings by examining which way the moss grew.

He was just kneeling down to inspect one of the trees when he noticed the cave. A craggy lump of rock jutting out from the forest floor, its surface almost completely obscured by dead leaves and weeds; its would have been easy to miss but for the grim blackness of the cave mouth. As he continued to stare, he became aware of a dull, flickering glow deep within the darkness, the light of someone's fire.

Mandred drew Legbiter from its sheath. The presence of fire indicated the presence of a thinking creature, one entirely different from the wolf he had followed so far and for so long. The most pleasant prospect his imagination could conjure was a band of brigands; at least they would be human. More likely the cave was infested with goblins, perhaps even a pack of skaven stragglers. The irony of that last possibility almost made him laugh.

Warily, he approached the cave. He strained to hear any sound, the scratchy whisper of goblin voices, the nasty hiss of skaven squeaks. The only noise that rewarded his alertness was the crackle of the fire. Tightening his grip on his sword, muttering a prayer to Ulric and another to Taal, Mandred made his way into the darkness.

The fire was a small one, burning in a little pit that had been gouged in the floor at the back of the cave. By its fitful light, Mandred saw that some manner of thinking creature had made the cave its home. Strings of dried herbs hung from the rock roof; animal skins covered the floor. One wall was given over to an assortment of gourds, woven baskets and old bones, their arrangement suggesting a deliberation beyond the witless whims of goblins and the bestial impulses of gors.

Mandred walked over to the assemblage of baskets and gourds. Removing the plug that sealed one of the gourds, he found the hollowed inside had been filled with a collection of wolf teeth. Carved into each fang was a sign, a rune that he recognised from the oldest Teutogen relics.

'Would you have your doom revealed to you?'

The voice caused Mandred to drop the gourd, scattering teeth across the animal skins on the floor. He glared at the darkness near the mouth of the cave, sword held at the ready.

The speaker emerged from the shadows, gliding towards him with an almost soundless tread. Mandred stared in astonishment as a beautiful woman stood revealed in the firelight. She was tall, her limbs well-muscled, her long hair endowed with a silvery-blonde hue he'd never seen before. There was a timeless quality about her face, a fusion of strength and softness that set his pulse trembling. Hers was a visage beyond the worldly pretensions of princesses and queens, a defiance of the mortal laws of age and decay. If he were a priest and allowed the distinction of communing with the goddess Rhya, he imagined her face would be akin to the woman he now gazed upon.

'I see you have cast the bones already,' the woman stated as she strode towards Mandred. She was near enough that he could smell the musky scent of her hair. She wore a simple garment of deerskin, cinched at the waist with a belt of dried gut, the brief skirt cut well above her knees. The luxuriant folds of a wolfskin cloak hung about her shoulders, tightened about her throat by a moonstone clasp. No shoes fettered her feet, yet Mandred could find neither scratch nor bruise upon her bare toes.

In a movement more graceful than Mandred would have thought possible for a human body, the woman knelt on the floor and quickly examined the teeth he'd upset from the gourd. Her hands passed over the wolf fangs, turning them over with the merest brush of her palm. Her eyes darted across the runes, flickering from one to another with the hungry fascination of a cormorant stalking fish.

'These tell me much about you, Mandred von Zelt,' the woman declared. In a single sweep of her hands, she gathered the teeth into her palm.

Hearing her speak his name broke the strange fascination that had gripped him. Mandred shook his head, but made no move to return Legbiter to its scabbard. 'What are you?' he demanded. 'A witch?'

The woman smiled up at him from where she knelt on the floor. 'Perhaps,' she purred. 'Or perhaps the fame of the Wolf of Sigmar is such that he is recognised even in the middle of nowhere.'

Mandred glowered at the woman. 'I am a follower of Ulric,' he declared. 'I have no truck with witches.'

Reaching to her breast, the woman pulled her deerskin vestment down, exposing the swell of her breasts and the symbol tattooed between them. It was the wolf-head emblem of Ulric, the same symbol that was woven into the ceremonial robes of Ar-Ulric himself.

'There are many ways to follow the White Wolf,' she said. Her choice of words sent a chill rushing along Mandred's spine. Was it mere chance that made her refer to Ulric by such title? Did she somehow suspect the strange path that had led him to her lair?

Mandred lowered his eyes, waving his hand at the witch. 'Cover yourself,' he commanded. The order brought a laugh bubbling from her lips, but she did as he asked.

'A man of violence, a dealer of death and slaughter, a warrior steeped in the blood of his enemies, yet you blanch at nakedness,' she mocked him.

'There are such things as decency and propriety,' Mandred stated. It was his turn to mock. 'They are the things that make men civilised. That set us above beasts... and witches.'

The woman jostled the teeth she held, sending an eerie clicking noise echoing through the cave. 'You may call me Hulda,' she declared. 'I am the Howl of Ulric. In better times, many sought my counsel. Now there are only a few.'

Mandred felt a curious sympathy when he heard the sorrow woven into her words. 'The plague has taken many,' he said. As he spoke, for the first time he considered the true extent of what had been lost to the plague. The toll in lives had been abominable, but now he contemplated what else had been lost with those lives: the ancient wisdom and traditions that had been exterminated with the people who kept them. This tradition of a forest oracle, a peculiarity of this part of Drakwald, how many were left who would keep it? How many of them had perished of the disease or fallen to the skaven who followed?

Hulda stopped rattling the fangs in her hand. 'The plague has taken many,' she agreed. 'Some through sickness, some through fear.' Cocking her head to one side, the seeress studied Mandred for a moment.

'The fangs have shown me where you have been, Graf of Middenheim,' she said. 'I have seen the road you travelled to get here... and why.' In a motion that was part lunge and part pounce, Hulda sprang across the floor, catching up the gourd in one hand and returning the teeth to it with the other. 'There is a terrible hunger inside you, Wolf of Sigmar,' she said. 'A hatred that burns for blood but which will never be quenched by blood.'

'How can I lead men?' Mandred asked, his voice betraying a note of despair. 'How can I ask them to follow me when all I can offer them is hatred?'

Hulda dipped her finger back into the gourd, removing a single fang. She held it up for Mandred to see the slash-like rune etched into the enamel. 'This is your sign. I read it when it fell to the floor. It is called Winterfire, the flame that freezes, the cold that burns. Never have I seen this rune matched to a man's soul. It betokens greatness.'

Mandred shook his head. 'I don't want greatness. I am unworthy of it.'

'Men do not choose the doom the gods have proclaimed,' Hulda said. 'Their destiny is written in the stars, in the mountains, in the song of the bird and the howl of the wolf. To deny destiny is the gravest insult to the gods.' Hulda smiled at him, a surprising tenderness in her manner. 'A small man seeks greatness, lusts after it, cheats and lies and murders to steal it. A great man shuns it, hides from it, begs it to pass to another. Which of these are you, Mandred?'

'But I am no leader,' Mandred said. 'I want nothing but to kill skaven. There is no hope, no future I can offer my people. Your bones have shown you. All that is in my heart is hatred. Men deserve more than that.'

Hulda set down the gourd. 'Then give them more. Give yourself more. Be the Winterfire, use the flame of hatred to bring hope, use the chill of rage to build tomorrow. That is the riddle of the rune, to use the power yet deny the essence of that power.'

'I am only a man,' Mandred insisted, clinging to that simple truth, trying desperately to deny the miracle of the Sacred Flame.

Hulda sprang to her feet. In a single bound she was beside Mandred, pressing the fang of Winterfire into his hand. 'Become something more,' she told him. Her eyes glittered as they stared into his. 'Destiny is a web that connects us all. If one strand fails, the skein may be undone. The fate of all men may rest upon the choices you make.'

Mandred clenched his fist, feeling the fang dig into his palm 'It is a grim burden,' he shuddered. His body felt as though a great weight were pressing down on him, threatening to smash him flat against the floor of the cave. Somehow, he felt that if he simply let the tooth fall out of his hand, the onerous duty would pass from him and he would be free.

Mandred tightened his hold on the fang. Hulda stepped back, her face aglow with admiration.

'A leader makes the right decisions,' she said. 'Not the easy ones.'

It was early morning when Mandred left the cave. Strangely, it seemed only a matter of minutes before he was back on the old familiar trail, the path he had quit when he'd started his pursuit of the white wolf. Had the beast led him in circles or had he simply imagined the chase to be far longer than the reality? He turned to look back, to find any glimpse of Hulda's cave, but the trees seemed to have closed in, blotting out even the trace of his own tracks.

'Your highness!' an anguished voice cried out from somewhere nearby in the forest. Mandred recognised the cry as belonging to his bodyguard Beck. Taking a last look in the direction where he thought Hulda's cave must lie, he cupped a hand to his mouth and called out to the knight. Immediately he heard the crash of armed men rushing through the tangled undergrowth. In only a few moments, the graf was surrounded by a bedraggled yet relieved group of rangers and woodsmen. Beck, it seemed, had appreciated his own limitations after all and gone to recruit those who knew the forest to conduct the search.

The men gathered around him as Mandred described his pursuit of the white wolf. When he came to relate his discovery of the cave, however, he found himself reluctant to mention Hulda, instead leaving it a mystery who might have made the fire or dwelt in the cave.

When he had finished, the men around Mandred celebrated his adventure and its happy outcome. Only Mad Albrecht, the veteran poacher and hunter was uneasy. A native Drakwalder, he professed to know these woods better than any of them. Gravely, he pronounced that Mandred was fortunate to have emerged from the forest alive.

'In Middenland, perhaps, the white wolf is a good omen,' Albrecht explained, 'but in Drakwald it is an ill sending. Long have the people of the forest whispered tales of a bloodthirsty monster that cloaks itself in the pelt of a great white wolf. It is a beast of unnatural cunning and impervious to mortal weapons. Many generations has it haunted these woods, and on nights when the moons are full its terrible howls can be heard even in the streets of Carroburg.'

Beck was quick to laugh at the poacher's story. 'A child's myth,' he said. 'A useful fable for keeping folk away from where the game is plentiful, eh?' The joke brought laughter from the other men.

Mandred didn't join the merriment. He looked back into the shadowy forest. He thought about what he had experienced. He thought about Albrecht's story.

And he wondered.

Altdorf, 1121

He never failed to feel the magnitude of his superiority whenever he stood upon the balcony and gazed upon the palaces of the noble and wealthy. They were his. Not just one of them, but all of them. The illusion of possession and ownership was a useful deceit, something to keep the old order pliable and complacent, docile and oblivious while their world was steadily and inexorably collapsing around them.

It was true, the nobles and aristocrats still had much power. Even in the midst of crisis and plague their wealth commanded respect. Too many commoners were accustomed to deferring to their blue-blooded masters. Servitude was all they had ever known, ambition had been as carefully culled from their minds as a mutant steer from a herd of cattle. They were too afraid of change to aspire for anything more. The promise of food and shelter was enough to kill their pride and smother their dreams. Like so many vampires, the nobility battened upon the complacency of their peasants.

But that world was changing. Before the Black Plague struck, the first seeds of change had been sown. In his merciless greed, Emperor Boris Goldgather had planted the crop, the tax upon the peasant soldiery, the *Dienstleute*. Unwilling to pay, many of the nobles had simply dismissed the peasant soldiers in their service, loosing upon the Empire thousands of embittered men. Commoners who had dutifully served their noble lords had been cast aside with utter disregard the moment their presence became an inconvenience to the treasuries of their masters.

Most of the displaced *Dienstleute* had descended upon Altdorf, petitioning the Emperor himself for food and work. The result of their protest had led to the Bread March and the massacre that followed. Those who had escaped the slaughter dispersed among the city's peasantry, each man spreading the word of revolution and a new society: one without aristocrats and nobles; a land where a man would earn his place by deeds, not breeding.

Adolf Kreyssig was the exemplar of such philosophy. Peasant-born, he'd risen to become the commander of the Kaiserjaeger, transforming it into the secret police of Emperor Boris. His position had become so powerful that he'd married into the House Thornig, noble landholders from Middenland. When Emperor Boris fled Altdorf for his Carroburg retreat, it was Kreyssig who'd been appointed Protector of the Empire in his absence.

Kreyssig smiled at the irony of such a title. Now that the reins of power were in his hands, now that Boris had so conveniently expired from the plague, the last thing he intended to do was protect the Empire. By inches and degrees he was going to tear it down and rebuild it in his own image.

He was indebted to Boris for more than just the authority he now wielded. More than any other man, Kreyssig had been privy to the machinations by which Boris had ruled. Assuming the throne while little more than a boy, Boris had been installed by the elector counts because he would be young and weak, the absolute opposite of the elderly and despotic Ludwig II. Boris, however, had a finely honed instinct for survival. If he was weak, he would use the strength of those around him, pitting one against the other, using their own power against themselves. Emperor Boris had built his tyranny simply by making himself indispensable as arbiter between rival princes and potentates. That many of these rivalries had been exacerbated by the Emperor himself never seemed to occur to those he manipulated.

What had worked so well for the Emperor now served the Protector. Kreyssig had commanded the attack that led to the Bread Massacre, earning him the regard of the nobility, or at least such regard as they might confer upon a commoner. But he had also carefully cultivated the unrest being spread by the survivors. At first simply as a way to expand the power of his Kaiserjaeger, presenting an enemy that would reinforce the necessity for the vicious organisation. Later, with Boris gone, Kreyssig had taken a deeper interest in the peasant movement. He'd acquired as much prestige as the nobles would allow him on their own. Indeed, Duke Vidor and other powerful nobles wanted to curtail Kreyssig's authority as Protector. It was the threat of peasant unrest and uprising that had stifled their efforts.

Then, almost like a gift of Providence, had come the skaven invasion. Kreyssig's erstwhile allies had proven themselves far more than a mere handful of degenerate mutants and far more duplicitous than he could have imagined. Their assault on the city had very nearly succeeded. But it had been turned back, and in such fashion that Kreyssig became a hero to the commoners, the man who saved them from monsters straight out of legend. The impression that the nobles would have abandoned Altdorf and its people to the skaven was unfair, but it was a sentiment that played into existing resentments. It was a story Kreyssig's agents spread among the peasants, exacerbating their jealousy and distrust of their lords. More and more, the nobility was recognising the might of the commoners they had looked down upon all their lives, the strength of the peasant mob to tear down even the oldest and greatest of them.

It was Kreyssig, hero of the people and surrogate for the dead Emperor, the man with connections to both the world of the peasant and the realm of the noble, who alone could mediate between the disparate groups. He alone was there to play the part of the arbiter…

A scowl worked itself onto Kreyssig's face. No, it wasn't quite true. There was another element at play. The Temple of Sigmar had been an important tool in establishing his support among the peasants. Through his efforts the Sigmarites had become the dominant force among Altdorf's religions. The bread the Temple distributed to the starving masses had earned them the favour of the peasants, allowing it inroads into every corner of the city. There was also a solid core of zealots, those who had been there to witness the battle against the skaven outside the very walls of Sigmar's Grand Cathedral. They were the ones who related in awed tones the bold stand of the Grand Theogonist upon the steps of the temple, the mighty hammer Thorgrim blazing with holy light as he brandished it on high. They were the ones who spread the legend of the Lady of Sigmar, calling down divine power to annihilate the skaven and scourge them from the city.

Kreyssig looked down at the grey cat he held in the crook of his arm as he thought about the Lady of Sigmar. She had been instrumental in that victory, without any doubt. Her magic, her arcane knowledge of the ratmen, her ability to play pious priest and arrogant noble like pieces on a game board. The cat Kreyssig held was part of her legacy, a way to warn him if skaven spies were around. Yes, Baroness von den Linden had been an important player in the salvation of Altdorf. But she'd been too ambitious. She would have set herself up as Empress, and Kreyssig had no illusions that she would have kept him around once that position was hers. Everything he had built up over the years she would have exploited, twisted to suit her own ends.

It was with the aid of Grand Theogonist Gazulgrund that Kreyssig had been able to escape the witch's coils. Baroness von den Linden, as the venerated Lady of Sigmar, had become a heroic figure to the people of Altdorf, eclipsing both the Imperial palace and the Temple of Sigmar. Her sorceries were anathema to the Sigmarite priesthood while her ambitions were a threat to the Protector of the Empire. With Gazulgrund's help, Kreyssig had eliminated the baroness. Using holy orisons to conceal his intentions from the witch, he'd locked her inside Boris's extravagant indoor apiary, leaving the enraged bees to destroy her.

Baroness von den Linden was gone. That still left Gazulgrund. Kreyssig was wary of the influence the Grand Theogonist had over the peasants. Even as he built up the Temple of Sigmar to suit his own purposes, Kreyssig was aware that he was endowing Gazulgrund with more and more power. It was becoming a bit less clear which of them was dependent upon the other, the Temple or the Palace.

Kreyssig lowered his gaze, staring down from the balcony at the imposing parapets of the Courts of Justice. Buried

beneath that imposing fortress were the secret dungeons of
the Kaiserjaeger. Locked within one of those cells was his
guarantee that Gazulgrund would do as he was told. So long
as the Grand Theogonist's daughter remained a 'guest' of
the Kaiserjaeger, the priest belonged to Kreyssig.

Through the Grand Theogonist, Kreyssig controlled the
Temple. Through the Temple, he controlled the peasants.
Through them both, he controlled the nobles.

In time, he would control the entire Empire.

Slowly, Grand Theogonist Gazulgrund walked across the
sparsely furnished cell that served as his private study,
advancing upon the little wicker cage resting atop a small
side table. The animal inside the cage hissed at him as he
stretched his hand towards it. The priest frowned at the
black-furred brute. There was no love lost between cleric
and cat. In the strictures of the Temple, cats were sympto-
matic of witchcraft and ill omen, described as emissaries
of Old Night in the apocalyptic writings of Arch-Templar
Dyre. No priest of Sigmar could feel entirely comfortable
around cats after reading Dyre. The animal, for its part, had
picked up on Gazulgrund's hostility and returned it in kind,
yowling and scratching at him whenever he came close.

Keeping the animal at all had been an act of submission
on Gazulgrund's part, a concession to the decree of Protector Kreyssig. Worried that the skaven might yet have spies
in Altdorf, that they might be planning a second invasion,
Kreyssig had ordered all persons of position to keep a cat
with them. The brute would warn if a skaven were near.
Gazulgrund's objections that the divine grace of Sigmar was
all the protection the Temple needed had fallen on deaf
ears. He'd sent a troop of Kaiserjaeger to the cathedral to
deliver the Grand Theogonist's cat, making it clear in no

uncertain terms that debate was not an option. That he'd selected a black cat for the priest, an animal even more closely associated with Old Night, was a calculated insult that wasn't lost on Gazulgrund.

The priest stared down into the hateful yellow eyes of the cat before drawing the heavy backcloth down across the cage, hiding the animal from view. He didn't like the reminder of Kreyssig's authority, of his dominance over the Temple. He could speak more freely without feeling the beast's hostile gaze upon him. And, especially this night, he needed to speak freely.

Returning to his desk, Gazulgrund sank down into his chair and tapped a tiny brass hammer against a bronze bell. A shrill, piercing note echoed through the study. In response, the door slowly opened and a shaven-headed monk peeked his head into the room.

'I will see him now,' Gazulgrund said, each word sinking like a leaden weight as he spoke. The enormity of what he was about to do, the implications of what he would order done, they were a burden not lightly contemplated.

The monk withdrew. The door opened wider and a man entered. He was garbed in black leather, from his gloves to his boots to the long cloak he wore. A heavy hood was drawn up over his head, obscuring his features in shadow. There was the clink of mail rattling with each stride the man took. As the door closed behind him, he reached up and drew back the concealing hood, displaying intense, hawkish features.

'It is my supreme honour to attend you, holiness,' the visitor declared, bending to one knee before the desk and the priest behind it.

Gazulgrund motioned the man to rise. 'You may find little honour in this audience after you have learnt why I

summoned you,' he announced gravely. 'My words will test
your resolve, they will push your faith in Lord Sigmar to the
utmost. Men, pious and true, have stood where you stand
now and they have recoiled in horror at my words. It is condemnation of neither your courage nor your belief if you
choose to depart now. If you stay to attend me and would
hear my command, know that the consequences must be
severe.' He waited a moment, but his visitor remained standing. The hawkish features displayed no trace of anxiety, only
curiosity. There was none of the trepidation he'd encountered before. Gazulgrund took that for a good sign.

'Templar-Captain Reinhardt Holz, you have served dutifully in the Order of the Silver Hammer for ten years.
Your career has been one of honour and fidelity. You have
devoted yourself to the Temple, to rooting out the enemies
of Sigmar and destroying them, whatever abominable form
they might take. The Warlock of Darckenburg, the Vampire
of Morrfeld, the obscene Cult of the Purple Hand in Nuln,
these have you exposed and exterminated in the name of
Mighty Sigmar.' Gazulgrund stared intently at the templar.
'However horrific the foe, you have never strayed from the
guiding light of Sigmar.'

'What nobler purpose can a man hold than to serve Lord
Sigmar,' Holz stated.

Gazulgrund glanced at the covered cat cage. It was curious
that Holz should quote from Dyre. Perhaps it was a sign
that he'd found the man who would not shrink from what
he would have him do, the atrocity that must be done if the
Temple were to endure.

'You have removed many threats to the Temple,' Gazulgr-
und said. 'Your bravery has never been questioned. Fearlessly
you have confronted evil and your valour in that arena is
beyond doubt. But it needs a different sort of valour to

protect the Temple now, a courage that demands far more strength than anything that has come before.'

'The Temple is mother and father, what threatens it must perforce threaten me,' Holz said, this time quoting from the sermons of Wolfgart Krieger, the man who had founded Holz's order in the days when Sigmar walked among men.

Gazulgrund was silent for several moments. He pondered the verse Holz had recited, impressed once more by the strange appropriateness of the choice. In his mind, in his heart, Gazulgrund had no doubts. He knew the course he was set upon was the correct one. If there had been any question, he would never have reached the grim decision he had made.

'To destroy evil is rewarding work,' Gazulgrund declared. 'It ennobles the soul, swells the heart with pride, eases the mind with accomplishment. There is no more satisfying labour than such good work.' The priest's expression darkened, his eyes becoming pinpoints of intensity. 'The task I would charge you with will bring no such reward. It will haunt you through your years, it will prey upon your mind and sicken your heart; your soul will be blackened and befouled. But know that it is necessary. Nothing you can do in this life will ever be more important. No threat to the Temple could ever be more perilous than the one I charge you to eliminate.'

The gravity of his tone, the weight of his words shook Holz, Gazulgrund could see that by the way the templar's eyes briefly widened, by the sudden breath he drew into his lungs. When Holz answered, it was with his own words, not those of some long-dead luminary of the Temple. 'Ask what you will, holiness. Whatever sacrifice I can make is too little to fulfil my obligations to the Temple.'

Gazulgrund opened a small teak box lying atop the desk.

From within, he removed a large jade ring. He saw Holz recoil slightly as he recognised it. He had often seen that ring on the finger of Grand Master Fahlenberg, the head of his order.

Gazulgrund stepped out from behind the desk. Solemnly he gripped Holz's left hand and slid the jade ring onto his finger. The priest nodded when he found it was a perfect fit. Surely another omen that his course was true, the path ahead right.

'You are now Grand Master of the Order of the Silver Hammer,' the priest decreed. 'The Templars are now at your command. They will acknowledge your command when they see you now bear the grand master's ring. I now burden you with the commandment that forced Fahlenberg to depart from the Temple. Some secrets, once learned, must either be embraced or...' He left the alternative unspoken. Far beneath the cathedral, bricked up behind one of the walls, Fahlenberg was perhaps even now breathing his last. It would have been too cruel to execute the old grand master without allowing him time to make his peace with Sigmar.

Holz nodded his head. 'The Grand Theogonist speaks with the voice of Sigmar,' he said, again reverting to scriptures, this time that of Grand Theogonist Marius. 'No man may deny the words of a god.'

'It is not evil that threatens the Temple,' Gazulgrund stated. 'It is not witch or warlock I charge you to destroy, but innocence. Those who are the stewards of Sigmar's faith, the leaders of his Temple are weak. They are creatures of the flesh, even as any man. That weakness jeopardises the Temple, tempts them to prostitute the name of Lord Sigmar. Such obscenity cannot be allowed! Such temptation must be scourged from the Temple!'

Gazulgrund set his hand on Holz's shoulder. 'It is a

dreadful duty I entrust to your order. There are wicked men who would seek to dominate this Temple through its priests. They would dominate those priests by threatening those they love. It is a cruel wisdom I have learned, but a man may love either flesh or god. If he would serve Sigmar truly and faithfully, he must deny the loyalties of flesh and blood.

'The Order of the Silver Hammer will cut the weakness from the Temple of Sigmar. The Templars will go forth and scourge the families of arch-lector and lector, prelate and bishop. Root and branch, the flesh must be culled. To protect the Temple from those who would exploit it, we must wash the Empire in the blood of innocence.'

Holz's face paled at the ghastliness of Gazulgrund's commandment, but he bowed his head in acceptance. 'Your will be done, holiness,' he said in firm voice.

'Send forth your men,' Gazulgrund told him, 'but there is one special task I will entrust to you and you alone. Here in Altdorf, beneath the Courts of Justice, there is a black pit of terror called the Dragon's Hole. You will descend into that pit. You will kill what you find there.'

The templar nodded gravely. The Order of the Silver Hammer was one of the few organisations outside the Kaiserjaeger who knew about Kreyssig's secret prison. Holz might not know who it was that the Protector had imprisoned, but the fact that she was noteworthy to both Kreyssig and Gazulgrund impressed her importance upon him.

A tear rolled down the priest's cheek as he quickly turned away from Holz. It was the last tear he would shed for his daughter, for the hostage Kreyssig had taken to bend him and the Temple to the will of a tyrant.

'Do your work swiftly, grand master,' Gazulgrund said. 'Do not let her suffer.'

—◄ CHAPTER IV ►—

Carroburg, 1119

Mandred watched as his council seated themselves around the charred, splintered table. They had Kurgaz and his dwarfs to thank for that bit of furnishing, a survivor from the demolition of Schloss Hohenbach. By some freak of chance, or perhaps some unfathomable whim of Ranald the Trickster, the table had been thrown clear when the castle went crashing down into the Reik. The dwarfs had discovered it lying at the foot of the Otwinsstein caught in the branches of a hoary old oak.

Despite the damage inflicted upon it, the quality and craftsmanship of the table was still abundantly evident. It was something that had been made for kings, perhaps even for emperors.

The Graf of Middenheim frowned at that last possibility. He'd hoped the table would lend a certain dignity and nobility to his meeting with his councillors. In such a savage setting as the ravaged rubble that had once been Carroburg the baser ambitions and greed of his vassals had been much too quick to be expressed. Thoughts of chivalry and duty seemed to have been forgotten in a realm ruined by war and decimated by plague. Trying to evoke, even in some small way the grandeur of a proper court, Mandred had hoped to arouse the nobility within his nobles, not encourage their lust for power with Imperial pretensions.

His humour only darkened further when two visitors to Mandred's council were escorted into the ruined temple by his knights. Gaudily arrayed heralds announced the richly dressed guests. The thin man in the ermine-trimmed cloak and sealskin boots was Count van der Duijn of Westerland. The woman in sky-blue gown and delicately coiffured hair was Baroness Carin of Nordland. Both of them had brought extravagant gifts for the Graf of Middenheim and his court. Some of his nobles had protested when Mandred refused to accept presents from the delegations.

Westerland was a realm that had been wracked by war long before the Black Plague visited death and destruction upon the rest of the Empire. The barbarian hordes of Jarl Ormgaard had descended upon the province in a fleet of dragonships. The Norscans had sacked, pillaged and burnt much of the land, killing and despoiling anything they couldn't steal. The once great city of Marienburg had been reduced to a shattered ruin, the lords of the land forced into their fortress on Rijker's Island while the barbarians dominated the rest of the province.

Nordland had fared equally poorly. The Black Plague had been especially disastrous to the coastal province, killing almost three-quarters of the populace. Norscan marauders had come from the sea to plunder and kill all along the coast. Beastmen had emerged from the great forests to ravage farms and villages, driving the survivors into the supposed security of the towns. As the towns filled with refugees, the plague wrought its grisly toll, slaughtering the Nordlanders by the thousands in the overcrowded conditions. The decimated communities had been easy prey when the skaven burst from their underground burrows. Most of the province now languished under their insidious lash.

These weren't lands that could afford gifts. Only the stubborn pride of their rulers made them think they could still indulge the extravagance of tradition. A chill ran through Mandred's veins as he pondered how nearly Middenheim had shared the fate of these lands. But for the harsh wisdom of his father, the stalwart courage of its people and the beneficent grace of Ulric, the City of the White Wolf would have been reduced to a wretched shambles.

'We welcome you,' Mandred addressed his visitors on behalf of his council, rising and extending his arm towards them in a show of friendship. 'Long and perilous has been your journey. We are humbled by the hazards you have risked and we are saddened by the dire circumstances that made those risks necessary.' As he spoke the formalities, evoked the almost cabalistic proprieties laid down by the etiquette of generations, Mandred could almost imagine himself back in the Middenpalaz listening to Viscount von Vogelthal conducting representatives of the Imperial court to his father.

The dignitaries waited until Mandred resumed his seat before they returned his greeting and assumed their own chairs. It was Baroness Carin who finally spoke, her prim, precise voice carrying with it only the slightest hint of accent.

'On behalf of Nordland, I thank you for such a warm greeting, Graf Mandred,' she said. She looked out across the faces of his courtiers, studying them before she spoke again. 'There is, however, a distinction between a true welcome and mere courtesy. I can see the concern that troubles your minds but which civility keeps from your tongues. Let me ease your doubts about our intentions in making this journey you so rightly adjudge long and perilous.' She looked aside at Count van der Duijn, waited for a nod from him before she continued. 'It is no secret that our lands have suffered terribly from calamity, but we do not come here as beggars seeking charity. The gifts we sought to bestow upon this court are given freely, without thought of restitution.'

'You come to us as equals then?' scoffed Duke Schneidereit. 'Your lands in ruin, your cities overtaken by monsters and barbarians and you claim...' The duke's fury wilted beneath the glower of his sovereign.

'It is hoped that her ladyship will forgive those among us whose pride is greater than their candour,' Mandred's tone was apologetic as he bowed towards the baroness. He directed a warning glance at his other nobles. 'After any conquest, in the wake of any battle, there burns a flame in some men. In the heat of the fray a man must be gripped by a certain boldness if he is to prevail. It is regrettable that this same boldness should cause some to forget that humility too is one of the knightly virtues.'

'A charitable sentiment, your highness,' Count van der Duijn remarked. 'But I must echo the words of my Nordland allies. It is not for charity that we have braved the Forest of Shadows and crossed the ruins of Drakwald.' This time it was the count who looked to the baroness for permission before continuing. 'We have come to do homage to the Wolf of Sigmar,' he said, his voice becoming as firm as stone and loud as thunder. 'We come to offer fealty to the mighty lord we would call our liege.'

From some among the council, the count's speech brought gasps of surprise, from others only scornful chuckles. Mandred maintained a stoic silence as he considered both reactions. The less farsighted among his nobles were thrilled by the prospect of controlling these neighbouring lands. To their imaginings of new fiefdoms in Drakwald they now added the vision of rich estates in Westerland and Nordland. Others among his council, those whose minds were of a more practical turn or more farsighted vision, could appreciate the onerous obligation the fealty of these lands would place upon Middenland and Middenheim. They would become responsible for these realms, bound to their protection and their defence. If they needed any example of how burdensome such responsibility would be they had only to look around them at the wreckage of Carroburg.

'The wolf who suckles the stray pup accepts it into the pack,' Ar-Ulric declared. 'But it must be wary lest the pack be weakened by its compassion.' The old priest looked over at Mandred. 'Too many mouths to feed brings ruin to the whole pack.'

At the graf's right hand, Hartwich countered Ar-Ulric's cautious philosophy. 'The pack must grow if it is to survive,' the Sigmarite said. 'If it abandons its own, then it is already a thing dead.'

'Try to save everything and you will save nothing,' Ar Ulric countered, his statement echoed by many wise nods from the seated nobles.

Again, Mandred considered both views. When he was a youth, his tutor had encouraged him to be careful in his deliberations. Grooming the young prince to one day rule a great city, his teacher had cautioned him that every problem had two sides. As he matured, however, Mandred realised how wrong such thinking was. Most of the world's problems were too complex to be limited by only two possibilities. He thought about Ar-Ulric's position. The wise old wolf urged caution, advising him to protect what was already won. He warned against reaching for more and thereby risking all. By the same token, he could see through Hartwich's counsel. The Sigmarite was a disciple of the first Emperor and to him the dream of that Empire was more than politics and power, it was a sacred duty. Mankind united beneath one crown, one voice and one throne. Such was the destiny Hartwich believed in. It was the vision towards which he strove to guide the man whose fate he believed was to rule.

Mandred thought of his strange meeting with the witch in the woods. He pondered the doom Hulda said the gods had proclaimed for him. He remembered her words, that a man who fled from power was the only man fit to wield it.

When the Graf of Middenheim voiced his decision, it wasn't the mere echo of the priests seated to either side of him, it wasn't the ambition of his nobles or the caution of his vassals. His choice was his. It belonged to him alone.

'I must reject the fealty of Westerland and of Nordland,' Mandred decided. He fixed his gaze upon the representatives of those realms. 'To accept your fealty would be to assume dominance over your people and your lands. That is something which I must reject.' He gestured to Hartwich seated beside him. 'There are some who would see me as Emperor, but I own no such ambition. The dream of Empire is not my own.'

With each word, Count van der Duijn sank a little lower in his chair, his face became a little more drawn and filled with despair. He had placed all his hopes in the army Mandred had raised, an army he had prayed he could turn towards the west, to use to drive the Norscans from his city as they had driven the skaven from Carroburg. Dejected, it took all of his dignity to keep from weeping before the nobles of Middenheim.

Baroness Carin was more composed, finding anger rather than despair in Mandred's denial of her offer. 'What then are your dreams, Wolf of Sigmar?' she demanded, challenge in her voice.

Mandred stood away from the table. Slowly he drew Legbiter from its sheath, displaying the runefang to the Electress of Nordland. 'Middenheim is realm enough to rule,' he said. Chastened, the baroness tried to look away from his fierce gaze, but found herself caught by the fire of his eyes.

'My dream,' Mandred said, slowly marching around the table, his footfalls like his words echoing through the wrecked temple, 'is a bold one. It is a vision that speaks for all men. It is a vision of lands fractured by divisions of greed and heritage brought together by shared hope and shared dignity. It is a vision built not upon the thrill of conquest and the desires of dominance, but one founded upon the pride that burns inside all men, be they noble or base.' His march brought him around to where the representatives were sitting. Mandred stared down at Count van der Duijn.

'I reject the fealty of Westerland,' Mandred repeated, then extended his hand to the distraught count. 'Instead, I beg the friendship of my brotherland. I ask that they accept the fellowship of Middenheim.'

Stunned silence held the room. Tears were in Count van der Duijn's eyes as he rose and seized Mandred's hand in his own.

'This is my vision,' Mandred declared. 'Not an Empire reforged in the flames of conquest, but of neighbours united in a coalition of mutual protection and respect. Look about you and see the destruction that is harvested by a people who stand alone. The same vile pestilence afflicts other lands, enslaves other peoples! Can we ignore their cries? Can we abandon them to the same vermin that sought to despoil our own homes? I say to you that the man who would contemplate such craven cowardice is a disgrace to his father and his grandfather and all the ancestors before him that ever walked proud beneath the sun.'

Mandred brandished Legbiter, letting its edge gleam in the sunlight filtering down through the temple's broken roof. 'Need we an Emperor?' he asked. 'That is a question for all men, all lands to decide. And it is a question that shall wait until the last skaven has been scoured from those lands!' Savagely, he thrust downward with the runefang, driving the blade into the charred surface of the table.

Their sovereign's passion brought the nobles from their chairs. They thrust their fists in the air, cheering this man who had walked through the Sacred Flame, this hero who had saved their city, this champion who had led them in the liberation of Drakwald. Perhaps they were too selfish, too small to share the vision that guided him, but it was enough that Mandred could see the path ahead. Where the Wolf of Sigmar led, they would follow.

Baroness Carin sat in silence as the nobles of Middenheim praised their graf. She too had been moved by Mandred's words and, as she gazed up at him, the flames of ambition were kindled in her eyes.

Lady Mirella was waiting for him beside the shattered image of Verena. There was a warmth in her smile that Mandred could feel in his very bones.

'When they built this place, the architect must have been well versed in the arcane secrets of acoustics,' Mirella stated. 'Even in here, I was able to hear you.'

Mandred shook his head. 'We'll have to find a different

place to hold council,' he mused. 'Somewhere better able to keep its secrets from stray ears. I can't have the whole camp learning what kind of simple-minded asses some of their noble lords are.'

Mirella closed her arms around him in a tight embrace. 'Then they couldn't take pride in the greatness of some of their noble lords,' she said, pressing her lips against his ear. He started to pull away as her kisses became more passionate.

'There is much still to do,' Mandred said. 'I must meet with Baroness Carin and Count van der Duijn to discuss plans for the campaign to relieve their peoples. I have to discuss the logistics of moving the army, of organising the Drakwalders who are able to fight and providing for those unable to march with us...'

His words were silenced by the soft fingers Mirella pressed against his mouth. 'Later,' she told him. 'It will all be waiting for you later. For now, there is this moment, this peace within the storm. Don't let it slip away. Let me share it with you.' She shook her head, apology in her voice. 'I'm not a powerful ruler or wealthy potentate. I don't have the wisdom of sages or the philosophy of priests. I've never worn armour or carried a sword. I am just a landless refugee, like so many others.' She set her head against his chest. 'There is so little I can offer you.'

Mandred's hand closed about her chin, tilted her face upwards so that he could gaze down into her eyes. 'More than gold and swords and philosophy,' he told Mirella. 'What can anyone offer another that is more precious than the love within their heart?'

The woman in his arms tightened her embrace, clinging to him with the desperate fear only love can know. Soon, she knew, he would again ride to war. Again he would be in the thick of battle, waging his crusade against the obscene enemies of mankind. Perhaps the gods would again bring him back to her unscathed, but after experiencing the tyrannies of Emperor Boris, she knew how fickle the beneficence of the gods could be.

No, she couldn't think of tomorrow. There was only now. This moment. This fragment of time they could share. This small sliver of life that belonged not to gods or nations, but to them and them alone.

Sylvania, 1121

Over the barren desolation of a haunted land, the silent height of Vanhaldenschlosse lorded over the terrain. A mad spiral of ancient stone steeped in the corruption of Morrslieb and the foulness of darkest sorcery, the tower emanated its own atmosphere of horror, the rank miasma of the eldritch and the profane. For all its aura of hoary age and primordial evil, the fortress was a recent construction, raised less than a decade earlier. Black magic and legions of supernatural labourers had erected the great tower in only a few months.

Those legions now lay strewn about the walls of Vanhaldenschlosse, exposed bones bleaching in the sun, rotten flesh drying and hardening into leather, acres of bonefields, thousands upon thousands of the unburied dead. The slaughtered husks of armoured Nachtsheer lay strewn beside the mangled shapes of Sylvanian peasants and the desiccated shells of prehistoric bog-men. Among the corpses were the inhuman carcasses of skaven by their thousands, elongated skulls rife with sharp fangs. Hulking among the legions of dead, rising from the bonefields like morbid hills, were the saurian vastness of vanquished dragons, strips of scale and flesh still clinging to their reptilian frames.

High overhead, carrion crows cawed and vultures wheeled. The scavengers were drawn to the stench of death and the sight of such a necrotic feast. Yet a force more primal even than their hunger kept them from descending, kept the wolves and jackals from stealing out from the woods. The beasts of field and sky could sense the arcane ember that lingered within each carcass. They could recognise the loathsome taint of sorcery that had once endowed these dead things with an abominable simulacrum of life. Their instincts warned them away, lest the natural life within their own flesh should stir those lingering embers. For what had once risen to the necromancer's call would never rest easy and might at any moment hearken to some sinister summons.

Birds and beasts shunned the wastes around Vanhalden-schlosse, but other things were more daring. Flitting across the bonefield, slinking from shadow to shadow, was a clutch of wiry figures draped in black. The shapes sometimes paused in their stealthy advance, sometimes made gestures to one another with hand-like paws before resuming their cautious journey. Like ghosts, the figures flitted through the desolation, converging upon the ominous majesty of the tower itself. Yet these were no ghosts, but creatures alive and driven by grim purpose.

Despite appearances, there was life within the black vastness of Vanhaldenschlosse. Life these black-draped killers had travelled far to extinguish.

Behind the sombre walls of Vanhaldenschlosse there existed a great hall, a mammoth vault with soaring ceiling perched upon the tips of pre-human dolmens. The eldritch vibrations of the standing stones sent a wailing crackle of aethyric energy swirling about the room. Like the pulsations of an unseen heart, the vibrations throbbed and ebbed. Each pulsation flickered as it was drawn out from the ancient dolmens, pulled to the centre of the hall where a crystal dais stood. Atop the dais stood a great seat, a throne built on a titanic scale. Skulls were the fabric of that throne, fused together with blackest magic, each brow stamped with arcane sigils and obscene hieroglyphs. In each eye socket, the dark flicker of a warpstone nugget lent its corrupt radiance to the profane power saturating the throne.

Nestled upon the throne like a black spider at the centre of its web was the master of the tower. No giant or titan, yet there was about the dark-robed figure such an aura of power that he was not diminished by his gigantic setting. The robes were those of a Morrite priest saturated in the vapours of betrayal and heresy. About his face was a mask of bone steeped in the horror of vengeance. And within the eyes, within the terrible eyes that stared from the sockets of the mask, there shone the glimmer of abominable purpose.

Am I the dream or the dreamer? The question had vexed the man who had once been Frederick van Hal the priest these past months. Van Hal, the man who from misery had turned his heart from Morr, god of death, and set his foot upon the black path of the necromancer, remaking himself as Vanhal, Scourge of Sylvania.

Long years had Vanhal rested upon his throne, allowing the vibrations of the dolmens, the vapours of warpstone, to seep into his spirit. By his sorcery he had harnessed the might of the magical fulcrum upon which Vanhaldenschlosse had been raised. His power had been such that he had turned forward time itself, hurling the fortress ahead many months to that moment when stars and moons were in their most propitious alignment. The resultant energies had been the fuel for spells not dared by mortal flesh in a thousand years. He had called the great wyrms from their graves, enslaved their decaying husks to his will, and unleashed them against the verminous foe that thought to destroy him.

The Battle of the Plague Dragons had annihilated the skaven host, but it had also drained Vanhal's powers, taxed his vitality. It had brought him to the borderland between life and death, the shadow world between the spheres. As he stood upon the edge of mortality, he could feel his passions crying out to him, striving to draw him back to the world of the living. Across the threshold he could see the shades of loved ones beckoning to him. Almost he could put names to once familiar faces, almost he could recall the emotions that had set him upon a path of horror and atrocity. Almost he could remember those who had been his family.

Between himself and the gardens of the dead, he imagined two mammoth pillars. One barred his way, stern and implacable. The other beckoned to him, drawing him to it like a moth to flame. As he approached, he found himself in a vast desert, a waste of sand dunes stretching to the far horizon. The pillars had dwindled to a pair of colossal stone feet, the statue they had once supported toppled and buried beneath the shifting sands. Between the feet was an inscription in the hieroglyphs of lost Khemri: a name so steeped in evil and horror that it was spoken only in whispers even a thousand years after the thing that had worn it was destroyed.

Vanhal felt an obscene affinity for that name, a ghastly kinship that leeched the warmth from his flesh. It was a name he had worn or would wear. The name of the black dreamer upon its black throne.

'No,' the necromancer hissed, raising himself from the seat of skulls. He was neither dream nor puppet. His will was his own; his mind was his own! He had chosen this path, it had not been chosen for him.

Vanhal looked about him, staring in wonder at the vast hall around him. He could see the aethyric vibrations dancing from the standing stones, could watch the skein of their energies swirling and dancing about him. He could see them twisting and writhing, fashioning themselves into hieroglyphs as they flittered through the chilly air. There were secrets wrapped in those symbols, obscenities too vile to be consigned to even the most degenerate tome. There were past and present, the dim shades of the future and the grotesque oblivion of eternity.

As the profane knowledge crawled into his brain, Vanhal could feel the embers of his humanity dying inside him. The last vestiges of kinship to man were being smothered, crushed with the bony talon of a monster that had made itself a god.

Only the dimmest, most primal part of Vanhal's brain was still conscious of the purely mundane nature of the hall around him. It was through veils of sorcerous distractions and esoteric thought that he saw the cloaked shapes creeping along the walls. Masked by a mental fog, the assassins pounced upon their prey.

The foremost of the killers leapt into the air, throwing its body into a tumbling roll. As it did so it threw forth its hand-like paws, flinging a menagerie of angular throwing stars at the necromancer. Iron saturated with warpstone powder, the missiles dripped corrosive poison, pitting the floor with their noxious venom as they hurtled towards their target.

Detached from the purely temporal, for Vanhal, the

assassin's shuriken flew absurdly slowly. Even in his distracted state, it was a small thing to conjure a corpse wind to buffet the little slivers of murder, to cast them back into the face of his would-be killer. The skaven assassin shrieked as it saw the throwing stars reverse direction. Its amazing reflexes allowed it to throw itself flat, but even its speed was unequal to the capricious magic of Vanhal. With but a thought, he shifted the angle of the necrotic wind and sent the shuriken slicing downwards into the prone assassin.

While he was disposing of the first killer, a second monster dropped at Vanhal from the ceiling, crooked blades clenched in both fists, a third knife wrapped in the coils of its naked tail. The assassin didn't cry out, didn't make any sound to betray its intention. Just the same, its advent didn't go unnoticed. Midway in its descent, the skaven was caught in the air, held in place as though an unseen hand gripped it. The ratman writhed and struggled as the restriction closed tighter about it. Soon squeals of agony and flecks of blood flew from its mouth. The sickening crunch of grinding bones shuddered through the hall, yet still the pressure didn't abate. The coils of spectral force were without mercy, clenching tighter and tighter until the pulverised assassin dripped to the floor in lumpy puddles of gore.

A third killer sprang out from the darkness. In its paws it clutched a great brass globe. Vanhal could perceive the sorcerous weapon as a baleful glamour, a hellish bonfire of malignant enchantments. The weapon never left the ratman's paws. Before it could hurl the sphere at the necromancer, his spells were already at work, crawling through the assassin's brain like so many maggots. Mesmeric paralysis held the skaven for a moment, then, with shuddering resistance, it lifted its paws on high and dashed the brass sphere at its very feet.

The assassin vanished in a coruscating ball of destruction, wrenched from reality and hurled bodily into the void between worlds, even its screams unable to escape the vacuum.

More assassins came leaping, crawling, slinking and stalking from the darkness. Singly and en masse, they strove to slaughter their terrifying foe. Singly and en masse, they were slaughtered.

When it was over, when his spells told him the tower was once more stripped of life, Vanhal muttered a lesser conjuration, endowing the least mutilated of his adversaries with a mockery of animation. The zombie skaven shuffled and staggered, stumblingly obeying their killer's commands. The undead began gathering up the remains of their less complete comrades, to cleanse the hall of the detritus of battle.

Vanhal leaned back in his throne, the fight already forgotten as he studied once more the profane hieroglyphs only the eyes of a master necromancer could see.

Deathmaster Nartik didn't stop until he was well beyond sight and smell of Vanhaldenschlosse. Sole survivor of the dozen master-killers Clan Eshin had dispatched to murder the necromancer, Nartik knew it was only the cape of elf-hair that had protected him, hiding him from Vanhal's magic. His faith in the cape's protection, however, only went so far. The vision of his death squad's massacre, of his own apprentices being butchered like mice, was enough to shake even the Deathmaster's confidence.

The contract Eshin had made with Bonelord Nekrot would have to be nullified. That would displease Grey Lord Kreep, but what else was there to do? Vanhal's magic was too much for the assassins to overcome. The lone killers

Nartik had sent into the tower had all disappeared and now this mass attack had met with disaster. The necromancer was simply too terrible to die. Nartik didn't like to think about Nekrot's claims that this was a weakened Vanhal they had been trying to kill. The very idea that the man-thing could be even more powerful was enough to make him forget the strict bodily control of an Eshin assassin and spurt the musk of fear.

Nartik ground his fangs together as he scampered through a dead forest and hurried to the hidden tunnel that would bring him back into the sprawl of the Under-Empire. Nekrot must have known! He didn't want the necromancer dead. It had all been a ploy on Mordkin's part to humiliate and belittle Clan Eshin! Yes-yes, that was the truth of the matter. It had all been a treacherous trap to kill the best of Eshin's assassins! Such was the report he would make to Kreep. Nartik hadn't failed in killing the target, he'd succeeded in escaping the trap!

The Deathmaster cast one last, hateful glance in the direction of Vanhaldenschlosse. If Nekrot really wanted the sorcerer dead, the Bonelord would have to do it himself!

─◄ CHAPTER V ►─

Carroburg, 1119

It was something of a shock to Graf Mandred, Hero of Middenheim and Saviour of Carroburg, when he pulled back the horsehide flap and started to walk into the tent. His face flushed with embarrassment and he started to withdraw. From the corner of his eye, however, he saw his helm standing atop a wooden stand. There was no mistaking that piece of armour, not with the fangs of a skaven chieftain still embedded in it.

'Forgive me,' Mandred addressed the woman sitting in one of his chairs and whose unexpected presence had thrown him into such confusion. 'I believe you have the wrong tent.'

Baroness Carin's face contorted into a disappointed pout. 'Do not say that you are turning me out.'

An awkward smile tugged at Mandred's mouth. It was difficult not to compare the baroness sitting in his tent with the one who had spoken to his council. As a visitor to his

court, her costume had been restrained, only allowing such
concessions to femininity as decorum allowed. She had
been a noble, even regal figure but at the same time distant
and chaste.

It would take a man with ice in his veins to offer the
same opinion as she appeared now. The crimson gown
she wore wasn't the billowy affair of court but a sleek garment that accentuated the delicate curves of her figure. If
there was a bodice beneath that gown, the baroness had
left it much looser, affording it no chance to hide the con-
tours of her amply female form. The coiffure of before had
been abandoned, leaving the noblewoman's hair to hang
about her shoulders in a dark cascade. Paints and powders complemented a face that was already possessed of a
natural gracefulness, changing the features from striking to
stunning.

Mandred felt guilty about letting his gaze rove across the
baroness's body for as long as it did. Even more so when
he noticed her sullen pout had softened into just the bar-
est suggestion of a smile, demure rather than wanton in its
expression of invitation. With the taste of Lady Mirella's lips
still on his own, he felt uncomfortably like a traitor for the
sensation that pulsed through his body.

He could see in Baroness Carin's eyes that she fully appreciated the impact her appearance made. Mandred wasn't
so naïve as to think her change of wardrobe and presence
within his own tent was mere happenstance. The base
ardour rushing through his veins cooled as he considered
the audacity of the noblewoman.

Reaching behind him, Mandred drew back the horsehide
flap. 'It has been a long and trying day,' he said.

Baroness Carin sighed and shook her head. 'We cannot
all of us fight our battles with sword and shield,' she said.

'Some of us must make do with such weapons as the gods have seen fit to provide.'

Mandred couldn't help but laugh at the frankness of her words. 'I think few opponents could deny you the field with such an arsenal at your command.'

'Only those who matter most,' the baroness said. She'd made no move to leave the chair. 'Those who can help my people.'

Mandred let the horsehide fall back across the doorway. His eyes searched the baroness's face, trying to find any hint of duplicity there. Had her words, like her costume, been carefully calculated, an invention to appeal to him? Or was it a genuine concern he heard in her voice?

'You inherited the title from Baron Salzwedel,' Mandred recalled. He turned his head towards the wall of the tent, staring in the direction of the Otwinsstein and the demolished castle. Salzwedel had been among the electors who had joined Emperor Boris in his refuge and who had perished with the tyrant when plague penetrated the walls of that refuge. He looked again at the baroness. How old was she? Perhaps twenty? Not much older, certainly, than when his own father had died and he had inherited the heavy burden of leading his people. It was one thing to grow into the obligations of leadership, quite another to have the role suddenly thrust upon you without warning.

'My younger brother was to inherit,' the baroness said. 'As far as my father was concerned, I was around only to tempt his most powerful vassals. He kept them loyal by dangling the prospect that one of their sons might marry into our family.' There was more than the mere suggestion of a smile now, but it was bitter and cheerless. She plucked at the bosom of her gown, wrinkling the material. 'I've had a lot of practice,' she said. 'It was only when the plague took my brother that my father thought of me instead of what he could buy with me.'

Pity for the baroness boiled up within Mandred. Before the emotion could overcome him, he strangled it. A man could be moved by pity, but it was a luxury a leader couldn't afford. Everything since he'd stepped into his tent had been plotted and strategised. Her clothes, her appearance, the coy hints that teased when they briefly flickered on her face, even the musky odour she wore, all of it had been designed to entice him. Why should he think her words any different? What was it she was trying to buy now?

Mandred paced away from the baroness. Stepping over to the upturned box, he laid his hand on his battered helm. Even if he'd failed to pry the skaven fangs loose, Beck had done a commendable job polishing the steel. It was like gazing into a mirror. He could see Baroness Carin sitting there behind him. He studied her reflection, watching her expression.

'The noblest are those who would sacrifice all for their people,' he said. His voice was soft and comforting but his eyes were steely glints as he watched the baroness's image. 'It is so rare to find a kindred soul. Long have I sought someone who would share my vision for the Empire.'

It was only for a heartbeat, but Mandred caught the triumphant smirk that broke through the baroness's carefully calculated ploy. His suspicions were justified. Unable to entrap him through passion, she now sought to snare him through his ideals. His hands were clenched into fists of rage as he rounded on her.

'The lowest slattern is the one who seeks to climb the highest,' Mandred snarled at her, his words clipped and cruel.

Baroness Carin didn't even blink at his accusation. 'For my people, I would seduce the gods themselves,' she told him.

There wasn't a trace of vulnerability in her tone now. Her voice was like the rasp of an iron blade across a whetstone, unyielding and unbowed. Posture and expression changed in subtle ways, stripping away the enticing invitation she had worn as though it were another garment. Her visage, her bearing, everything about her had an unmistakable aura of command.

'Get out,' Mandred growled, all civility and propriety gone. When she didn't move, he stormed across the tent. His hand closed about her arm, drawing her to her feet with a savagery that surprised even him.

'Not until you listen to me,' the baroness said.

'I've heard all I care to hear,' Mandred told her, dragging her towards the door.

'But not all I have to say.' Mandred wasn't certain how she managed it, but a simple twist of her wrist and she slipped free of his grip. She stood there, massaging the spot he had held so roughly. Briefly, he felt shame that he had done her harm, imagining the bruises that must even now be forming underneath the sleeve of her gown. Then he reflected that a seductress would be accustomed to rough use. Certainly she was accomplished at slipping free from a man's fingers.

'Do I need to have you removed?' Mandred asked, matching the glare his visitor directed at him.

'I will leave,' the baroness said. 'But not until you've listened to me. I want to explain to you why the Electress of Nordland so brazenly steals into your tent.'

Mandred smiled coldly. 'I'll find out who admitted you,' he assured her. 'If I limit myself to just staking them out for the wolves, they may consider themselves blessed by Shallya.'

'My purpose coming here wasn't what you think,' the

baroness told him. She laughed cynically. 'Thanks to my father's guile I have learned that the surest way to influence a man is to make him love you.'

'And what did you intend to accomplish with such influence?'

'The salvation of my people,' she answered without hesitation. 'Believe nothing else I have said to you this night if you will only believe that. Your army is the only power in the north with strength enough to save us. You can free Nordland and Westerland both.'

'I have said my army will do so,' Mandred told her.

Baroness Carin shook her head. 'How will you free us?' she asked. 'As conquerors, or as liberators? Will you toss us our freedom like a bone thrown to a dog?' She waved her hand, gesturing at the walls of the tent. 'Look out there at the people of Drakwald. You've freed their land from the skaven, but you haven't given them what they most need. What I've come here to beg you not to deny my people or the people of Westerland!'

'Something given away has no value,' she explained. 'What pride can the Drakwalders take in the freedom you've brought them? They had no part in it. They didn't earn it. They didn't win it for themselves.'

She saw the impact her words had made, the doubt that had struck at Mandred's vision. Like a predator scenting prey, she pounced upon that vulnerability. 'Allow my people and the people of Westerland to share in what you would win for them. Let them hold their heads in pride and declare that they too played their part.'

'Your lands are broken, your people scattered or enslaved,' Mandred pointed out. 'What part would you have them play?'

'It is true,' the baroness admitted. 'Our peoples are scattered and broken. We need the strength of your army if we are to be free. We need the sword only that mighty host may wield. But let it be Nordland, let it be Westerland that guides that sword. Together with Count van der Duijn, I have conceived a plan that will free both our lands and allow our peoples their portion of the glory.'

Mandred motioned her back to the chair. 'You are right,' he told her as she sat down. 'You aren't leaving until I've heard what you have to say.'

He was reminded of Warrenburg as he walked through the squalid refugee camp. The misery of Warrenburg had been born in the plague; the misery he saw around him had been inflicted by the skaven. It was difficult to decide which was worse. Wherever Mandred turned, he seemed to find some new horror. An old woman dragging herself along the ground like some sort of human slug, the scabrous stumps of her legs scarred by the marks of verminous teeth. A little boy shivering at anyone who came near him, cowering in the corner of a broken wall, crying out not with a whimper but with the rodent squeaks of the monsters who had enslaved him. The broken wreckage of a once hulking man, scarred holes where his eyes had been, his face branded with the scratchwork letters of the skaven.

Everywhere the bestial cruelty of the ratmen was on display, a parade of atrocities that stabbed at Mandred's conscience. If he had acted sooner, if he had stirred his army from Middenheim earlier, how much of this misery could these people have been spared?

As he looked around him, Mandred saw too the evidence of what Baroness Carin had told him he would find: the listless shame of survival when so many others had perished, the apathy of men who had lost everything, the guilt of a people stripped of their pride. He wasn't so credulous

that he failed to see that Baroness Carin and Count van
der Duijn would profit greatly by his implementation of
their plan. By insinuating themselves so intimately with
the liberation of their provinces, they would strengthen
the foundations of their own power. Yet he could not
deny that a people who found pride in their leaders was
a people who found pride within themselves. He thought
of how his father had made Middenheim strong through
his leadership.

The plan Baroness Carin and Count van der Duijn had
hatched between them appealed to Mandred. It possessed
the right mixture of boldness and cunning. Mandred's
army would march into Nordland, striking for the port
of Dietershafen. Once the town was liberated from the
skaven infesting it, they would use the shipyards there to
restore Nordland's navy, refitting the ships that had been
savaged by the ratkin. The army would winter in Dietershafen while the people of Nordland made ready their
ships. In the spring, the revitalised fleet would carry the
army to Marienburg. Jarl Snagr Half-nose and his barbarians would expect an attack by land, but they imagined
only their own kind still roamed the Sea of Claws.

It was the Marienburg part of the plan that rested ill
with Mandred. The Norscans, however barbarous, at least
were men. With so much of the Empire in the thrall of
the ratkin, it offended him to expend time and resources
– to say nothing of lives – fighting his fellow man.
Indeed, his misgivings were such that he'd left their meeting without giving the baroness a firm decision. He had
to think about the campaign ahead, had to ask himself if
his zeal to free Dietershafen and his reluctance to attack
Marienburg owed itself to the arena of logistics and tactics or if it was simply the hatred inside him, the burning

hunger to destroy the ratmen wherever they could be found. He thought again of Hartwich's warning about the two wolves.

As he walked among the human debris of Carroburg, Mandred closed his eyes and prayed to Ulric for the wisdom to do what needed to be done.

When he opened his eyes, the first person he saw was a grubby, filth-covered woman. Tattered rags draped loosely about a body that had been starved into a scarecrow shape. The face was worn and haggard, ravaged by the twin evils of brutality and privation. The hair was grey from dirt and dust, but here and there a patch as white as driven snow managed to peek through. The piteous wretch was wandering amid the rubble, turning over fallen stones, peering behind broken windows.

She was just another of the flotsam discarded by the crimson tide of war, yet something about her drew Mandred. There was some unshakable feeling of familiarity, almost a sense of kinship. He watched her for a moment as she stumbled about the ruins, calling out in a weak, cracked voice. 'The doktor! Have you seen the doktor?'

Mandred went to her. The accent in her voice wasn't that of Drakwald, it belonged to Middenheim! When he joined her beside the burnt-out husk of a barn, she looked at him with dazed, confused eyes.

'The doktor. Have you seen the doktor?' she asked him.

As he stared down into her pleading face, Mandred felt a shock course through him. He knew this woman! She had been a regular visitor to the Middenpalaz. Her father had been Baron Thornig, Middenheim's representative to the court of Emperor Boris.

'Princess Erna?' Mandred asked, almost frightened by the idea that this ragged, starveling creature could be the vibrant, kindly woman from his memories. He saw the confusion on her face become panic when she heard her name. Before she could run, Mandred grabbed her arm. He shuddered at its bony thinness, comparing it in his mind to the fleshy vitality he had felt beneath his hand when he had caught hold of Baroness Carin.

'The doktor said he died from the plague!' Erna cried, her eyes wide with terror. 'He died from the plague!'

Mandred kept his grip on her. With his free hand he drew back the hood of the cloak he was wearing. He had borrowed the simple wool garment from Beck, using it to shroud himself in anonymity as he moved among the refugees.

Erna flinched as he threw back the hood, then a little ember of recognition seemed to shine in her eyes. Suddenly she dropped to the ground, falling to her knees in courtly deference. 'Your Grace!' she gasped. It was strange to hear himself addressed in such a manner, but he reflected that when she'd left Middenheim, she'd known him as Prince Mandred, not Graf Mandred.

The genuflection of the ragged, tattered figure drew the notice of the refugees around them. Timidly, they crept towards Mandred, maintaining a wary distance, unable to believe their liberator was among them. First one, then another of the wretched figures fell to their knees, their heads bowed.

Mandred raised Erna to her feet, hoping that by doing so the others would also stand. Their obeisance made him feel guilty. After all they had endured, that they should still remember to humiliate themselves at the feet of a noble was perhaps the cruellest barb of all.

'It's all right now,' Mandred soothed Erna. 'You've come home.'

She started to pull away, fright again filling her wasted features. 'I can't,' she said. 'I mustn't. I have to find the doktor.' She lowered her voice, leaning close to Mandred. 'He's my friend,' she whispered. She nodded as though to convince herself. 'We have a secret,' she added. 'One I can't tell anyone else. I must find him so I can tell him our secret. He has to know I haven't forgotten.'

Mandred remembered the young princess he knew, tried not to let that memory become the sad creature he now held. 'What is the doktor's name? I'll help you find him.'

Erna blinked at him, puzzled by his words. 'We can't find him,' she said. 'They took him away.' A horror shone in her eyes as her wounded mind connected the words she spoke to the memory they represented. Sobbing, she collapsed against Mandred's chest. 'They took him away,' she repeated. 'He didn't want to go, but they took him down into their burrows. They took him into the dark and he didn't want to go.'

Gently, Mandred led the sobbing woman away. He praised Ulric that he'd found her, that he'd been led to this single mote in a sea of suffering. A face and a name had been given to those languishing under the verminous tyranny of the skaven. He had seen what it meant to fall into their clutches: Erna the kindly princess reduced to the crazed creature he now held. Whatever could be done to restore her body and her mind would be done, he made this vow to himself.

He made another vow too. He would exterminate the skaven, whatever the cost. It wasn't hatred now; it wasn't Hartwich's Wolf of Death. No, it had grown beyond that, become something greater and more terrible.

Something that could lead him only to victory or death.

* * *

Skavenblight, 1121

'Choose three.'

Seerlord Queekual's snarl echoed through the murky cave, catching in the shadows and crawling into every crack and crevice. Doktor Moschner trembled at the sound, shivering in the filthy ratskin robe the skaven had given him to protect against the subterranean chill. He looked over the dozens of naked, scrawny humans. Once, as personal physician to Emperor Boris, he had been accustomed to consorting with only the highest strata of society, the very elite of the Empire, those of only the noblest blood and pedigree. In the black depths of Skavenblight such petty distinctions as class and breeding quickly crumbled away. Men were naught but chattel to the verminous underfolk, livestock to be exploited to the fullest and then, ultimately, consumed. The skaven cared nothing if the man being subjected to their horrors was once a wealthy baron or lowly mendicant. All were the same to the inhuman monsters: prey.

Moschner stepped away from the crude stone table he had been labouring at, careful to keep his eyes averted as he passed Queekual, bobbing his head in the deferential manner that conveyed respect to a high-ranking ratman. He had always been quick to adapt to the fashion and style of the Imperial court in Altdorf, to adopt whatever wisdom was en vogue at the moment when prescribing for the Imperial household. He had thought he'd overcome that facility for self-preservation when he'd turned against the excesses of Boris Goldgather. But whatever pride, whatever righteous indignation at the abuse of his fellow man had emboldened him against the cruelties of a human emperor had evaporated before the tyrannies of an inhuman sorcerer. It wasn't necessarily a fear of death that made Moschner submit – it was fear of the kind of death Queekual could bestow.

Nervously, the doktor walked towards the black-furred guards flanking the group of humans. They bared their fangs at him, claws clenching more tightly about the hefts of their spears. Moschner quickly covered his mouth with his hand, hiding the nervous smile that had worked itself onto his face. Among themselves, a show of teeth was a sign of challenge so the skaven were quick to read the same in the smiles of their slaves. If not for the presence of Queekual, Moschner knew he would have been beaten for his lapse of verminous etiquette.

'Three,' Queekual hissed again, the Seerlord's tone crackling with impatience.

Moschner nodded his understanding and hurried to inspect the slaves. They were dirty, reeking of the filth and squalor of the pens. Most bore the bruises and lesions of their captivity, a few sported still more serious hurts. Wounds, however, were the least of Moschner's concerns. Using a long stick, he poked and prodded the naked wretches, examining armpits and throats for any trace of the plague. He felt ashamed that he hoped the slaves were infected. The disease might be cruel, but it would kill them much quicker than the skaven.

'Well?' Queekual demanded, his ire vicious enough to make the skaven guards squeak.

Moschner turned his head, risking a glance that almost met the Seerlord's gaze. 'What happens to the ones I don't accept?' he asked, surprised that he didn't choke on his own bold words.

Queekual slammed the butt of his horned staff against the

floor. 'Pick-quick,' he growled, a green glow creeping into his eyes as his temper rose.

'Why only three? I may need even more help,' Moschner persisted. 'What you ask of me isn't easy!'

The Seerlord slammed his staff against the floor again. He held up his other paw, displaying a crooked claw. 'Now doktor-thing picks only one!' he declared. 'Speak-squeak again and I kill-burn all-all!'

There was no doubt in Moschner's mind that the ratman meant what he said. The skaven were callous with the lives of their own kind – he had seen that often enough. They thought no more of killing a slave – be it man, dwarf or goblin – than a man thought of squashing a bug. Bobbing his head in deference once more, Moschner looked again at the slaves arrayed before him. He tried to ignore the pleading, hopeful stares. The slaves were too cowed to implore him with their voices, but they could still beg with their eyes. That was torture enough for the doktor as he studied them.

'Him,' Moschner finally said, pointing his hand at a tall blonde-haired man standing at the back of the company. Despite the cruelty and privation the skaven must have imposed on him, the man's physique still conveyed a sense of power. More importantly, there was still a gleam of pride in his eyes. Alone of all of them, he didn't beg Moschner with his eyes.

Queekual brought his claws together in a hollow clap. At his gesture, the guard-rats began to herd the other slaves away. The Seerlord turned back to Moschner. 'You have a helper now. I expect-want progress. Fast-quick!' To emphasise his command, Queekual lashed the floor with his naked tail. Moschner kept his head lowered until the terrifying ratman exited the cave.

'Thank you.' The words came in a parched whisper. Moschner looked around to find the tall slave beside him. He motioned for the man to stay where he was and hurried to the niche in the wall where he kept the provisions Queekual allocated to him. He came back with a water-skin. Greedily, the slave quenched his thirst, only relenting when the skin was half-drained. A guilty look crossed his features and he thrust the depleted skin towards Moschner.

'It's all right,' Moschner assured him. 'Our beneficent masters keep me well supplied. Drink all you want.'

The slave took him at his word. Only when the last drop had been wrung from the skin did he return his attention to Moschner. 'Thank you again,' he said, his voice rendered more human this time. 'I am called Schroeder. Until three months ago I was a knight in the Order of the Black Rose.' A flicker of pain shot through him and he pressed a hand to his forehead. 'Was it three months? Can a man suffer so much in so little time? Can the gods allow such hell to persist?'

Moschner stared in alarm as Schroeder's wits began to wander. He cast an anxious glance at the mouth of the cave where Queekual's warriors stood guard. He wasn't certain if the beasts understood Reikspiel the way their master did, but even so they could not fail to notice a madman whatever language he spoke. After so long alone, Moschner didn't want his only companion taken from him.

'I am Doktor Wolfius Moschner, lately of Carroburg,' he introduced himself, approaching Schroeder with extended hand. The absurdity of such formality in such circumstances brought a hearty laugh from the knight. More importantly, it focused his straying mind.

'Pfeildorf was my home,' Schroeder declared. 'Before the underfolk came,' he added with bitterness. He stared hard at Moschner, suspicion erasing the gratitude in his eyes. 'Why do they treat you so well? What service do you provide them?'

Moschner could not mistake the challenge in the knight's tone. A soldier thought in very simple terms. His worldview was limited to ideas like friend and enemy... and traitor.

'The ratkin captured me in Carroburg after they seized the city,' Moschner explained. 'The horned one is a sorcerer. He is taking any healers he can find among their captives and using them to conduct research.'

'What kind of research?' Schroeder demanded.

Moschner motioned with his hand, leading the knight deeper into the cave. 'It will be faster if I show you,' he explained. Schroeder followed his lead, every muscle in his body twitching with the expectation of treachery.

'This is what he wants me to study,' Moschner said, waving his hand at the confusion of cages scattered about the back of the cave. Inside each cage a living slave had been stuffed. Not a human slave, nor a dwarf nor even a goblin. These were slaves culled from the dregs of skavendom, ratkin who had been subjugated by their own kind. It took Schroeder only a moment to recognise what common bond the imprisoned skaven shared.

'They have the plague,' he gasped in fright.

Moschner nodded. 'That is what Queekual wants me to study. Apparently the underfolk aren't immune to the disease that has wrought such havoc among humanity, though the symptoms are far less pronounced.'

'And this Queekual wants you to find a cure?' Schroeder growled, not bothering to mask the contempt in his voice. 'How could any man agree to help such monsters when his own people are being slaughtered and enslaved?'

'You don't understand!' Moschner snarled back, bristling

at the horrible accusation. 'The ratmen are already resistant to the plague! Left on their own, only one in ten would die, though the paranoia of their kind ensures the sick aren't given such a chance if they're discovered.'

'What does your sorcerer expect then?' Schroeder asked.

Moschner repressed a shudder. 'Something that goes against every oath I swore when I joined the Guild of Physicians. He wants me to make the plague more lethal. Not for men,' he hurried to explain when he saw the knight clenching his fists. 'He wants the plague's qualities against the ratkin improved.'

Schroeder was silent a moment, letting Moschner's words sink in. When he spoke, it was to utter a bark of laughter. 'Truly the gods favour us, doktor! These long months I have prayed for a way to strike back against the ratkin and now, through you, I am given an opportunity beyond my prayers!'

'I don't understand,' Moschner stated, alarmed that the knight's wits might be deserting him again.

'This task the sorcerer has given you!' Schroeder said. 'Can you not see? Do you not understand? The fiend intends to unleash a plague against his own kind!

'Work hard, doktor. Tell me what I must do to help. Because together we are going to kill a lot of skaven!'

⤛ CHAPTER VI ⤜

Nordland, 1119

The Army of Middenland marched with lighter step once the desolation of Drakwald was behind them. They were passing through their own land now, the trees that pressed close to the Old Forest Road were familiar to them, the songs of the birds that flittered through the sky were ones they knew. Many a soldier cast a wistful, longing look down one of the small tracks and trails that joined the road, picturing the comfort of hearth and home that waited for him somewhere down that path.

There were no deserters. However fierce the longing for their homes, even the lowliest spearman nursed within him an equally fierce sense of duty. Drakwald, the destruction of Carroburg, the suffering of those enslaved by the ratmen, these were lessons burnt into their hearts. Fighting the skaven, purging them from the lands they had conquered, had taken on the aspect of a crusade. Prevail or perish, those were the thoughts in every man's mind. Destroy the skaven so that the homes they left behind would not suffer the fate of Carroburg.

It was with pride that Mandred rode in the vanguard of his army. He rode in the company of the Knights of the White Wolf, the elite of Middenheim's warriors. They presented a fearsome aspect, their bodies locked within plates of red-painted steel. Hammers of iron hung from their saddles, vicious mauls that in the hands of a knight could pulp a skull in a heartbeat. Their warhorses, all of them enormous destriers selected for strength and stamina by the horse-breeders of Middenland, were adorned in quilted caparisons that hung down to their fetlocks. The steel barding that would normally have guarded the powerful animals was stowed away during the long march, a concession to the strain the added weight would impose even upon such steeds. In gentler times, against more civilised foes, squires would have led the warhorses to the battlefield. The knights would ride simple coursers until the time when battle was nigh. Only then would they mount the giant destriers, unleashing the full force of the animals in the brutal spectacle of a cavalry charge.

These were dark times, however, and the enemy was insidiously savage. No man who had fought in the Battle of Middenheim could forget the murderous cunning of the skaven, their penchant for deception and trickery. Honest battle was anathema to them. The creatures preferred ambush to battle, massacre to combat. Only with their grisly warlords threatening and goading them, only with the advantage of numbers and terrain, would the vermin be induced to fight.

Such an enemy knew nothing of honour, of the proprieties of war. They would gleefully exploit any advantage, no matter how churlish and vile. The only defence against an enemy who might strike from anywhere was vigilance and preparedness. As the column moved north, Mandred's knights wore their armour and rode their destriers. His bowmen kept their bows strung and at their sides. Spearmen marched with their shields loosely strapped to their backs, so that in case of a sudden attack the man behind might swiftly avail himself of the shield of the soldier in front. Macemen marched among the wagons, each dienstmann encased in full armour. A series of rotations allowed some of the macemen to rest in the wagons, but never more than a quarter of their number at any time. Swordsmen and axemen, restricted by far less cumbersome mail, were expected to march without such periodic respite.

Rangers, poachers, bandits and woodsmen ranged along the sides of the column as it marched, stealing into the trees, scouting the land for any sign of a lurking foe. They came from the depths of Middenland and from the forsaken interior of Drakwald. Nordlander scouts accustomed to prowling the Forest of Shadows and who had come to join the Baroness Carin. Veteran Hochland hunters, fleeing their own skaven-infested lands to lend their blades and bows at the service of Graf Mandred.

As grave as his concerns for flank and rear, it was the path ahead that most worried Mandred. Dozens of his best trackers had been sent before the army, men who could trail a vole through a briar and follow the week-old path of a beetle over a slab of granite. Several times Mad Albrecht or some other sentinel in forest-green would come drifting back to the column to report activity ahead. Sometimes it was merely to say they'd seen a herdsman moving his flock across the road, at others it was to announce that some small band of Nordlanders was waiting ahead either to join the army or to sell it provisions.

Nothing, no matter how inconsequential, escaped the notice of Mad Albrecht and his scouts. It was therefore a shock when the horses at the front of the column suddenly began to buck and whinny. The knights in their saddles tried to quieten the frightened steeds even as archers moved forward, nocking arrows to their bows as they watched the trees.

The fright of the horses persisted long enough that the entire column came to a halt. Try as they might, the knights couldn't calm their normally disciplined destriers. With each passing moment of delay, Mandred's patience wore a little thinner. Beside him, Beck easily read his master's mood.

'Let me see what's wrong, highness,' Beck suggested. 'You shouldn't expose yourself...'

The advice, however, only increased Mandred's displeasure. Annoyed, he spurred his white stallion forwards, bulling his way through the press of knights. As he neared the front of the column he could see the frightened horses stamping the earth, shaking their heads and gnashing their teeth. He was reminded of a hunting expedition when he was little. They'd hobbled their horses in a meadow while cleaning the deer they'd brought down. The horses had suddenly started to panic, much as the destriers were now doing. The cause of their fear had been a large panther, the predator revealing itself only when it rushed across the meadow and sank its claws in one of the animals.

Riding to the front of the vanguard, Mandred almost expected to see the same panther come lunging out from the trees. There was something ironic about an entire army being forced to stop its march because a hungry cat was spooking their horses.

Here was another irony too: for all the distress the destriers were experiencing, his own mount didn't so much as nicker. Mandred found that as he moved forwards, the other horses also became quiet. He was about to make a comment to Grand Master Vitholf, congratulating him on finally getting the animals under control, when he noticed movement on the road ahead. He gazed in disbelief at the lone figure that came prowling towards the column. Such was his doubt that he glanced to the knights around him, wondering if they could see it too or if the presence was only in his mind. The way some of the warriors gawked in fascination, he knew they saw her too.

It was Hulda, the witch from the woods, self-professed oracle of Ulric. How she could have travelled so far and so fast, crossing hundreds of leagues from the Drakwald to this place, was something that made the hairs on his neck stand on end. Magic, whatever shape it took, was an unsettling thing.

'Hail to you, Wolf of Sigmar!' Hulda called out.

Mandred looked around uneasily to see if Ar-Ulric was nearby before he returned the woman's salutation. He doubted if the old priest would appreciate a witch in their camp. At best, it would strike him as heretical. Mandred wasn't so certain. The powers of the gods weren't so limited as to be restrained by the dogma of their temples. Was it so impossible that Ulric might speak through this woman in some way? The wisdom she had shown in their previous meeting caused Mandred to believe Hulda was exactly what she claimed to be.

'Hail to you, Howl of Ulric,' Mandred greeted her. He nodded his head towards the knights around him. 'Was it you who frightened our horses and brought my army to a halt?'

The witch came striding forwards, each step exhibiting the same graceful, almost unearthly flow that Mandred remembered so well. Hulda didn't deign to answer his question. Of course it had been her magic that had upset the horses, just as it had been her magic that allowed her to slip through Mad Albrecht and his pickets.

'I would speak with you and give you counsel,' she declared. Her eyes suddenly shifted away from Mandred, focusing instead on the clutch of riders who came galloping out from the column to join the graf.

It was a mixture of Middenland nobles, *Dienstleute* officers and knightly commanders who had ridden up to join their leader. Among them, Mandred was surprised to see Baroness Carin and several of her retainers.

'Witch! Harlot of Old Night!' Ar-Ulric's voice trembled in the fury of his outrage. Mandred feared the old priest would tumble from his saddle, so violently was he shaking. Beck actually rode over to him, reaching up to keep him from falling. Ar-Ulric shrugged him away, not even deigning to look at him as he continued to stare balefully at Hulda.

Before the priest could unleash another stream of invective, Hulda made a gesture with her hand. Mandred didn't quite catch what it was, but its effect upon Ar-Ulric was dramatic. It was as though he'd been poleaxed by an ogre. The fury that had gripped him but a moment before seemed to evaporate. He stared at the woman with an expression of confusion and wonder. Not another word did he say. He simply turned his steed's head and rode back into the body of the column.

Hulda watched him for a moment, and then turned her eyes upon Mandred. 'You intend to follow the Old Forest Road?' she asked, though from her tone, it was apparent she already knew the answer.

'We are taking the army into Salzenmund,' Mandred told her. The fortified town had become the centre of Baroness Carin's diminished realm. Before she'd made her perilous ride to Carroburg, she'd had her vassals assemble provisions and supplies for the army she hoped to bring back with her. They'd be dearly appreciated by an army that had been marching across three provinces.

Hulda frowned at his statement. 'You must not go to Salzenmund,' she said. 'The skaven know what this woman has planned,' she pointed a finger at Baroness Carin. 'Their spies know about your army. They wait and watch for it to arrive.'

'Impossible!' the baroness shouted. 'My people are loyal! They wouldn't betray me to the ratkin!'

Mandred gave the baroness a sympathetic look. He'd seen for himself the perfidious ways of the skaven. No place was safe from their prying ears. It didn't need a human traitor for them to have discovered her plans.

'It would be like them to turn your own stronghold into a snare for us all,' Mandred told the baroness. He thought of the fight deep within the dwarf halls below Middenheim. 'I have seen such trickery before.'

Baroness Carin threw up her hands in exasperation. 'Then what do we do? Turn back? Abandon my people to these monsters?'

'If you follow the road and go to Salzenmund, the skaven will be waiting for you,' Hulda repeated. 'But there is another way. A way to turn their trap against them.'

'Ridiculous!' the baroness exclaimed. 'The only path an army can navigate is the Old Forest Road and it passes through Salzenmund.'

'There is another way,' Hulda said. 'A way unknown to the ratkin. While they wait in ambush outside Salzenmund you can strike at their nests in Dietershafen.'

Baroness Carin turned towards Mandred. 'Your highness, this is my land. Believe me when I tell you there is no trail such as this witch has imagined.'

There was a challenging quality about the smile Hulda turned upon the baroness. 'There is the Laurelorn Forest,' she said. The words were almost a whisper, yet they had an impact upon the Nordlanders as though they were the roar of a titan. Their faces grew pale, their eyes darted anxiously from one another, a few of the men even made the signs of Taal and Manaan to ward them against ill omen.

'The… the Laurelorn is haunted,' Baroness Carin explained. 'Any who stray within it never return. Not alive. Not sane. Better the skaven than whatever horror lurks within the forest.'

Mandred appreciated the fear in the baroness's voice and the effect that fear was having upon his own men. Before it could grow and spread further, he quickly turned towards Hulda. 'Can you protect us against the ghosts of the forest?'

Hulda nodded 'I can guide you. The path is perilous. Those who lose their way…' She left the warning unspoken. 'But you will be unseen by the skaven.'

Mandred smiled at that last point. It would be richly satisfying to take the skaven by surprise for once.

Baroness Carin waved the riding crop she held at Hulda. 'Surely you aren't going to listen to her? You're not going to trust a witch to lead us?'

Mandred's voice was loud when he answered her, loud enough to carry far down the column. 'She isn't leading this army, I am,' he said. 'Many of these men have invested their trust in me before. They have trusted me to tell them where to fight and how to fight. They have trusted me to ride with them into battle. Now I ask you, I ask them to trust me again. If we fight the skaven at Salzenmund, even in victory we are undone. It will take time to re-gather our strength, time the ratmen infesting Dietershafen will use to make ready for us.

'The Laurelorn offers a way to cheat the ratmen, to attack them where they think themselves safe!' Mandred shook his fist in the air as though strangling a skaven throat. 'I mean to teach them nowhere is safe while one man yet draws breath! I *will* teach them that lesson, even if I must ride alone through the forest!'

The thunderous cheer that rose from his soldiers told Mandred that whatever might await him in the haunted Laurelorn, he wouldn't face it alone.

Stirland, 1121

Screams tore the night air, cries of agony and horror that echoed through the darkness. It was the death rattle of Kleinbad and eighty-four of the eighty-seven who called the village home. Rugged, hardy specimens of Stirland's peasantry, they had survived the worst onslaught of the plague, they had endured years of famine and marauding masterless *Dienstleute*, they had escaped the depredations of opportunistic goblins and prowling beastmen. After nearly a decade of survival, Kleinbad had begun to think of itself as protected by the gods, shielded by the sympathy of Rhya and the indulgence of Taal.

If the gods had protected Kleinbad, then such beneficence had run its course. Nothing stayed the black riders who swooped down upon the community, swords slashing out in butchering sweeps, hooves stamping down in bludgeoning blows. Down the muddy lane between the sunken wattle-and-daub grubenhausen the invaders rode, killing anything that tried to flee. After them came dismounted attackers, spears crashing against barred doors, mailed fists

dragging terrified peasants from their homes. The villagers
wailed and shrieked, crying out for mercy. The headman
braved the stamping hooves to reach the square at the centre of the community, to dig with his bare hands at the base
of an old oak tree. Desperately he pulled the treasure the
peasants had hidden, the bribe with which they hoped to
buy their lives.

One of the riders paused, eyes blazing behind the visor of
his steel helm. The headman raised his hands towards the
invader, showing him the fistfuls of grain. The rider's hesitation came to an end, his sword chopping down into the
peasant's shoulder. The mortally wounded man flopped at
the base of the tree, his life's blood soaking into the grain
scattered across the ground.

No inhuman threat could have visited a more complete
doom upon Kleinbad than that which was inflicted upon
the village by monsters who were all too human. The Sylvanian Nachtsheer, the sell-sword army of Count Malbork
von Drak, were more thorough than any beastman, more
vicious than any goblin, more exacting even than the ratkin
as they annihilated the little farming community.

There was no pity on the face of Dregator Iorgu Turul as
he watched his footmen herd the peasants into the square.
He had served the von Draks too long to have any pretensions of conscience. To survive in the service of a cruel and
ruthless master, a soldier learned to be as callous as those
issuing his orders. Though he had himself been born in
a village not terribly dissimilar to Kleinbad, the dregator
felt no kinship with these people. He had risen above his
peasant beginnings and he would take a certain amount of
pleasure in displaying just how far he had come by carrying
out the voivode's commands to the letter.

The wailing sobs, the pleas for mercy as the peasants were

shoved and clubbed into the square only increased the dregator's contempt for them. These were the snivelling curs who would rule over Sylvania? These cowardly Stirlanders, begging to crawl on their knees when they should be willing to die on their feet? The ancient hatred of Fennone for Asoborn burned in Iorgu's veins, the call of barbarian ancestors hungry for blood.

Blood they would have. Count von Drak's orders would allow nothing less. Iorgu pointed with the gilded baton he bore, the dragon-headed symbol of his rank. A moment he let his gaze linger upon the weeping, terrified villagers. Savagely he slashed the baton through the air.

'No survivors,' he growled. The black-clad Nachtsheer were swift to execute Iorgu's command. Horsemen came galloping back into the square, chopping down peasants with their swords. Those who tried to flee back into the streets were spitted on the spears of footmen or smashed into bloody ruin by steel maces and oaken cudgels. The massacre continued for what seemed an eternity. Each scream brought a cruel smile to the dregator's scarred face. Justice for the oppression of Sylvania.

When the carnage in the square reached its peak, Iorgu called out to the sergeants among his footmen. 'Bait the trap,' he hissed. The dregator's eyes glittered in the blaze of burning hovels as the Nachtsheer put Kleinbad to the torch. A detachment of grim-faced soldiers, their uniforms hidden beneath the folds of long leather aprons, stalked among the dead, hacking and chopping with the massive cleavers they bore. Each group was accompanied by a mercenary with a monstrous spiked mace. Wherever the butchers encountered a victim who wasn't quite dead, the maceman would finish the job before they started their desecration of the dead.

Horsemen prowled about the village, reaching into saddle bags and dropping rusty trinkets and scraps of mouldering cloth on the ground. Rubbish culled from an ancient Styrigen barrow mound, it was this hoary garbage that would be the final proof to bait the Stirlanders.

Iorgu scowled and wheeled his horse around that he might stare down at the villains who would bring the first evidence to Wurtbad and the grand count. If his regard for the slaughtered peasants had been one of contempt, it was a thousand times worse for these men. A traitor, even a useful one, was an abomination. How much worse when the traitor was moved not by ideal or emotion, but by simple greed. These three men had betrayed their community, their families and neighbours for the promise of gold. Only a fool would trust such men. Neither Count von Drak or Dregator Iorgu was a fool.

'Have we not served you well, your lordship?' the oldest of the traitors asked. They were very much alike in their appearance, dusky men with long noses and pale blue eyes. An uncle and two nephews, shepherds who had lost their livelihood when the village headman ordered their flock killed so that the peasants might survive the harsh winter of 1118. Revenge had perhaps played its part when they responded to the intimations of a wandering Sylvanian tinker, but it was von Drak's gold that had won their cooperation in the end.

'A traitor is a double-edged blade,' Iorgu mused as he glared back at the scruffy peasant. 'Trying to cut with it, one must be careful about getting nicked by the reverse edge.'

The peasant was unctuous in his protestations. 'We have taken the voivode's coin,' he stated, injecting a tone of injured pride to his words. 'We know what is expected of us. We will alert Baron von Kleistern, tell him that a legion of skeletons and zombies descended upon the village and killed everyone.'

Dregator Iorgu nodded as he heard the peasant recite the story he had been told to deliver. 'And what, pray, would happen if Baron von Kleistern should offer you more gold to tell him what really happened here?'

All three of the peasants looked at one another, their faces betraying the same look of disbelieving shock as that of a deer that suddenly scents a lurking hunter. One of the younger men turned to run. Before he got twenty paces, an arrow from a Nachtsheer archer brought him tumbling into the mud.

The old shepherd threw himself to the ground, hands clenching tight about the stirrup holding Iorgu's boot. 'Mercy, your lordship! We are loyal!'

The dregator kicked the man away, sending him sprawling into the muck. 'Save your words! The voivode wants something more substantial to ensure your fealty!' He raised his gilded baton. The little dragon sculpture glittered in the firelight as Iorgu waved it overhead. From the darkness, a cloaked figure emerged. Leaning heavily upon a gnarled oaken staff, Arch-Druid Caranica marched towards the dregator and the men cowering before him. High priest of Ahalt the Drinker, bloodthirsty god of wild places, Caranica's features were hidden behind the hollowed out deer-skull he wore. A sickle, shapeless beneath the patina of gore coating it, was tucked beneath the sash he wore. As he approached, a stink of blood and death preceded him.

'They will obey,' the druid promised in a voice that was like the rustle of dead leaves. Removing the sickle from his belt, Caranica walked over to the writhing peasant with a Nachtsheer arrow in his breast. A moment of bloody work and the sickle was slick with the man's lifeblood.

A foul smile curled the wizened face visible beneath the jaw of the deer-skull. Slobbering growls rasped past the druid's sharpened teeth, sounds more akin to those of beasts than men. As Caranica growled, a fell vapour began to gather around the bloody sickle, endowing it with an obscene light. The fresh blood upon the ceremonial blade began to steam and bubble, writhing as though possessed of some atrocious vivacity.

The treacherous peasants retreated when the druid advanced towards them. Only the spears of the Nachtsheer kept them from fleeing. Forced to stand their ground, the men screamed as Caranica slashed their forearms with the glowing sickle. Their screams grew louder as the enchanted blood crawled off the blade and into their veins, vanishing into their bodies like a crimson maggot.

'The mark of Ahalt is upon you,' Caranica told the men. 'Your lives belong to the Drinker now! Defy him, betray him, and the beasts of forest and field shall make sport with your bleached bones! You may escape the eyes of men, but there is no escaping the eyes of a god!'

Caranica laughed as the terrified peasants were released. The men fled into the night, thinking only to escape the presence of the ghastly druid. Later, as they felt the Blood of Ahalt crawling inside them, they would remember what was expected of them. They would tell their liege lord what Count von Drak wanted.

'How will you remove Ahalt's curse?' Iorgu asked. He had no liking for sorcery and even less when it masqueraded as religion. In better times, his Nachtsheer would have been hunting down animals like Caranica, not working with them.

The druid cocked his head and stared up at Iorgu, bewilderment in his eyes. 'Remove the mark of Ahalt?' he asked, as though it were the stupidest question in the world. 'It was my understanding that we only need these men for a few days, a few weeks at the most. After that time...' He made a helpless gesture with his arms. 'Blood will have blood and the Drinker is always thirsty.'

Dregator Iorgu shuddered at the calm way Caranica explained what he had done. What the druid would do again, for there were other villages with other traitors that had a role to play in Count von Drak's plan, his scheme to make Grand Count von Oberreuth believe Stirland was being invaded.

Invaded by the undead hordes of the necromancer Vanhal.

⎯⟨ CHAPTER VII ⟩⎯

Laurelorn Forest, 1119

Fear, anxiety, uneasiness, whatever name he chose to call it, not a soldier in the column was unmoved by the fearsome tales the Nordlanders related to their allies in hushed whispers: stories of ghoulish lights that could be seen dancing among the woods; accounts of ghostly shadows that stood watch just within the forest, waiting for their prey; discoveries of bloodless corpses, torn and mangled in unspeakable ways, dangling from the treetops. The descriptions from the Nordlanders became more grisly with each step they took towards the shunned forest.

When the army finally came within sight of the Laurelorn, many of the soldiers laughed at the horrors the Nordlanders had conjured. In their minds they had pictured gnarled trees with skeletal branches clawing at the sky, vast swathes of bramble and thorn, stinking quagmires of slime. What they found instead was lush greenery, vibrant and fulsome. Birds sang from the branches of mighty oak and stalwart ash. Rabbits scampered beneath berry bushes, bees buzzed about patches of marigold and daisy. There was nothing untoward about the forest, no festering terror. If anything it was more pleasant and marvellous than any forest they had seen before.

The horror of the Laurelorn, however, wasn't a thing that could be seen. It was something that had to be felt, something that had to be experienced.

'I have prayed to Lord Sigmar that you are right about this...' Lady Mirella's voice faded, reluctant even to whisper the word that had formed in her mind.

Beside her, Graf Mandred felt the doubt in her voice stab at him. 'Witch,' he finished. 'You've been talking with Arch-Lector Hartwich again.'

Colour flushed into the noblewoman's face. 'He's been too busy ministering to the needs of Princess Erna to consult me,' she said. 'But it is no secret that he doesn't trust your friend. I don't either. There are many who don't.' As she said the last, her gaze strayed to the Nordlanders and their leader, Baroness Carin.

'She's very beautiful,' Mirella stated, her voice soft and tinged with melancholy.

'Hulda?' Mandred frowned. 'There's something compelling about her. Compelling... yet also frightening.'

Mirella turned away from her scrutiny of the baroness, pouncing upon Mandred's words. 'Then you *don't* trust her,' she gasped.

Mandred was quiet a moment. It was so difficult to put his feeling into words. 'No, it's something deeper than trust. Faith, perhaps. Maybe that's why she frightens me. I'm not the only one though. Ar-Ulric can't say three words when she's near, yet at the same time he can't take his eyes off her.' He pointed to the edge of the forest where the old priest stood alone, watching the trees. Hulda had trotted off into that forest less than an hour before, warning Mandred to keep his army out of the Laurelorn until she returned. Throughout her absence, Ar-Ulric had maintained a silent vigil. It was hard to read the priest's attitude. Was he concerned that Hulda wouldn't return or was he more concerned that she would? Ar-Ulric had been a fixture of the Middenpalaz and Middenheim for as far back as Mandred could remember. In all that time he had never seen the priest in such a light. For the first time, there was an uncertainty in his manner, a hint of doubt in his dogmatic resolve.

'Perhaps your highness would be advised to heed the council of Baroness Carin,' Beck suggested. The knight remained at a respectful distance from Mandred and Mirella, yet near enough that the bodyguard could defend his master at a moment's warning.

Mandred arched an eyebrow at Beck's interruption. 'You appear to have taken an interest in the baroness,' he said. 'Someone admitted her to my tent before we left Carroburg. I've wondered who could be so bold as to forget themselves like that.'

Beck turned towards his master, the scar running beneath his eyepatch vivid against his skin. The puckered wound seemed to point accusingly at Mandred when the knight spoke. 'My duty is to the Graf of Middenheim. It has always been my duty,' Beck stated. He inclined his head slightly towards Mirella. 'If I pay undue consideration to Baroness Carin, it is because others close to your highness exhibit their own concern.'

When Mandred looked at Mirella, he saw the rush of colour that rose to her cheeks, the hasty downward cast of her eyes. He smiled at his misunderstanding. It wasn't the beauty of Hulda that worried her.

Before Mandred could reassure his lover that nothing existed between himself and Baroness Carin, a commotion at the front of the column drew his attention. Mad Albrecht and a few of his scouts, posted just ahead of the main body of the army were breaking from their cover, bows drawn as they slowly worked their way back to the column. The wiry Drakwalder shook his head anxiously as he approached his sovereign.

'It's too quiet, your highness,' Albrecht reported. 'All of the little rustlings and noises of the small animals scurrying about have gone silent. Even the birds have flown away.' He saw the confusion on Mandred's face. Albrecht pointed to a starling clearly visible in a tree nearby. 'Not here,' he explained, then pointed a not-quite-steady hand back at the edge of the Laurelorn. 'There,' he said, his voice just falling to a whisper.

Almost in concert with Albrecht's report, the lone figure of Hulda came prowling out of the forest. As before, her approach had gone unobserved by the scouts, lending her appearance an eerie suddenness. She paused only once, glancing at Ar-Ulric, before she walked in sinuous grace to Mandred.

'The way has been prepared,' she stated. 'You may enter the forest. The horsemen must walk their steeds and take pains to keep them calm. There must be no fire of any sort. The path will be marked. Any who stray from it... must be left to the forest. Take neither wood nor game, even a single fallen leaf will be perilous.'

Mirella faced Hulda, staring hard into the witch's eyes. 'If this place is so dangerous, why do you lead us there?'

'It is because it is dangerous that I lead you here,' Hulda said. 'It is because it is dangerous that it offers safety.' Teeth gleamed white as she smiled at the Reikland noblewoman.

'Those who remember their respect, and my warnings, will see the other side.' She turned away from Mirella, regarding Mandred with a severe expression. 'You must go first,' she told him.

Beck bristled at the very suggestion. 'If you think we're going to allow his highness to walk alone...'

Hulda rounded on the angered knight, her own gaze blazing with such fierce challenge that Beck was taken aback. 'I did not say alone. The graf may bring whomever he chooses. But he must go first. Only then may the column follow.' She turned, glancing back at the Laurelorn. 'It is what the forest demands.'

Mandred nodded slowly. 'Then it is what I must do,' he said. 'Whatever awaits us here can be no worse than running into the skaven at Salzenmund.' He reached to his belt, checking that Legbiter slid free in its scabbard, the only display of uneasiness that broke his otherwise firm demeanour. 'Pass Hulda's warning to the officers. Tell them to ensure that every man in the column has been instructed how to behave.'

'You must take a guard with you,' Beck insisted, still watching Hulda with his one good eye. 'We cannot risk our leader.'

Mandred heard the anxiety in his knight's every word. Despite the peculiar feeling of belief he had in Hulda, he couldn't help but share Beck's doubt. From her manner and her words, Mandred felt that they were dealing with something that went beyond her control, something that had to be appeased before they could proceed.

'Volunteers only,' Mandred told Beck. 'No men with families,' he amended his statement. The order brought a grim nod from the knight.

'Volunteers,' he repeated, staring past the graf to the forest beyond. For all its apparent beauty, it was quickly becoming the imposing place the Nordlanders had warned about.

Slowly, Mandred and his escort approached the forest, following Hulda as the witch led them towards a pair of immense oaks, their branches twining and merging into a living archway. Moss hanging from the trees created a green veil.

What lay behind it, Mandred felt, was something beyond the ken of men.

The atmosphere within the forest was murky, the light subdued by the verdant canopy overhead. Graf Mandred's small group had walked only twenty paces into the Laurelorn before they were met. His escort consisted of Beck and Ar-Ulric, Kurgaz Smallhammer and Mad Albrecht, half a dozen Knights of the White Wolf, an exceedingly terrified liaison from the Nordland contingent and a few rangers from Drakwald. Leading the way was Hulda, picking a path through the lush undergrowth with an ease that made even Albrecht and the rangers seem clumsy. By command of their sovereign, the men entered the forest without drawn weapons, but there wasn't a hand that didn't keep an easy grip about the heft of a hammer or the grip of a sword.

Seemingly from nowhere, three figures appeared ahead of Mandred's group. They were tall, slimly built people, human in form but endowed with an almost ethereal quality of beauty and poise. When they moved it was with the same careless grace as water flowing in a stream or sunlight filtering through a cloud. They were arrayed in smooth breeches of emerald green, loose shirts of jade and light boots that appeared smoother and finer than the softest calfskin. Curious cloaks, apparently woven from leaves, clung to their shoulders, bound by neither clasp nor chain, but simply merging with the shoulders of their shirts.

The humans were dumbstruck, unable to do anything but gaze in wonder and admiration as these almost spectral creatures manifested from the lush greenery. It was Kurgaz who found his voice and gave a name to the forest people. 'Elves,' the dwarf growled, spitting the word off his tongue as though it were the vilest abomination.

The elves turned their heads almost in unison, first directing an indifferent stare at Kurgaz, then turning back to Hulda. 'We did not agree to the presence of diggerlings,' one of the elves intoned, his reproach carrying with it a sharpness that somehow accentuated the mercurial tonalities of his voice, rendering his command of Reikspiel at once precise yet conveying a curious accent, as though perhaps the elf hadn't spoken this tongue in so long that his command of it belonged to generations long dead and buried.

Hulda stared back at him. 'I was unaware that it was *your* decision to make,' she countered. Turning, she gestured to Mandred. 'This is the one they have named "Wolf of Sigmar." It is he who seeks passage through the forest.'

The elf didn't bow or acknowledge Mandred's rank in any way, though it was obvious he was fully aware of the titles the human held. 'You would bring dwarfs into this place?' the elf challenged. He deliberately ignored the burst of hostility that streamed from Kurgaz's mouth and the warhammer the dwarf had started to pull free from the sling across his back.

Mandred met the elf's strangely piercing gaze. For all their beauty, there was a ghastly alien quality about the eyes of an elf, a window into a mind as different from that of a man as a man's was from a lowly ant. He could feel the weight of incredible depths of time studying him, weighing his every twitch and breath, judging him in ways he couldn't begin to imagine, much less understand.

Some of the old idealism rose to his tongue, the impulsiveness that had once caused him to ride into the plague-infested squalor of Warrenburg and to fight depraved cultists on the very walls of the Ulricsberg. Mandred forgot all the careful diplomacy and candour of his court and his position, falling back upon the one thing he felt was all too easily obfuscated by the proprieties of state. What he told the elf was the simple truth.

'I march against the foul ratkin who infest the lands of men,' Mandred told the elf. 'Those who would help me in this noble work, I am honoured to call friend. Those who would forsake their own homes and their own people to help mine reclaim their homes from this vile enemy are more than friends. They are brothers.'

No flicker of expression crossed the elf's face, but it was clear from his speech that he had caught the barb of accusation in Mandred's words. 'All creatures have their obligations to the land,' he said. 'It is how we choose to interpret those obligations that defines us. We have forsaken the path of smoke and the wheel. To embrace those who yet walk that path is not permitted to us.'

Kurgaz spat on the forest floor. 'The perfidy of elves. Tell you to shove off and then make you feel like the one who should be ashamed!'

'Of all peoples, the dwarfs should appreciate what we have sacrificed to find a place for ourselves,' the elf retorted, for the first time a flicker of emotion crossing his serene features. 'We have withdrawn from the world that would have consumed us, found our own sanctuary.' The elf looked away, becoming attentive as the trees creaked and groaned. Calm settled onto his face as he addressed Mandred once more.

'We are sympathetic, but we will not fight your wars,' the

elf stated. 'It is enough that we do this for you. We have begged the forest permission to allow you passage. Know that you trespass here under the strictest sufferance. The path has been marked, but understand that any who allow themselves to be lured from the path will not return. Do not look for them. Do not tarry. If you once stop, if you once linger, there is no protection we can offer you.'

'Protection?' Mandred asked. 'Are your people so hostile to my kind that they would attack us?'

'It is not my people who threaten you here,' the elf said. The creaking groans of the forest seemed to swell to louder volume though none could feel any wind rustling through the woods. 'Stay on the path. Do not stop. Do not linger.'

Mandred shook his head. 'It is impossible. It will take us weeks to cross your forest. The army will need to camp, to rest.'

The elf was unmoved by the statement. 'Do not stop,' he warned. 'You move in the eye of a storm. If it descends upon you, you will be lost.' His expression became impossibly grave, more dour than the most doleful Morrite priest Mandred had ever seen. 'There is something more, something you must do to appease the forest.' An actual shudder passed through the elf's body. He gestured to the undergrowth the men had trampled in their advance. 'There must be recompense for the scars left by your passing. The forest demands a sacrifice.'

A wail of horror escaped the Nordland liaison, and the man had to be restrained by two of the White Wolves to keep from running away in a fit of abject fear. Kurgaz drew his hammer, glaring at the elves, fairly daring any of them to move towards him. Mandred stared accusingly at Hulda.

'You knew of this?' he demanded. The anger in his voice was fed by a feeling almost of betrayal.

'It comes easy to tyrants to demand sacrifice from others,' Hulda stated. 'It comes harder to those who would be leaders. To sacrifice themselves is less bitter to them.'

Mandred stood in silence for a moment, fuming at Hulda's deception. Before he could say anything, before he could decide between forcing a path through the forest regardless or going around and daring the attentions of the skaven, Albrecht had loosened his sword belt and let it drop to the forest floor. Hesitantly, the former poacher walked towards the elves.

'Albrecht!' Mandred shouted at the man.

The Drakwalder turned and gave his sovereign a wistful look. Then he threw back his shoulders and walked more boldly to the elves. Exhibiting a surprising degree of respect, two of the elves led the man off into the trees where he was soon lost to sight.

Mandred drew Legbiter from its sheath. Before he could order those around him to rescue Albrecht, he felt a firm hand close on his shoulder in a restraining grip. He almost expected Hulda's hand to be there and was surprised to find that the hand was Ar-Ulric's.

'Do not cheapen what your friend has done for you,' the priest said. 'Allow him this moment to repay what you have done for him. An act of pure selflessness is the most sacred thing. The gods themselves will pay tribute to Albrecht.'

The groaning of the trees was becoming more agitated now. To Mandred's ears there seemed an unspeakable suggestion of hunger woven into the cracks and pops of swaying branches. He shuddered at the loathsome expectancy of the noise. Mad Albrecht, the refugee from shattered Drakwald, a man just crazed enough, beholden enough, to give his life for his adopted monarch.

There was no scream, no cry, no sign of what happened

to Albrecht. The poacher's fate was something that was felt, a mocking shudder that seemed to course through the grass beneath their feet and the leaves overhead. Mandred knew his friend was gone, knew it as certainly as if he had watched Albrecht's throat slit before his eyes.

'The skaven will pay,' Mandred swore. 'They will pay for every drop of Albrecht's blood.' He glared at Hulda, then at the elf. 'My army is going to cross your forest. You have warned us, now let me warn you. Let anything try to stop us at its peril.'

The elf bowed in acknowledgement of the message. 'Your words have been heard. I will try to make their meaning understood. If you are fortunate, they will be satisfied with what they have already taken.'

As the army moved into the forest, the trees seemed to close in around them. Soldiers muttered anxiously to one another, scarcely daring to raise their voices in more than the feeblest of whispers. The horses were led by their dismounted riders, blankets thrown over their heads to prevent the animals from seeing anything that might set them into a panic. The normally stoic dwarfs marched in a tight phalanx, weapons at the ready, eyes scanning the enclosing greenery fearfully. At Hulda's urging, the dwarfs left their pipes in their pockets, heeding the witch's warning against even the slightest flame.

There was no question of scouts or rangers creeping ahead of the force. Even the most misanthropic of the former poachers and huntsmen longed for the presence of his fellow man. They clung to the column with the same eagerness as the infantrymen and camp followers, taking some slight comfort from those around them.

Comfort, but not security. The elf's allusion to the eye of a

raging storm struck Mandred as a chillingly precise appreciation of what their passage through the forest was like. The
'path' the elf had told the army to follow wasn't anything
visible. It was instead a sensation, a feeling that squirmed
through the mind of man and beast alike. A soldier would
know when he strayed from the path allowed to him by the
forest when he felt the hairs on his arms prickle, when his
pulse suddenly quickened. It was all the warning given. It
was all the warning needed. None who felt it failed to divert
their march back into the unseen cordon laid out for them.

Beyond the invisible barriers of that cordon, the trees
pressed close to the path. Their branches reached down like
skeletal talons, their roots spilled across the earth like giant
serpents. Leaves fluttered down from their boughs, evoking
in Mandred's mind the memory of an angry mob throwing
garbage at a criminal locked in a pillory.

Small animals and an amazing variety of birds regarded
the column from the branches, an eerie sentience seeming to shine in their eyes as they watched the men march
by. Beyond the trees, there were ponderous crashings and
thrashings as though mammoth shapes were stirring in the
depths of the forest. Sometimes, just from the corner of his
eye, Mandred fancied he saw a face peering at him, inhuman
countenances of weathered wood and moss. Sometimes he
saw a gnarled arm beckon to him. Always, when he stared
directly at these apparitions, they would assume the innocu-
ous form of a tree trunk or a fallen log. Mandred wasn't sure
which vision, however, was the illusion.

Shouts of alarm, cries of panic sounded throughout the
march as men discovered comrades who had gone missing. Despite the terror around them, there were some who
allowed themselves to be lured from the path. Mandred
even caught Beck straying towards the trees, convinced he'd

heard a woman's soft voice calling out to him. It was a voice Mandred, walking just beside him, had been unable to hear.

As the day began to darken, all in the column dreaded the thought of spending a night in the ghastly Laurelorn. The Nordlanders were especially upset. It took a cordon of White Wolves and dwarfs to keep Baroness Carin from ordering her men to make a break for the countryside. Mandred sympathised with her. The idea of camping in the forest was terrifying. At the same time, he had come to appreciate the awful power of this place. He was convinced that if the Nordlanders did try to force their way out then none of them would ever be seen alive again.

As the terror of spending the night in the Laurelorn was reaching the proportions of a general panic, as Mandred was debating the impossibility of the injunction not to stop and not to tarry given to them by the elves, there came a sudden lessening of the brooding intensity of their surroundings. With a suddenness that was as unexpected as it was unanticipated, the forest opened out into a grassy plain.

At first, Mandred believed they had simply reached some incredibly vast clearing deep in the forest. Then the cries of disbelief and incredulous moans that sounded from the Nordlanders made him aware of the truth. Some of the natives of the province recognised this terrain, knew it to be land far from where they had entered the Laurelorn. Impossibly far. They recognized the hills and valleys of the northern fiefdoms, the burned-out shells of windmills and the toppled heap of an old Jutone castle.

In only a handful of hours within the haunted forest, the Army of Middenland had crossed a distance that should have taken them weeks. They had entered the Laurelorn at the southern extremity of Nordland. Now they found themselves only a day's march from Dietershafen on the coast.

'Do not question ancient magic,' Hulda advised him. Mandred gave a start, unaware that the witch had come up beside him.

'This is why you wanted us to go through the Laurelorn?' he asked, gesturing to the sprawl of countryside before them. 'You knew this would happen?'

Hulda bowed her head. 'The forest was eager to be rid of you, so it sped your passage through it.'

Mandred scowled. 'Not all of us,' he said, thinking of Albrecht and all those who had been lured from the path. How many had there been? Dozens? Scores? It would need an accurate head count, a roster of the army to be certain. Mandred dreaded knowing how many the forest had claimed. How many he had led to such a strange death.

'The price of such magic is high,' Hulda conceded. Her expression became grave as she added. 'It is a price that must always be paid.'

'The cost is too high,' Mandred said.

Hulda cocked her head to one side, puzzled by his attitude. 'How many would you have lost had you walked into the skaven waiting for you at Salzenmund? Even with my warning? And you would still be far from your objective. The hunger of the Laurelorn has been cheap. Or are the only deaths you can accept those which happen on a battlefield?'

Mandred turned away from her, his fists clenching at his sides. 'The only deaths I can accept are those of skaven.'

Altdorf, 1121

Already it was being called 'the Night of the Holy Knives'. Messengers from across Reikland and from as far away as

Nuln had been riding into Altdorf to bring tidings of the wave of murder and massacre that had exploded across the land. In an Empire already ravaged by plague and war, a few isolated deaths would have gone unnoticed. This, however, went far beyond something that could be ignored. Hundreds were dead, killed in a single night. Given the size of the Empire and the perils of travel, the dead might number in the thousands if the same slaughter had been carried out in Averland and Nordland, Sylvania and Ostermark.

Kreyssig sat on the Imperial throne, feeling his stomach tighten as the officers of his Kaiserjaeger marched into the council chamber and delivered each new report as it was brought to the palace. He could easily picture each victim; it was no stretch of the imagination, simply a quick consultation of his own memory. A week before he'd been summoned to the Courts of Justice by the gaoler who maintained the Catacombs, the private dungeons of the Kaiserjaeger. The guards who had been posted in the Dragon's Hole were dead, dispatched by sword and dagger. Kreyssig had worried that his prize prisoner, Grand Theogonist Gazulgrund's daughter Gudrun Schoppe had been rescued by some agent of the priest's.

What he found instead was far more disturbing. The woman was laid out in her cell, her throat slit from ear to ear. It was obvious someone had dallied to compose the body, folding her hands across her breast and placing a simple wooden icon between her dead fingers. It was a Sigmarite hammer, and the message being conveyed couldn't be any clearer. An agent of Gazulgrund had been here, but he hadn't come to rescue Gudrun. He'd come to break the hold Kreyssig had over the Grand Theogonist, to break it in such a way that he would never be able to reclaim such power again.

If Gazulgrund's decision to execute his own daughter was chilling, what followed was absolutely terrifying. Across the city other murders were discovered. Murders of little men, murders of important men, some killed by blade, others by bludgeon. The uniting factor in the deaths, beyond the synchronicity of their timing, lay in the little wooden hammers their killers had placed in their folded hands. It was only when Kreyssig learned that the wealthy von Reisarch family, relations of Altdorf's Arch-Lector von Reisarch, were among the dead that he suspected an even more horrible connection. It took only a short investigation for his spies to confirm his suspicions. All of the dead, or at least those who had been the targets of the attacks as indicated by the icons stuffed into their dead hands, were the kinfolk of highly placed members of the Temple of Sigmar. They had been fathers and mothers, brothers and sisters, wives and children of Sigmarite priests.

Gazulgrund had severed the hold Kreyssig had over him and, with the same stroke he was ensuring that no other priest in the Temple could be coerced in similar fashion. The utter ruthlessness, the cold-blooded calculation of a massacre on such a scale was horrifying even to someone of Kreyssig's amoral ethics. These weren't strangers the Grand Theogonist had ordered killed; these were the families of his own priests. His own daughter.

The scale of the massacre grew with each passing hour. Beyond Altdorf, Gazulgrund's killers had seemingly been at work in every town and village. Anyone with direct blood ties to one of the Temple clergy had been murdered, always with the same little wooden hammer in their dead hands. The lengths to which Gazulgrund had gone to protect the Temple from outside influence went beyond anything a sane mind could conceive.

As more reports reached his ears, Kreyssig appreciated the terrible mistake he'd made when he'd thought Lector Stefan Schoppe would make a pliant and easily dominated Grand Theogonist. Normally a keen judge of character, he'd grossly underestimated the man he himself had made supreme authority of the Sigmarite faith. He'd never suspected that beneath the priest's humility there might burn the fire of a true religious fanatic.

How could he control a man who genuinely believed he was the instrument of his god's will? How could Kreyssig reason with a man who had ordered the slaughter of entire families? In elevating Stefan Schoppe, Kreyssig realised now that he'd created a monster he couldn't control.

The Temple of Sigmar had been made strong with Kreyssig's help. He knew only too well how strong. He'd planned to use the clergy to rouse the peasants for the eventual overthrow of the nobles. He appreciated fully the hold the Sigmarites had over the commoners now. While it had been firmly under his control, he had been pleased to let the Temple's power grow.

Now, things were different. Gazulgrund had even delivered a sermon in the Great Cathedral, admitting to what he called the 'Sacrifice of the Innocents'. He spoke of those murdered by his killers as martyrs, justifying every drop of their blood as an offering to Sigmar. He disparaged the worldly ways of the clergy and spoke of a need to return to a spiritual purity in order to revitalise the Temple and renew the sacrament between Sigmar and the Empire he had built. The great famines, the terrible Black Plague, the insidious skaven themselves, all of these were tribulations set upon the people as a warning that they must repent their iniquities and return to the faith of Sigmar. The priesthood, being nearer to Sigmar, naturally had to aspire to a greater piety and selflessness than their flock. The earthly ties of blood and family had to be severed that their minds might be focused solely upon the divine.

Strangely, while there was dissension and even outrage among the clergy – and many of the most outspoken of these dissenters mysteriously vanished in the weeks after the massacre – Gazulgrund's sermon found fertile soil in the hearts of the commoners. When the Grand Theogonist spoke of martyrs and sacrifice, he gave the impression that all was done for the good of the peasants, to relieve the suffering that ravaged their communities. By restoring the grace of Sigmar to the Empire, he promised to scour away these calamities, to bring back the days of peace and plenty for those who would keep the faith. The very barbarity of the massacre cried out to the peasants in a voice of thunder. This was the length to which Gazulgrund would go to ease their suffering, to intervene with Mighty Sigmar. The other temples might promise similar things, but Gazulgrund had done more than simply make promises, he had put action behind his words. He had given his own daughter's life that his own soul and his own mind might be made pure enough to facilitate a greater communion with their god.

The peasant mob, that great weapon Kreyssig had thought to wield against the nobles, now belonged to Gazulgrund.

There was no power in Altdorf that could oppose the Grand Theogonist now. Kill him? The thought brought a bitter laugh to Kreyssig's lips. That would only make him a martyr as well, and his death might ignite the peasants into full revolt. Even if he could put down such an uprising, it would mean the end of Kreyssig's authority. If he were forced to neutralise the peasants, he would lose the threat that kept Duke Vidor and the other nobles under his thumb. They would fall on him like a pack of wolves and carve him to ribbons.

The cat resting in Kreyssig's lap became agitated, raising its head and arching its back in a sudden display of alarm. The Protector rose from the throne, looking anxiously around him for any secret place one of the ratmen might be concealed. His anxiety turned to a disgusted sneer when he saw the animal swatting at an insect. He watched the cat for a moment, leaping to and fro as the bug buzzed around its head. A bee of some sort. They were a nuisance in the palace, persisting despite strenuous efforts to eradicate them. Kreyssig suspected they were coming from Boris's old apiary, some tiny hole in the walls. It was tempting to send someone down there to cleanse the chamber, but doing so would mean breaking down one of the walls and Kreyssig wasn't anxious to explain what they'd find inside. Baroness von den Linden should be left to rest in peace. The last thing he needed was the Lady of Sigmar's corpse reappearing while the Grand Theogonist was whipping up the rabble.

Kreyssig sat back on the Imperial throne. Killing the witch might have been a mistake. Though her own ambitions had been dangerous, she at least was strong enough to oppose Gazulgrund. The Grand Theogonist knew it too, that was why he had persuaded Kreyssig to dispose of her. Even then, Gazulgrund had been preparing for the Night of the Holy Knives. He'd been preparing for it ever since he'd taken the name Gazulgrund, christening himself after the dwarf god of death. He knew killing Gudrun would break Kreyssig's hold over him. Baroness von den Linden had represented the only threat to him. With the peasants championing her as the Lady of Sigmar, the witch could fight Gazulgrund on his own ground.

To break Gazulgrund's power, Kreyssig would have to engage the priest in that spiritual arena. It was a fight he was ill-equipped for. His were the weapons of fear and intimidation, not hope and faith. He might be a hero to the people of Altdorf for vanquishing the skaven, but they would never entirely forget that he was also the Commander of the Kaiserjaeger and the man who had been the Emperor's Hound.

Kreyssig drummed his fingers against the pearl-inlaid arm of the throne as a thought came to him. He might not have the ability to fight Gazulgrund on his own terms but perhaps there were others who could. Reports had reached him from Drakwald and Middenland about the Graf of Middenheim. There were wild stories about some sort of miracle relating to Graf Mandred, and his subjects had taken to calling him the 'Wolf of Sigmar'. He was reported to have fought the skaven in Nordland and was marching his army into Ostland. Such was his hatred of the ratmen that many claimed he was going to drive them from every province in the Empire.

Such altruistic pretensions didn't fool Kreyssig. Mandred was making a bid to make himself Emperor, to buy the Imperial crown with skaven carcasses. It would be only a matter of time before he turned his army towards Altdorf and tried to realise that ambition. A healthy greed for position and power was something Kreyssig could understand and exploit far more readily than the religious mania of Gazulgrund. To eliminate the Grand Theogonist, he was prepared to make overtures to Mandred. After all, the Middenheimer would need a powerful ally in Altdorf if he were to legitimise his rule. To ensure his own survival, Kreyssig had to ensure that ally was himself.

Yes, he would pit the Wolf of Sigmar against the High Priest of Sigmar, match them like two dogs in a fighting ring, play the heroic campaigns of the one against the pious sermons of the other.

Kreyssig struck at the bee as it came buzzing past his face. Angrily he kicked the cat away as it came leaping into his lap in pursuit of the insect. The bee made one last pass, and then went buzzing off down the hall. The Protector of the Empire chided himself for allowing the bug to capture his attention.

He had far greater annoyances to dispose of than an errant bee.

⤙ CHAPTER VIII ⤚

Nordland, 1119

After the terrifying ordeal of the Laurelorn, it was with profound relief that the Army of Middenland made camp in the Rol Valley. Once the valley had been home to dozens of villages, farming communities which had prospered in the rich soil. Vast swathes of grain had filled the slopes, transforming the valley into a swaying sea of gold whenever a brisk northern breeze blew down into it. Entire flotillas of Nordland ships had set out for Marienburg with their holds filled with grain, bearing back the wealth and wares of Westerland's capital. It was a lucrative trade, one that would have made Nordland the breadbasket of the whole Empire had dark times not conspired against the province. First had come the Norscan conquest of Marienburg and Westerland, denying them the rich market that had served them so well. Then had come their invasion of Nordland itself. Though the barbarians had been thwarted in their ambitions for Nordland, the havoc they wrought had left terrible scars on the land. The Rol Valley had been the scene of Jarl Ormgaard's last stand, the rich farmlands scorched black in the flame of war. The nobles of Nordland had just set their peasants to clearing away the wreckage of Ormgaard's marauders and restoring the prosperity of the valley when the Black Plague came. The soil might be as rich as ever it had been, but now there were too few to work it and too few to buy the crop to make such labour worthwhile. The Rol had been abandoned to rot.

The stands of grain growing wild in the valley were quickly trampled under by the great host of men and beasts that now marched into the depression. The blackened husks of huts and granaries became bivouacs for soldiers; the decaying frames of barns became stables for horses. Weed-choked shrines to Taal and Rhya and seafaring Manaan were cleared by pious warriors, gathering about them small encampments of men desperate to placate the gods and beg some token of divine protection from them.

Mandred established his own headquarters in the toppled husk of a timber fort that had been ransacked by the Norscans almost a decade before and never rebuilt. Two of the outer walls remained sturdy and serviceable, affording at least some small measure of protection against any sudden attack. Though there were no signs that the skaven had afforded the Rol any degree of interest, it was never foolish to take precautions where the ratkin were concerned. The rangers and scouts attached to the army were even now patrolling the edges of the valley, watching for any sign that their presence had been noticed and that the enemy was stirring from their nests in Dietershafen. Hard, capable men one and all, they followed their orders with less enthusiasm than they had shown before. More than most, these men of the wilds had been unsettled by their experience in the Laurelorn and to that shaken confidence the sacrifice of Mad Albrecht had to be added. The Drakwalder had become something of a leader to these men and it was only in his absence that his importance was truly felt.

Mandred considered that sacrifice and the disappearance of nearly a hundred others during their passage through the Laurelorn. The appreciation of such loss poured iron into his heart, making it impenetrable to the cautious advice of his council. His generals urged for a respite of three days, time for the army to recover from their long march and the ordeal in the forest. To take the men into battle as they were, with only a single night's rest, was perilous they warned.

'It would be more perilous if the skaven learn we are here,' Mandred countered. He thrust his finger at the map of Nordland stretched across the table before him. It was a remarkably detailed illustration of the province, executed by one of the Tilean masters fifty years ago, commissioned no doubt on monies earned off Rol Valley grain. Beneath the graf's finger, the slashed course of the valley snaked its way towards the coast, ending well before the cliffs and salt marshes. Near its far end, depicted as a tower of blue ink, stood the city of Dietershafen. 'While we keep to the valley, we may be safe from their eyes and noses, but we cannot trust too much in such security. Kurgaz warns that the ratkin are steeped in black sorceries and witchcraft. What man can say how such fell magics may be employed?'

'But if we march now...' Grand Master Vitholf threw up his hands. 'Even among my White Wolves, morale is low. It is worse among the *Dienstleute* and the peasant conscripts. The Nordlanders are close to desertion and the Drakwalders look as if they would rather fall on their own blades than...'

Mandred slammed his fist against the blue tower of Dietershafen. 'They are men, and no man worthy of the name

will forget what has been done to his land. Middenheim,
Nordland and Drakwald, all have suffered the scourge of
the ratkin. This army is weary because it has marched long
and hard, its courage has faltered because it has experienced unnatural horrors. Yet where you see weakness, I
find strength. These men *have* endured all of this. They *have*
pushed themselves this far. You say push them no farther.
You say that their strength is spent. I say let these men but
see the enemy, let them but smell his rancid stink, and a fire
shall burn within them! They *will* remember why they fight
and they *will* glory in the opportunity to do so!'

Many of Mandred's nobles nodded in agreement. They
had seen before the extraordinary efforts their sovereign
could summon from his warriors. They had seen him push
men beyond their endurance, pushed them past any reasonable expectation. And they had seen him prevail through
such methods.

'Where will you be?' Baroness Carin wondered. Since quit-
ting the Laurelorn, she had recovered much of her carefully
calculated composure. There was just the right balance of
royal indifference and emotional concern in her tone to do
homage to both her position as Electress of Nordland and
her personal interest in Mandred.

Mandred didn't hesitate in his answer. 'I ask no man to
go where I wouldn't lead him,' he said. The Nordland and
few Drakwald nobles on the council protested his intention to take personal command of the army, but those from
Middenheim were resigned to their sovereign's convictions.
Whether riding with the Knights of the White Wolf or
marching shoulder to shoulder with Kurgaz's dwarfs, the
graf would be there in the thick of battle. Though they hated
to see him put himself at such risk, none of them could
deny the effect his mere presence had on the soldiers. Never

had they seen peasants fight so fiercely as those who saw Mandred's banner flying before them and knew their great hero was near.

Baroness Carin smiled at his statement. 'You risk much for Nordland. It is one thing to see you risk your army to return Dietershafen to me, but I am humbled that you would endanger your own life. What reward can I offer such bravery?'

'Let us first win back Dietershafen,' Mandred said. He drew back the map of Nordland, exposing a second map detailing the city and its environs. He looked up, meeting the baroness's gaze. 'You are certain of the fog?'

'Only priests are ever certain of anything,' she countered, 'but at this time of year the fog has always rolled in with the dawn. The Breath of Stromfels, they call it, for it has brought many a ship smashing upon the breakers.' The baroness leaned across the table, tracing her finger along the perimeter of the city. 'Often the fog will crawl beyond the walls, leaving only the highest towers clear. They can be seen, like castles in the clouds, from leagues away.'

Mandred frowned as he considered that point. 'If the skaven post sentries in the towers they can see us advancing no matter the fog.'

'The ratkin have poor vision in daylight,' Kurgaz said. 'They are vermin of the dark.'

'They might have human sentries,' Arch-Lector Hartwich cautioned. His time with Princess Erna had sapped the Sigmarite's stamina, leaving him looking withered and drained. His ministrations to the noblewoman had been beneficial to her, restoring her physically and repairing some of the damage dealt to her mind. At the same time, his attentions were sapping his own vitality.

'I have learnt much about our enemy from Princess Erna,'

Hartwich explained. He bowed deferentially to Kurgaz. 'No offence to our dwarf friends, but the princess has lived among these creatures. She knows the way these vermin conduct themselves. They are arrogant in their strengths and paranoid in their weaknesses. If a human would serve them better in these watchtowers, then you will find a human there serving them.' The priest shook his head sadly. 'Many men would gladly serve these monsters to spare themselves even a fraction of the cruelties these beasts would inflict upon them.'

Mandred turned his eyes back to the map, pondering the terrain beyond the city. 'The skaven have established fields outside the walls,' he mused, tapping his finger against the marks drawn by Baroness Carin's scouts. 'Crops to feed their teeming hordes.' He stepped away from the table, waving his hand at a stalk of wild wheat sprouting up from the cracked foundations of the tower. 'Tunnel-crawling vermin would know nothing of sowing and reaping. They would leave such tasks to the slaves they have taken.

'The fields outside Dietershafen must be at least as ripe as this,' Mandred said. 'Ready for the harvest.' He laughed. 'Ulric favours us! Let every soldier in this army gather the wheat that grows wild in the Rol. Let him weave it into his armour, into his surcoat, into the barding and mane of his steed. Let him conceal himself in a cloak of wheat. The sentries, be they human or vermin, will be watching for the glint of steel, but they will think it is only the wind should the fields be disturbed by naught but moving grain.'

'A bold plan, your highness, but it will deceive none once we draw close to the city,' Duke Schneidereit objected.

'When we are close enough to be seen, the fog will conceal us,' Baroness Carin said. Her eyes shone with approval and admiration. 'The first the ratkin will know of their peril is when we are already within the walls. Nordland owes you much, Graf Mandred.'

Mandred chose to ignore the suggestion that was laced into the baroness's voice. Instead he continued to describe his plans for his generals. Baroness Carin barely seemed to hear him, though her attention remained riveted upon him.

From his place on the periphery of the council, Beck watched the baroness as she gazed upon Mandred. As he listened to the graf make his plans, Beck began to quietly make some of his own.

Ar-Ulric climbed the wall of the valley, scrambling up the slope with an agility that belied his years. The priest was a servant of a fierce and warlike god. To allow his physicality to decay, to allow his vigour to deteriorate would be to be unfit to serve his god. When a priest of Ulric felt his years overwhelming him, he would choose a successor and make a pilgrimage into the wilderness. If he was wrong about himself, he might return. Otherwise it was better to die alone in the wild rather than become an embarrassment to Ulric.

When he reached the top of the slope, Ar-Ulric looked back into the Rol. No campfires betrayed the presence of the army nestled within the defile. Mandred had ordered a cold camp, concerned that light and smoke would betray their presence to the skaven. A cautious leader, shrewd and wary as his father had been. Truly it was a remarkable man who had been baptised in Ulric's Sacred Flame.

The Wolf of Sigmar. Ar-Ulric almost laughed at the presumptuous title Hartwich had bestowed upon Mandred, yet at the same time it felt strangely appropriate. He hesitated to use the word 'ordained', yet such was his personal conviction. The Ulrican faith didn't accept the divinity of Sigmar, but they did revere him as a mighty champion of their god.

Whatever Hartwich's own intentions, the title he had given Mandred worked from either perspective.

He turned away from the valley, lifting his eyes to the heavens above. Sickly Morrslieb was but a faint glimmer on the horizon while Mannslieb blazed full and bright. Ar-Ulric could hear wolves howling to the moon from their distant forest lairs. It was a chilling, primordial sound, one that unsettled the blood of any man. Especially those who were of the Teutogen race.

Ulric was a god of men, but he was also god of the wolves. In the dim days of their ancient past, the Teutogens had struggled for the favour of Ulric, vying against their rivals in the forest. Man and wolf. Wolf and man. Ever the competition for territory and game, ever the struggle to dominate. In those ancient times, many strange compacts had been forged between wolves and men, between mortals and gods.

Ar-Ulric threw back his head. From the depths of his lungs, a fierce howl pierced the night. He waited for a time, letting silence wrap itself around him. The wolves in the distant forest had stopped howling, instead breaking into rapid, frightened yips as they withdrew deeper into their territories. The sound of their retreat gave Ar-Ulric pause. What he cried to was as abhorrent to beast as it was to man, a thing with one foot in each world.

It took all of Ar-Ulric's courage to repeat the howl. How he remained where he stood, waiting alone in the dark for the summons to be answered, he could never say. Perhaps it was Ulric lending him strength. Perhaps it was simply that he was too afraid to move.

She came trotting out of the darkness, a great white wolf. There was a terrible cunning in her eyes, an understanding that went beyond the instinct of beasts. They were eyes Ar-Ulric had seen before. As she came towards him, the wolf didn't snarl or growl, didn't bare her teeth. She simply loped along until she was a few yards away. Settling down on her haunches, the wolf watched Ar-Ulric with an eerily human attitude of expectation.

It wasn't lost upon Ar-Ulric that he was within leaping distance of the powerful animal, that one spring would set those jaws about his throat. Such knowledge didn't disturb him. It wasn't the prospect of death that made his blood curdle, it was the shape that death had taken.

'I hoped, I prayed that I was wrong,' Ar-Ulric told the wolf. 'I had even dared believe your kind a mere myth, an old parable, allegory for the viciousness inside all men.' He paused, staring gravely into the icy eyes of the wolf. He didn't feel foolish conversing with this animal. He knew she understood his every word.

'Your kind are recorded in the oldest legends, those from before the Ulricsberg was discovered, before we made friends of the dwarfs. *Ulricskinder*, the Children of Ulric, those able to walk between the shapes of men and wolves. Things both beast and man yet neither.'

The white wolf licked her fangs, ears flicking in a twitch of irritation. The fearsome intelligence in her gaze bore into Ar-Ulric's face.

'My ancestors believed your kind blessed by Ulric,' the priest continued. 'They rendered up their children to you, sacrificed them as Mad Albrecht was surrendered to the Laurelorn. When the moon was bright, they would cower in their caves and wait while your kind prowled the night, taking what they would. It took a long time for them to learn the truth. To understand that your kind weren't blessed by Ulric, but cursed by him. It took them many generations to recognise the werewolf and drive it from his lands, whatever shape it chose to wear.

'Now you return from the dark of legend to dominate men once more.' Ar-Ulric reached into his robe, withdrawing a sprig of holly. The white wolf cocked her head and stared at the little plant. 'I will not let you destroy Mandred. He is the chosen of Ulric. He is the hope of men. I deny your claim as an oracle. I deny your claim to speak for Ulric. Most of all, I deny you Mandred. I will not...'

In a white blur, the wolf sprang at Ar-Ulric, her great weight dashing the priest to the ground. One of her paws raked against his hand, sending the sprig of holly tumbling down into the valley. The fur where the paw had brushed against it was singed, a little wisp of smoke rising from the scorched toe pads and claws.

Ar-Ulric felt the wolf's fangs at his throat, pressing against his skin. 'Kill me, monster,' he hissed at the animal. 'Destruction has ever been your way. Kill me, and there will be none to know you for what you are.'

The jaws about his throat didn't tighten. Instead he felt the harsh rasp of the wolf's tongue as it licked his skin. Slowly, the animal loosened her grip. Just as slowly, she backed away, never letting her eyes stray from the prostrate priest.

Ar-Ulric pressed his hand to his neck, stunned to find that the skin wasn't even broken. 'You will have cause to repent your mercy,' he said. 'I will not be deceived. I know you for what you are and I will remain vigilant. I will not let you harm Graf Mandred.'

The white wolf bent low on its forelegs, approximating an eerie semblance of a curtsey. She fixed Ar-Ulric again with her pale eyes, then turned and dashed off into the darkness.

Ar-Ulric continued to rub his neck. 'I pity you, woman,' he said, his voice soft and sombre. 'But pity will not keep me from doing what must be done.'

* * *

Sylvania, 1121

Ghoulish silence dominated the macabre corridors and ghostly chambers of Vanhaldenschlosse, the eerie desolation of an open grave.

Cautiously, Lothar von Diehl approached the morbid throne of skulls. His magically attuned eyesight could see the streams of energy rising from the ancient dolmens about which the walls of the chamber had been built. He could see the coruscating bands of obscene force wrapping themselves around the gruesome entity ensconced upon that ghastly seat. He could read a little of the eldritch symbols that the energy formed itself into as it was drawn to the body of the master necromancer. Like whispers from a dark and primordial epoch, they sent Lothar's very spirit shuddering. Some things were too profane for even a matricidal heretic to contemplate.

The litter of mutilated assassins had been cleansed from the hall, but Lothar could feel the violence of their deaths clinging to the stones. He could hear the ghostly echo of their bestial screams; he could smell the noxious tang of their polluted blood. In a place like Vanhaldenschlosse, the residue of death had a firmer foundation in reality than the vibrancy of life.

'Speak,' Vanhal commanded as his apprentice crept towards the throne. The master necromancer's voice was an eerie hiss, a tone from beyond the mortal veil.

For a second, Lothar's noble pride resisted the order. To be spoken to in such fashion by a mere peasant was an insult beyond bearing. He was more than some simple grave-robber! He was *Baron* von Diehl of Mordheim, able to trace his high-born ancestry almost to the time of Sigmar! Who was this fallen priest to treat with him as an equal, much less a superior?

Lothar swallowed his pedigree and bent his knee before the ghoulish throne. With bowed head, he addressed the one man in all the world who could fill his heart with fear.

'Master, an army poises itself to move against us,' he reported. He cringed as he saw one of Vanhal's eyes staring down at him from behind the necromancer's mask of bone. 'Not an expedition of Sylvanians, master, but an army from Stirland!'

Vanhal made a dismissive wave of his hand. 'They are men. They are mortal,' he declared.

Lothar nodded his head, but his words weren't entirely in agreement with the fallen priest. 'Surely the Stirlanders know this. For them to be so bold as to threaten our – your – occult power...'

Vanhal lifted himself from the throne, dissipating the bands of energy coiling about him. Slowly he descended towards his apprentice. 'Continue,' he told Lothar.

'They would not dare such action if they did not have, or at least think they possess, the means to oppose your magic.' Lothar raised his head, meeting the ominous gaze of his master. 'It has happened before. Great Kadon was destroyed by brutish orcs. Mighty Nagash was vanquished by a naked savage calling himself a god.'

Vanhal stalked towards his apprentice. 'What is your counsel? What do you advise so that your master might be spared the fate of Kadon and Nagash?' There was a sneer, a challenge in his voice, a threat as keen as a naked blade.

'You must confront them before they are ready,' Lothar said. 'Don't wait here for them to come to you and unleash whatever magic they believe can overwhelm your power.

March your legions out to them. Strike them down in their own lands; slaughter them in their own homes. Make your vengeance so terrible that not for a thousand generations will the men of Stirland dare to whisper your name!'

Lothar could feel the piercing gaze of his mentor, feel the necromancer's power probing the corridors of his mind. He trembled under that fearful scrutiny, struggled to maintain the mental barriers, which were his only defence. At his full power, Vanhal would have easily stripped away Lothar's defences. In his current diminished capacity, however, there was just a chance that the apprentice would be able to retain his secrets. It was a chance he had gambled more than simply his life upon. Punishment from Vanhal would extend well beyond the grave.

'That is the course you advise,' Vanhal mused. There was a trace of suspicion in his voice that made Lothar shudder inwardly. He reassured himself that it was only suspicion and nothing more tangible. Nothing certain. Vanhal didn't really know of Lothar's betrayal.

Vanhal marched through the great chamber. A wave of his hand evoked phantom spheres of light to illuminate his way. A spectral wind swept through the hall as the master necromancer made his withdrawal. He hesitated at the winding stair that climbed to the roof of the tower. 'Come, Lothar,' Vanhal beckoned, his pallid hand standing stark against the sombre folds of his robe. 'Together we shall set an example to remind all mortals of their place in this world.'

With faltering step, Lothar followed his grim master. Even diminished, there was a terror burning inside Vanhal, a malignance that was beyond measure. He was nightmare made flesh. The vessel of apocalypse.

Lothar's heart quivered as he mounted the steps and ascended with the diabolic force he had accepted as his master. The fiendish power he had been insane enough to think he could betray.

Vanhal stood upon the parapets of his fortress, his form reduced to a shadow by the gibbous light of Morrslieb overhead. It was with sickness in his stomach that Lothar looked upon the sky, recalling the awful vision he had seen here, the fearful testament of his master's power. It was impossible to forget a sorcerer who could shred the fabric of time itself in order to feed his enchantments. The echoes of that terrifying invocation were all around him, whispering and moaning in the stones of Vanhaldenschlosse. The necromancer had promised to make the fortress a permanent magical fulcrum, an eternal engine of arcane power.

What Lothar could do with such resources made his heart swell with avarice. What Vanhal would do with such power made his soul shrink in terror.

All around the tower, from the base of the foundations to the fog-wrapped forest in the distance, stretched a vast bonefield. The decaying debris of war, the residue of carnage, the sprawl of bleached bones and blackened flesh was of an enormity that beggared contemplation. The dead from the Battle of the Plague Dragons, both the vanquished and the victorious, lay strewn about Vanhaldenschlosse like the neglected toys of a morbid god. Lothar knew the carrion affected the aethyric vibrations, colouring the magical energies flowing through the fortress, transforming them into necrotic vapours and spectral whispers. Death was both the result and the source of Vanhal's power, a ghoulish spiral that fed upon itself.

Ever growing.

Ever hungry.

Vanhal stepped to the edge of the roof, balancing himself

upon the precipice. He stretched forth his pallid hand. Years of aethyric energies had leeched his flesh of all colour, leaving the skin translucent. Veins and arteries were visible beneath his ghostly skin, yellow bones pressing close against the surface. Yet there was no sense of weakness in the necromancer's emaciation, only an awful and irresistible sense of destiny. Fate made manifest.

The master necromancer hissed the hoary words of dim antiquity, shaping the Khemran tongue into patterns never imagined by the liche-priests of lost Nehekhara. A mosaic of obscenity wove itself around Vanhal as he evoked his magic. The chill of sorcery caused frost to gather about the black masonry of Vanhaldenschlosse and sent an aurora of witchfire crackling across the sky.

A ghostly gale plucked at Vanhal's robes, snapping the tattered vestments about him like the wings of some mammoth bat. The necromancer ignored the menacing pull of the wind, ignored the precipitous fall only a hairsbreadth from his feet. The physical world had faded from his consciousness. All that remained was his great conjuration.

Upon the deathly desolation below, a terrible activity now became manifest. An undulation swept across the bonefield, the unburied dead shifting like the waves of some ghastly tide. Skeletal arms reached to the heavens, fleshless jaws snapped and clamped. One by one, then hundred by hundred, the slaughtered and the slaughterers raised themselves upon bony legs and turned inwards to face the tower. A silent horde of abomination, profane legions from beyond the grave. By their hundreds, by their thousands, the undead awaited the command of their master.

Vanhal stiffened. For the first time Lothar had an inkling of weakness in that awful personage. A bead of sweat dripped from the fallen priest's palm, a quiver snuck into his invocations. Small things, but they spoke to Lothar of a strain he had never seen before. Below, he watched as four of the great necrotic mounds that had once been dragons shifted and stirred. The headless bulk of Graug was the first to rise. Two of the other dragons, the most recently dead of the beasts Vanhal had summoned from the fabled Plain of Bones beyond cursed Nagashizzar, also reared into a macabre semblance of life. The fourth dragon, however, collapsed back to the earth, its bones flaking and crumbling into ash as the dark energies that had attempted to revive it dissipated and fled back into the aethyr.

During the battle with the skaven, Vanhal had conjured dozens of the mighty wyrms to do his bidding. Now it was beyond him to maintain even four of the beasts. Lothar tried to hide the thrill of excitement, the lustful anticipation that swelled inside him.

Vanhal turned from the edge of the roof, his eyes boring into Lothar's. The master held his hand towards the apprentice. Lothar tried to resist, but there was no defying the imperious demand in that gaze. Step by reluctant step, he crossed the roof and joined Vanhal. The moment he reached the fallen priest, Vanhal's icy clutch closed about his own hand.

Instantly, Lothar felt himself reeling. He could feel something draining out of him, flowing from his spirit into that of his master. The ghoulish embers of Vanhal's eyes blazed with revivified fire. The master necromancer turned back to the bonefield and the thousands of slaves awaiting his command.

New words rasped from Vanhal's lips. Like some human parrot, Lothar found himself repeating those intonations without any conscious volition. Dimly, faintly at first, phantom strains of melody impacted the nobleman's hearing, a cacophony of eerie melody that seemed to crawl into the blackest corridors of his soul.

Lothar knew this music, the cadence from the beyond. It was a conjuration of Vanhal's own devising, a ghastliness he called the Danse Macabre. Lothar had witnessed its effect before, watched it impart upon the risen dead a horrifying vivacity.

'Oh thou profaner of souls. Oh thou defiler of the tomb. Thou Mighty One of Uatep.' The invocation boomed like thunder from the parapets of Vanhaldenschlosse, the voices of master and apprentice merging into a single tone. 'Let not these limbs be without movement. Let them not pass away. Let them not suffer from corruption. Make supple these limbs. Make strong these sinews. Refill these hearts with persistence. Restore these souls with perseverance that they may walk again the kingdom of Khem in all thy majesty and terror and wear once more the mantle of life.'

A tremor passed through the deathless legions below. With awful vitality, they turned away from the tower, forming themselves into companies of fleshless warriors, snatching up splintered shields and rusty blades from the bloodied battlefield around them. Decayed roars wheezed from the leathery carcasses of the dragons as they lifted themselves into the night on ragged pinions.

'Now they will know the terror that waits in the darkness. Now they shall see the doom that waits for them in the shadows. Blind, ignorant, they shall all die for presuming to defy the might of a god.'

The words were Vanhal's. The tongue that gave them voice was Lothar's.

In that tiny corner of his mind that hadn't been subsumed by the essence of his master, Baron Lothar von Diehl screamed.

⤛ CHAPTER IX ⤜

Dietershafen, 1119

Much of the ground floor of the Seafarer's Guild had been gutted, doors torn down, walls knocked out, pillars toppled. Sections of the floors above had come crashing downwards during the demolition, precipitating a crazed network of support beams and rigging to keep the rest from collapsing. One exterior wall had been blown out entirely, the room extended into a rickety expansion cobbled together from discarded lumber and deck planks scavenged from Dietershafen's shipyard.

The purpose behind such deranged architectural adjustments reposed in the middle of the cavernous sprawl of the Guild's ground floor. It was a hulk of copper pipes and tubes, bronze flywheels and iron gears, crystal lenses and ratskin belts. Enormous tread-wheels bulged in haphazard disarray among the confusion of machinery, scrawny rat-men locked inside the cages as they frantically used their legs to propel the revolving platforms beneath their feet.

A great curl of wire, spiralling upwards into a set of horns, loomed above the contraption, crackling with electricity as the slaves spun the tread-wheels.

As it danced between the horns, the electricity took on the shrill, squeaky intonations of a distorted skaven voice.

'Man-dread not come,' the disembodied squeak whined. 'Can't sniff-see man-army. Sword-rats get hungry-bored. Want-like sack Salzen-nest soon-soon. Want-like much-much.'

Sythar Doom, Warplord of Clan Skryre and Grand High Techno-tyrant, bruxed his fangs in annoyance as he heard the report. The nugget of warpstone that powered his mechanical heart burned a bit hotter as the ratman's rage surged through his veins. After his humiliating defeat in Altdorf, he wasn't about to let the humans trick him again. Before, he had made the mistake of considering the urgings of his minions, listening to their treacherous counsel. He wouldn't make that mistake again. They would bide their time, they would adhere to his plan and if any of the mouse-fondling maggots dared spring the trap early...

Energy crackled about Sythar's metal fangs as he turned towards the nearest of the slave-wheels that powered the Warpsqueaker. His own invention after he had appropriated the research of an almost-clever underling, the machine allowed transmission of vocalisations uttered by those who'd undergone the proper surgeries. One day, devices such as the Warpsqueaker would be found throughout ska-vendom, wherever the shining brilliance of Clan Skryre had established a presence, allowing instant communication between the far-flung hench-rats of the Grey Lords. It was to be regretted that warpstone poisoning took such a toll on the slaves needed to power the device. A human would last roughly an hour, a dwarf three or four times as long and

an orc longer still, if one could keep the dumb brute motivated. No, the most efficient were skaven slaves, and even
these would suffer fatal exposure after two days. Watching
the occupants of the nearest cage, Sythar considered it was
probably getting close to the stage where their fur would
fall out and the sores on their skin start to ooze. He'd have
to remind the warlock-engineer responsible to have them
switched out as soon as this annoying report from his minions under Salzenmund was complete.

Sythar Doom's natural eyes had rotted away long ago,
replaced with lenses of polished warpstone and arcane
technology. They burned with a grisly crimson light as he
focused them upon the Warpsqueaker. The machinery was a
dull, scarlet shadow in the ratman's synthetic sight, the arcs
of electricity appearing as grisly green flashes.

'Listen-obey!' Sythar snapped, his fangs crackling with
energy as they gnashed together. 'Wait-watch! The army
of Man-dread will come. The man-things have no tunnels.
They must use roads, must crawl across the surface. My spies
will see-sniff them. They will tell when the humans near
Salzen place! Man things need rest and food and think to
find both in Salzen-place. Instead, they will find death!'

Sythar chittered happily as he envisioned the carnage
when the human army walked into his trap. The might of
Clan Skryre and half a dozen vassal clans would rise from
their burrows to exterminate the feared Man-dread. Killing the feared slayer of Vecteek the Despotic would be an
accomplishment to shake the halls of the Shattered Tower.
The Grey Lords would bare their throats to the skaven who
killed the despised Man-dread. Though Sythar was far too
sensible to risk himself in a direct engagement with the
terrifying warrior, it would be his plan, his genius, that
brought about the human's doom.

A great tumult rose from the streets outside, a clamour of confusion that drowned out the response crackling from the Warpsqueaker's transmitter. Sythar Doom spun away from the immense invention, murder in his posture. Someone would pay for this interruption! If they were human, he'd have their bones ground into bread! If they were skaven, he'd wear their pelt as a scarf... and have their bones ground into bread!

Glaring at the attendant warlock-engineers, the fierce warplord began to stalk to the great doors of the guildhall. He had only gone a few paces, however, when his ears began to twitch and his tail began to squirm. The sounds of disorder were growing louder and more persistent. He could hear the boom of explosions, the whoosh of warp-fire being expelled from flame-spitters, the crack of jezzails being fired.

Sythar Doom spun back around, baring his fangs at the Warpsqueaker. Those treacherous flea-maggots! They'd been whining about impatience and boredom, complaining that they wanted to attack the humans. All of it was lies! They'd allowed Man-dread and his army to march right past them without raising a paw to stop him!

The humans weren't in Salzenmund, they were attacking Dietershafen!

'Destroy that... that foolishness!' Sythar roared at the warlock-engineers. The technorats stared at him in confusion for a moment. When their cruel overlord drew an oversized pistol from his belt and sent a sizzling lance of warp-lightning burning through one of them, they quickly regained their sense of priority. With hammer and spanner, the skaven threw themselves at the offending Warpsqueaker, savaging it with the viciousness of starving rats.

Sythar Doom wished he hadn't been so hasty killing the

inventor of the treacherous device, because he dearly wanted to kill him now. A brilliant device, one that would reshape all skavendom! An instrument for treasonous underlings to work their betrayals from afar, to squeak their lies without hiding the duplicity in their scent and the deceit in their posture!

This betrayal wouldn't succeed. Sythar was too cagey to place all of his trust in anything or anyone. Plans within plans within plans had been the philosophy that had allowed Clan Skryre to prosper. Let the humans enter the city; let them carve their way deeper into Doom's domain. Every step would bring them only closer to their own destruction.

When Sythar had claimed Dietershafen for Clan Skryre, it had been with a definite purpose in mind. The shipyards had been quickly converted for the use of his allies, the ship-rats of Clan Skurvy. Even now, a flotilla of Skurvy ships equipped with the murderous inventions only Clan Skryre could provide was sitting at anchor in the bay. They watched for enemy ships, fleets from across the Sea of Claws, but it would be a simple thing to turn them around and bring their weapons to bear against Dietershafen.

That thought brought another chitter of malignant laughter from the warplord. Not only the weapons of Skurvy's ships could be turned away from the sea. Seizing upon that idea, leaving his underlings to complete the demolition of the Warpsqueaker, Sythar scurried from the guildhall, intent upon reaching the defences he had prepared for the protection of Dietershafen.

Defences he would now use to smash the city flat!

Legbiter flashed in a butchering sweep, cleaving down to crush the collarbone of the skaven halberdier who leapt out from the fog. Black blood exploded from the ratman's torn flesh, the creature wilting to the roadway to be crushed beneath the stamping hooves of Graf Mandred's destrier.

'No quarter! No mercy!' Mandred shouted, bringing his sword stabbing into the breast of a second ratman. A kick of his boot flung the flailing creature from his blade, knocking down a cluster of skaven charging behind it. Mandred spurred his warhorse into the tumbled creatures, splintering bones and smashing skulls before the monsters could recover. All around him, frightened squeaks and bestial screams rang out, wailing from the thick grey mantle of fog that blanketed the city.

There was no blessing the gods could have bestowed upon Mandred's army that could have been more welcome than the fog. The Nordlanders held that they had never seen the Breath of Stromfels range so far inland, and seldom had they seen it so thick. Visibility was measured in feet, all beyond that range reduced to vague shapes behind the mist. The wet dankness of the fog confounded the keen noses of the skaven. For the first time in their war against the vermin, the Middenheimers found themselves on a level field with their monstrous foe.

Or nearly so. The beasts were still inhumanly quick and agile, capable of frenzied bursts too swift for the human eye to follow. At the same time, they were cowardly, cringing creatures devoid of any loyalty to anything greater than their own skins. The ratmen wouldn't press an attack once they saw their enemy wasn't to be overwhelmed easily.

From the start, the skaven had been taken by surprise. Under cover of the fog, Kurgaz Smallhammer and his dwarfs had stolen right up to the walls of Dietershafen, crept right to the great gates of the city and planted the explosive charges that sent those gates hurtling into the sky. The thunderous blast had been the clarion call for Mandred's army. Into the fog had charged his cavalry, a thousand horses and more spilling down the streets of Dietershafen in an avalanche of steel and flesh. After the cavalry came the host of footmen and peasant conscripts, some clambering onto the walls to clear them of stunned skaven sentries, others smashing into the houses and shops to clear them of any verminous occupants.

The fog, the great and glorious fog, made the human advance swift and irresistible. The skaven, their keen senses stifled by the mist, were disorganised and confused. As they swarmed out to meet the attack they did so as individual packs and mobs. The weight of numbers wasn't there, the cruel discipline of their despotic leaders wasn't behind them to drive them into the terrified desperation that alone could make them press home their attacks. When they came boiling out of the fog, they did so without any concept of how numerous their foes might be. Vision and smell dulled, all they could do was to listen to the cries of battle. And when those cries were the fierce roars of enraged men and the dying whimpers of butchered skaven, the monsters would break and run, scampering back the way they had come, blocking those still with the heart to bring battle to the humans.

Great was the slaughter as Mandred led charge after charge into the packed masses of ratmen. The white caparison of his warhorse was black with the blood of vermin, the surcoat of his standard bearer became foul with the fluids of dying skaven, and his own beard became matted with clots of gore. Still the slaughter continued. The crunch of warhammers splitting skulls and smashing ribs, the crack of bones pulverised beneath the iron-shod hooves of warhorses, these became like a perpetual roar in his ears. Resistless as the pounding tide, the Knights of the White Wolf followed their sovereign down the streets of Dietershafen.

Narrowly did Mandred escape disaster. Pressing one routed pack of skaven too closely, he discovered the fratricidal brutality of these monsters. A great sheet of green flame came rolling out from the fog, sweeping over the rat-men, incinerating them in a wash of molten fire. So great was the heat that for an instant the fog itself was burnt away. Before it could come sweeping back in, Mandred saw what looked like a beer-monger's wagon at the end of the street, a clutch of skaven swarming about it, pushing it up the lane. Stalking before the wagon, its body draped in an all-enclosing smock of oiled leather, was a muscular ratman with a strange metal nozzle gripped in its paws. Hoses led away from the nozzle back to the immense wooden barrel in the bed of the wagon.

The operators of the fire-thrower hadn't been able to see the humans through the fog, instead they had targeted the panicked squeaks of their own comrades. Unleashing the caustic flames of their weapon at the sound, they had trusted they could destroy the enemy along with their own fleeing troops. By a slender margin, their ghastly tactic had nearly succeeded.

Mandred forced himself to wait while the fog closed in again, watching as the skaven worked frantically to push their grisly weapon forwards. As soon as the curtain of fog came back, he turned his horse and bolted down a side street. 'To me! To me!' he cried, his shout taken up by Beck and his standard bearer. The Knights of the White Wolf followed after him, the *Dienstleute* behind them galloping after. Mandred took the first turn, wheeling his horse about to the north. His steed trampled the skaven jezzails they found lurking in the lane, smashing them before the beasts could bring their guns to bear. The graf cursed even so slight a delay as he turned his horse again, charging down a street parallel to the first diversion. From the scorched road he had retreated from, screams of men and horses sounded, accompanied by the fiery whoosh of the insidious skaven weapon. Mandred tried not to think about the men who'd been caught in that grisly green fire. Instead he focused on the path ahead, the path that would see those men avenged.

Mandred burst from the fog like some phantom nemesis from the gardens of Morr. He was back on the street he had originally fled, but his diversion had brought his command around behind the skaven fire-thrower. He glared at the wagon, at the shackled ratmen pushing it forwards, at the chittering engineers operating its murderous mechanisms. The vermin were gloating in their fiendish massacre of human horsemen, frantically trying to bring their weapon forwards to slaughter the cavalry filling the street beyond those they had already immolated.

Clenching his teeth, Mandred galloped into the skaven war machine. Legbiter carved a gory path along the slaves chained to the left side of the wagon. Across from him, he could hear Beck's blade at work on those to the right. The leather-cloaked ratman at the fore of the wagon spun around, eyes going wide behind the goggles it wore. Frantically, the beast aimed the nozzle of its weapon at Mandred and the knights galloping behind him. Oblivious to the way its spin had twisted the hose behind it, the skaven drew back the lever fitted to the top of the metal nozzle.

The ratman shrieked as the twisted hose burst behind it, showering it in an oozing green demi-fluid. The leather coating it wore resisted the splash for a moment, then greasy smoke rose from its body. The skaven flailed about frantically as the caustic filth burnt through the leather and sizzled into the fur and flesh beneath. Mandred reined back his warhorse, content to watch this monster experience the same agony it had visited upon the men it had slaughtered. Around him, Beck and the other knights massacred the other skaven engineers, working their own vengeance upon the vermin.

'To me, men of Middenheim! To me, men of Nordland!' Mandred shouted into the closing fog, calling out to the horsemen he had left behind. 'We have but sipped from the chalice of slaughter! There is much work ere the cup be drained!'

There was much slaughter, as Mandred had vowed. Every street, every corner was infested with skaven. The momentum of the human assault was blunted by the fear that following the vermin too closely would lead them into the waiting mouth of another fire-thrower. Twice, they saw the grisly glow of green fire shining behind the fog as the skaven turned their war machines against their own. Each time, Mandred took his knights down a side street and led his men against the flank or rear of their foe.

There were other horrors waiting in the fog. Packs of jezzails, unable to snipe their targets from afar, instead emptied their weapons in withering fusillades before scampering back into the concealing mist. Mandred's horse was shot from under him in one such attack, a replacement drawn for him from among the chargers of his knights. More perilous were the grisly, almost insect-like ratmen who carried huge casks strapped to their backs and sent plumes of green smoke spilling from the hoses they carried. The fog seemed to catch the smoke, depriving it of the impetus it needed to reach any but the nearest of foes. After watching one knight coughing up flecks of his own lungs after inhaling the green vapour, Mandred gave a prayer of thanks that the fiendish weapons were denied their full potential.

Such obstacles weren't enough to turn the battle. Street by street, the humans were cleansing Dietershafen. When their advance brought them to the canals separating the Old City from the New City, they herded hundreds of routed skaven before them. The panicked creatures shrieked and whined as they were pushed into the canal. Men looked on as the brutes were swept away by the current or dragged under by their own arms and armour. Many of the creatures were drowned by their own flailing comrades, shoved under by panicked ratmen trying to pull themselves clear of the water.

It was a grim spectacle, but one that Mandred watched with a feeling of vindictive satisfaction. The sensation was spoiled, however, by the sight of some ratmen managing to drag themselves onto the docks on the far side of the canal, scrabbling up the steps into the New City. Sternly, the graf gave the order that sent his knights galloping across the bridges into the New City. The skaven rout was such that the bridges were undefended. That alone was enough to tell Mandred his enemy was beaten.

Victory, however, wasn't enough. The skaven had to be exterminated. He couldn't claim the day to be won until he had seen the last of the beasts put to the sword.

Spurring his own horse onwards, Mandred charged into the New City. Here, even more than in the Old City, the marks of skaven defilement were everywhere. Houses had been gutted, plundered of wood and thatch until only the stones of their foundations remained. Plaster walls were gnawed and stained with the scratch slashes that served the skaven as script. Human bones hung from dead trees on cords of rat-gut, a grisly warning to the slaves of the ratmen. Mandred vowed that for the skull of every man hanging from those trees, the heads of a dozen skaven would be spitted on the harbour wall.

Those ratmen who were caught in the streets of the New City were dispatched with the rekindled ruthlessness of an avenging scourge. The soldiers and knights who now roved the streets had their rage rekindled with every mark of skaven defilement. They forgot their fatigue and their wounds in their lust to see the enemy destroyed.

It was then, in the midst of overwhelming triumph, that a new terror descended upon the human army. From within the fog came a great whirring sound, the shriek of metal grinding against metal. Then, from some corner of the New City, a deafening crash, the obscene sound of wood and stone being crushed. Screams of men and horses and even skaven wailed through the streets.

Mandred spurred his horse towards this calamitous sound, urging the men behind him to new effort against whatever outrage the skaven now loosed upon them. Whatever he had expected, he was stunned when he galloped through the fog and his horse stumbled into a great crater. The graf was rattled by his fall, landing hard on his side. His destrier snorted and thrashed, struggling to regain its feet. The beast had slid a dozen feet along the side of the pit, its sideward twist sparing it from crashing headlong to the bottom another dozen feet below.

'Your highness!' Beck cried, leaping from his saddle and hurrying down to render what aid he could to his master.

Mandred struggled free from his horse, the loose earth beneath him allowing him to slide clear as the animal tried to right itself. He started to wave Beck back, to let his bodyguard know that he was all right. Words and gesture were lost, however, when his eyes strayed upwards.

Through the fog, a horrific sight was descending. Impossibly gigantic, vaster than any dragon or giant told of in the most outrageous legend, a great claw came hurtling downwards to rip at the streets of Dietershafen and bring destruction to Mandred and his army.

Skavenblight, 1121

The enormous warp-lantern cast its green glow across the Grey Chapel, the masked Luminary attending the device leaping frantically about the confusion of controls littering the contraption. It was a matter of life or death for the warlock-engineer that this invention function as it should: a shining example to the Lords of Decay that the technosorcery of Clan Skryre would light the way to skavendom's future.

There had been over a dozen Luminaries of the Shattered Tower since the embarrassing defeat of Warpmaster Sythar Doom in the man-thing warren of Altdorf. The Grand Technorat of Skryre had been vicious enough following that humiliation, killing underlings in especially gruesome fashion for even the least provocation. The failure to achieve the victory entrusted to him by the late Supreme Despot Vecteek had resulted in a serious loss of face for Clan Skryre at a time when the warlock-engineers could least afford it. Their cold science was losing the fight for the minds of skavendom, beaten back by the promises of Clan Pestilens and their diseased superstitions.

The Luminary risked a quick glance across the chamber, easily spotting his dread master sitting among the villainous Lords of Decay. Sythar Doom's mechanical jaws flashed as sparks rippled about his fangs, the enchanted rubies that served him for eyes glowed from the shadows. A ghoulish glow shone beneath the folds of his black robes, the dull susurrus of the power plant wired to his heart wheezing in time to his pulse. The arcane bionics had suffered from the latest tragedy to afflict Clan Skryre. Aiding the ship-rats of Skurvy to secure a man-thing port and their shipbuilding facilities, the warlock-engineers had been routed by the army of a creature whose name was being heard more and more in the halls of the Shattered Tower. A king-thing called Man-dread, the same king-thing that had slain Vecteek and Deathmaster Silke. Now the king-thing was making war against the skaven, driving them from the surface lands they had won by right of conquest.

Sythar Doom drummed his claws against the cold stone council table, barely heeding the schemes and intrigues of his fellow Grey Lords. He was brooding on the falling fortunes of his clan and the diminution of his own power. He was thinking of who was to blame, who he should take vengeance upon. When he raised his head and sniffed in the direction of the warp-lantern, the Luminary made certain to look as busy and indispensable as possible, careful to keep his breathing soft and shallow. His predecessor had perished for no greater slight than that of breathing too loud.

To the Luminary's relief, Sythar Doom soon forgot his flunky, turning instead to regard the Grey Lord now addressing the rest of the Council. His paws folded together, the Warpmaster turned a careful ear as Seerlord Queekual spoke. Like Skryre, the fortunes of the grey seers had suffered from the rapid advancement of Clan Pestilens. With the death of Seerlord Skrittar, the ancient prophets of the Horned Rat were in a position of vulnerability for the first time in living memory. Unable to defy the heretical dogma of the plague monks, unable to overcome the great treasure brought back by Plaguelord Vrask Bilebroth, unable to deny the efficacy of Poxmaster Puskab Foulfur's Black Plague, the grey seers were a waning power. It was only a matter of time before Arch-Plaguelord Nurglitch petitioned for himself to assume the Seerseat beside the vacant throne reserved for the Horned Rat Himself, only a question of when the plague monks would declare themselves the true voice of the skaven god.

Seerlord Queekual was in an even less enviable position than Sythar Doom. The question that rose to the Luminary's mind was whether the Grand Technorat would seek to join his resources with those of the grey seers in alliance against the plague monks or if he would pounce on the weakened sorcerer-priests and take from them what power they still possessed.

Knowing his fearsome master as he did, the Luminary imagined Sythar Doom might be scheming to do both.

'This Man-dread is a warning, a portent of doom visited upon us by the Mighty Horned Rat! He is a scourge sent to remind all skaven that they have strayed from the true faith,' Seerlord Queekual paused in his pronouncement, letting his gaze linger on the three green-robed heretics sitting at the other side of the crescent-shaped table. 'We have allowed strange ideas and alien beliefs to pollute us. At the very moment when the Horned Rat offers us our inheritance, we spurn him and chase after the diseased delusions of lunatics.'

'Those diseased delusions have done more to further our conquests than all your prayers stacked from snout to tail!' growled Bonelord Nekrot, his sepulchral moan sending a chill through the Grey Chapel. 'Prayers did not bring Skrittar victory against the dead-things! Prayers did not burn the wyrm-wings out of the sky!' Nekrot gnashed his fangs, flecks of foam dripping to the floor. 'Tell me, Queekual, will prayers bring back my dead warriors? Will they call back their corpses from the mage-things that now enslave them?'

Seerlord Queekual glared at the grisly Nekrot, the warlord's bleached fur and bone armour showing stark amid the shadows. Only a few years ago the Bonelord of Mordkin would never have dared speak to a grey seer in such a manner, much less the Supreme Seerlord. Queekual could understand Nekrot's misguided resentment, blaming the entire Order of Grey Seers for the tragic miscalculations of Skrittar. What he couldn't understand was the morbid rodent's boldness. After the Battle of the Plague Dragons, the cream of Mordkin's fighting strength had been decimated. The grave-rats weren't prolific enough to have bred back that strength already and Queekual had heard no rumours of Nekrot enslaving weaker clans to replace the difference.

A quick glance towards the three plaguelords made Queekual lash his tail in fury. He saw the wicked gleam in Vrask's eyes, the momentary arrogance of his posture. Pestilens was behind Nekrot's boldness, offering Mordkin some hellish alliance. Perhaps even now Mordkin was being initiated into the pestiferous Pestilent Brotherhood, that assemblage of deluded clans who believed themselves equal partners in the fortunes of Pestilens when in truth all they shared were the diseases and heresies of their new masters.

It was a ghastly thought, Mordkin in thrall to Pestilens. The plague monks would then control a third of the seats on the Council – more if Warmonger Vrrmik decided to allow Nurglitch to sit upon the Seerseat and interpret the will of the Horned Rat!

Queekual stilled the tremor of panic pounding in his heart. Let the heretics have their moment. The higher they climbed, the more inevitable their fall. Nothing nurtured hatred, envy and fear so much as success. Once the rest of skavendom saw the plague monks exposed for what they were, once they appreciated that they would have no share in the triumph of Pestilens, the whole rotten burrow would come crashing down!

The Seerlord twitched his whiskers and turned away from Nekrot. 'It was the cowardly, treacherous lack of faith in the Horned Rat on the part of Mordkin that brought disaster upon Skrittar. Your dalliance with the strange beliefs that have been allowed to take root in the Grey Chapel.' Again, he made a point of drawing attention to the three plaguelords.

Great Warlord Vrrmik leaned across the table from the Tyrant's Chair at the left hand of the Black Throne, his eyes glistening with malice. He was a hulking, brutish skaven, black warpstone armour guarding a pelt that was white as snow. With the decline of Rictus and the death of Vecteek, it was Mors and Vrrmik who were ascendant now, dominating the Council in much the way his predecessor had. Queekual had spent great wealth on Eshin spies trying to learn which way Vrrmik would lean in a contest between the grey seers and Pestilens. Like Vecteek, Vrrmik was proving too cunning to fall into any direct alliance, preferring to work through puppets and proxies.

'The Black Plague has brought the kingdoms of men low,' Vrrmik hissed. 'Even the grey seers must admit the service Poxmaster Puskab has provided the Under-Empire. My armies range across the surface, seizing food and slaves. My loyal subjects prosper as never before.'

Queekual was silent a moment, studying the other Grey Lords before continuing. 'The clans grow too attached to their conquest. They act like man-things, carving out fief-doms and dominions on the surface.'

'There is much-much meat above,' Rattnak Vile chortled, rubbing his paws together in a display of unashamed greed.

'We are breaking the man-things to our will,' Murderlord Raksheed Deathclaw snarled through the red cloth hiding much of his face. Warlord of Clan Skully's legions of killers, 'The Old Rat Under the Mountain' was the deadly rival of Shadowmaster Kreep and the assassins of Clan Eshin. The loyalty of Eshin always brought with it the enmity of Skully. 'They till their fields, grow their crops for us now. Would the grey seers have us eat mushrooms and mice?'

Queekual leaned back in his chair. 'I would have you remember the misfortune of Clan Verms. Remember the price paid by those who dally with heresy. The power that conquers may also destroy.'

Poxtifex Nurglitch stirred from his seat. 'It is only the enemies of the Horned One who need fear the power of Pestilens.' The plaguelords seated to either side of him quickly echoed the thinly veiled threat.

The Seerlord didn't answer Nurglitch. Instead he cocked his head towards the Black Throne. He waited until the murmur of conversation dropped away, until the tension in the Grey Chapel was thick enough to gnaw. He waited until he was certain every member of the Council was watching him commune with the Horned Rat. For all their antagonism and hatred, none of them was certain that the grey seers weren't touched by their god.

Queekual let the silence drag on. Abruptly he bobbed his head in deference and tilted his neck to expose his throat to the Black Throne. It was a gesture of abject submission, the sort of thing expected of a slave, not a Lord of Decay. The impact of such a sight didn't go unappreciated by the Seerlord's audience.

Rising from the Seerseat, Queekual cast his condemning

gaze across the ranks of the Council. 'Persist in your confusion at your peril,' he declared. 'We have given you our warning.'

As he turned his back to the Council and marched from the Grey Chapel, Queekual knew the Lords of Decay would remember this prophecy of doom. They might doubt his intentions, question his ambitions. But it wasn't the Seerlord they were watching. Their eyes were on the empty Black Throne.

And in their minds the Council of Thirteen wondered if the Horned Rat had truly spoken to His High Prophet.

It was the first seed of doubt. Soon that seed would grow into a mighty tree and its roots would stretch throughout the Under-Empire.

─◄ CHAPTER X ►─

Dietershafen, 1119

Like the talon of a rampaging god, the claw reached down from the fog. There was another ear-splitting cacophony of destruction as it obliterated another street, as it crushed men and horses between its mammoth extremities.

'Ulric have mercy!' Beck gasped. Mandred shared the knight's horror as they watched the claw retreat upwards into the fog, its talons opening to shower debris and bodies across the New City. What beast was this that the ratmen now turned against them? What daemon conjured from the blackest pit?

Mandred throttled the fear inside him, strangling it before it could overwhelm him. 'Ulric listens only to the brave,' he told his bodyguard as he started to climb from the pit. Whatever abomination the skaven had brought against them, they couldn't allow it to drive them from the city. If victory was snatched from his army now, he knew there would be no coming back. Dietershafen, indeed this whole part of Nordland, would be lost, conceded to the skaven.

'We cannot fight that!' Beck declared, pointing his hand at the sky.

Mandred looked away from the scarred knight, staring up at the rim of the pit where more of his warriors had gathered. There was no mistaking the terror in their faces. Only their fierce loyalty and belief in him had kept them from fleeing. Even that devotion was hanging by a thread. When the graf spoke, his words were meant for them as much as they were for Beck.

'This is not our home,' Mandred said. 'We can turn away and leave it to the skaven. We can abandon our brothers to slavery and atrocity at the paws of these beasts. We can go crawling back to Middenland. And when the skaven again come, when they bring this great horror against our homes, who will there be to stand with us? Who will help us fight?' He shook his head, his voice descending into a defiant growl. 'No, it is here we make our stand. A man can die but once. Do we die on our feet or on our knees?'

There were no cheers, no shouts of admiration, but Mandred could see that the conviction of his words had impressed itself upon the hearts of his men. He saw it in the clenching of their jaws, in the tightening of their fists. He saw it in the fatalistic gleam in their eyes. It wasn't hope he had kindled in these men. It was duty, the ancient pride of every warrior that makes him understand that a man's death can be more important than his life.

Again, they heard the whirring grind of metal hissing from the sky. The mighty claw struck downwards once more, bringing with it havoc and carnage. With a ghoulish groan, it rose through the fog, discarding those it had destroyed like so much offal.

'I go to find the monster, to sell my life choking on its

blood,' Mandred declared. 'Who walks with me through the Gates of Morr?'

It was a grim company who followed Mandred through the ravaged New City. Everywhere they saw the marks of the skaven monster, the horrendous craters gouged by its claws. Debris and mangled bodies were everywhere. The metal shriek of the gargantuan talon as it tore at Dietershafen was obscene in its steady rise and fall as it wrought still greater havoc.

As Mandred's followers advanced through the fog, they gathered to themselves small bands of survivors hiding amid the devastation. It was the same devotion to the graf that drew these men out from the grip of their fear. It was the same appeal to duty and honour that bound them to him as he pressed deeper into the New City, hunting the murdering titan.

The hunt yielded only a few bands of terrified skaven, frantic vermin who were quickly cut down. For all its enormity, there was no sign of the giant monster itself. Mandred could hear the whirr it made as it moved through the fog, the ghastly din as its claw ravaged the city. Was the thing some flying beast, some vast kindred of dragon and griffon? If so, how had the tunnel-haunting ratkin found it and mastered it?

As the whirring clamour again shrieked overhead, Mandred motioned his followers to silence. Carefully he studied the dreadful noise, listening intently to its cacophony. He almost laughed when he understood the truth. Turning to his men, he told them his suspicion. 'That is no beast of flesh and blood the ratkin set upon us. It is one of their damnable machines. I know not what shape it takes. I do not pretend to know how it operates. All I know is that the creatures who command it are naught but more of the vermin. Find them, kill them, and their machine will kill no more.' He paused, forcing himself to forget the devastation being wrought. Closing his eyes, Mandred tried to imagine what sort of ghastly machine the vermin could have built. The image of the hoists on the walls of Middenheim, employed to haul heavy loads of timber and stone up from the base of the Ulricsberg, their jibs reaching far out over the side of the mountain. The most splendid of these devices, built by the dwarfs of Karak Grazhyakh, was powered by a windlass and able to pivot upon its base so that the angle of ascent could be adjusted to accommodate larger loads. Once, however, the load of stone had been too great, snapping the hooks and sending the cargo plummeting back down the side of the mountain. The destruction inflicted upon the earth below reminded Mandred of the devastation now being wrought against Dietershafen.

'Is there some high place, some vantage from which the skaven can command this part of the city?' Mandred asked his warriors.

One of the men who had followed Mandred through the fog, a Nordlander, stepped forward. 'There is Manaan's Lantern,' he said. 'It is a hill that overlooks the harbour. A tower sits atop it and a light was always kept burning there to guide ships through the fog.'

Mandred doubted the ratkin had kept up the practice. No, he suspected the vermin had put the hill and the tower to a far different purpose. 'Can you lead us to this place?' he asked the Nordlander. The soldier looked around him, trying to get his bearings. The destruction was too vast, however. Ashamed, he finally shook his head.

The grinding shriek of the claw growled overhead through the fog. Mandred scowled at the violent din as the talon wrecked further ruin upon the city. 'Then we will let the snarl of this infernal machine guide us to its masters,' he decided. Grimly, he led his men into the grey rubble of Diet-ershafen, pursuing the ghastly shriek of the war machine. By degrees, the men began to appreciate the cadence of the sounds, associating different pitches with the claw's ascent and others with its hideous descent. Each man held his breath when he heard the claw ascend, dreading that when it came hurtling downwards once more it would strike the very ground he stood upon.

Gradually, Mandred noted that what parts of the street had been spared the ruinous attentions of the claw were begin-ning to slant upwards. The ground was sloping towards some height. Perhaps Manaan's Lantern itself. The sun was beginning to burn away the fog and as the misty veil was withdrawn, he could make out the vast shape of a rocky mound looming above them. As more of the fog cleared, the blocks of an ancient tower were revealed. Once it might have acted as a beacon for ships at sea, but the skaven had set the building to more fiendish purpose.

The top of the tower had been levelled, expanded into a sprawling wooden platform, a deranged confusion of support beams slanting down from its bottom to grip the walls of the tower. Most of the platform was consumed by a great framework of metal, thrusting up and out like the skeletal arm of a steel giant. Huge tread-wheels operated the pulleys fixed to great chains, strange motors that belched black smoke were fitted to the turntable upon which the crane was based. With a grinding roar, the whole base would rotate, spinning the arm around, turning it so that it stretched out across a different section of the New City. On the end of the arm was the gigantic claw, each talon the size of a river barge. Chains coiled away from each of the immense digits, snaking their way back to a network of smaller tread-wheels attached to the sides of the arm. In each basket-like tread-wheel, tiny figures could be seen scampering, running forwards to open the talons, running backwards to close them.

'There is our monster,' Mandred hissed, glaring up at the tower. Beckoning to his men with the deadly length of Legbiter, the Graf of Middenheim led them around the base of the hill to the causeway leading up to the tower.

Fortune favoured the attackers. Manaan's Lantern had never been conceived as a defensive fortification by its builders, so neither wall nor gate protected the approach to it. The skaven had neglected to erect any defences of their own when they transformed the lighthouse into a ghastly weapon. All that blocked their path as Mandred led his men charging up the sloping road was a pack of skaven spear-rats. The vermin fought savagely at first, but their bestial ferocity was no match for the fury of men who had been tormented by the mechanical claw, had watched comrades butchered by the insidious weapon. Upon the narrow confines of the hill, the greater numbers and speed of the ratmen counted for nothing, the discipline and strength of the humans for much. As the fight descended into a massacre, many of the skaven threw down their weapons and flung themselves over the rocky sides of the hill in a desperate bid to escape.

The fight was still raging around the hill when Mandred and several of his knights broke through into the tower itself. Only a handful of ratmen tried to stop them as they rushed up the winding stairway. The black-furred monsters were bigger than their kin outside, but fared no better. Their mangled carcasses tumbled down the steps behind Mandred's irresistible momentum.

When they reached the roof of the tower, the enormity of the mechanical claw was impressed upon the men. The great steel arm towered over them, thrusting itself into the sky as though it might impale the sun. The turntable upon which it moved was on a cyclopean scale, hundreds of human slaves toiling to turn the great winch that operated it and made the whole crane rotate. Dozens of vicious skaven, whips clenched in their paws, prowled on a walkway above the slaves, snarling down at them in a debased mixture of Reikspiel and their own foul tongue.

Mandred's men launched themselves at the slavemasters, cutting many of them down before they were even aware of the attack. Mandred himself targeted the grotesque ratman who seemed to be master of this infernal machine, a corpulent monster attired in a heavy fur robe and with a strange confusion of wires and tubes running from its scarred snout to a box lashed across its chest. The creature's paws were flying about a riotous confusion of levers and pulleys scattered across a broad console that seemed to have been crafted from the remains of a harpsichord. Pipes and tubes slithered away from the console, snaking upwards into the metal crane.

Some betraying sound caused the fat skaven to spin around as Mandred rushed at it. The monster bared its fangs in a savage snarl, one paw digging into the bag it wore hanging from its shoulder. A glass sphere was soon in its claws and the beast chuckled evilly as it hurled the strange missile at Mandred. The chitter of vicious anticipation turned to a squeak of terror when the sphere crashed through the ramshackle flooring of the platform to plummet into the tower below. Whatever grisly death lurked within the globe went with it into the darkness.

Mandred leapt over the gap in the floor, swinging his runefang in a cleaving stroke as he lunged at the ratman. Wires and tubes snapped as his sword slashed across the monster's neck and sent its scarred head flying from its shoulders.

As the brute's twitching corpse collapsed to the floor, Mandred glared up at the ghastly machine. It would visit no more death upon his army.

Even as he made that vow to himself, a flash of light drew Mandred's eyes back to the city below. The fog was clearing rapidly. He could see the full extent of the havoc wrought by the claw upon the New City. Now, however, there was another menace, one that threatened the much larger Old City. Sorcerous green fire blazed among the houses. While he watched, a second fire erupted, then a third and a fourth. Orbs of glowing green light, eerily similar to the sphere the dead ratman had hurled at him but far greater in size, were raining down upon Dietershafen. It took but a moment, a single turn of his head, to find the source of the gruesome barrage. A dozen ships floated in the harbour, ugly warships whose lines displayed the same deranged principles of construction and vandalism as they had seen visited upon Manaan's Lantern. Each ship in the skaven fleet had upon its decks an enormous catapult. It was from these that the wicked creatures loosed destruction upon the city.

Victory, so near, was being stolen from Mandred's army. The perfidious ratmen had decided to burn Dietershafen rather than lose it to the humans. Out in the harbour, the skaven ships were impervious to attack. There was nothing the humans could do to oppose them.

Unless…

Mandred looked back at that tower of steel and down at the turntable beneath his feet. He smiled as the thought came to him. The ratmen had built this gigantic claw to defend Dietershafen, to use it against attackers from the sea. Now, by the mercy of Ulric, he would put this obscene weapon to the purpose for which it had been intended.

'Beck!' Mandred shouted as he saw the knight rushing up to join him. His bodyguard had been caught in the fighting on the hill and had only now broken free to find his master. The reunion was destined to be a short one.

Mandred waved his hand down at the rubble of the New City, to a square where the stolid shapes of Kurgaz and his dwarfs could be seen hacking their way through a mob of skaven. 'I need you to bring Kurgaz here,' he told Beck. 'Have him bring his engineers, anyone who might have some idea of how to operate the claw.'

'Your highness, I do not…'

Mandred brushed aside Beck's concern. Now wasn't the time to worry about any one man, even a graf of Middenheim. Not when an entire city was at stake. 'Bring the dwarfs,' he ordered. 'If we can't turn this claw against those ships, all will have been for naught. We'll be powerless to do anything but watch Dietershafen burn.'

From the deck of *Fleetmaster Skarpaw's Vengeful Fang of Avenging Violence and Inevitable Domination over Clan Sleekit* Warplord Sythar Doom watched as his minions rolled another cylinder of burning death into the basket of the warpcaster that was bolted to the roof of the ship's wheelhouse. After the slight design flaw encountered during his attack on Altdorf, Sythar had set his most capable warlock-engineers to increasing the safety of the warpcaster. The machine itself, of course, was perfect. It was a design of Sythar's own creation only slightly adapted from the catapults deployed by lesser races. Adjustments to the warpcaster itself weren't negotiable; even the mere suggestion was treasonous and a quick way for a mouse-livered opportunist to get himself carved up into burrow-pork.

A particularly crafty underling named Toksik Gnaw had provided the answer. Since the skaven conquest of Wolfenburg, Toksik had been collecting the man-things calling themselves alchemists. He had been using them to further his own researches, providing him with new insights into the very nature of warpstone. His studies had helped to ease the concerns about the warpcaster. Instead of redesigning the machine, he'd redesigned the ammunition. The warpstone explosive was now housed in a casing of lead, rendering it docile. After being loaded into the basket, however, an artillerist would smash a flask of acid over the projectile. The acid would eat through the lead and, as it dripped into the warpstone explosive, cause a violent reaction. Not only did Toksik's solution make the ammunition safer to handle, but it also enhanced the destructive ability when the missiles crashed into their targets.

Sythar almost regretted hiring Deathmaster Nartik to dispose of Toksik, but any minion *that* clever was simply too dangerous to keep around.

'Burn-burn! Kill-kill!' the slurred squeaks of Fleetmaster Skarpaw were more like listening to a cat being strangled than someone speaking. The grizzled pirate was prancing about the warpcaster, savouring every turn of its gears, every whine from its motors. Whenever he thought he could get away with it, he stroked the wooden framework with the few fingers still clinging to his right paw.

Sythar felt a surge of disgust at his erstwhile ally. Skarpaw had been outraged at the prospect of destroying Dietershafen and its shipyards, irrationally demanding that Clan Skryre expend its resources to recapture the place. At some point in the argument, the foolish Fleetmaster remembered he was talking to a Grey Lord, one of the despotic Lords of Decay. There was a subtle change in the ship-rat's scent as he took his dissension into the bottom of a bottle. The fermented mushroom juice had done wonders for his attitude if not his wits. From angry protest he'd descended into drunken exuberance as Clan Skryre's weapons levelled the city.

The fog was clearing quickly now. Sythar had waited until it started to burn away before ordering Clan Skurvy's ships to attack. He wanted to see with his own optics the extent of the destruction a concentrated barrage from half a dozen warpcasters could inflict. If he had to lose Dietershafen, at least he could exploit the opportunity to its fullest and conduct some field tests. There was also the practical side to consider: the more extensive the destruction the better his sales pitch would be to the next clan he offered the warpcaster to.

Sythar gazed out across the ships in the harbour. There hadn't been enough time – or warpstone in Clan Skurvy's coffers – to outfit more than six of the ships with warpcasters. Most of the vessels were simply captured human ships. Only Fleetmaster Skarpaw's flagship was one of the new ironclads Clan Skryre had designed. Immense plates of iron bolted to its sides, two gigantic paddlewheels fastened to its sides and powered by a warpstone furnace buried deep in the ship's hold, the flagship represented a new height of design, surpassing anything that had ever put to sea. Sythar was more than a little angry that he'd sold it for as little as he had, but he consoled himself that the next one would be far more expensive. If Clan Skurvy didn't buy, then of course there was no reason he couldn't approach Clan Sleekit. Indeed, maybe the plague monks would be interested. They certainly had the warptokens to pay for such advanced engineering.

Thoughts of advanced engineering caused Sythar to turn

his head back towards Dietershafen. This time he didn't look out over the Old City, where the incendiary warpstone missiles were setting the streets ablaze. Instead he looked at the New City, at the cratered moonscape that had devastated nearly the whole of the waterfront and much of the residential and market districts. The Far-Claw, a magnificent achievement, a murderous feat of engineering and fiendishness! It was a pity such a weapon, by its very size, was compelled to be a fixed installation.

Observing the carnage caused by the Far-Claw, Sythar regretted he'd never been able to use it the way it had been intended. From the hill, the claw could command the whole of the harbour.

If he'd still possessed organic eyes, Sythar would have blinked in surprise as the Far-Claw began swinging around, turning away from the city. The long steel crane stretched out over the harbour, the enormous metal talons poised above one of Clan Skurvy's ships. Before the crew fully appreciated its peril, the chains holding the claw were loosed and the gigantic mass came slamming downwards like the fist of an angry god.

The destruction was incredible. The ship was pulverised, its hull pitted, its back broken. Fore and aft snapped, drifted away in separate masses of splintered wood before slowly rolling belly up. Shrieking skaven were thrown into the sea, scrabbling frantically at the wreckage floating around them in an effort to escape the water. Slowly, the huge claw rose from the depths, bits of the ship it had annihilated clinging to its fingers as the chains lifted it back into the air.

Horrified silence settled across the harbour. The warpcasters on the other ships no longer hurled their missiles at Dietershafen. Instead, their captains unfurled sails, broke out banks of oars and began a frantic retreat out to sea.

The crew of the flagship started to do the same. Sythar was forced to gun down three of them before they decided to listen to the enraged Grey Lord.

The audacity! To use his own weapon against him! To turn the Far-Claw on his allies! Sythar's blood boiled at the thought that some treacherous underling was even now helping the man-things bring the Far-Claw against Skurvy's ships. Vengefully, he ordered the warpcaster crew to load the catapult and target the hill. He hissed in disgust when the first shot fell short, impacting against the rocks well below the base of the tower.

Before a second shot could be hurled at the tower, the Far-Claw came hurtling down from the sky. The seamanship of the ironclad's crew was admirable. Even in the face of such a terrifying assault they managed to manoeuvre their ship. Instead of smashing clean through the vessel, the huge claw simply grazed the side, catching one of the paddlewheels. The wheel was ripped from its moorings, sent to the bottom as a twisted mess of metal impaled upon the Far-Claw's talons.

Loss of the paddlewheel caused the ship to develop a rapid list to starboard as the imbalance of the remaining wheel's weight threatened to roll the vessel. Frantic ship-rats armed with hammers, axes and anything else they could get their paws on rushed to the paddlewheel, thinking to break it free. The desperate effort, however, came to naught.

As he fought to keep his footing on the pitching deck, Sythar watched in horror as the warpcaster's ammunition was sent rolling towards the bottles of acid. Even in the depths of drunkenness Fleetmaster Skarpaw appreciated the threat, hurling himself at the lead balls to intercept them. However, in his drunkenness, the pirate failed to appreciate what the heavy lead balls would do to a body of flesh and bone.

Sythar Doom dove for the ironclad's side, racing away from the disaster he knew must follow the collision of lead sphere and acid flask.

The entire aft end of the ironclad vanished in a burst of green fire, a pillar of flame that soared hundreds of feet into the air. Its entire back blown to atoms, its buoyancy hopelessly obliterated, the forward section of the ship vanished beneath the waves, the suction of its sinking dragging many of the skaven survivors with it into the briny darkness.

The surviving skaven ships conspired to still greater efforts to escape into the Sea of Claws, spurred on by the violent demolition of their flagship.

The Battle of Dietershafen was over.

Stirland, 1122

The town of Silberwald was swollen with refugees. Even at the height of the plague and the skaven depredations that had followed, the settlement had never suffered from such an inundation of humanity. Shacks and tents stretched all around the town's timber palisade, engulfing the fields and pastures beyond the walls. Acres of forest had been felled to feed the fires and build the hovels of the refugees. Every effort by the town militia and the handful of *Dienstleute* in the service of Silberwald's liege lord, Duke Reinhard, to restrain the tide had been thwarted. Against such numbers there was nothing so few men, no matter how well armed and disciplined, could do.

For many years, tales of what was going on in the neighbouring province of Sylvania had been trickling into

Stirland. Wild stories of marching skeletons and armies of decayed zombies had met with derision and scorn. Morrite priests and secular authorities had dismissed such tales as exaggerations, fables to frighten the Stirlanders and make them forget the duty owed to them by their Sylvanian subjects.

Now those black fables had exploded across the frontier and plunged Stirland into panic. Villages all along the border had been decimated by midnight marauders, exterminated by the deathless hordes of Vanhal.

Vanhal! The name once considered nothing more than the bogey of ignorant, inbred rustics had become anathema. Few among the peasantry dared even whisper the name now lest by speaking it they should draw the attentions of its merciless owner. Publicly, the nobles did their best to discredit the fearsome mythology that had grown up around the necromancer, claiming him to be nothing more than a murderously clever warlock preying upon the weak. In private, however, the nobles spent small fortunes acquiring talismans and charms that might fend off Vanhal's sorceries.

Invaded first by the refugees, the mass of humanity gathered about Silberwald had brought a second invasion. The knights and soldiers of Grand Count von Oberreuth and his vassals marched to the town. Where the local authorities had failed to bring order to the ragged host, von Oberreuth's army soon took charge. Sergeants prowled among the refugees, detaching those hale enough to carry a spear. A simple armband of green was all it took to mark the startled peasants as soldiers. After a dozen hangings, none of the chosen men dared to desert. It didn't need Vanhal's advance to visit death upon them.

* * *

'An impressive muster,' observed Dregator Iorgu as he studied the sprawl of the military encampment that had displaced much of the refugee squalor outside Silberwald. He pointed his baton towards an open field where barrel-chested sergeants tried to drill some discipline into their newly recruited peasant soldiers. 'A bit rough around the edges. Do you think these peasants will fight?' The dregator looked aside at the mounted warlord beside him. The cold gleam of the voivode's eyes sent a chill down Iorgu's spine. People tended to die in very unpleasant ways when Count von Drak was in such humour.

'They will fight,' Malbork declared. 'They will fight because they have no choice. Von Oberreuth has chosen a good place to fight. He intends to engage Vanhal in Fellwald. The trees are dispersed enough to allow for cavalry yet still thick enough to provide shelter from Vanhal's dragons.' The voivode paused, stroking his thick moustache as he considered the prospect of facing dragons on the field of battle. It was the sort of conceit that belonged to legends, the fabric of heroic ballads. But then so did an entity of such terrible power as Vanhal.

'They will run,' Iorgu sneered, trying to mask his own trepidation.

Malbork bestowed upon the dregator a withering smile. 'They will fight,' he repeated. 'They will fight because their wives and children stay behind in Silberwald. If we do not turn back Vanhal, if they do not fight to their utmost, the necromancer will butcher their families. Root and branch.' He barked a vicious laugh. 'It never ceases to amaze how those with the least quality in their blood will struggle hardest to perpetuate their line.'

Dregator Iorgu shifted uneasily in his saddle. To ensure the loyalty of his Nachtsheer, Count von Drak made it a custom to take the children of his officers hostage. He scowled as he glanced back at the Stirlander peasantry training in the field. For all his rank and privilege, he was no better off than these unwashed clods. The approach of riders gave him a distraction from his grim thoughts.

'Excellency, it seems Count von Oberreuth has at last taken note of our arrival,' Iorgu said, directing the voivode's attention to the horsemen.

Count von Drak drew a sharp breath through clenched teeth. It had been insult enough that his liege lord had kept the Sylvanian force waiting for the better part of an hour, but now when von Oberreuth finally deigned to receive Malbork it was by way of Baron von Waldberg-Raabs. Sending a tax collector out as his emissary was a gesture eloquent in its calculated diminishment. Von Oberreuth was reminding Malbork of his subservient position.

The voivode curled his lip in a sneer. Let the damnable grand count enjoy his supremacy while he could. Once the armies of Stirland and Vanhal annihilated each other, there would be no force strong enough to deny Sylvania the independence she had so long coveted.

Baron von Waldberg-Raabs drew his horse up short before Malbork and Iorgu. 'Greetings from his lordship Grand Count Karl von Oberreuth, Prince of Wurtbad, Margrave of Waldenhof, Duke of Woerden, *Overlord* of Sylvania.' The emphasis on the last title wasn't lost on the voivode. While he was still scowling at the reminder, the baron cast an appraising glance at the black-clad footmen and cavalry arrayed on the road behind von Drak. 'His lordship was waiting for the rest of your company to arrive before receiving you.' He waved his hand at the Nachtsheer. 'Surely these aren't all the men Sylvania is contributing.'

'These are soldiers,' Iorgu growled at the baron, forgetting the deference due the man's noble rank. 'Veterans of ten long years of fighting the undead. Each of them is worth a dozen of your peasant trash.'

Baron von Waldberg-Raabs didn't deign to respond to the dregator's agitation. Instead he made a show of trying to count the number of Sylvanians. 'Three hundred? Surely a man of Count von Drak's leadership could rally more fighters to his banner? Why I saw more men toiling away at fixing your castle!'

'I should strip my lands bare and leave them defenceless?' Malbork snapped. 'What if this invasion is only a clever ruse? What if Vanhal intends to draw us out, then strike at the very heart of Sylvania? How would I meet my obligations to his lordship then?'

The baron shrugged. 'I suppose we shall have to make do with your, frankly, distressingly small contribution to the cause. Fortunately his lordship has less timid allies.'

The statement brought a narrowing of Malbork's eyes. He had paid little attention to the man who rode up with Baron von Waldberg-Raabs before. Now he made a careful study of the fellow. He was a big almost brutish specimen, his hair long and unruly, his beard thick and plaited in an almost dwarfish manner. The pelt of a white wolf was draped across his armour and the massive destrier beneath him was of a breed foreign to the Empire's eastern provinces.

'Grand Master Vitholf of the White Wolves,' the baron introduced the knight beside him. 'He is the representative of Graf Mandred von Zelt of Middenheim. It seems Graf Mandred's army has been scouring the skaven from Ostland. Now he offers to put his troops at Count von Oberreuth's disposal that we may purge Stirland of the undead scourge.'

Count von Drak bowed his head to Vitholf, everything in his manner the very picture of appreciative courtesy. Only

Dregator Iorgu wasn't fooled. He could see the expression in Malbork's eyes. It was well for Vitholf and the baron that they were in Stirland and not Sylvania.

It was that fact alone that kept them among the living.

'Aid-help, yes-yes?' the frightened squeak issued from the dejected little ratkin who grovelled at the warlord's feet. 'Promise-say mighty Mordkin save-guard brave-loyal Skab!'

Bonelord Nekrot brought his foot smacking against the beggar's snout, claws raking across the thin fur of the rat-man's nose. The emissary leapt back, yelping in pain. An intoxicating mix of fear and blood saturated the skaven's scent. The smell filled the underground grotto, the plundered ruin of an ancient barrow. The beady eyes of Nekrot's warriors shone in the darkness, reflecting the gleam of worm-oil lanterns, illuminating their grisly hunger.

A flick of his claw and Nekrot let his grave-rats pounce upon the stunned messenger. The Skab-rat was gory ribbons almost before he could shriek, ripped asunder by the cannibalistic fangs of Mordkin.

Clan Skab! The fool-meat had thought to prey upon Mordkin's vulnerability after their battle against the mage-thing Vanhal! They had wrested from Mordkin some of the surface holdings bestowed upon them by Vecteek. They had seized some of Mordkin's lesser burrows and warrens. Now, when their warriors were being decimated, when they were being driven from the surface by the Man-dread, now they sought alliance with Mordkin? Such audacity deserved to end in catastrophe!

Nekrot ran his paw across the bleached bone armour covering his body. Crafted from the butchered remains of the last Bonelord, the armour was a symbol of the permanence of his clan. Mordkin had defied the fearsome power of the

Accursed One and emerged from the bowels of Cripple Peak
stronger than before! What did they need to fear from their
fellow skaven?

Naturally, it helped when their fellow skaven were credulous enough to accept words of treaty and alliance. When
Man-dread first set upon Skab's holdings, Mordkin had
promised them aid. If the Skab-rats had been stupid enough
to believe Nekrot intended to honour such promises, that
was their problem!

The Bonelord turned away from his feasting grave-rats,
settling himself in the smashed crypt he had adopted as
his personal nest-throne. The sepulchre's cool stone surface
felt inviting, the pleasant scent of lingering decay made his
mouth water. It was a testament to how hungry his warriors
were that they'd devoured Skab's messenger so quickly. Normally they would keep a carcass for a few weeks so it could
properly ripen.

There would be chance enough to indulge such appetite
soon, however. Clan Eshin had proven incapable of killing
the Vanhal, but at least they had maintained a careful watch
on the hated mage-thing. Deathmaster Nartik's blades
might be dull, but his eyes were proving sharp.

Nartik had brought back word that Vanhal was marching against the man-things. There was the promise of a
great battle soon. The prospect pleased Nekrot no end.
Let the humans and undead batter themselves into pulp.
Once both sides were weakened, once the two armies were
reduced to bloodied tatters, Mordkin would sweep in and
destroy them all!

A string of drool dripped from Nekrot's fangs as he imagined what the marrow inside Vanhal's bones was going to
taste like.

Nothing had a better savour than vengeance.

─◄ CHAPTER XI ►─

Dietershafen, 1119

Mandred paced across the confines of his tent, feeling as though the canvas walls were closing in on him. Several times his foot got caught in one of the furs strewn across the ground, nearly tripping the distracted Graf of Middenheim. Even here, on the plain beyond Dietershafen the stink of skaven hung heavy in the air. The reek was stifling, obscene in its persistence. Given the extent of the ratmen's assault on the Empire, there were some who now speculated that the vermin had inflicted the Black Plague on mankind in some unholy fashion. To Mandred's mind, the stench of the skaven themselves would have been enough to spread sickness among men.

That Baroness Carin and her retinue could bear to be down in the old palace, a place that was absolutely filthy from years of verminous infestation was something Mandred found astounding. The polluted rubble was worlds away from the splendour of her castle at Salzenmund, yet she condescended to surround herself with this squalor. It was a testament to her iron resolve and her political acumen. She knew the bold message her habitation of the palace would send. The proper lords of Nordland were back; Dietershafen was once more in human hands.

The message was noble, but the reality was bitter. Dietershafen was almost as ruinous as Carroburg had been. Three-quarters of the city had been obliterated by either the giant mechanical claw or by the fires started by the naval bombardment. Before Mandred led his army into Dietershafen, the skaven had packed the city with human slaves. The blessing that so many had managed to escape the carnage of battle had become a curse now that the logistics of feeding such a multitude had been added to their problems. The former slaves were packed into every building that had survived the fighting, sometimes in such numbers that they slept upon the floors in great heaps, like so many exhausted dogs.

Simple humanity demanded that the supplies Baroness Carin had stockpiled in Salzenmund be brought to Dietershafen. Only the most callous of his advisors had demurred. Among them was Count van der Duijn. He insisted that the supplies be devoted solely to the troops. The Westerlander clung to the old plan of using Dietershafen to stage a naval assault against the barbarians in Marienburg. He was blind to the many ways the situation had changed, refusing to see or hear anything that would delay the liberation of his homeland.

Mandred could sympathise with Count van der Duijn to a degree. It was a terrible thing to have your land occupied by foreign conquerors. Taken within the whole, however, Marienburg was fortunate its conquerors had been at least a debased sort of humanity. The scope of atrocity perpetrated by the skaven against those they'd conquered was almost beyond comprehension. To the thousands of starved, beaten and maimed slaves the ratmen had left behind must be added the thousands more who, like Princess Erna's doktor, had been dragged away to the subterranean world of these monsters. Even more horrifying were the accounts and evidence of how the ratmen dealt with those too weak or sick to toil for their verminous masters. However debased they might be, the Norscan barbarians weren't eating their captives. Mandred had argued with his council that Marienburg would have to wait while the ratmen still infested so much of the Empire. It was an argument that he won easily.

Beyond the immediacy of freeing those enslaved by the skaven there was the bald fact that the plans developed by Count van der Duijn and Baroness Carin were no longer practical. To mount an attack on Marienburg, they would need a great fleet and a port that could service such an armada. Baroness Carin was the first to confess that Nordland could no longer provide either. The destruction inflicted upon Dietershafen would take years to repair; certainly the shipyards couldn't be put in order until the next summer, at earliest. Replacing the ships demolished or stolen by the ratmen would take even more time. In three years, perhaps, they would have the resources to liberate Marienburg from the sea.

Three years for the army to sit idle, bivouacked in Nordland while they waited for the ships to be built. Three years to allow the enemy to recover from their defeat, to marshal their forces and strengthen their defences. Three years for still more men to be slaughtered by their bestial overlords.

It was a situation that Mandred wouldn't allow. Brooking no dissension, he'd made his position clear. The army would secure Dietershafen and recuperate through the

winter from the long march and the fierce battle. During
that time, detachments would range across Nordland to
clear out such pockets of skaven as might yet be lurking in
the towns and villages.

Once the spring thaw came, they would move eastwards.
While the great city of Mordheim, crown jewel of the Ostermark was yet in human hands, defended by a vast army of
Ungol mercenaries, Roppsman horse archers and *Dienstleute*
from across the Empire, much of Ostland and Hochland
were in the possession of the foul ratkin. The mountain city
of Wolfenburg had been under siege by the skaven for two
long years. Breaking the siege, liberating the capital of Ostland, would be the next objective of Mandred's army.

It was his decision, one that he shared with no one else.
The enormity of that choice rested heavily on Mandred's
shoulders. He had listened to the arguments against such
action even if he hadn't allowed his convictions to be
swayed by them. Count van der Duijn's position was clear,
but there were other voices who raised more reasonable
objections. Some felt that they should consolidate what had
already been won, warning Mandred against over-extending
his advance. Others cautioned that to bring sufficient forces
to bear on Wolfenburg would mean a perilous reduction
in the troops left behind to garrison Nordland. If the skaven did return, they might win Wolfenburg only to lose
Dietershafen.

Surprisingly, it had been Baroness Carin's voice that
spoke loudest against such reserve. With the evidence of
what skaven dominance meant, she felt any hesitation was
unconscionable. Wolfenburg would be rescued; Ostland
would be freed. If it meant the loss of Nordland, then her
people would die fighting rather than submit to the ratmen again.

Arch-Lector Hartwich had enjoined the council to have faith in Sigmar and the other gods, to remain true to the nobility within the blood of man. Ar-Ulric had echoed Hartwich's sentiments, though the old priest lacked his usual fire and verve, seeming unsettled in mind and spirit. It had been the Sigmarite's rather than the Ulrican's appeal to religious sensibilities that finally impressed Mandred's council. He watched as the gaze of each noble strayed from Hartwich to their graf. It was easy to see the thought burning behind each man's eyes, the memory of that instant of miraculous intervention. Those who had been there, who had watched Mandred step from the Sacred Flame unharmed while the skaven assassin was utterly consumed, had no doubt in the power of the gods. They had seen it.

It was somewhat ironic then that the man who had been the direct focus of that miracle should be so plagued with doubt and fear. The esteem of his fellow man, their willingness to accept his commands, to stake their lives on his words, these were like millstones chained about him. Mandred could feel their weight dragging at his every step, stifling his breath, smothering his brain. What was it Hulda had said? A tyrant glories in power, a leader is humbled by it?

As though thinking of the wolf-witch had conjured her from the darkness, Hulda emerged from behind the hanging tapestry that partitioned Mandred's tent. The graf shook his head, throwing up his hands in frustration.

'Beck must fear for the perpetuation of my line,' Mandred declared. 'Every time I turn around he's letting a beautiful woman sneak into my tent.'

Hulda paused, tilted her head back and sniffed at the air. There was an amused sparkle in her eye when she returned her gaze to Mandred. 'Was it he who invited the Lady Mirella?' the witch wondered.

Colour rushed to Mandred's face and there was more than a touch of embarrassment in his laugh. 'No,' he admitted, 'her ladyship was here by my invitation. I rather think Beck disapproves.'

'No doubt he believes Baroness Carin to be a companion more befitting your station,' Hulda said. 'Even the Graf of Middenheim must observe certain proprieties,' she cautioned.

Mandred shifted uncomfortably. He was willing to give of himself for his people and he had accepted that there were sacrifices he would be called upon to make. Even so, he didn't like being reminded about those obligations. Determinedly, he changed the subject.

'You have scouted Salzenmund?' he asked. When Mandred had determined to bring Baroness Carin's supplies to Dietershafen, a chief concern had been the disposition of the skaven hidden there. He didn't pretend to understand what sort of magic the witch possessed or how she had discovered the skaven ambush to begin with, but he hoped she could use those same powers to discover if the monsters were still there.

'The ratkin are gone,' Hulda reported. She smiled, displaying her strong white teeth. 'They learned what happened here. They didn't want to share the same fate, so they retreated back into their tunnels. You may have the caravan sent whenever you like.'

Mandred started pacing again, his mind working out the details of how best to handle moving so much food through a starving land.

'Let tomorrow's daemons fight among themselves,' Hulda suggested to the troubled graf. 'The evils of the future will wait for you to find them.' The sparkle came back into her gaze. 'You might ask Lady Mirella's counsel. Her smell is strong. She can't have been gone long. Certainly not long enough to be already abed. She wouldn't be disturbed if you sent for her.'

Perhaps because the suggestion was so appealing to him Mandred took umbrage at Hulda's words. Directing a stern gaze on the witch, he spoke his mind. 'What is it between you and Ar-Ulric? You seem to have a terrible fascination for him. I've known the priest since I was a boy and I've never seen him so... uncertain. There are some in the camp who say you have bewitched him. Is that true?'

Hulda's gaze matched the harshness of Mandred's accusation. 'Idle tongues work more mischief than idle hands. The discord between myself and Ar-Ulric is a matter of doctrinal differences. We each honour Ulric in our own way. I know his way. He *believes* he knows mine.'

'And what does he believe?' Mandred asked.

'Ask him,' Hulda said as she stepped towards the doorway. 'I would be very interested to hear how much he dares tell someone else.

'I've already heard how much he dares to tell himself.'

Skavenblight, 1122

Locked within the dank burrows beneath Skavenblight, the only illumination coming from worm-oil lamps and candles rendered from rat-fat, Wolfius Moschner had degenerated into a living scarecrow. In those rare moments when he saw his image reflected in a bucket of water or mirrored in the glazed eyes of a dead skaven, the physician found it hard to accept that the person he gazed upon was indeed himself. His arms had shrivelled into bony sticks, ribs pressed against his pallid skin; his face was a wrinkly mess of loose skin and blotchy sores.

'The gods pay me back for my hedonism,' Moschner said, his voice a scratchy whisper. He ran a skeletal hand along one cheek, watching the process in the reflection of a blood-filled bowl. The sanguine fluid made the image both horrible and fascinating. Like the fabled stare of the gorgon or the compelling gaze of a serpent.

'Oh how proud I was of my fine things!' Moschner declared, shifting around on his wooden stool to speak directly with Schroeder. 'The Emperor provided me with everything. The best clothes, the most delicate sweetmeats! I was attended by the Barber Imperial and my tresses were shorn with golden shears. I wanted for nothing... save perhaps my dignity.'

Schroeder reached into the wickerwork cage, employing a barbed hook to drag out the corpse lying inside. He shook his head at the despair in the doktor's voice. These morose fits had become more frequent of late. It wasn't hard to guess the cause. The reason was impaled on the end of the knight's hook. Dissatisfied with the progress Moschner had been making, Queekual had expanded the doktor's field of study. The inhuman fiend had provided Moschner with a new kind of specimen for his studies – human slaves. Something to compare the progress of the plague on Moschner's skaven test subjects.

The hideous results of that strategy languished in cages all around them. When the captives had first been brought to Moschner, their screams and cries had pressed him to the edge of madness. Queekual had solved that distraction, however, in typically fiendish fashion. The mouth of each captive had been sewn shut with cords of rat-gut, leaving just enough space between the lips that the sludge-like swill the skaven gave them to eat might be forced down their throats. Utterly without empathy for their own kind, the skaven could not understand the pity the lot of these wretches evoked in other men. It was, Schroeder felt, the most chilling aspect of the underfolk.

'Now I have nothing,' Moschner declared. 'When I watched Emperor Boris die, when I defied him and cast aside the honours he had bestowed on me, I thought at least I might regain my dignity. I thought I might be able to walk the streets of Altdorf with my head held high. But the skaven leave nothing, dignity least of all.' He stared down into the bowl of blood, not the black filth of skaven veins but the humour found within human ones. He tried not to think of the man the blood had been drawn from, to forget the weakness that would afflict him as his body withered under the caprices of maladjusted humours. He tried to focus as Schroeder told him to. He tried to think only of the work, only of the end result his labours must yield.

'Is… is the herdsman well?' Moschner asked, setting down the magnifying crystal and covering the blood bowl with the clay tablet on which he had been scratching his notes.

Schroeder pretended not to hear the question, concentrating instead on removing the dead captive. If he dragged the body to the cave entrance, the guard-rats would remove it. He didn't like to think what they did with the corpse when it was gone.

'I asked if the herdsman is recovering,' Moschner repeated, anger creeping into his tone. 'Check on him!' he added, slapping his withered hand against the table.

The knight released the hook and let the corpse flop to the floor. Grimly, he stalked towards the cage where the man in question was kept. 'You need to forget about these people,' Schroeder scolded him. 'None of us matters. We are already dead. Have been since we were brought into Skavenblight. All that matters is your work and what you can do here.'

'Look in on him,' Moschner shouted, the effort wracking his body in a fit of coughing. He could hear agitated squeaks in the tunnel outside, but he didn't care if he upset Queekual's guards. All that mattered now was assuaging his own sense of guilt.

A sour look on his face, Schroeder navigated the tangle of cages, recoiling when an especially lively skaven slave tried to nip at him from behind the bars of its prison. When he reached the herdsman's cage the knight threw back the bolt and opened the tiny door. A moment only he lingered there, before turning back to Moschner. 'He's dead,' Schroeder reported, his voice conveying all the emotion of solid stone.

Moschner reeled, almost falling from the stool. Dead? Another victim! Another black mark upon his soul! Drawing the man's blood had been too much, one abuse too many for him to endure. Moschner thought back to when the herdsman had been brought to him. Rendered mute by the skaven, rendered illiterate by the indifference of his noble liege lords, the prisoner had been clever enough to draw in the dirt beneath his cage to convey his story. Such cleverness in the face of brutality that had broken knights and nobles had impressed the doktor. It had spoken to him of some indomitable endurance deep within the human form, a quality he prayed he might find hidden somewhere inside himself.

Now the man was dead, killed by Moschner's own cruelty, by the abominable demands of his studies. For what had he died? To placate the insane ego of Queekual? To further research that profaned every oath sworn by every doktor who ever lived?

'No more,' Moschner whispered. He stared at the bowl

of blood he had been studying. 'No more,' he cursed in a louder voice. With a sweep of his arm he sent the vessel flying from the table, spattering the floor with gore. 'No more!' he raged, flinging himself to his feet. Dimly he heard Schroeder shout at him, could hear the big knight crashing against the cages as he rushed for the doktor.

How many times had they helped one another so? The knight and the physician, pulling one another back from the brink of madness, reminding each other of the purpose that drove them on. Not this time. Moschner wouldn't let Schroeder's words pull him back. He could endure no more. Better a gruesome death than an obscene life.

Moschner rushed to the mouth of the cave, screaming his defiance. The guard-rats scurried into his path. Not daring to enter the cave itself, they pointed their spears at him from the edge of the tunnel, hissing and squeaking in their loathsome parody of speech.

The doktor did not relent. A red fury propelled him into the waiting guards, a crazed recklessness that would have impressed a Norscan berserk. The ratmen recoiled before the deranged human. Moschner had always suspected they'd been given orders not to harm him, just to keep him in his prison. Now he exploited their reluctance. When one of the skaven lowered its spear, he lunged at the vermin. Wasted as he was, he was still able to wrap his arms about the beast's neck, to squeeze and strangle. Positioned as he was, the ratman could bring neither fangs nor spear against him. The agony of verminous claws raking his back only sent him into a greater fury.

'Look out!' The warning came from Schroeder. Before Moschner could react to the warning, he felt a terrific impact against his skull. The other guard had slammed the butt of its spear against his head. His grip on the choking skaven slipped away as he wilted to the floor. The next instant he felt a clawed foot kick against his ribs.

Before he could be abused further, a shrill bestial scream rang through the tunnel. Through his bleary gaze, Moschner could see Schroeder standing over the sprawled body of one guard-rat, a bloodied pestle clenched in his fist. The other guard-rat, the one the crazed doktor had half-strangled, was coughing and sputtering on the ground. Before it could recover, Schroeder caught up one of the spears and ran the creature through.

The knight turned away from the dead skaven and pulled Moschner to his feet. The doktor tried to turn around, to flee into the tunnel, but Schroeder's grip was too tight. 'It's no good!' he yelled at the physician. 'There's no escape! There are leagues of tunnels, thousands upon thousands of underfolk! The only chance, the only hope is to complete your work. That's the only thing you can do to make restitution to all the victims of these fiends.'

Moschner glared at Schroeder and tried again to pull away.

'Please, doktor, you must do this for me,' Schroeder said. 'Make my death worth something. Kill as many of these bastards as you can.' The next instant, the knight buried his fist in Moschner's gut. He carried the stunned doktor back into the cave, laying him down beside the table.

The doktor had an impression of Schroeder staring down at him, then the image faded into the blackness of unconsciousness.

When Moschner awoke, it was the terrifying figure of Seerlord Queekual standing over him. In the sorcerer's paws was Schroeder's severed head. Queekual said the knight had killed the guards and tried to escape while Moschner was asleep. He hadn't got very far before skaven trackers sniffed him out and brought him down.

Queekual left the head with Moschner as a reminder of what would happen should he try to follow the dead man's example.

It was a needless lesson. With Schroeder's last words still ringing in his ears, the last thing Moschner wanted to do now was escape.

⤚ CHAPTER XII ⤚

Averland, 1123

The mood within the hunting lodge Mandred and his commanders had taken over for their headquarters was tense. After the long campaign through Ostland, the liberation of Wolfenburg, the fighting against both skaven and Vanhal's undead in Stirland, many of his nobles had grown weary of the war. They urged Mandred to secure what had been gained, to disperse the army and send the men back to their homes.

It was an argument Mandred had heard many times, and it was an argument that never failed to fill him with contempt for those who made it. Only a week before, these same men had walked the streets of Woerden, seen with their own eyes the misery the town had been reduced to by their skaven conquerors. The ratmen weren't simply a rival baron, a mortal human enemy to be fought between spring and the harvest. They were an insidious pestilence, a plague every bit as heinous as the Black Plague itself. Where they conquered, they despoiled, stripped the land bare, enslaving the populace and taking many of them down into their burrows – never to be seen again. There was no question of coexistence with this vermin, no possibility of simply conceding territory to them and hoping they would be content. No, the skaven had to be hounded out, pressed relentlessly, exterminated until not a single one remained. Nothing less could ensure the security of the Empire or even just a small corner of the Empire. It had to be all or nothing, because this inhuman foe would never relent. Given the chance to recover, allowed any respite at all, they would be back. Kurgaz said the dwarf Book of Grudges was riddled with wars against these monsters, wars that stretched back thousands of years.

The peasants understood. Their ties to the land were more intimate than those of their noble lords. It struck Mandred as bitterly ironic that the men who owned the land had less understanding of it than those who served them. Not simply how to till the soil or bring the cattle to pasture, but an actual appreciation of the land as a living, vibrant thing. For too many of the nobles, their holdings were merely something to generate an income; their interest in it began and ended with the coin each harvest generated.

Then there were the opportunists, those like Baroness Carin who saw in the conflict a way to gather power for themselves. Mandred had been impressed by the noblewoman's strength and determination, but her calculating politicking was something that evoked his contempt. Wherever his army marched, Baroness Carin ensured that concessions were made to Nordland and Middenland, pacts and treaties that would favour those realms once the fighting was done. She sought to profit from the war, that was clear enough, and her inclusion of Middenland in those spoils was also obvious. She'd made it clear several times that her interest in the Graf of Middenheim was more than platonic.

There were many who were already whispering that Mandred should become the next Emperor, that the House von Zelt should be the new keepers of the Imperial crown. Baroness Carin was cautious in voicing her own support for such a future, probably because it would be unseemly for a woman who hoped to become Empress to inveigle herself in the question.

Mandred glanced in her direction and saw Baroness Carin return his gaze with a stalwart nod of approval. Whatever her ambitions for the future, now, in the present, she was a staunch ally. He turned his gaze towards General von Weichs, the commander of the Stirlander contingent, and Dregator Vladislav from the Sylvanian levy. Both soldiers were obviously ill at ease, uncomfortable with marching their troops into another battle, yet at the same time well aware that inaction would threaten their homelands.

Elder Boldo Hoop from Mootland was more reserved than the delegates from his neighbours. Possibly since the Black Plague had limited its attentions to humans and failed to infect halflings, the skaven had avoided any intrusion across the boundaries of the Moot. That had engendered among the halflings an isolationist attitude, most of them content to remain in their peaceful oasis while disease and war raged around them. At the same time, the Moot's good fortune had turned it into a potential breadbasket for Mandred's army. The supplies of food he'd negotiated for would be far more vital than any military support the halflings could offer. Even so, Mandred had welcomed the hundred-odd archers who formed the All Volunteer Mootland Anti-Rat Brigade.

Less helpful were the contingents from Talabecland and
Ostland. They were eager to return to their homelands now
that neighbouring Stirland had been cleansed of the ratkin.
With their borders secured, these forces felt their part in
the war was finished. Count von Drexler of Talabheim had
even argued that Mandred's force should turn to Hochland,
scourge the skaven from that province and secure the whole
of the north before attending to the infested south. Count
van der Duijn, of course, continued to press for a strike
against the Norscans in Marienburg, even in the face of
reports that the barbarians were withdrawing of their own
accord, their ranks decimated as the Black Plague finally
reached their enclave.

Mandred listened to all the arguments. His decision was
already made, had been made before he set foot in the
lodge. The council was here to argue for the positions of
their respective lands, to make their voices heard. Mandred
knew it was important that the rulers of Ostland and Talabheim felt their opinions had been heard, that their advice
had been given due consideration. Indeed, if a good enough
reason could be made, Mandred did not believe himself so
conceited in his power that he couldn't be swayed by a solid
argument.

No such argument had been offered, however. Leaning
across the table, Mandred thanked the assembled generals
and nobles, paused a moment to honour the counsel of
Ar-Ulric and Arch-Lector Hartwich, and paid his respects to
Kurgaz and his dwarfish allies.

Then, the Graf of Middenheim settled back in his chair
and declared what he intended to do. 'The skaven infestation of Averheim threatens this entire region,' he said,
directing his words particularly at the Stirlander and Sylvanian emissaries as well as Elder Hoop. 'It is the core of the

ratmen's occupation of Averland, the nest from which their armies plunder the province and enslave its people.' He turned and nodded to Kurgaz. 'It has been opined that the skaven armies that have been assembled here are so large because the ratkin seek to make an assault against Zhufbar and engage their hereditary foes, the dwarfs. However, it is equally possible, now that so much of the north has been cleansed of their evil, that the skaven will loose these armies into the very lands we have spent so much blood to liberate.' He pointed at the leaders from Ostland and Talabecland. 'Do not think the skaven will be content with simply holding Averland and the rest of the south. Do not even think they will be satisfied with retaking Stirland or capturing Sylvania. Even if you are so craven as to allow your fellow men to languish in bondage to the ratkin, you will not be safe. In a month, a year, the skaven will come for your lands and there will be no one to stand and help you defend them.'

'If you are wise, you will attack while the skaven are massed in Averheim,' the suggestion came from Kurgaz. 'I've seen that city. I know how tightly it is packed inside its walls. The numbers of the ratkin will work against them if they are trapped inside those walls.'

'Nor can the vermin afford to bring their complete strength against an attacker.' For the first time since the meeting had started, the wolf-witch Hulda approached the table. Ar-Ulric gave her a stern glance, but too many of the other commanders at the table had benefited from the accuracy of her prognostications to gainsay her a place among them. The wild-looking woman swept her piercing gaze across the table. 'The skaven have yet to break the defenders within the Averburg. The old quarter remains in human hands and continues to endure the siege of the underfolk. Several times the Averlanders have managed to sally from behind the old walls, wrecking havoc among the ratmen. If Averheim is attacked from without, the skaven will still fear an attack from within.'

Count von Drexler remained unconvinced. 'From what I have heard, the skaven massed in Averheim are more numerous than anything we have seen. A larger army of the monsters than conquered Carroburg and Dietershafen or laid siege to Wolfenburg. It will take a massive effort to relieve the city, and we face the very real prospect that, even if we are victorious, our army will be too weak to remain an effective fighting force.'

Mandred nodded. 'I agree, that is a possibility. But if the army is too weak to fight the skaven at Averheim, how will it be strong enough to stop the ratkin when they eventually leave Averheim and strike north?' He let the question linger for a moment, letting the truth of his words impress itself on each mind. 'No, if we cannot break the monsters here, we won't be able to break them later when our forces have been dispersed to guard our homelands. It must be now if we are to prevail.'

As he walked away from the hunting lodge towards his own tent, Arch-Lector Hartwich was struck by the appearance of several armed riders moving through the army's encampment. Throughout their long march, the army had added small bands of fighters to its ranks. Usually these were the retinues of some petty lord, small companies of mercenaries or displaced *Dienstleute*, even the occasional bandit gang. The riders he now observed were markedly different.

There were about three dozen of them, all kitted out in heavy suits of plate armour, the metal blackened to a dull, sooty colour. As striking as the black armour was, it was the ghoulish masks each of the horsemen wore that made them so remarkable. The steel masks of their helms were cast in the semblance of leering skulls.

A quick enquiry from a passing Middenheim officer revealed to Hartwich that these men called themselves the Knights of the Black Rose. They had ridden all the way from Wissenland where they had been campaigning relentlessly against the skaven around Pfeildorf. Their leader was a man named Aldinger from Nuln, though his accent was that of Reikland.

As he watched the sombre procession ride past him, Hartwich was struck by the familiarity of the way they marched their horses, how they held their lances at a slight tilt with the butt resting against the left stirrup. It was like watching Grand Master von Schomberg's Reiksknecht on parade.

While Hartwich was watching the knights, one of the armoured riders broke ranks and galloped towards him. Dipping his lance respectfully towards the priest, the warrior addressed him in a precise, clipped tone. 'You are Arch-Lector Wolfgang Hartwich?' the knight asked.

'I am,' Hartwich said. 'Would I be speaking to Grand Master Aldinger of the Knights of the Black Rose?' It was a guess, but the trace of Reikland in the rider's voice made Hartwich think it a good guess.

'Captain Aldinger,' the knight corrected him. 'The Knights of the Black Rose are too poor for a grand master. A captain suits our needs well enough.' From behind the sockets of his steel mask, Aldinger's eyes took on a cunning aspect. 'There is a second captain who rides with us, though he is not of our order. He is waiting for you in your tent. I must ask a question of you, your excellency. Is he safe there? Is what he has brought safe?'

Hartwich was silent for a moment. The import with which Aldinger asked his question, the gravity of his voice told him exactly who this other captain must be and the nature of what he had brought with him. 'Sigmar has brought them this far,' Hartwich said. 'I do not think we will lose either of them now.'

Aldinger saluted the priest, satisfied with his answer. Wheeling his horse around, he galloped to rejoin his command. Hartwich watched him ride off for a moment, then hastened down the rows of tents and pavilions to where his own shelter had been erected.

Throwing open the flap, Hartwich found himself looking on a man he hadn't seen in nearly a decade. Captain Erich von Kranzbeuhler looked as strong and vibrant as the day he'd encountered an outlawed Hartwich in the backwaters of Reikland. Both of them had been beyond the law then – Erich had been a commander in the abolished Reiksknecht and a chief participant in the plot to overthrow Emperor Boris.

More than the man's escape, it was what he'd escaped Altdorf with that made him important. As Hartwich looked at him, the priest didn't need to say a word. Erich already knew the question that was uppermost in the priest's mind.

Carefully, the knight unwrapped the bulky object he had carried across half the Empire, the treasure he had hidden for ten years in the wilderness.

Hartwich dropped to his knees and gasped in awe as he found himself staring down at the holiest of Sigmarite relics: Ghal Maraz, the Hammer of Sigmar Himself.

'We must keep this,' Hartwich gasped. 'No one must know. No one must see.'

Erich frowned. 'I thought you would bestow Ghal Maraz upon Graf Mandred. There are many who already call him Emperor. The warhammer would make that claim still more legitimate.'

Hartwich nodded. 'Yes. And that is why it must remain hidden. Be kept secret. We cannot allow its presence to be felt until the right moment. The man who holds Ghal Maraz can make himself Emperor, but first he must build the foundations for that Empire.'

Beck scowled as he stood outside Graf Mandred's tent, listening to the soft voices of his master and the Lady Mirella. The knight scratched at the scar running down from his missing eye. When he was irritated the old wound would begin to itch. It was a complaint he'd noticed ever since the liberation of Woerden. Of all the fresh scrapes and bruises, the ugly gash left by a spear in his right thigh, he found it ironic that an injury suffered years before should be the one to vex him.

The graf! Beck couldn't understand what his master was thinking, dallying with Mirella, a landless vagabond from Altdorf when Baroness Carin could be his for the asking. She was a woman of his own station, a ruler who would bring the wealth of Nordland with her. With the shrewd baroness at his side, Mandred could well and truly become what many were already calling him: Emperor.

Yet he spent his few quiet moments with Mirella! It was a situation Beck couldn't understand. Mandred wasn't like other men, free to follow the whims of his heart. He understood that he was first and foremost the ruler of Middenheim, that when he wed it must be to the advantage of his people. Growing up, he'd been reminded again and again of his duty to the people he ruled. How he could forget that, forsake his obligations simply to lie in the arms of a...

Beck left the thought unfinished. The graf might know what he was doing. He might be toying with Mirella in order to excite the jealousy of Baroness Carin. Yes, now that he considered the idea, the knight was certain he had the truth of it.

To take his mind away from the voices inside the tent, Beck reached into his pocket and dug out the trophy he'd claimed from the skaven warlord of Woerden. It was a curious stone, when the light hit it just right it shone a brilliant green, at other times it seemed blacker than black. The skaven had worn it on a chain about its neck. Beck had taken it because its shape reminded him of a wolf's head. As a good Ulrican, he'd taken that as a good omen and kept the stone as a lucky charm.

It felt strangely warm in his hand as he turned it over in his palm. Absently, Beck reached his finger up to his eye and began to scratch at the scar.

The old wound was itching again.

Stirland, 1122

Fear. Since becoming voivode and merciless despot of Sylvania, Count Malbork von Drak had thought he understood all there was to know about fear: how to evoke it; how to inflict it; how to use it; how to control it.

Now, as he sat astride his warhorse and watched the obscene legions of Vanhal marching across the fields bordering Fellwald, Malbork appreciated for the first time how little he really understood about fear. His heart was pounding against his chest as though it would burst. His breath came in short hot gasps while the blood in his veins seemed to have been turned to ice water. He could feel his stomach churning beneath his mail, threatening to make him sick even before battle was joined.

The Sylvanian troops had been positioned on the left flank of von Oberreuth's army, delegated to the position of least concern to the grand count. Despite Malbork's hopes that Stirland and Vanhal would decimate one another, his noble pride chafed at the blatant insult in such a deployment. Louder than any decree, the grand count was proclaiming his distrust of the voivode.

The Great Host of Stirland was arrayed along the tree-line, its pickets clearly visible to the approaching undead, but not so far from the forest as to be beyond the defence of its thick canopy. Von Oberreuth's troops were largely peasant conscripts, commoners drafted from every village and farm between Wurtbad and Waldenhof. They made for a sorry spectacle, their only uniform a strip of green tied about the sleeves of their woollen tunics, their only weaponry a shaft of sharpened ash or yew. The conscripts were ranked in great square blocks, living walls of humanity arrayed to deny the advance of Vanhal's deathless horde.

The real strength of von Oberreuth's army was hidden behind and between the massed conscripts. Footmen, *Dienstleute* armoured in mail and bearing cruel maces and vicious axes, their kite-shaped shields quartered in the green and gold of Stirland. Horsemen, their lances held at the ready, their steeds draped in the panoply of war. Most impressive of all were the knights, their scale armour covered by gaudy tabards declaring the noble lords to whom each warrior owed fealty. Malbork had heard that the knights had been promised fiefs of their own should Stirland carry the day. Von Oberreuth was no fool. He was looking beyond today's battle, preparing for the future when he might need a new class of petty noble to support him against the ambitions of the old aristocracy.

In the vanguard of the army were the White Swords,

resplendent in their snowy tabards, the plates of their armour painted a milky colour to match the coats of their magnificent destriers. The White Swords were the elite of Wurtbad, a martial society that drew its membership from the oldest Asoborn families. They were the paladins of Stirland, sworn to defend the province with their dying breath. Upon the nasal of each helm was daubed the sign of Rhya the Mother and Taal the Father, eternal emblems of the gods who watched over the Land Across the Rivers. Von Oberreuth belonged to the White Swords and had taken his place among the paladins for the coming battle. It was a gesture meant to inspire the army he led. Whatever dangers they must face, the grand count would face them first.

Of course, those who followed the grand count wouldn't have the benefit of two Morrite exorcists riding beside them, but that was a small detail von Oberreuth didn't think they needed to know.

Malbork turned his sceptical eye from the White Swords and his liege lord and instead gazed across the assemblage of troops that formed the Great Host's right flank. He had to confess that Graf Mandred had dispatched an impressive force to aid Stirland. Two, perhaps even three thousand infantry, all of better calibre than von Oberreuth's peasant conscripts, many of them rivalling the *Dienstleute* for quality. Here were hairy Middenlanders with cowhide armour and brutal mattocks, grizzled Middenheimers with chain shirts and steel swords, pale Nordlanders with barbed spears and tall helms, dusky Drakwald archers and grim Hochland axemen. A company of boisterous Ostland spearmen broke into bawdy song, defying the hideous undead with a show of scornful cheer. Their jest was muted by the sombre chants of a flagellant mob, blood dripping from their bare backs as the fanatics lashed themselves with scourges.

The cavalry of Mandred von Zelt was equally diverse. Dour Verenan Templars draped in black, savage Roppsmen from the icy wastes of Kislev, the lightly armoured lancers of Wolfenburg and the heavy horsemen of Krudenwald. Like von Oberreuth, Mandred had his elite troops, in his case the crimson-armoured Knights of the White Wolf. It was easy enough to spot the Graf of Middenheim among his men. He alone was without the white wolf pelt that swung from the shoulders of his knights. Perhaps such an affectation was unnecessary. The men in Mandred's army were already calling him 'the Wolf of Sigmar'.

All told, the Great Host was equal to its name. Never had Malbork seen such a vast army. At least not of living men…

The foe that now marched indefatigably towards the forest was more numerous than Malbork had believed possible. Rank after rank of bleached bone and rusted armour, troop after troop of fleshless horses carrying skeletal riders. Vanhal's legion was as numberless as the stars in the sky. Tattered banners and rotten flags waved above the undead horde, crows and vultures circled above them, drawn by the omnipresent stench of death. Spear and sword, bow and axe, lance and flail, the skeletons came, giving voice to no shouts, no song, no chant. Only the dry rustle of leathery flesh against decayed bone, the clatter of crumbling armour jouncing against morbid frame.

At the core of the legion, like the hub of some obscene wheel, was the necromancer himself. Malbork could see the fiend's black cloak and the skull-like mask. Even from a distance, his skin crawled at the impression of malefic power emanating from the sorcerer. Vanhal was borne aloft upon a writhing, wailing nimbus of spectral energies, a great pillar of enslaved spirits, their essences fused to form an abominable chariot beneath the necromancer's throne.

Vanhal raised his arms high and as he did so, three vast and ghastly forms swept down from the sky, the wasted, putrid carcasses of dragons, preserved and animated by the necromancer's foul arts. Shouts of alarm greeted the descent of the dragons, cries of horror that were silenced by the blare of trumpets. At the signal, the Great Host retreated into the shelter of the trees while bowmen advanced between the ranks and loosed a volley into the hurtling monstrosities.

Arrows by the hundreds whistled up into the reptiles, stabbing into their withered scales and corrupt flesh. The beasts responded with gouts of stinking putrescence, a brew of diabolic corruption that seared its victims to the very marrow. Scores of men fell shrieking beneath the toxic breath. Unable to drop the beasts with their arrows, they were left helpless before the rampaging dragons.

The sacrifice of the archers provided an opportunity for a particular element within Graf Mandred's force. Rushing onto the field and taking up a position to the flank of the swooping dragons, a regiment of burly dwarfs hastily brought their curious weapons to bear. The dwarfs aimed their weapons – long tubes of steel fixed to stocks of wutroth – skyward. Each warrior set the end of a smouldering cord of hemp against a small opening just behind the steel tube. A moment later, a deafening roar boomed from dozens of firearms as each gunner sent a ball of lead exploding into the decayed dragons. Where the undead brutes had shrugged off the impact of arrows, the dwarfish bullets pulverised bone and shredded flesh. One of the wyrms plummeted to the earth, gouging a great pit as its mass pounded into the field. The sound of the reptile's bones breaking brought a resounding cheer from the Stirlanders and their allies. The remaining dragons wheeled away, retreating back across the line of Vanhal's advancing legion.

Malbork looked back at the necromancer, hoping to see some reaction from the fearsome Vanhal to the routing of his foul dragons. The skull-masked sorcerer remained implacable, as emotionless as the skeletons he commanded. A gesture and the dragons began circling over the undead host. Not routed, simply withdrawn. It occurred to Malbork that their foe had more tactical acumen than he would have credited him. The dragons had been a probing attack, simply a test of the Stirlander line. Mandred's deployment of the dwarfs had exposed one of the teeth hidden inside von Oberreuth's army.

At another gesture from the necromancer, the entire deathless legion came to a halt with preternatural precision. One breath they were moving, the next they were as still as a mountain, a solid mass of carrion arrayed before the forest. Vanhal leaned forwards upon his spectral throne. For an instant, it seemed to Malbork that the fiend stared directly into his eyes. He shuddered at the contact, feeling the devilish mockery in the necromancer's glare.

Then there came a flurry of motion from the centre of the undead host. Marching out from between the ranks of silent skeletons were scores of armoured monsters. Flesh blackened and withered by millennia clung to the ancient bones, the bronze armour caked in verdigris, crumbling a little more with each step the horrors took. There was something troubling about that armour, something naggingly familiar. Malbork's vexation resolved itself when he heard Dregator Iorgu draw a frightened gasp.

'Impossible!' Iorgu exclaimed. 'It wasn't real! It wasn't real!'

The wights continued to march, and from the Stirlanders a despairing moan rose. 'The old kings,' they wailed. 'The old kings march to reclaim their land!'

Malbork stared again at Vanhal, understanding now that terrible mockery. He had thought to provoke war between his enemies by convincing Stirland that Vanhal had set the ancient Styrigen dead upon them.

Now, Vanhal was making Malbork's lie a reality. He had called the dead from their barrows. The Styrigen wights had risen to take their revenge against the Asoborn conquerors.

⤚ CHAPTER XIII ⤙

Averland, 1123

Arch-Lector Hartwich led the outlaw knight down a winding path between the pavilions of the great and the mighty. Clustered at the very core of the encampment, the tents of the nobles and dignitaries were a spectacle, their gaudily painted banners snapping in the winds, bright pennons fluttering from support poles. Soldiers wearing the liveries of a hundred noble houses stood guard outside the tents, leaning against spears and halberds as they watched each passer-by with a suspicious glare. The enticing aromas from a dozen private kitchens wafted through the air, almost blotting out the omnipresent stink of horse dung and human sweat.

'Where are we going?' Erich asked the priest for what seemed the hundredth time since they'd quit Hartwich's own pavilion. This time, however, instead of brushing him off with an injunction to be patient, Hartwich stopped and turned towards the knight. There was a worried look in his eyes.

'I am taking you to where I think you can work a great

good,' Hartwich said after a moment of inner reflection. 'Yes, I think Sigmar must indeed have guided you here, in His mercy. But now that we stand upon the precipice, I find myself wondering if I have the right to ask this of you.'

Erich smiled and slapped his gauntlets against his armoured thigh. 'You've asked nothing of me so far. Aside from hiding in a cave for years on end, my only human contact a Taalite priest.'

'Haerther is a wise man. I knew he would keep you safe,' Hartwich said.

'He stayed with me for a time after I took shelter with the Knights of the Black Rose, but mysteriously left us one day, vanished as completely as if he'd never been,' Erich said.

Hartwich nodded knowingly. 'Haerther is more comfortable among the trees and meadows, the wild places where he can be closer to Taal. He's little good around people for very long.' The priest frowned as his mind turned back to the subject at hand.

'Erich, I am going to ask your help to heal a great hurt,' Hartwich said. 'I've tried my best, but it needs a strength more profound than what I can bestow.'

The knight slapped his gauntlets against his thigh again, this time with a bit of irritation behind the gesture. 'You're speaking in riddles again,' he accused.

'Princess Erna Thornig is in this camp,' Hartwich stated, his words blunt and to the point. 'She was rescued from the skaven in Carroburg. Graf Mandred himself found her.' The priest felt a pang of guilt when he saw the way Erich's face lit up at the mention of the princess. He remembered watching them together, all those years ago when they'd all been involved in Prince Sigdan's conspiracy against the Emperor. He'd been praying the light he'd noticed then hadn't been dimmed by the cruelties of time.

Now that he saw it yet burned, at least in Erich's heart, Hartwich felt his guilt increase a hundredfold. He reached out and set his hand on Erich's shoulder. 'Prepare yourself,' he cautioned. 'The princess isn't the same woman you left in Altdorf.'

Erich shook his head and said sombrely, 'The woman I left in Altdorf I thought to be dead, murdered by that maggot her father arranged for her to marry.' He knew it was vile to hold a grudge against the dead, but he still resented Baron Thornig's callousness in using his own daughter as a means of removing Adolf Kreyssig.

'There are some things worse than death,' Hartwich warned. 'Things that make even a priest lose hope.' He stared hard at the knight. 'If there is any feeling for you left in her, it may awaken when she sees you, and in awakening stir the rest of her mind. She may need your strength to support her for a very long time.'

'She will have it for as long as she wants it,' Erich vowed. Hartwich nodded and led him on towards a tent that stood by itself. Even the fact that she was being supported by Graf Mandred wasn't enough to make anyone pitch camp next to a madwoman. Two dwarf guards stood before the tent, the only warriors in the camp with the stomach for such duty.

Hartwich led Erich past the sentries and into the sparingly appointed space beyond. The knight gasped in disbelief when he saw the white-haired, pallid woman. It was like looking at the echo of the Erna he had known in Altdorf. She was lying upon a pile of furs, idly rocking back and forth while pulling clumps of goose-down from a pillow.

'She has suffered much,' Hartwich explained. 'First at the hands of Kreyssig, then as a witness to the cruelties of Boris. Finally there came the long years as slave to the skaven.'

Erich felt the flicker of hope die inside him. 'What can be done?' he asked.

'Pray,' Hartwich said, but the priest was looking past the knight, watching the woman rocking back and forth. At the sound of Erich's voice she had perked up. Now she was looking in their direction.

'Captain? Is it my captain?' Erna asked. When she saw Erich turn back around, a piteously jubilant smile stretched across her face. Dropping the pillow, she lurched onto her feet and stumbled on her stiff legs towards him.

'Go to her,' Hartwich encouraged the perplexed knight. Erich nodded and did as the priest said, meeting Erna halfway across the tent, catching her in his arms.

'It is you,' the princess cried, tears rolling down her cheeks. 'Adolf said he killed you.'

Erich smiled at that. It would be just like the swine to claim he was dead just to inflict that little extra measure of torment on his wife. 'I don't die so easily,' he told her.

Erna drew away from the embrace, staring intently into Erich's eyes. 'I killed him,' she said.

The knight smiled awkwardly. It was common knowledge that Kreyssig was alive and well in Altdorf, still acting as Protector of the Empire. Indeed, he was something of a hero to the people there after fending off a skaven attack.

Erna understood the incredulous expression. Her brow knitted angrily. 'I killed him,' she insisted. 'Doktor Moschner was there. He saw me do it.' She glanced around warily. 'I wouldn't tell anybody because it is a secret but I want you to know. I killed him.'

'That is all she worries about, this man she says she killed,' Hartwich explained. 'She always says it is a secret only the doktor knows. Sometimes she also explains that the doktor was taken away by the skaven.'

Erich sighed. 'The things Kreyssig must have done to you for you to murder him in your mind,' he said, his voice almost reduced to a sob as he reached out to stroke Erna's colourless hair.

Again, the princess pulled back. Ironically, there was an uncomprehending look on *her* face. 'Not Adolf,' she said, her voice dropping to a conspiratorial whisper. Her next words, soft as they were spoken, still had an impact like thunder as they left her lips.

'I killed Emperor Boris.'

Graf Mandred paced about the confines of his tent, listening again to the report that had just reached him from his scouts. It was about the worst news he could have expected. For this reason, he'd summoned only his closest confederates, the men who had been with him the longest. Even his most ardent supporters like Baroness Carin were excluded from this select group.

'You've heard the reports,' Mandred challenged his councillors once the scouts finished repeating the information. 'What is your advice?'

'An army marching behind us on our flank,' Ar-Ulric said. 'It threatens the entire campaign against Averheim. Instead of catching the skaven between us and the Averburg, this force would trap us against the walls of Averheim.'

'Do we know who they are,' Duke Schneidereit asked. 'Perhaps it is another volunteer force from Stirland or Sylvania?'

'More likely a skaven column,' Grand Master Vitholf suggested. His face grew grave as he voiced another possibility. 'It could also be a fresh army from Vanhaldenschlosse.' After their battle with Vanhal, not a man in Mandred's army liked the prospect of fighting the undead a second time.

Kurgaz growled into his beard as he suggested yet another

dire prospect. 'Most of the greenskins have been battering away at the dwarfholds in the mountains,' he said, 'but it's always possible some horde of goblins decided to call it quits and look for easier prey.'

Mandred's fingers clenched about Legbiter's grip. 'Whoever they are, we can't have them on our flank.' He grimaced as he thought of the other problem at hand. 'We can't delay the attack on Averheim. Any delay and I think the contingents from Ostland and Talabecland will go home. We have to strike, and strike soon.'

Grand Master Vitholf stepped over to his graf. 'There's only one thing to do then. You'll need to send a company of cavalry to engage these troops on our flank. Attack swiftly, retreat quickly and lead them off away from the army.'

'It will be a dangerous duty,' Mandred cautioned.

Vitholf laughed. 'That, your highness, is why I am volunteering the Knights of the White Wolf for the job.'

The shrieks of a score of skaven scratched at the air as a jagged chunk of masonry came hurtling out from behind the towering walls of the Averburg. Packed in tight formations around the besieged fortress, every rock lobbed by the defenders wrought a hideous toll from the attackers.

Great Warlord Vrrmik, He who is Twelfth, bruxed his fangs in satisfaction when he caught the scent of the dead and dying ratmen. The humans had directed their artillery against Clan Skab's positions again, proving Vrrmik's wisdom in rotating them there. It would make for a formidable object lesson if Skab's warriors were decimated here. The scum should have stood their ground in Woerden and fought to the last fang instead of turning tail and scampering away after their warlord was killed.

Vrrmik leaned back in his palanquin, a massive throne

that had been stitched together from a number of tapestries plundered from the homes of the nobles and then lashed to a jumbled frame that included the altar from a shrine to the goddess Rhya. The altar stone was a bit onerous for Vrrmik's bearers to shoulder, but the warlord found the smell of the stone as delightful as the texture of the tapestries, so the slaves really had no choice in the matter.

Well, they had one choice, Vrrmik reflected, running his white paw down the haft of the enormous mattock he'd stolen from the dwarfs inside the Ulricsberg. He'd named the thing Skavenbite in recognition of his new position as Vecteek's successor. With the diminished power of the grey seers, more than ever the occupant of the Twelfth Throne was ruler of the Grey Lords and master of the Council of Thirteen.

There were challengers of course, chief among them the other great warlord clans, Skab and Rictus. Several thousand warriors from each of those clans had been brought to Averheim, determined to win for their warlords some measure of the victory when the Averburg finally fell. It was important to them that Vrrmik and Mors be denied the credit for subduing the city.

Such scheming, however, played right into Vrrmik's paws. Between Averheim and Woerden all the towns were defended by skaven from Clan Mors, skaven who wouldn't engage Man-dread's army as it moved southward but would instead retreat. Vrrmik would open the way for Man-dread to reach Averheim. There, the man-things would obligingly slaughter the treacherous clanrats of Skab and Rictus. Once the decimation of his rivals reached a point where they could safely be considered no longer a threat, Vrrmik would attack with the full might of Mors and the diseased weapons of his ally, Poxmaster Puskab Foulfur.

The humans would think themselves winning a great victory in Averheim, but in fact they would merely be stepping into a carefully laid trap. Prey just waiting for Vrrmik to pounce.

Altdorf, 1124

Adolf Kreyssig and an honour guard drawn from the ranks of the Kaiserknecht sat their horses beneath the ponderous stone arches of the Reikstor, the great gate on the western bank of the River Reik that afforded entrance to Altdorf from the province of Reikland. Rain pounded against the battlements overhead, streaming down from the maws of stone gargoyles and lead-lined culverts. The downpour had sent all but the most determined travellers retreating indoors. What little traffic remained, largely traders desperate to reach the city before market day and refugees from the eastern provinces seeking the security of the capital, was being diverted away from the Reikstor by companies of armed militia. Kreyssig wanted the gate kept clear for a very special visitor from the east.

The years since the Night of the Holy Knives had been eventful. The dominance of Gazulgrund and the Temple of Sigmar had grown despite Kreyssig's clandestine efforts to undermine it. Even when he'd cut off the supplies of grain being diverted to the Temple, the Grand Theogonist's power had continued to grow. His cynical belief that a policy of 'bread for prayer' was behind the dramatic rise of the Sigmarite congregations had proven woefully wrong. There was much more at work than the disbursement of food to hungry peasants, a force that was so alien to the opportunistic Kreyssig that while he could recognise it and even exploit it he was unable to understand it. That force was simply faith, the stubborn perhaps even desperate willingness of the commoners to believe in something greater than their noble lords and their servile existence.

Elsewhere, however, other forces were at play. Forces Kreyssig was able to understand. Graf Mandred's campaign against the skaven had swept through Nordland and Ostland, down into Stirland and Sylvania. Wherever the Wolf of Sigmar gave battle, the ratkin were deposed, sent scurrying back to their subterranean lairs. Mandred was hailed as hero and liberator by those he freed from the cruelties of the skaven. Even in the Imperial court there were those who said Mandred von Zelt was the man to reunite the shattered Empire.

Mandred's army had been active in Averland, campaigning to break the skaven occupation of Averheim. The latest reports to reach Kreyssig had the army turning northward now, marching towards Talabecland and Hochland. If Mandred added these territories to those already beholden to him, there would be no stopping any claim he made upon the Imperial crown.

Kreyssig had ambition, but he was shrewd enough to know when it was useless to stand against the tide of history. Unless he fell in battle, Mandred would become the next Emperor. The Hohenbach dynasty was gone, it would be the von Zelts who would build the future. If he wished to occupy a place of prominence in that future, Kreyssig knew he had to act swiftly. He'd dispatched emissaries to Mandred's army, sending the graf overtures indicating the Protector's willingness to support him and help pave the way for his coronation as Emperor.

Those emissaries had returned, bringing back word that

Mandred was sending his own messenger to discuss the details of an alliance with Altdorf. Kreyssig's agents had followed the progress of that messenger, bringing back word at every step of the man's journey. The last report to reach him made it clear that the expected dignitary would arrive by way of the Reikstor this day unless he stopped somewhere to take shelter from the rain.

Kreyssig wasn't willing to gamble on the timidity of Mandred's representative. There were those in Altdorf, chiefly Duke Vidor and his cadre of nobles, who would see any contact between the Protector and Mandred as a show of weakness. They would seize upon any perceived vulnerability to depose the hated commoner from his position. Until he had established a new role with the graf, made secure a new position in the coming regime, Kreyssig couldn't afford for anyone but himself to have access to Mandred's emissary or for anyone to even be aware of the man's presence in Altdorf.

Hence, the powerful and despotic Adolf Kreyssig sat beneath the archway, listening to the rain and watching the road. He drew the folds of his bearskin cloak tighter around himself against the chill in the air. The rain might be good for the crops, but it was eroding his patience.

On the road ahead, two riders appeared, immediately arresting Kreyssig's attention. One rider was a tall man bundled in a rain-soaked woollen cloak. The other rider, mounted upon a mule, was shorter but far broader of shoulder. Even at a distance, it was clear the second rider was a dwarf. Kreyssig's spies had told him that the emissary was travelling in the company of a dwarfish bodyguard. The keenest anticipation held Kreyssig as he watched the militiamen wave the two riders towards the Reikstor.

Spurring his own steed, Kreyssig rode out from the shelter

of the arch to greet the emissary. It would help establish a thread of commonality if he exposed himself to the elements as the messenger had done, showing the man that whatever Kreyssig's position he was eager to work with the Middenheimers and their allies. All his life, Kreyssig had seen how much easier people were to manipulate when they believed in the existence of a common bond.

'Welcome to Imperial Altdorf,' Kreyssig announced, removing his hat with a flourishing sweep of his hand. As he bowed his head, his sharp eyes studied the two riders. The dwarf was a grim, cheerless figure, his head shaved into a single strip of hair that had been stained a brilliant crimson and greased into a spiky crest. In defiance of the elements, he travelled with neither cloak nor cape, nor indeed any shirt upon his back, instead preferring to journey bare-chested in order to display the whirling tattoos inked into his skin. The Protector's greeting brought only a brusque huff of acknowledgement from the dwarf as he blew drops of rain from his beard.

The other rider, the human emissary, was covered by a grey cloak, the hood drawn up over the man's face. As Kreyssig stretched out his hand in welcome, the emissary drew back the hood. The colour drained out of Kreyssig's face when he saw who it was.

'It has been a long time, Adolf,' Erich von Kranzbeuhler said, each word spoken with such cold precision as to curdle the blood.

Kreyssig recoiled, waving his hat in a frantic gesture to summon the honour guard to his side. Von Kranzbeuhler! A man who by all rights should be dead. He was a member of the outlawed Reiksknecht, the order of knights who had opposed the massacre of the Bread Marchers and later conspired to depose Emperor Boris. When he'd last seen von

Kranzbeuhler, it had been in the sewers beneath the Imperial palace trying to escape with Ghal Maraz. The rebels had
stolen it from the palace and were trying to keep it from the
possession of Boris Goldgather, thereby stripping his reign
of some of its legitimacy. Kreyssig had nearly lost his life
trying to recover the relic.

The outlaw knight smiled coldly when he saw the shock
on Kreyssig's face. 'No ghost, Adolf. I am real.' He reached
beneath his cloak, bringing out a roll of vellum. Carefully,
shielding the scroll with his body from the rain, Erich
unrolled it just enough to expose the waxen seal fixed to the
bottom of the document. There was no mistaking that seal.
It was the insignia of Middenheim's royal house, the symbol
of Graf Mandred.

'Call back your dogs,' Erich warned as the Kaiserknecht
started to draw their blades. 'As you can see, I am the man
you have been expecting.'

A thin smile worked itself onto the Protector's face. His
shock at seeing his old enemy was profound, but even
more profound was the message Mandred was sending
by dispatching this knight as his representative. Very few
people would know about what von Kranzbeuhler had
stolen. Mandred must know that Kreyssig was one of them.
Without saying a word, he was letting Kreyssig know where
Ghal Maraz was and announcing his intention to claim the
Imperial crown. If von Kranzbeuhler had brought Sigmar's
Hammer to Mandred, his claim would be seen as ordained
by the gods themselves. No one would even try to stand in
his way.

Kreyssig waved aside his guards, snarling at them to withdraw back under the archway where the noise of the rain
would deafen them to the words he would trade with von
Kranzbeuhler. 'I will not insult you by protesting that what I

did I did for the Empire, that I was only following the orders of Boris Goldgather.'

Von Kranzbeuhler nodded his appreciation of such courtesy. 'A villain who takes pride in his accomplishments is a rare thing. Such honesty in a blackguard is rarer still.' It was not lost on Kreyssig that the knight's hand had dropped to the hilt of his sword.

'You would dearly like to kill me, wouldn't you?' Kreyssig taunted. 'But you are in service to Graf Mandred now and your sense of duty won't permit you to indulge yourself. Mandred's army must be stretched thin after so many conquests. I don't think he would risk war with Altdorf. Certainly not over some personal grievance harboured by a vagabond outlaw. However fine the presents that outlaw might have brought him.'

The knight's hand clenched into a fist, striking against his thigh in a show of frustrated anger. 'His highness desires friendship with Altdorf,' Erich stated. 'He is concerned with exterminating the skaven threat and is worried that he will lose precious time if he has to conquer Altdorf as well.'

'And what does he offer for Altdorf's friendship?' Kreyssig asked. 'I suppose that he won't allow me to remain as the Emperor's steward. But I'm not a greedy man. I would be content with a less lofty title.' He sneered at von Kranzbeuhler. 'I believe the role of Prince of Altdorf is still vacant.'

Erich bristled at the remark, fully aware that it had been Kreyssig who had thwarted Prince Sigdan's coup against Emperor Boris and thereby had been responsible for the prince's death. He retaliated for the mocking barb with one of his own.

'Your wife sends her tender regards,' the knight hissed.

Kreyssig flinched as though he'd been physically struck.

Erich laughed at the despot's surprise. 'Yes, Princess Erna

is alive. She escaped the fate of Boris Goldgather and his guests. As we speak, she is the welcome guest of Graf Mandred's court. She is eager to see you again. You will find her quite changed, Adolf. She's not the same woman you tortured and imprisoned.'

Kreyssig turned his horse about. 'Come,' he ordered as he walked towards the Reikstor. 'You must be tired after your long journey. The courtesies of the Imperial palace are at your disposal. After you have rested, we will discuss what Graf Mandred is willing to offer and what I can provide in return.

'Affairs of state first. Old reunions will have to wait until a more providential time.'

Von Kranzbeuhler followed Kreyssig through the Reikstor. 'I am at your convenience,' he promised. 'I look forward to it with the keenest anticipation,' he added as his fingers again closed about the hilt of his sword.

—◄ CHAPTER XIV ►—

Averland, 1123

Against the night sky, the fires burning inside Averheim cast a hellish glow. It was akin to staring into the maw of a gargantuan dragon, the ruined towers and temples of the city standing in black silhouette against the flames like the jagged fangs of the monster. The dull, distant clamour of battle raging about the besieged Averburg was transformed into the reptile's hiss and roar, distorted and strangely magnified by its circuitous passage through the streets.

Mandred had learned long ago the wisdom of engaging the ratmen in the clean light of day whenever possible. Since they were tunnel-haunting beasts, the skaven eye was especially sensitive to sunlight. Given their preference, the vermin would fight in darkness. At Wolfenburg, the creatures had gone so far as to drag grass and timber to the walls of the city, burning it so that they might wage their siege beneath a mantle of smoke. It seemed the ratkin were following the same tactics here.

Desiring every advantage over the foe, Mandred ordered a halt when his army neared Averheim. With the day nearly spent they would need to wait until daybreak before starting their attack against the skaven. Timber palisades were quickly erected against any assault by the ratmen across the plain outside Averheim and a battery of scouts and sentries was dispatched to watch for the enemy while the rest of the army struck camp.

Most curious among Mandred's precautions were the iron rods his troops pounded deep into the ground. Twenty feet long, the rods were struck again and again until only two feet remained poking up from the earth. At each sunken rod, a dwarf was stationed, with one hand resting on the top of the rod. It was a precaution that had been adapted from the methods used by the dwarfs to warn them of the presence of skaven in their tunnels. Vibrations in the earth would be conducted through the metal rod and detected by the hand resting against it. If the ratmen were burrowing beneath the encampment, the dwarfs would feel the vibrations.

It was towards midnight when the dwarfs gave the alarm. Sleepy-eyed men spilled from their tents, hurriedly strapping on their swords and donning shirts of mail. The alert spread swiftly through the encampment. Kurgaz himself rushed to Mandred's tent to warn the graf.

'Skaven,' the dwarf said, investing the name with such hatred that he had to spit after uttering it.

Beck helped Mandred into his armour, strapping the steel breastplate about the nobleman's chest. Mandred frowned at his bodyguard's own wardrobe, a linen nightshirt and a pair of boots. 'See to your own armour,' he told the knight.

Beck shook his head as he removed a vambrace from the armour rack. 'My duty is to guard your life,' he said, then rapped his knuckle against the steel plate he held. 'This will do a better job than I could ever do.'

'See to your armour,' Lady Mirella ordered Beck, rushing forward to take over the outfitting of her lover. Beck was hesitant to relinquish his labour. The noblewoman scowled at him. 'Many are the times I helped Prince Sigdan into his armour before a tourney,' she told the knight. 'He never suffered for my attentions.' Reluctantly, Beck withdrew, hurrying off into the night to find his own tent.

While Mirella strapped him into his armour, Mandred spoke with Kurgaz. 'Can you tell how close they are, or how many?'

'There's some miners could tell you how heavy each rat in the pack was by the way the stake wobbles,' Kurgaz said. 'But we don't have anybody that good with us. All we know is that they're close enough to make the ground shiver, and that's a damn sight too close.'

Mandred nodded grimly. 'If we knew where they'd break surface, we could cut them down as they brewed up from their hole.'

'Aye, that we could,' Kurgaz said. 'As it stands, however, we'll just have to wait for them to poke their noses out.'

At that moment, screams and shouts rang out from across the encampment. The skaven had poked their noses out, not from a single hole but from dozens. Cursing bitterly, Kurgaz unslung the warhammer from his back, the brutal weapon he'd adopted ever since Drakdrazh was stolen by the skaven.

Mandred hastily pulled away from Mirella. Catching up Legbiter from where it rested alongside the armour stand, he ripped the runefang from its scabbard and tossed the sheath aside. The echo of his hatred blazed up in his eyes, but it was subdued by a far more important feeling – concern for the men whose lives were imperilled by the skaven assault.

'Ulric grant me strength,' Mandred prayed as he followed Kurgaz out into the carnage of battle.

'Ulric grant me strength!' the cry whistled through the bloodied face of Ar-Ulric as the old priest brought his axe cleaving down into the verminous skull of his attacker. A stagnant, retched broth of foulness bubbled up from the robed ratman's head, a treacle too pestiferous to be called blood. The stricken thing collapsed at his feet, gnashing its fangs violently as it snapped impotently at its killer. While the thing was yet in its final death throes, another of the vermin sprang forward, trampling the dying skaven underfoot in its rabid fury to close with Ar-Ulric.

The wolf-priest was all but surrounded now. Four of his Teutogen Guard were down, slain not by the rusted blades and cudgels of the robed skaven but by the diseased fumes billowing from the grisly censer one of the monsters bore. As the foulness had wafted across them, each of the brave warriors had collapsed, vomiting up blood and flecks of tissue as the filth scorched their insides and corrupted their flesh.

The censer bearer itself had fallen soon afterward, overcome by the fumes of the very weapon it carried. The hooded ratman lay in a heap beside the men it had slaughtered, like a dog laid out at the feet of an ancient hero. The creature's death, however, had done little to cheer the men fighting to defend the shrine of Ulric. Four of their number were killed almost at the onset of the fray, leaving only six to hold the shrine. Already they had cut down a score of the ratmen, yet for each skaven they killed, three more seemed to boil up from the hole to take their place.

By accident or design, the burrow the plague monks had

been digging had opened up almost directly beneath the shrine. The stone statue of Ulric in his manifestation as the God of War had nearly fallen into the pit as it opened. Indeed, the statue had been purposefully toppled from its plinth by Ar-Ulric to prevent it from being knocked into the stygian darkness. With more of the creatures swarming from similar holes throughout the encampment, Ar-Ulric and his Teutogen Guard found themselves alone.

The heavy armour of the Teutogen Guard preserved them against the snapping fangs and stabbing blades of the ratmen. The plague monks threw themselves upon the warriors with a reckless ferocity they'd never encountered in skaven before. Foam dripped from the mouths of the ratmen, their eyes glazed with a feral madness. Again and again they would fly at the men, regardless of their own hurts. When one of the guards was finally overcome, felled by a slash across his neck, the skaven pounced upon him, hacking his warm flesh until the shrine was coated in blood.

Sight of the bestial savagery enflamed the outrage of Ar-Ulric and his remaining men. Howling the name of their god, they surged into the plague monks. Over and again, the priest's axe flashed down, hewing asunder the diseased bodies of his foes. For an instant, the slaughter wrought by Ar-Ulric seemed to impress even the crazed minds of the rat-monks. The frenzied attack faltered. The creatures turned back towards their hole.

Before the plague monks could rout, another of their number crept out from the pit. He was a wizened, shrivelled-looking ratman, his green robes embroidered with strange sigils and arcane runes. Great antlers spread from the sides of his skull-like head. The creature glared balefully at Ar-Ulric with blemished eyes that looked like scabrous pools of pus.

A tremor of fear pulsed through Ar-Ulric as he beheld the
monster. From those who had been rescued at Carroburg
had come stories of this noxious beast: Puskab Foulfur,
the loathsome Poxmaster of the skaven. The Black Plague,
the survivors whispered, had been crafted by this inhuman
sorcerer. If true, Ar-Ulric gazed upon a monster that was
responsible for more death and destruction than any mortal
creature since the age of Nagash the Accursed.

Puskab chittered malignantly at his fleeing minions. He
stretched forth his paw and one of the plague monks collapsed, the flesh across its body bubbling like water brought
to a boil as buboes erupted across its hide. The plague
priest's object lesson had its effect on the other skaven.
Squeaking and snarling, the monks returned to the attack.

More than the effect Puskab's profane magic had upon
his verminous minions, it was the effect it had on Ar-Ulric's
own guards that incensed the priest. Where but a moment
before the warriors had been viciously throwing the ratmen
back, now they recoiled before the monsters, falling back
step by tremulous step. Ar-Ulric strangled the fear inside his
own breast. Hefting his axe, he brought it cleaving through
the neck of one plague monk and broke the jaw of a second
with the return sweep of the weapon. Throwing back his
head, he howled the name of Ulric.

The howl was answered by a white-furred fury. A great
white wolf with pale eyes leapt out from the darkness, lunging into the ratmen with tooth and claw. The creatures,
only a moment before emboldened to the point of frenzy
by Puskab, now squealed in fright. Ar-Ulric froze, gazing in
open wonder at the wolf's avenging assault. Alone among
the stunned men who watched the wolf butcher a path
through the plague monks, he recognised the creature as
the other self of Hulda the *Ulricskind*. Horror at the witch's

transformation warred with gratitude for her defence of Ulric's shrine in the old priest's heart.

Puskab Foulfur spun around at the onset of Hulda's attack. The plague priest drew away from the rampaging white wolf, seizing one of his acolytes and holding the squirming monk between himself and the huge animal. At the same time, however, Puskab began to work his own magic. Grisly green flames erupted from the tips of his branching antlers; his blemished eyes glowed with a spectral light. Throwing open his jaws, Puskab spewed a stream of corrosive magic at the wolf. Instead of his foe, his foul magic caught two of his skaven instead, melting the screaming monks into steaming puddles of fur and bone.

Ar-Ulric rushed at the plague priest before he could send a second bilious gout at Hulda. His axed hewed into the monk Puskab was using for his shield, striking the wretch down. Even as Ar-Ulric drew back his arm for another attack, Puskab opened his jaws and sent a stream of caustic filth splashing into the old man's face. Ar-Ulric's scream became a liquid bubble as he collapsed to the ground, his face reduced to the smoking ruin of a skull.

A low growl brought Puskab spinning around. The plague priest squeaked in terror as the white wolf pounced at him. Exhibiting ability far beyond his wasted appearance, Puskab leapt back into the hole, hurtling down into the blackness of the burrow below. As he did so, Hulda's jaws clamped tight about the plague priest's naked tail. A twist of her lupine head as Puskab fell into the burrow and the scaly appendage was torn out by its roots.

The other plague monks quickly followed their leader in retreat. Hulda and the Teutogen Guard let them flee. Men and wolf alike gathered about the corpse of Ar-Ulric. While the warriors gathered up the priest's body, the wolf sank down onto her haunches and raised her head to the heavens.

Hulda's mournful howl echoed above the encampment, ringing out above the din of battle, commending the spirit of a brave man into the keeping of his god.

Mandred sank down onto his knees, pounding his fists into the bloodied ground inside his tent. Beside him, Kurgaz and the other warriors who had fought with him in the battle kept silent.

The plague monks had been driven from the encampment, routed before they could wreak much havoc. The purpose of their attack seemed to have been to get at the food stores, but in this they had been thwarted by the fast action of Captain Aldinger and his Knights of the Black Rose. Overall, the ratmen had inflicted few casualties, with fewer than a hundred dead and not many more than that wounded. Among the casualties, however, was the spiritual centre of the Middenheim host, Ar-Ulric, the grizzled old High Priest of Ulric. His loss was one that shook the entire complement, a loss scarcely alleviated by the tales of the Teutogen Guard, stories about a great white wolf that had suddenly manifested and tried to save Ar-Ulric.

Mandred was stunned by the death of his old councillor and spiritual mentor, and even more alarmed by the eerie manifestation of the white wolf associated with the priest's death. The animal that had so often crossed Mandred's path once again appearing from nowhere and returning just as suddenly into the aethyr. It was a circumstance that vexed his mind with both regret and dismay. He'd thought the wolf a sending of Ulric, yet the beast hadn't been able to save the old priest from the skaven.

Within Mandred's tent, however, was the mute evidence of the cruellest cut the monsters had inflicted upon the army's leader. It was difficult at first to make out precisely what the gory heap of meat lying on the floor was. When the outlines of a body revealed themselves, few were grateful for such resolution.

Beck pushed aside the flap of the tent and hurried to his master's side. He stopped short when he saw the butchered corpse on the floor. 'The skaven,' he said, his voice less than a whisper.

Mandred looked up, his eyes blazing with rekindled hatred, with the malignance of unbridled vengeance. 'Form the men into their companies,' he ordered. 'Let every soldier gird his armour and take up his sword. I want anyone able to bear a weapon ready to march at first light.'

The graf turned his eyes back to the mutilated body that had been Mirella less than an hour before.

'We ride with the dawn,' Mandred growled. 'Woe to the man who shows these vermin any mercy, for he will find none in me.'

Stirland, 1122

The Great Host's battle-line faltered as the ancient wights marched forwards. An aura of unspeakable and primordial evil clung to the Styrigen dead, the accusation of ancient revenge and forgotten outrage. Ghostly fires blazed from the sockets of each skull, shining with the infernal hatred of a vanquished race.

Terror closed upon the hearts of the Stirlanders, Grand Count von Oberreuth's army stood upon the edge of panic. It needed but a moment more to rout the entire force.

From the Great Host's right flank, a small company of

riders emerged. Foremost among them was a bearded man, the open face of his helm resembling the jaws of a wolf. The crest that rose above that helm was a new symbol, that of a rampant wolf holding a great hammer in its paws. It was the symbol of the leader who had rallied the whole of the north to his cause, the man who styled himself the Wolf of Sigmar. With Graf Mandred rode two old men, one dressed in the vestments of a Sigmarite arch-lector, the other wearing the high robes of Ulrican priesthood.

'Men of Stirland!' Mandred's voice rang out as he drew rein before the faltering Great Host. Some trick of acoustics or magic magnified that voice, projecting it deep into the forest, causing it to ring even in the ears of Count Malbork's Sylvanians far on the left flank. 'Fear no darkness, sons of Queen Freya! The blood of the Asoborns burns pure in your veins! Do not betray that legacy! Show Ulric and Sigmar, Taal and Rhya that you are worthy of your ancestors!' With a flourish, Mandred threw back his cloak, exposing the bared length of Legbiter. The runefang shone with arcane brilliance as he held it aloft. Grimly, he pointed the blade at the advancing undead. 'Do not fear these grave-cheating ghouls! Remember it was your ancestors who sent them there! Remember that Sigmar gave this land to you, not to them!'

From throats that had been frozen in fear a moment before there now rose a thunderous cheer. Peasant conscripts and armoured *Dienstleute* brought spear and sword crashing against their shields, a sound of such violence that it boomed like the bellow of an avalanche. Upon his spectral throne, Vanhal gazed in wonder at the spectacle. For an instant, the entire deathless legion was still as the master necromancer puzzled over this mere mortal who would defy all the powers of Old Night.

The cheering army fell silent when Vanhal raised a

wizened hand and pointed his bony finger at Graf Mandred. All could sense the hideous power when it erupted
from the sorcerer's talon. A phantasmal force sped towards
the Middenheimer, gathering a miasma of shape and form
as it hurtled towards him. As it swept through the ranks of
unmoving skeletons, bones exploded into dust, the decayed
powders drawn into the morbid cyclone.

Mandred's panicked horse threw its master from the
saddle and galloped away. The steeds of both priests bolted
as Vanhal's deathly spell came hurtling onwards, withering
the grass beneath it as it flew towards its victim.

Rising from his sprawl, Mandred poised himself upon
one knee and held Legbiter before him. There was no fear
in the graf's eyes, no doubt upon his countenance, only the
grimmest resolve.

The necromantic bolt crashed against the ensorcelled
blade of Legbiter, evaporating like so much mist and fog.
A patina of bone powder drifted to the earth, sizzling for
a moment before the last dregs of arcane power faded into
nothingness. Mandred stood, glowering down at the ecto-
plasmic residue. Then he glared across the field, locking eyes
with the ghoulish gaze of Vanhal. Defiantly, Mandred again
pointed his runefang at the necromancer.

A second cheer erupted from the mortal army, dwarfing
the first shout to insignificance. 'For Stirland!' Count von
Oberreuth roared as he spurred his destrier forwards. The
White Swords charged after him, the rest of the Stirland
horse following suit. Boldly they rode towards the Styrigen
wights. In a crash of armour and bone they slammed into
the ghastly creatures. With lance and sword they brought
the loathsome undead a second and more final death.

The Battle of Fellwald had been joined.

* * *

Malbork von Drak scowled as he watched the carnage unfold. Von Oberreuth's horses were decimating Vanhal's undead, exterminating them on an appalling scale. It had been his plan to have the two forces decimate each other, not have the Stirlanders simply walk over the monsters.

'Excellency, shall we assist the grand count?' the question came from Dregator Iorgu. Malbork clenched his fist, more angry at the appropriateness of the question than anything else. The way the battle was shaping up, the necessity of protecting the left flank was vanishing. Already Graf Mandred's troops were closing from the right and engaging the undead. If the Sylvanians didn't follow the Middenheimer's example, it was certain that von Oberreuth would demand an accounting.

The voivode started to answer Iorgu, to give the order for the Nachtsheer to advance, when a cold shiver ran through him. Looking away from his henchman, he studied the battlefield. Something was happening there, something that the commanders in the thick of the melee couldn't see. The dead that Graf Mandred and the grand count had left littering the ground behind their advance were stirring. Shattered bone was knitting itself back together; mangled skeletons were raising themselves from their own dissolution.

It didn't take the witchsight of a warlock to see the sorcerous power exuding from Vanhal's body. It was like gazing upon the emanations of some black and necrotic star, ebony tatters of power that snaked and slithered along the ground to restore a profane mockery of life to the undead and the mortal men they had vanquished.

Cries of terror and warning rose from the infantry still sheltering in the woods, but the alarm came too late. The fire from human archers and dwarf gunners was too little to stem the disaster. Hurtling down from the sky, a headless dragon vomited burning putrescence from the stump of its neck onto the phalanx of Middenland foot knights who would have marched to the relief of their embattled comrades. Under the dragon's assault, the infantry fled back into the forest.

Malbork shuddered, appreciating now the diabolical tactics of the necromancer. Vanhal had allowed his forces to be decimated, drawing his mortal foes ever deeper into an infernal trap. With every yard they advanced, the cavalry left a yard of corpses behind them. Now, as the necromancer's baleful power saturated the land, the attackers found themselves enmeshed in a solid ring of enemies. A cordon of merciless skeletons now converged upon the horsemen from all sides. As he watched, Malbork saw the second of Vanhal's dragons come diving down, incinerating dozens of knights, indifferent to the scores of skeletons that melted beneath its breath. Even as they fell, the steaming bodies of the dragon's victims stirred and lurched to their feet.

'I think,' Malbork said as he stroked his thick moustache, 'we shall stay precisely where we are.' The voivode didn't bother to restrain his laughter. After today, at least von Oberreuth would no longer be a problem and if Lothar von Diehl managed his side of their compact, Vanhal wouldn't be a worry much longer either.

So rapt was he in watching the havoc unfolding before the eaves of Fellwald that Malbork didn't see the frantic Sylvanian scouts when they came galloping towards their voivode. His first awareness of their approach was when his bodyguards formed ranks around him, wary that some disloyal peasant might have taken it in mind to assassinate their despotic master.

The scouts, however, had a different enemy in mind. As the foremost of the riders drew rein before the voivode, he began to stammer a confused account of being attacked in the hollow they were watching. Malbork listened to the terrified babble for a moment, then spurred his steed forwards, brushing aside his protectors. 'Make sense or I'll hang your guts in a tree,' he growled at the scout.

By way of explanation, the frightened man turned around in his saddle and pointed a shaking hand towards the hollow. As he did so, scurrying shapes emerged from the shadowy vale. Shouts of alarm rose from the Nachtsheer when they saw the things, watched the fading sun glisten from bleached bone and rusty steel.

A flank attack? Had Vanhal added such a deployment to his strategy? The thought chilled Malbork, but as he watched more of the enemy come out of the darkness, the truth seemed even worse. These were no undead, the exposed bone they saw wasn't the skeletons of wights and wraiths but rather the macabre armour worn by living creatures, things every bit as monstrous as Vanhal's obscene creations.

It seemed another faction had seized upon Malbork's idea of letting Stirlander and undead exterminate one another. Seized upon it and made it their own.

The creatures lurking underneath that bony armour were unmistakable. The same monsters that had ravaged and plundered most of the Empire. The loathsome ratmen were come to destroy both armies.

The only thing standing in their way was the tiny company of Sylvanians.

━◄ CHAPTER XV ►━

Averland, 1123

Graf Mandred sat upon his white destrier before the massed ranks of his cavalry. The horsemen would make a probing attack against the walls of Averheim to determine where the fortifications were weakest and where their siege engines – catapults from the human realms, cannon brought down from the mountains by dwarf mercenaries – would be most effectively concentrated. The infantry, kept busy through the night assembling the massive towers of hide and timber that would allow them to assault the battlements directly, were catching a much-needed rest. Their part would come after the cavalry and artillery had done their jobs.

Mandred stared at the sprawl of Averheim. By night it had looked like some hellish inferno aglow with daemonic fires. The sight by day was even more disheartening. The once great city looked like a blackened wound, the burnt-out rubble strewn about the landscape like a great carcass. Already a thick plume of smoke stretched into the sky from the bonfires the skaven were setting. Closer to the city, Mandred knew the smoke would blot out the sun, affording the verminous monsters the darkness that was their element.

'Gaze upon this place, my brothers,' Mandred enjoined the troops who followed him. 'Lock this vision in your hearts; bury it in your souls. Look on the corpse of Averheim and know that this will be the fate of your cities and your homes. If we falter, if we fail this day, all we have fought for will be for naught. The ratkin will be resurgent, their hordes will sweep across the land in a great blight and usher in a darkness even the gods will not wipe away. We are the last shield of mankind, the last sword of the light. To us is given the honour of breaking the shadow of the rat. To us is given the glory and the burden. Let each man prove worthy of the task the gods have entrusted to him!'

A fierce cheer rose from a thousand riders, a roar that boomed across the plain like thunder. Like thunder too was the pounding of hooves as the horsemen galloped towards the blackened city.

As he rode towards the walls, Mandred could see the skaven sentries scurrying about behind the battlements, squeaking and shrieking the alarm to their commanders. The vermin had no archers – in the blighted underworld they infested there was no need for such skill. The absence of bowmen among their swarms was keenly felt by the rat-men now. The bark and crack of a handful of jezzails was the only opposition the monsters could offer as Mandred's cavalry swept across the plain. It was only when they got within a few horse-lengths of the walls that masses of emaciated ratkin armed with crude leather slings appeared on the walls and were able to offer any sort of challenge. Their bullets, however, were hastily loosed and poorly aimed. The skaven slaves had no hunger for battle, no great heart to defend their cruel masters. Moreover, their courage evaporated when they saw the human riders galloping straight towards the battlements, armour shining in the sun, pennants fluttering in the breeze. The awesome sight made the creatures shrink back against the crenellations, stirring themselves only when the abusive whips of their overseers forced them into action.

Across the length of the walls, Mandred saw much the same scene. Focusing upon the besieged Averburg, the skaven had left only the dregs of their army to defend the walls behind them. More, the ratkin had done little to repair the damage inflicted upon those walls in their initial attack. A gatehouse in the western approach had been so sloppily mended that one of its walls was simply a pile of rubble that had been dragged out from the city and heaped against the side of the fortification. One look at the slovenly construction and Mandred knew where his army would make its attack. Even the moat that ran along the western wall had been drained, its bottom sown with what looked like a crop of runty corn stalks. If it didn't suit his own purposes so well, Mandred would have been appalled by the sheer arrogance of the ratkin.

'Sound the recall,' Mandred ordered the trumpeter riding beside him. While the knight blew into his horn, the graf turned in his saddle and motioned to the banner bearer following behind him. The knight nodded and pulled a cord on the standard he carried, unfurling a yellow flag. It was a sign that would be seen by the artillery assembled across the plain, alerting them that the graf had chosen their target.

Even as Mandred's cavalry galloped away from the wall, the catapults and cannon began their barrage. He smiled at the craftiness of the dwarfs. To deceive the skaven about their intentions, the artillery would be directed against several places along the wall. Only a quarter of the total barrage would be focused on the real target until the advance of the infantry and their siege towers made such deception pointless. Then the full might of the barrage would pour down upon the gatehouse and the wall around it. If everything worked to plan, the skaven defenders in that position would be pounded into complete disarray and the monsters would be too late to rush reinforcements to secure the area before Mandred's forces came pouring in.

The graf watched as the first boulders and cannonballs came slamming into Averheim. He reached to his arm, fingering the strip of bloodied cloth tied about his armour, a piece cut from Mirella's bloodied dress. There would be a reckoning this day, he swore it by all Ulric and Sigmar and any other god who would listen. The ratmen had much to atone for, but this day, this day he consecrated to the woman he had loved and who had been taken from him by the cringing monsters.

Whatever god the skaven owned, that foul being would be meeting a great many of his pestiferous children soon.

Vrrmik kept to his subterranean burrow, listening with keen anticipation as each messenger brought more details to him about the battle being fought overhead. The great warlord stroked his whiskers and chittered in delight. Everything was proceeding exactly as his brilliant plan had anticipated.

The midnight assault by Clan Pestilens against the human encampment had achieved its purpose magnificently even if Puskab Foulfur had failed to poison the army's food stores. Vrrmik had anticipated that it would take the threat of starvation to goad the humans into swift and desperate action. He was surprised that it had needed nothing more than the attack itself to provoke Man-dread into immediate attack. It was an important lesson to bear in mind, this recklessness of the humans to react to any attack by staging one of their own. Vrrmik could liken their reaction only to the mindless belligerence of ants when their nest had been disturbed.

Whatever the cause and whatever the reason, Man-dread was playing right into Vrrmik's paws. As each scout came scampering back to him, the Grey Lord chortled a little more loudly. The slaves holding the outer walls had been overrun; the humans had brought up their foot troops and were invading the city.

He almost wished he could be there to smell the terror in the scents of Warlord Hakrr and Warlord Ransik when they found humans pouring into the rear of their armies. The hordes of Clan Rictus and Clan Skab were ringed around the Averburg, so keen to steal the victory from Clan Mors that they'd completely ignored the thinning of Vrrmik's own forces laying siege to the stubborn human fortress. Most of those Vrrmik had left behind were slaves and warriors from thrall clans, losses that Mors would easily replace.

But it wasn't the decimation of his skaven rivals alone that excited Vrrmik. Soon he would cut the pelt from Man-dread, this annoying human who had caused so much distress to the Under-Empire. In some ways, Vrrmik felt obliged to Man-dread. Indeed, if the human hadn't already existed he thought he would have had to invent him. Man-dread's attacks had sapped the strength and injured the pride of many clans, among them even the mighty Pestilens itself. He had proven useful in curtailing the reckless ambitions of lesser skaven, of reminding them of their place within the hierarchy of Skavenblight.

Now, however, Man-dread had made the mistake of crossing claws with Clan Mors. His usefulness was almost at an end. Having been built up as the great threat to skavendom, it was time for the human to be sacrificed to the greater glory of Vrrmik.

Vrrmik closed his paws tighter about the heft of Skaven-bite as he listened to the frantic report from the exhausted messenger who had scurried all the way from the cellars near the Averburg to the great warlord's hidden lair. He bruxed his fangs together in delight as he heard the news. Man-dread's troops had reached the rear of Warlord Ransik's clanrats. Even better, the humans within the fortress were sallying forth to engage Warlord Hakrr's stormvermin.

Vrrmik reared up to his full imposing height. A steady diet of specially prepared meats and cheeses infused with warpstone dust had swollen his musculature to a degree where his fur had abandoned the effort to clothe the bulging biceps and triceps, leaving great patches of his body naked to the skin. His armour, festooned with spikes and warpstone charms, exuded the scent of slaves slaughtered only that morning so that none of his warriors could fail to detect the smell of their warlord. A bladed tail-ring encircled the scaly appendage as it lashed to and fro behind the monster's back.

'Attack-maim! Destroy-die!' Vrrmik growled at his clanrats. The murderous hammer he bore came smashing down, reducing the head of the messenger into a bloody mist with a single blow. The violent display urged his warriors into a frenzy of activity.

Light streamed down into the tunnels as the skaven pulled aside the camouflaged covers. Hidden by the stalks of black corn growing in the loose layer of dirt strewn over them, the mats were dumped into the burrow and the skaven swarmed up into the dry moat outside the walls of Averheim. Warning trumpets blasted from the human encampment far across the plain as the teeming hordes of Clan Mors surged up onto the surface.

The warning was sounded too late. Even as the human soldiers who had stayed behind to protect the breach turned to see why the alarm had sounded, the skaven were among them. Not the weak, half-starved slaves who had defended the walls, but armoured clanrats and stormvermin. The horde swept across the horrified men in a tidal wave of slashing blades and snapping jaws.

Vrrmik advanced with his warriors, exulting in the raw power of Skavenbite. A sweep of his hammer and a human was flung twenty feet into the air, his body crashing to earth in a puddle of splintered bone and ruptured flesh. An over-hand blow of the warhammer and an armoured knight was driven into the ground like an iron nail, his feet so firmly embedded in the flagstones that a second strike from the weapon ripped his legs off at the knees.

More than the havoc inflicted by his hammer, it was the terror the carnage evoked that set Vrrmik's blood racing. The savoury smell of fear in the scent of his minions, the stink of terror in the sweat of the humans. Vrrmik was a demigod of death and destruction, a living engine of slaughter and ruin.

Furiously, Vrrmik drove his horde on into the human ranks. His trap was sprung; Man-dread's army was caught inside Averheim, pinned between the stone walls and the hordes of Rictus and Skab. Mors would press the humans further into the toils of the other clans, equally happy with whichever side suffered losses. There was only one death Vrrmik refused to concede to the other skaven, one death that he would deny even his own warriors.

The keenest noses among the scavenging troglodytes of Clan Skrittlespike followed close beside Great Warlord Vrrmik, their senses trained to pick out one scent from among the countless smells and odours in the air. Their purpose was to sniff out Man-dread himself and guide Vrrmik to him.

When Man-dread perished, it would be beneath the mangling sweep of Skavenbite. When the hope of humanity was slaughtered, all would recognise Vrrmik as the butcher of that hope.

Man and skaven alike would bow in terror before the might of Vrrmik.

Skavenblight, 1122

'Scurry-hurry! Quick-quiet!' the squeaking hisses of Queekish came uneasily to Moschner's tongue. He felt unclean even trying to shape such sounds. Squeamishness, however, was a quality he didn't have the luxury of indulging. Not anymore. Not if he was going to reduce Skavenblight to a charnel house of disease and destruction.

He watched as the three skaven slaves, scrawny specimens that had been supplied to him as test subjects, attacked their labour with frantic urgency. Moschner watched them carefully, wary lest their haste should blot out their sense of caution. Previous experience had taught him that a single reprimand from him would send the slaves into fratricidal frenzy. If any of them thought another was going to spoil its chance to escape, the results would be swift and brutal.

The skaven were secured in a large cage at the back of the cave. The walls were much too tough for a human or dwarf to excavate barehanded, but a skaven could gnaw through iron with its fangs if given enough time and incentive. To

the best of his ability, Moschner had endeavoured to provide the creatures with both.

Every hour, Moschner expected his plans to collapse
around him. The audacity of his scheme frightened even
himself. Every time he was visited by Seerlord Queekual he
was certain the ferocious sorcerer had seen through his ploy.
However, the abject terror he felt during such visitations
served to encourage the ratman's megalomaniacal pride. In
his arrogance, Queekual was oblivious even to the possibility that this terrified little slave might have the courage to
plot against him, that so frightened a wretch would be bold
enough to lie to his face.

The lie still held, but Moschner knew he was on borrowed time. There was only so long he could rotate the
skaven test subjects from cage to cage before Queekual
noticed. There was only so long he could pass off specimens not yet exposed to the plague as early-stage victims
of the disease.

The secret hidden by the lie was one that would have
thrilled Schroeder. Moschner could take no such pleasure.
He felt like a Shallyan acolyte shaking hands with a diseased
disciple of the Fly Lord. What he was doing represented
the sundering of every oath he'd sworn as a physician and
healer. That he had succeeded in his ghastly labour only
made it worse.

The improved strain of Black Plague Queekual demanded
had become reality several weeks ago. That was the secret
Moschner couldn't afford to let his terrible patron discover.

He still had only the vaguest idea of what the Seerlord
intended. That the monster wanted this disease to unleash
against his own kind was obvious, but what Queekual
hoped to achieve was a mystery to Moschner. Whatever it
was, he was certain that it brooked no good for mankind.

That was why Moschner had been playing for time. That was why he had removed the healthiest of his skaven specimens to the rear cages, had given them crude digging tools fashioned from the fangs of their dead kin. That was why he had encouraged the ratmen to dig, had helped them hide the loose earth in the bellies of dead slaves. The earth below Skavenblight was a labyrinth of tunnels and passages. It couldn't be long before the ratmen broke through to another chamber. When they did, they would be free, free to scatter and hide among the teeming hordes of their monstrous society.

Free to escape and bring the new strain of plague to the rest of the ratkin. For what none of the slaves knew was that they'd already been exposed to the disease, that they were in fact simply the latest in a long chain of skaven that had been pressed into the doktor's plot. If they broke through before the worst symptoms crippled them, they would go free. If not, Moschner would move their sick carcasses to different cages and wait for a fresh batch of specimens to take up the work.

'Scurry-hurry,' Moschner repeated as he marched away from the diggers.

He would give Queekual his plague, all right. But not in the way the sorcerer expected.

Seerlord Queekual clutched the mummified cat's-paw tighter. A relic from the ancient tombs of Khemri, it was a powerful talisman against sickness and decay. Warlord Nekrot had worn it once and Queekual's agents had secured it for him when the unlamented Bonelord met his end before the malefic magics of Vanhal. He was certain of the talisman's efficacy, having tested it on a dozen apprentices and adepts. They'd resisted exposure to the very worst diseases, so Queekual was prepared to accept that the talisman performed in the manner expected of it.

Even with the talisman's protection, the horned ratman cringed when he leaned down and scrutinised the miserable captives sprawled at the bottom of their cages. He held a brick of pungent cheese to his nose to blot out the offensive odour of rot and disease. The stench of plague was as unmistakable as the physical symptoms. While he watched, one of the captives twitched violently and was still.

'That one has just died,' Moschner-man reported. The slave consulted his clay tablet, nodding his head in deference to the Seerlord's exalted position. 'The specimen was exposed to the new stock only eighteen food cycles ago.'

The report had Queekual leaning close to the bars despite the smell and his own fear of the plague. Eighteen food cycles? Twenty-four hours as humans reckoned time! The sorcerer wiped a string of drool from his fangs. It was astounding, to think the disease could kill so quickly! It went beyond his greatest expectations.

'I was smart-wise to keep you alive when all the others disappointed me,' Queekual declared, preening his whiskers with two claws while the rest continued to grip the block of cheese. He gestured with the paw gripping the mummified talisman. 'All the others, witches and priests, herbalists and barbers. All of them failed. All of them died.'

Moschner bowed in the expected gesture of submissive gratitude. He lifted the clay writing tablet. 'I have written down the formula for you,' he said. 'You understand how to read Reikspiel as well as speak it?'

The skaven swung away from the cage, his fur bristling at the condescension in Moschner's tone. 'Give-bring!' Queekual snarled, flinging the block of smelly cheese to the floor. The doktor was the very model of a humble slave as he crept forward and deposited the tablet in Queekual's waiting paw.

'Follow those instructions and you will be able to create more of the plague any time you like. All you need is some fleas and polluted blood. And a little patience.'

Queekual stared down at the tablet, his mind awhirl with the possibilities, the potential he gripped in his paws. He held a force mightier than anything Clan Pestilens possessed, a force powerful enough to bring all skavendom to its knees! Yes, the hordes of the Under-Empire would learn what it meant to defy the word of their god! Queekual would loose this new disease on all those who stood in his way. He would reshape the Under-Empire as a theocracy led by the grey seers with himself as Ultimate Hierophant!

The Seerlord's eyes narrowed. His tail twitched in the dirt behind him. Of course, if he were to deliver skavendom from calamity, there couldn't be any evidence linking him to that calamity.

Queekual shifted the tablet under his arm. Retrieving his staff from where it leaned against the wall, he regarded Moschner with a fanged smile. 'You have done good-good,' he hissed. 'Now I gift-give your reward!'

The head of Seerlord Queekual's staff blazed with coruscating bands of arcane energy. The blinding dazzle of light leapt from between the metal horns, striking out and immolating Moschner in a burst of sizzling annihilation. When the light faded, all that was left of Queekual's hapless slave was a pile of smoking ash and a few charred bones.

'Destroy-burn!' Queekual snarled at the guard-rats outside as he marched from the cave. 'Burn everything! Leave nothing!'

Soon, all traces of Moschner and his work would be obliterated. Then Queekual could begin his great work, the task entrusted to him by the Horned Rat Himself. There could be no question of his triumph, of the ruination of his enemies.

If he had noticed an empty cage at the back of Moschner's cave, if he had seen the tiny, crude tunnel leading away from it, Queekual might not have felt so confident.

⤙ CHAPTER XVI ⤚

Averland, 1123

Terror swept through the human forces as a second mighty host of skaven appeared at their rear. The breach in the walls of Averheim was now sealed up by a solid mass of verminous flesh. The ratmen attacked in a great chittering horde, driven to the point of frenzy by the threats of their leaders and the smell of fear on their foes. While the vanguard of Mandred's army, the knights and mounted warriors, slammed into the skaven besieging the walls of the Averburg, striving to link up with the defenders within the old fortress, the infantry supporting his assault threatened to collapse. Peasant militia, mendicant flagellants, mercenaries and bandits, the troops had the will to fight, the heart to follow Mandred on his quest to free the Empire from the shadow of the ratmen, but they lacked the training and discipline which alone could stand before the bestial onslaught of Clan Mors.

There was one exception, one rock that stood steadfast

before the sea of despair and panic that raged around it, a stolid wedge of defiance that spread across the streets. Fleeing men broke before the immovable walls of flesh and steel, funnelled down side streets and alleyways, channelled off in directions where their route wouldn't reach the soldiers battling around the Averburg and make a shambles of their efforts to smash the skaven lines.

The ratmen pursuing the fleeing humans crashed against the shield-walls like a loathsome tide. Like a tide, too, they broke against the unyielding rock they crashed against, flowing backwards and rolling forwards in an unending wave of feral savagery.

'*Khazukan Kazakit-Ha!*' the fierce cry boomed through the streets as each wave of skaven crashed against the shield-wall. The dwarfs of Grungni's Tower, the hardest and most steadfast warriors in Mandred's army, had been unable to maintain the pace of the long-legged humans in their rapid advance through the city. By degrees, the dwarfs had been left behind by the spear of Mandred's assault forces. Now they assumed a new role: that of the army's shield.

Standing shoulder to shoulder with his kinsmen, Kurgaz Smallhammer glared at the oncoming skaven with eyes that were ablaze with hate. These beasts had killed his brother, had profaned the halls of Karak Grazhyakh, had stolen the great hammer Drakdrazh. Many were the grudges for which these vermin would atone and not the blood of a thousand of their pestiferous kind would be enough to wash away that debt.

Kurgaz brought his axe flashing down into the skull of a crook-nosed ratman, splashing its brains across the beasts behind it. He slammed the spiked boss of his shield into the breast of another skaven, feeling the spike pierce its squirming flesh as he drove it back upon the bodies of its comrades. His boots became sticky with the black, stinking blood of the vermin, his beard clotted with the gore of the beasts he killed and still it was not enough.

'*Khazukan Kazakit-Ha!*' Kurgaz repeated. 'Beware! The dwarfs come for blood!' The ancient war-cry resonated through the bones of each bearded warrior who heard it, swelling their hearts with ferocity. It echoed through the glands of the skaven, withering their valour and sending fear pulsing through their veins. Foot by foot, yard by yard, the indomitable shield-wall advanced, throwing the skaven back, pushing them in upon themselves. The bodies of hundreds of ratkin lay strewn in the wake of the dwarfs, crushed beneath their steel-shod boots as they marched ever forwards.

Inevitably, the reeling ratmen threw more forces into the fray. The vermin squeaked in horror as robed plague monks came charging through their ranks, swinging censers that exuded noxious vapours. Scores of ratmen perished as the corrosive smoke seeped down into their lungs, scorching their insides and leaving them to choke on their own blood. Frantic ratkin flung themselves with renewed desperation at the dwarfs, but despite the savage desperation in their attack, they found the shield-wall as impregnable as ever.

As the last of the panicked clanrats fell, a small group of dwarfs rushed out from the shield-wall. They charged towards the censer bearers, seeking to keep them and their deadly smoke away from the rest of the formation. Several of the plague monks fell as the dwarf skirmishers flung hand axes into their diseased bodies, others perished under the heavier battleaxes and warhammers of their enemies as they charged into the lethal clouds of decay. The brave warriors knew they would perish with the monsters, brought down by the noxious smoke, but they died gladly in the knowledge that by their sacrifice, the rest of the formation should be preserved.

The failure of the plague monks brought a new tide of skaven swarming down the street. Brawny, black-furred monsters wearing heavy armour and wielding an assortment of cleavers, axes and halberds, the elite of Clan Mors crashed into the dwarf line. Foam dripped from their fangs, blood dripped from their eyes and noses as the abhorrent black hunger drove them into a murderous frenzy. The stormvermin threw their own comrades onto the blades of the dwarfs, using them as living shields so that they might leap forwards and drag the embattled dwarfs down.

Into this carnage, this maelstrom of death and butchery, stalked a monstrous white skaven. Kurgaz froze when he saw the beast, his mind retreating back through the years to the dark mines of Karak Grazhyakh and the ratkin warlord that had killed his brother and stolen Drakdrazh. He was uncertain if this was the same creature, for if it was then the monster had become still more massive and muscular in the years since their last encounter, swelling into something that resembled a troll as much as it did a skaven.

Then Kurgaz saw the immense hammer the creature bore, saw the havoc the ratman dealt when he brought it crashing down into the dwarf line. Armoured warriors were tossed into the air as though they weighed nothing, iron shields folded as though made from tin beneath the sweep of the ratman's hammer. Kurgaz's lip curled back in a snarl of outrage as he realised that the weapon was Drakdrazh, its splendour and dignity defiled by bands of warpstone and the scratch-mark sigils of skaven runes.

Roaring his outrage, Kurgaz bulled his way through the stormvermin, smashing them down, crushing them beneath his boots. Desperately he forced his way towards the white warlord. The huge ratman swung around, its lips peeling back from its yellowed fangs. The brute uttered a mocking chitter as it brought the head of Drakdrazh sweeping around.

Kurgaz, in his fury, had forgotten the incredible speed with which the skaven could move, even a monster such as the white warlord. Drakdrazh crashed into the dwarf's chest, flinging him high into the air. He crashed in a heap among the bodies of his slain comrades, blood bubbling up from his mouth. Blinking through the pain, Kurgaz struggled to regain his feet. His grip on his axe broken by his fall, he groped among the dead for a weapon.

The mocking chitter again sounded in Kurgaz's ears. Groggy from his injury, he struggled to focus his eyes on the hulking beast as the warlord lumbered over the dead and the dying. The ratman's eyes glittered malignantly as it came to finish the prey who had somehow survived the blow of its hammer.

Kurgaz lurched to his feet, spitting a mouthful of blood onto the ground. If he were to die this day, by Grimnir, he would do so on his feet!

The warlord turned suddenly, its snout raised as it sniffed the air, its ears pressed close against the sides of its head as it detected a scent both familiar and frightening. Any thought of finishing Kurgaz was abandoned as the warlord started to back away.

Dimly, through ears still ringing with the violence of Drakdrazh's strike, Kurgaz heard the sound of hooves and the blare of a trumpet.

The skaven had taken too long to break through the dwarfs. Mandred was bringing forces around to engage the ratmen closing in upon the rear of his army.

* * *

Great Warlord Vrrmik shook his head in disbelief as he caught the scent of Man-dread in the air. There was no mistaking that smell, hadn't he engaged the best thieves Clan Eshin could provide to steal garments cast off by the human warlord so there could be no mistaking the creature's scent? What alarmed Vrrmik was that the scent was so near. Man-dread should be off fighting Rictus and Skab, obligingly annihilating Warlords Ransik and Hakrr for him. He should be so far away that only the heightened sense of smell of Skrittlespike cave-rats should be able to pick him out.

It was part of Vrrmik's great plan that he should be the one to kill the feared Man-dread and wear the creature's pelt as a trophy, but that plan called for the human's army to be overwhelmed and annihilated, crushed between the valiant warriors of Clan Mors and the scabrous traitors of Clans Rictus and Skab. The plan was to decimate the human's followers, leaving them strewn about him in mounds of dead and wounded, to sow despair and terror in Man-dread's heart, to shatter his mind with the understanding that his army was destroyed and that everything he'd fought for was lost.

This... this wasn't the way Vrrmik had expected things to be. The smell of horses and man-thing knights, the clamour of hooves as the cavalry came charging towards his stormvermin. The fatigue and exhaustion of his warriors as they reeled from the effects of the elixir they'd imbibed to help them smash their way through the dwarfs.

The dwarfs! Their stubborn defiance had spoiled Vrrmik's cunning plan, yet why should Man-dread leave such bold warriors so far from his assault forces? Unless of course he knew of Vrrmik's trap! Unless some simpering traitor had warned the humans, perhaps so that Rictus and Skab would be spared the full fury of their attack! Or maybe it went still deeper than that. Puskab Foulfur and his less than fruitful attack on Man-dread's camp, his inability to poison the human food stores and drive them into the panicked desperation that was key to Vrrmik's battle plan! Yes, that was it! Clan Pestilens jockeying to usurp Vrrmik's position! Not content with three seats on the Council of Thirteen, the plague priests coveted the Twelfth Throne itself, to sit beside the Great Throne of the Horned One!

From the rear of Vrrmik's warriors, in the direction of Averheim's outer walls, came the stink of fear musk and the frightened screeches of hundreds of skaven. Something was unfolding at the walls, some new threat to Vrrmik's elaborate trap! The flicker of a suspicion grew in the great warlord's mind. The horsemen Man-dread had sent away from his camp. Where had they gone? To fetch new forces? To bring another human army against Vrrmik's rear?

The clatter of hooves was nearer now. Snarling, Vrrmik roared at his stormvermin to fling themselves at the enemy as a company of knights came charging down the street. Their advance was hindered somewhat by their timidity, trying to circle around the surviving dwarfs. The skaven suffered no such weakness, trampling their dead and dying underfoot as they rushed at the enemy.

Vrrmik rushed towards the hated scent of Man-dread. If he could kill the human leader, he might yet overcome the man-things, route them from the field even as they tried to close their trap around him!

The great warlord lashed out with Skavenbite, the mighty hammer smashing down the only knight between himself and Man-dread. He snarled as he looked upon the human warlord, rage boiling up inside him as he realised that even he, Mighty Vrrmik, was intimidated by this infamous adversary.

Man-dread's eyes narrowed when he saw Vrrmik and he

dug his spurs into the flanks of his steed. The man came galloping towards Vrrmik, the sword in his hand aglow with magic.

Skavenbite struck out as Man-dread came charging towards Vrrmik. The awesome power of the magic hammer obliterated the head of the horse, sending its carcass crashing against the wall at the other side of the street, pinning its rider beneath its dead weight.

In the same instant, however, Man-dread's blazing sword came slashing down. Vrrmik felt his head exploding in pain, blood gushing down his neck. He clamped a paw to his head, felt the jagged gash where his right ear had once been. Chittering in pain, the smell of his own blood now combining with the musk of fear rising from the glands of his followers, Vrrmik's savagery collapsed into blind panic.

He might have fought down the horror coursing through his veins. Indeed, Vrrmik took a few vindictive steps towards Man-dread's fallen horse. Then he saw the human pull himself out from underneath his dead steed. He saw the unbridled rage in the man's face, the blazing fury in his eyes, the malevolence in his scent.

It was too much for Vrrmik. Uttering a frenzied howl, ordering his minions to shield his retreat, Vrrmik rushed back towards the moat. Gone was the idea of victory and glory, of punishing traitors and eliminating rivals. The only thought in Vrrmik's bleeding head was escape. To live to plot and fight and kill another day.

For there would be another day. Vrrmik would make certain of that. Man-dread would suffer for the audacity of striking skavendom's greatest warrior!

When next they met, there would be no mistakes. Vrrmik would make certain of that!

* * *

Altdorf, 1124

The private chambers adopted by the Protector of the Empire were situated at the very heart of the Imperial palace. They had been designed as a vault to hold treasure, engineered as a stone box with thick walls and stout double-doors of iron-banded oak. Ceiling and floor were of granite blocks some three feet thick. The walls were thicker still and reinforced with iron rods.

Despite the efforts at refinement, the lavish rugs and tapestries arrayed about the vault, it was still a cold and cheerless place. There was no hearth, so heat and light were entrusted to bronze braziers. Circulation was poor in the tomb-like chamber and it needed a strange contraption that was part bellows and part windlass to keep the fresh air flowing and disperse the smoke from the braziers. That device was an invention of the dwarf revenue collectors who continued to serve Kreyssig as they had the Emperor before him. Reviled as 'gold grubbers' by noble and peasant alike, the dwarfs had been engaged for such duties by Boris when it was discovered that they couldn't contract the Black Plague and so could venture boldly among even the most severely afflicted districts in Altdorf. They still performed their duties with exacting precision and fidelity. If not for their strange codes of honour, Kreyssig would have happily inducted the dwarfs into his Kaiserjaeger. As it stood, he had to limit them to tasks that wouldn't offend their exacting sensibilities.

Kreyssig leaned back in his chair, tapping his foot impatiently as his manservant Fuerst scurried about him with a razor and scraped the stubble from his cheeks. The servant was nervous, fussing over his master with only the most

timid, delicate strokes. Fuerst scowled at the braziers and
the sputtering light cast by their flames. He cursed the
numbing cold of the vault. He lashed out with his foot as
one of Kreyssig's cats rubbed up against his leg, nearly causing him to stumble and nick his master with the razor.

'I wish you would take other accommodations,' Fuerst
complained. 'It feels like being buried alive down here.'

'You know my reasons,' Kreyssig reproved his servant.
Fuerst grimaced, closing his eyes against the image of ratmen creeping behind the walls. Here, in the vault, they were
safe from such intrusions. The only way the skaven could
reach this chamber was by way of the door, and Kreyssig
had a dozen of his best Kaiserjaeger standing guard in the
corridor outside. The same held true for any human assassins, be they from Gazulgrund, Vidor or Mandred.

Fuerst bowed in apology. 'It is difficult to attend you
properly here,' he said. 'The light is poor, the cold makes my
hand shiver...'

'And your thoughts are troubled,' Kreyssig stated, craning
his head back so that his servant could shave his throat.

Fuerst hesitated. 'What you are doing... are you certain it
needs to be done?' He hurried to appease the irritated glare
Kreyssig directed at him. 'It is not... I know you've thought
it through. You always do. But the danger involved...'

'A man who risks all may gain everything,' Kreyssig told
Fuerst. 'By sending that outlaw to me, Mandred has made
it clear that he is not going to negotiate with me. He will
dictate terms. He has Ghal Maraz now, and coupled with
what he has already done – not to mention that ridiculous
"miracle" he supposedly benefited from in Middenheim –
even Gazulgrund won't be able to deny him the Imperial
crown.'

'You might still be given something,' Fuerst said. 'The

people of Altdorf celebrate you as a hero. That has to be worth something.' He hurriedly pulled the razor away as Kreyssig shook his head.

'Too many tongues have already poisoned Mandred against me,' Kreyssig said. 'Von Kranzbeuhler, that strumpet Erna, even that scum Hartwich. I knew I shouldn't have trusted Thorgrad when he said plague had taken Hartwich. Mandred has more dead men in his court than that necromancer in Sylvania!' He chuckled grimly. 'No, I shall be fortunate if Mandred's beneficence extends so far as to spare my life.'

'But to break your alliance with him…'

Kreyssig gave a dismissive wave of his hand. 'You forget, it will not be *me* who breaks the faith. Why do you think I kept von Kranzbeuhler and the dwarf here and sent one of my own men to carry the treaty back to Mandred?' All the humanity evaporated from his face, leaving only a reptilian visage of mercilessness. 'I have two problems: Gazulgrund and Mandred. I must remove the first and prevent the second from becoming Emperor. The only way to accomplish that is to assassinate the one and place the blame on the other.'

Fuerst drew back, his hand trembling again. 'You don't mean to use that, that *thing*?'

'Too unpredictable,' Kreyssig said. 'I couldn't trust it to do what needs to be done. No, I'll make it look like von Kranzbeuhler did it. The fool conveniently still wears the armour of the Reiksknecht and we have plenty of that lying around from when Grand Master von Schomberg was executed and his rabble outlawed. It will be easy enough to disguise one of the Kaiserjaeger. He'll strike down Gazulgrund and escape in the confusion. Von Kranzbeuhler will be captured and blamed.'

'He will protest his innocence and Graf Mandred will support him,' Fuerst objected.

Kreyssig laughed. 'He won't have a chance to say anything. After he's captured, he'll accidentally fall into the hands of the peasants. As attached as they are to Gazulgrund, they'll rip him to pieces with their bare hands before he can say six words to them! When I accuse Mandred of ordering his man to kill the Grand Theogonist, the peasants will turn on him too. Murdering the High Priest of Sigmar will blot out all the victories, all the omens. Mandred will be fortunate if he can keep Middenheim from deposing him, much less become Emperor.'

'If something should go wrong,' Fuerst persisted.

'Nothing will go wrong,' Kreyssig declared. 'Nothing will be left to chance. The Palace Guard are even now taking charge of von Kranzbeuhler and the dwarf. They'll be removed to safer accommodations until I need them.

'All I need now is for Mandred to finish mopping up the skaven in Hochland. Then the final pieces will fall into place.'

Blood was dripping down the side of Erich's face as he was half-pushed, half-dragged down the corridors of the Imperial palace. A leather cosh had opened his scalp and rattled his senses. It was difficult for him to focus his gaze or get the ringing to fade from his ears. By contrast, the tang of blood in his mouth from the tooth he had knocked out when he struck the floor was shocking in its distinctness and there was a weird smell in his nose, which his muddled mind kept telling him was the aroma of the colour blue.

'Come to your senses, manling!' a gruff dwarfish voice bellowed. The rattle of chains punctuated the dwarf's angry outburst.

Erich managed to turn his head and focus his vision enough to see his comrade being dragged along beside him. Kurgaz Smallhammer's brawny body was wrapped in heavy chains, his face bruised and bloodied. Despite the chains coiled around the dwarf, the four guards who had taken charge of him were taking no chances. As they walked, one of the soldiers kept the edge of his blade against Kurgaz's throat.

Painful memories rose from the fog inside Erich's skull. It was his fault that the dwarf had been captured. Left to his own devices, Kurgaz would have chosen death over surrender. When the Palace Guard burst into the room the emissary and his bodyguard had been given, Kurgaz had been the first to engage them, braining one soldier with a chair and breaking the leg of another with a powerful kick of his boot. While the slayer was on the attack, Erich made the mistake of trying to reach the table where his sword was resting. One of the guards caught him before he could reach the weapon, stunning him with a blow to the head.

Though the shamed dwarf longed for death in battle, he submitted to capture when he saw Erich helpless before their enemies. More important than Kurgaz's vow to redeem his honour with a glorious death was the duty that had been entrusted to him by Graf Mandred. He was Erich's protector and as such couldn't allow harm to come to the knight.

'Manling! Do you hear me!' Kurgaz growled.

Erich had to spit blood from his mouth before he attempted to answer. 'My apologies, friend,' he said. 'I overestimated Kreyssig's sense of honour.' His statement ended in a grunt of pain as one of the soldiers carrying him brought a fist cracking against the knight's head.

'Silence, traitor!' the guard snarled. 'It is by Protector Kreyssig's mercy that you are still alive.'

A grim grin crossed Erich's features. 'Then he must have a good reason for needing us alive,' he sneered at his captors. 'I already know Kreyssig doesn't know the meaning of mercy.'

The guard struck at Erich again, this time smacking his fist into the knight's face. The assault brought fresh thrashings and curses from Kurgaz. The soldier brutalising Erich turned and glared at the slayer. A cruel glint came into his eyes.

'Protector Kreyssig said to keep the traitor,' the guard mused. 'He didn't say anything about needing the dwarf.'

The Palace Guard stopped their march through the halls. A wicked laugh spread through their ranks. There were seven of them. The two holding Erich maintained their grip on the knight, turning him around so he could watch the murder of his companion. The guard with the sword at Kurgaz's throat drew his arm back while the four men holding the chains tightened their grip.

The soldiers stopped at the sound of armoured troops marching down the hall. They turned and looked in confusion as half a dozen dwarfs slowly walked towards them down the gloomy corridor.

'What do you gold grubbers want?' one of the guards demanded. He looked over at the two captives and added in a sardonic laugh. 'These two already paid their taxes.' The jest brought laughs from the other soldiers. Kreyssig had maintained Emperor Boris's policy of using the plague-resistant dwarfs to collect taxes in Altdorf. It was the only thing the men in the Palace Guard felt the creatures were good for.

The dwarfs continued their slow, silent march towards the soldiers. They didn't share in their laughter. Indeed, the expression on their bearded faces was anything but jovial.

'*Khazukan Kazakit-Ha!*' As the fierce cry echoed through the hall a heavy hammer came sailing through the air, smashing into the arm of the swordsman. The guard shouted in pain, his weapon clattering to the floor.

The dwarfs suddenly charged down the corridor, dragging weapons from their belts. 'Gold grubbers!' one of the guards cursed, ripping his sword from its sheath and lunging forwards to receive the first of the attackers. His slashing sword glanced off an armoured pauldron while the dwarf's return with a vicious axe stroke left the man lying disembowelled on the floor.

The reluctance of the Palace Guard to abandon their prisoners and meet the dwarf attack in force made the fight woefully one-sided. First two, then three of the soldiers were felled by the axes and hammers of the dwarfs. The last man trying to hold the chained Kurgaz was dropped by his own captive when the slayer suddenly lunged at him and brought his thick skull crashing into the soldier's forehead. The stunned guard wilted to the floor, dragging the chained Kurgaz down with him.

The last guard holding Erich drew his dagger and pressed it to the knight's throat. Defiantly, he glared at the dwarfs. 'Back!' he snarled. 'Back or I'll kill him!'

There was a chilling indifference in the expressions of the dwarfs. Their leader, a broken-nosed fighter with a long black beard simply shrugged his broad shoulders. 'Kill away,' he said. He jabbed a thumb at Kurgaz lying on the floor. 'I owe a debt to Smallhammer here, not the manling.'

From the floor, the slayer cried out to the dwarf leader. 'Dharin, I have given my word to protect the human!'

Dharin nodded and fixed his stony gaze on the guard. 'That makes it different,' he declared. 'Cut the manling, and my clan will swear vengeance on your bloodline. We'll not rest until your children's children's children have cause to curse your name.' He shrugged again. 'Or you can drop the knife and run away.'

The guard licked his lips nervously. His eyes flashed from one dwarf to another, finding the same brooding malignance on each face. He watched helplessly as two of the dwarfs began to free Kurgaz from his chains. Imagining what the slayer would do to him if he made good his threat was what decided him at last. Shoving Erich towards the dwarfs, the soldier turned and fled up the corridor.

'Looks like we're out of a job,' Dharin said, reaching to his left arm and ripping off the armband that marked him as an Imperial revenue collector. The other gold grubbers chuckled at the remark and removed their own armbands.

One of the dwarfs had recovered the keys to Kurgaz's chains from a dead guard. The moment he was free of the bindings, the slayer stomped over to Erich and used the keys to remove the knight's own manacles.

'It was lucky for us that your friends happened along,' Erich said, bowing to Dharin in gratitude.

Kurgaz quickly corrected the knight. 'Dharin Rockhome is no friend. He's the most bitter enemy my family owns.'

'And the Smallhammers are recorded in our Book of Grudges for their insults,' Dharin declared. 'Your blood will not be enough to wash away that debt, but at least it will be a start.'

Erich blinked in disbelief. 'You… you saved us just so you could kill Kurgaz?'

Kurgaz shook his head. 'It's not that simple, manling. I've taken the Slayer Oath. If Dharin kills me, he must take up my vow. He's too fond of gold to do that. All the Rockhomes are.'

'I can still give my ancestors the satisfaction of watching you die,' Dharin snarled back. 'Just knowing there's one less Smallhammer in the world will ease their burden.' He shook his head. 'We must be quit of this place. The guard who ran away will be sounding the alarm.'

'They'll already have closed the gates then,' Erich observed. 'And I doubt if Kreyssig has left the old route to the sewers open after my last escape from this place.'

'Those tunnels were built by dwarfs,' Dharin said. 'Do you think any shoddy human construction can keep us out of them?'

≺ CHAPTER XVII ≻

Averland, 1123

At Arch-Lector Hartwich's urging, Graf Mandred agreed to receive the representatives from Altdorf in the tiny Sigmarite chapel within the old fortress of Averburg. Only days after his fight with the skaven warlord, Mandred's body felt like one big bruise. The rush of battle, the rage of war had carried him through the fray after the beast's magic hammer decapitated his noble steed. With the battle won, those revitalising energies had deserted him, making him keenly aware of the hurts he had suffered.

Mandred stared at the Sigmarite iconography on the walls. For an Ulrican like himself, he still found it strange to be surrounded by the trappings of a god he had always considered something of a foreigner. It was only through his travels across the Empire that he had begun to appreciate the importance of what Sigmar represented, the greater meaning the god held for mankind as a whole. The old gods, deities like Ulric and Taal and Rhya, were in many ways localised gods. Middenland was the home of Ulric; he was their patron. Nordland and Westerland claimed Mannan; Stirland favoured Rhya; Talabecland and Drakwald venerated Taal; here in Averland it was Verena. Each land, each people, claimed a different god as their own. Sigmar alone was a god for the whole of the Empire, a god meant to bring unity rather than divisions. He was the god a broken land needed now more than ever.

Mandred smiled as he considered what Ar-Ulric would have said about such an idea. Most likely, he would have regarded it as some manner of heresy, a slight against the White Wolf's power and authority. After all, he would have reminded Mandred that in life Sigmar himself had venerated Ulric.

Even so, Mandred had to admire Hartwich's cunning. From the first, the priest had manoeuvred him into a closer relationship with Sigmar, proclaiming him as 'the Wolf of Sigmar' when he emerged from the miracle of the Eternal Flame. Peoples and lands who might have felt threatened by a manifestation of Ulric, lands with long histories of strife with the Teutogens, had more readily accepted a miracle that could be attributed to Sigmar instead. Hartwich the priest wasn't half so clever as Hartwich the politician.

Now the delegates from Altdorf and the Imperial court had arrived. Mandred had heard much from Princess Erna about her husband, Adolf Kreyssig, the man Emperor Boris had proclaimed Protector of the Empire in his absence. Since the arrival of Erich von Kranzbeuhler in the camp, Erna had recovered much of her mind and her memory. What she'd revealed to him about Kreyssig, what parts of her story both Hartwich and Erich could substantiate, made him cool in his reception of the delegates.

Even without Erna's story, Mandred couldn't forget that

Kreyssig's emissaries had waited until after the Battle of Averheim was decided before riding out from their camp to meet with him. Hulda said that from the look of their encampment, they had been there for more than a week. They could have met with Mandred well before the battle had they been so inclined. Most likely, they had been told to wait, to see which way the battle went, to see how weak Mandred's position was before they came to him.

Mandred smiled as the Reiklanders came marching into the chapel. He'd taken care to fill the place with representatives from all the lands he had liberated, with the men and women he could count as his friends and allies. He ensured that they would see the Count of Averland, his head bandaged from the injuries he had received in the last hours of the battle to free his capital. He made certain that the exiled Reikmarshal von Boeckenfoerde had a prominent place on the dais where Mandred waited to receive his visitors. It had been von Boeckenfoerde's mercenary army riding out from Mordheim to join forces with Mandred that had so alarmed him days before and caused him to dispatch Grand Master Vitholf and the Knights of the White Wolf to intercept them in the belief they were a skaven column or a fresh legion of undead from the necromancer Vanhal. The sudden appearance of von Boeckenfoerde's forces outside Averheim had helped to break the ratmen and send them into full retreat. Von Boeckenfoerde hadn't sat back to see how the battle would end, he had ridden into the fray to help turn the tide.

The Altdorf delegation bowed as they approached the dais. One of the noblemen displayed the signet ring on his hand, a ring that bore the Emperor's seal. Only two men were permitted to entrust that seal to an emissary, the Emperor and his appointed Protector. 'We bring greetings from Protector

Kreyssig of the Imperial Throne to Graf Mandred of Middenheim,' the Altdorfer said.

Arch-Lector Hartwich stepped out from the front pew and walked across the chapel until he stood between Mandred and the delegates. 'By what authority do you wear that ring?' he demanded.

The nobleman bristled at the scorn in Hartwich's tone. 'By the authority of Protector Kreyssig!' he snapped.

'And by what authority is he Protector?' the priest demanded.

'By decree of the late Emperor Boris!' the Altdorfer snarled back.

'Then your authority comes from pretenders and dead tyrants,' Hartwich declared. He pointed at Mandred. 'There stands a ruler whose authority has been bestowed by the gods.'

The Altdorfer smiled. 'Even in the Imperial Palace we have heard stories of fables... I mean miracles.'

'The incredulous will not believe a miracle unless they have seen it with their own eyes,' Hartwich said. 'That is why Lord Sigmar has granted Graf Mandred a sign of His favour no man can contest!'

Even Mandred was stunned by the vehemence in Hartwich's voice, surprised by the belligerence of his tone. Certainly he understood the priest's loathing of Kreyssig and the murderous Grand Theogonist the Protector had installed as the highest cleric of Sigmar in the land, but this went beyond what he could accept. Diplomacy demanded that care was taken in how Kreyssig's men were received. In his proper wits, Hartwich would have been the first to acknowledge that fact.

Mandred was about to admonish Hartwich before the assembled nobles and dignitaries when he suddenly stopped. The priest had turned away from the Altdorfers and was walking towards Erich who had risen from his seat. The knight held a bulky object wrapped in a purple cloth. Reverently, Hartwich took the object from him and marched back towards the dais.

'Tell me, what is the living relic by which an Emperor's rule is sanctified? What is the link that binds him to Sigmar?' Hartwich could see the confusion on the faces of most of the emissaries, but the man wearing the signet ring had grown pale. He at least knew the answer to the priest's question. Hartwich turned away from Kreyssig's men. Lifting his voice, he instead addressed the nobles gathered in the chapel.

'Ghal Maraz!' he declared, whipping away the purple cloth, exposing the ancient warhammer forged over a thousand years before for Sigmar himself. Richly etched and engraved, the head of the hammer supported by carved griffons, the pommel at the end of its spiralling grip fashioned into a conclave of skulls, the relic blazed with an inner light, a golden glow that suffused the air around it with a divine aura. 'Skull-splitter!' Hartwich's voice rose into a roar. 'The Hammer of Sigmar!'

An awed silence held the assembly, a silence that wasn't broken until Hartwich turned and dropped to his knees before Graf Mandred. 'Ghal Maraz, come to us by the will of Sigmar into the hands of the man who will lead His Empire out of darkness and back into the light!'

Almost timidly, Mandred approached the kneeling priest. Hesitantly, he reached down to take up Sigmar's Hammer, wondering to the last if he dared such a thing, if he was truly worthy of such honour.

Then, as his hand closed about the spiral grip, as Mandred felt the magic within the hammer flow into him, he knew he would never doubt again. It was the same sensation he had felt in the Eternal Flame, the holy power of the gods.

Raising Ghal Maraz in one hand, Mandred basked in the jubilant cries of those who had followed him, those whose lands he had liberated and whose people he had saved.

Only the men from Altdorf were silent, their faces pale with fear. Even if they didn't feel it, they recognised the power of the symbol Mandred held.

The power to unite the whole Empire.

Kurgaz knelt amid the ashes outside Averheim's west gate, the place where the city's rulers had cremated the carcasses of the skaven dead. He could think of no better place to do what he had to do.

Grimly, the dwarf drew the knife from his boot. Tears of shame streamed down his face as he stared at the earth. A ritual such as this was supposed to be observed within a proper shrine, preferably the Great Shrine in Karak Kadrin. It was a magnification of his guilt that such a pilgrimage was impossible for him. Any day might see Mandred's army resume its campaign against the ratkin. When the humans marched, Kurgaz would march with them. He had little enough honour left to him; he wouldn't allow that to slip away as well.

The dwarf closed his eyes, seeing again the ghoulish white skaven, the defiled Drakdrazh in its paws. The creature that had killed his brother, that had stolen the sacred relic of his clan, a weapon that had been handed down from father to son since the War of Vengeance ages ago. He had vowed to find that monster, to kill it or die in the attempt. He had succeeded in neither. He was alive, and so too was his bestial nemesis.

There was only one answer for such shame.

Kurgaz brought the knife against the side of his head,

pressing it against his scalp until he could feel a trickle of blood running down his neck. His voice lowered to a respectful whisper, he prayed to Grimnir, begging the ancestor god to accept the offering of his hair, his honour and his life. From memory, Kurgaz recited the Slayer Oath as he used his knife to scrape the hair from the sides of his head.

Life had no value to him now. The only redemption Kurgaz could still claim was to die a noble death, to set before Grimnir the carcass of some mighty foe. Only then could he hope to enter the halls of his ancestors. Only then could he blot away the shame he had allowed to stain the name of his clan.

Cautiously, Beck picked his way among the tents and pavilions erected by Mandred's triumphant army. Amid the vast host it was impossible to go anywhere unobserved, but he wanted to avoid anyone who might recognise him if possible. There might be awkward questions later if somebody remembered seeing him where he was going.

The knight turned his face and inspected a stack of spears when a pair of White Wolves went marching past. The warriors seemed caught up in their lively debate over the combat abilities of Aldinger and his Knights of the Black Rose, but there was always a chance that they might be more aware of their surroundings than they seemed. Beck preferred not to tempt fate even with the most remote opportunity to work mischief. Too much depended on his success.

Beck scratched at his scarred face, trying not to think too closely about what it was that his eye patch now concealed. He knew there were those who would call it the Dark Stigmata and condemn him as a disciple of Old Night should they learn of the strange changes that had come over his wound.

The knight had his own ideas about the cause of his affliction. He'd seen the way Ar-Ulric regarded the 'oracle' Hulda. There were many in the camp who held her to be more witch than priestess and several who laid still more sinister accusations against her. For his own part, however, Beck wasn't certain. It was undeniable that Hulda's strange powers had been beneficial to Graf Mandred. The possibility that those same powers were protecting the graf from the same sort of affliction as the one his bodyguard was suffering had so far restrained Beck from taking any action. It was enough to keep a sprig of wolfsbane in his pocket next to his stone talisman.

Proceeding through the camp, Beck hurried towards a different sort of affliction, one that he could and would protect Mandred from. He'd been there after Hartwich's dramatic presentation of Ghal Maraz to the graf, been privy to the far more private audience he'd held with the emissaries from Altdorf. He listened as the emissaries offered an alliance between Kreyssig and Mandred. The Protector would support any claim Mandred made upon the Imperial throne in exchange for certain concessions. Baroness Carin had encouraged the alliance, pointing out that with the certain support of the electors whose provinces Mandred had helped liberate and the endorsement of the Protector, there was no force in the Empire that would prevent him being installed as the next Emperor.

The argument might have swayed Mandred but for the venomous counsel of Princess Erna. Why the half-crazed adulteress should hold any influence over the graf was a mystery Beck couldn't explain. All he did know was that without her, Mandred would be more open to an alliance with Kreyssig. The wedge that had come between himself and Baroness Carin would be removed.

Beck's hand tightened about the grip of his sword as he approached Erna's tent. He paused outside for a moment, listening to the sound of voices inside. She had her lover in there, that outlaw knight Erich. So much the better. He'd need someone to blame for her murder, and the knight would make a perfect patsy.

Carefully, Beck slipped into the tent. He could see the princess seated on a divan, her feet propped in the air. Erich was waiting on her, bringing her wine and cold mutton from a table set against the side of the enclosure. His back was to the entrance; her eyes were on him. Quickly, Beck drew his sword and rushed at the knight. He could afford for Erna to make some noise – everyone knew she was mad and they wouldn't think too much of a few screams – but he couldn't have Erich giving an alarm. Not until the deed was done, anyway.

Erna's startled gasp as she saw Beck rushing towards Erich gave her lover just enough time to turn. Instead of crashing against the back of his skull, the iron pommel of Beck's sword slammed into the side of his face. The result was the same, dropping the man to the ground, though instead of being insensible, the blow only stunned him.

Beck kicked Erich as he started to rise and then rushed towards Erna with his sword. He found his charge turn into a sprawl when Erich's hands clutched at his foot and tripped him.

'Damn you, Reiklander!' Beck cursed. 'I need you alive!' He punctuated the statement with a brutal kick to his foe's head.

'Why, murderer?' a voice snarled from behind Beck. The knight looked up to see Hulda standing between him and the princess. 'Did you decide there weren't any skaven you could blame this atrocity on?'

Beck rose to his feet, a vicious smile on his face. He reached into his pocket. 'I don't know how you got here, witch,' he said, 'but I came prepared for you just the same.' He held the sprig of wolfsbane towards her and laughed as she drew back. 'Ar-Ulric was right, wasn't he?' the knight laughed.

'Now you will kill us all?' Hulda accused, keeping Erna behind her, preventing the princess from rushing to her injured lover.

Beck nodded. 'Him because now he's heard too much. Her because she stands between Graf Mandred and the greatness that should be his.'

Hulda eyes gleamed hatefully at Beck. 'You have killed for that reason before,' she said. 'Your scent was on Lady Mirella's body, and there was no smell of skaven around her. I had no proof I could bring to Mandred, but from that moment I have watched you.'

'For all the good it has done you,' Beck said. 'If you meant to avenge Mirella, you've failed, monster.' He nodded his head, reaching a decision. 'You are as much a threat to Graf Mandred as any of them. If the people found out what you are, Hartwich could bestow a hundred relics on the graf and they'd never make him Emperor!'

Hulda looked away from Beck, staring past the knight at something over his shoulder. 'You heard?' she asked.

'I heard,' Mandred's voice was little more than a hiss. Beck spun around at the sound of his master's voice. 'You killed Mirella?' he snarled at his bodyguard, then disgust curled his lip as he remembered another woman who had been close to him. 'Did you kill Sofia too?'

'You were beside yourself with grief,' Beck explained. 'She had the plague. You'd have caught it yourself if I...'

'Enough!' Mandred roared. 'I have heard enough, murderer!'

Beck cringed at the fury in his master's voice. 'Please, highness, all that I have done I did for you!' The knight recoiled when he saw no pity in Mandred's enraged gaze. When the flap of the tent was pulled back and half a dozen Teutogen Guard swarmed into the tent, Beck turned and threw himself at the far wall of the enclosure. His sword slashed out, cutting a great gash in the wall. Before any of the guards could seize him, Beck was through the gap and running off into the rubble of Averheim.

Mandred glared at the rent in the wall. 'I want him found,' he snarled, tears in his eyes.

'I want him to answer for his crimes.'

Stirland, 1122

Bonelord Nekrot, Corpsemaster of Clan Mordkin, gnashed his fangs together with such fury that it rattled the teeth in the jaws of his skeletal helmet. Worthless, treacherous grave-rats, incapable of restraining their pestiferous hunger for a few hours more! He should have the entire pack skinned alive and their bones made into toys for newborn pups! They'd allowed the scent of rotten meat and decayed bone to overwhelm their brains, rushing up from their concealed burrows to glut their hunger on the dead-things. In so doing, they'd run straight into a lurking force of humans.

Nekrot glared at the embattled ratmen. He was sorely tempted to leave the treasonous vermin to their fate. Only the realisation that to do so would mean cancelling his plans to visit gruesome revenge on Vanhal dissuaded him from such a course. The ambush was spoiled; the only option now was to attack in force, quickly, savagely and with all the merciless terror of starving rats.

A snap of his claws and the gang of slaves cowering at the warlord's feet lifted to him the dragon horn. Plundered from the carnage outside Vanhaldenschlosse, the armourers of Clan Mordkin had pounded slivers of Seerlord Skrittar's sacred bell into its sides. A hollowed nugget of warpstone served as a mouthpiece and when Nekrot wrapped his lips about it he could feel the raw magic sizzle against his flesh. It was no light thing to call upon the divine power of the Horned Rat.

When Nekrot blew into the mammoth horn, a dolorous note shuddered through the hollow. Each passing breath intensified the sound, causing trees to crack and the earth to tremble. Skaven were thrown from their feet as the cacophony washed over them, but their enemies fared even worse. Horses toppled, smashing their riders against the ground. The baggage train beyond the Sylvanians was scattered like so much rubbish, thrown to the four corners of the forest by the violent susurrus.

Nekrot ripped the horn from his lips, shreds of burned skin clinging to the poisonous mouthpiece. The warlord clenched his paw against his smouldering lips, trying to ease the pain. Absently, he kicked one of the slaves, feeling a little better when he heard something snap. With the paw not massaging his muzzle, he waved the warriors of Mordkin forwards. If they struck fast, they could slaughter the humans before they recovered from the Whispering Horn. As he watched the horde scurry past, Nekrot wondered how many of the over-eager vanguard lying strewn across the ground would be trampled underfoot.

The Bonelord hoped the casualties were high.

His belly felt empty.

* * *

Raw horror gripped Count Malbork von Drak as he struggled to free himself from the thrashing weight of his
toppled horse. All around him the screams of panicked men
and animals impacted against the discordant ringing in his
ears. Instinctively, he tried to look past the prone bodies of
his guards, trying to see what Vanhal was doing, what the
necromancer had done to wreak such magical havoc. Only
when the chittering horde of skaven was descending upon
the reeling Nachtsheer did the voivode appreciate that the
dreadful magic had been unleashed by the ratmen themselves.

Isolated bands of soldiers fought to hold the verminous
mob back. Theirs was a hopeless struggle, but Malbork
hoped they might delay the skaven long enough to afford
him some chance to escape. To die in battle was something
he was prepared to accept, but to be butchered beneath the
paws of such filth! That was a peasant's death!

The stricken horse continued to thrash above him, grinding his right leg against the ground, refusing Malbork's every
effort to bring the beast back to its feet. In despair, he drew
his dagger and slashed it across the animal's throat. The
horse screamed and crumpled against its master. Malbork
cried out in agony as the dead weight pressed against him,
but without the horse's struggles he at least had some hope
that he might pull himself free.

A glance over his shoulder robbed him of that hope. A
snarling ratman, its muzzle flecked in blood, the spiked
mace in its paws caked in clumps of gore, came skittering
past the beleaguered soldiers. The creature chittered malignantly at Malbork, then dove in for the kill.

The voivode shifted away from the descending bludgeon
and stabbed upwards with his dagger, catching the beast in
the groin. The skaven uttered a yelp of shock and collapsed

in a writhing heap, black blood spurting from its punctured body. Malbork forced himself to look away from the
hideous brute, to concentrate on wrenching his leg from
beneath his fallen steed.

As he began to despair, the weight against him seemed to
dissipate. Malbork blinked in wonder as his horse began to
twitch, as the animal kicked its legs and started to rise. His
wonder turned to horror when he saw the dead glassy eyes
and the rictus-like grin. Now he could see the snake-like
ribbons of unholy power seeping into the animal's body,
endowing it with a profane semblance of animation.

Before the zombie steed could lift itself fully from the
ground, Malbork dragged his leg from the stirrup. Pant-
ing in terror, he watched as the animal stumbled onto its
hooves and pawed at the earth. More snakes of sorcerous power were slithering along the ground, sinking into
whatever dead flesh they encountered. Frozen with horror,
Malbork watched as the skaven he had killed staggered into
grotesque life and retrieved its mace from the ground.

A firm grip seized the voivode from behind. Malbork
whipped around with his dagger, but Iorgu caught his hand
before he could deliver the blow. 'Excellency, you must call
the retreat!' the dregator yelled, his words barely penetrat-
ing the ringing in the voivode's ears. 'Vanhal has turned his
legion away from von Oberreuth. If we do not run now, we
shall be caught between the skaven and the undead!'

Malbork's lip curled in an ugly snarl. 'Let the Nachtsheer
die! That is what they are paid to do! Their deaths will allow
us the opportunity to escape.'

Iorgu's grip tightened about Malbork's hand. Cold fury
blazed in the former peasant's eyes. 'You can't abandon
your men!' he roared.

With a twist of his wrist, Malbork broke Iorgu's hold and

sent the dagger plunging into the dregator's breast. 'Stay with them then,' he hissed at the dying man. Even as the words left his tongue, the voivode saw the tendril of darkness seeping into the murdered man's flesh. Crying out in terror, Malbork reeled away from the revivified dregator.

Dragging his injured leg, Malbork fled across the field towards the trees, praying he might reach their shelter before the deathly legions of Vanhal came crashing down upon the Sylvanian camp. Behind him, even through the clamour of the skaven horn, he could hear the stumbling steps of Dregator Iorgu as the zombie pursued its killer into the forest.

The skeletal horde marched away from the Stirlanders and their allies, ignoring the mortal foes as though they weren't even there. The surrounded cavalry broke free, riding back into the shelter of the trees. A ragged cheer went up from the allied camp as Graf Mandred returned to them. For the Stirlanders there was only a limping steed with an empty saddle to mark the fate of their grand count.

Vengeful archery punished the undead as they turned northwards and away from Fellwald. Dwarf gunners emerged from the trees, firing their weapons at the dragons overhead, peppering the beasts with bullets until they flew beyond the range of their weapons. Behind them, like the track of some vast and decayed snail, the undead left a litter of broken bones and mutilated bodies.

Upon his spectral carriage, upon his throne of wailing ghosts, from behind his mask of bone, Vanhal watched as his legion marched towards the real battle. The deceptions of Malbork von Drak and Lothar von Diehl, the challenge of Graf Mandred and Grand Count von Oberreuth, these had been useful to the necromancer. They had provided the bait that would draw his greatest enemy from hiding. Once before, he had dismissed the verminous ratmen as being of no consequence. That had been a mistake, one that had cost him dearly. One thousand years of shapeless oblivion.

Vanhal shook his head, trying to clear the weird image from his mind. An illusion of memory, a nightmare struggling to make itself real. Yet where had it come from? Some ancestral spark, some mad delusion conjured by the brain of Lothar von Diehl?

The necromancer dismissed the distraction. The provenance of the illusion was of no consequence. What did matter was the annihilation of the skaven. Once they were extirpated there would be no more assassins slinking into the halls of Vanhaldenschlosse, no more thieves stealing into his fortress to plunder the warpstone from its walls. There would be only peace and silence, the quietude of the grave.

The ratmen were engaged with the remnants of the Nachtsheer and the newly risen dead Vanhal's magic had animated. Even so, their numbers were vast, mighty enough to form a battle-line to oppose the tide of undead he was bringing to bear upon them. The necromancer made a pass of his hand through the air, bidding the abhorrent dragons in the sky above to swoop down and shatter the skaven formation.

As the dragons descended, the destructive cacophony of the horn sounded once more. The blast of magic caught both dragons, sending their wormy bulks crashing to earth, bowling them across the ground like a landslide of reptilian flesh and saurian bone. Hundreds of skeletons were pulverised as the dragons rolled over them. What had been a vast legion of the undead was shattered.

Vanhal stretched forth his hand as one of the dragons

came tumbling towards him. The vast bulk exploded into a shower of decay, passing to either side of the necromancer like ocean waves crashing about the base of a rock.

The necromancer glared across the carnage. He paid no notice to the squeaking, jeering swarm of skaven who now skittered across the battlefield and dragged down those pockets of undead yet standing. His eyes were focused on the morbid warlord who had conjured such magic. There, he knew, lay the real threat.

Mustering his energies, Vanhal sent his phantom palanquin shrieking across the terrain, boiling over shattered undead and marauding skaven alike. Whatever the wailing spirits touched was scorched and withered, left rotting upon the barren ground. The jubilant squeaks of the ratmen turned to howls of horror and they broke before the advance of the ghostly throne.

Bonelord Nekrot was just putting his scorched lips to the horn to evoke its magic for a third time when Vanhal's enslaved spirits brought the necromancer raging through the skaven lines. Before the skaven warlord could react, a blast of arcane power caused the Whispering Horn to crumble in his paws. The vengeful ratman squealed in terror as spectral hands lifted him from the ground and dragged him to the ethereal mound of enslaved ghosts. He was dumped at the very feet of the man he had struggled so hard and for so many years to kill.

Vanhal smiled behind his mask. Now all the old betrayals would be avenged. Stretching out his hand, he began to draw the life from Nekrot's body, leaching his vitality like a sponge. He held the warlord in his power, killing him inch by inch, letting the once mighty skaven hear the shrieks of terror rise from his minions, letting him watch as they scampered back to their holes.

Before he had drawn the last dregs of life from Nekrot's body, Vanhal broke the spell. The Bonelord was doomed, he had only moments to live, but they were moments the necromancer intended to savour.

Nekrot knew he was dying, and that knowledge fired his ratty heart like no other power could. With all the viciousness of a cornered rat he lunged at the necromancer.

In the moment before Nekrot's fangs closed about the necromancer's throat, Vanhal withdrew his consciousness from the body of his apprentice Lothar, the shape he had worn like an old cloak while his own body rested within the walls of his fortress.

He wanted Lothar to experience with his own mind the last murderous seconds of Nekrot's vitality. It was really the least Vanhal could do to repay his apprentice's clumsy effort at betrayal.

The last sound Vanhal's spirit heard before it went hurtling back to Vanhaldenschlosse was Lothar's anguished shriek as he understood what his master had done to him and felt Nekrot's fangs sink into his flesh.

─< CHAPTER XVIII >─

Averland, 1123

The great hall of Averburg's keep bore the scars of the skaven siege. Once a grand arcade of marble pillars and tiled floors, now only the soiled echoes of its past opulence remained. Graf Mandred recognised the putrid corrosion left behind by the impact of a warpcaster's glowing pellet. Whatever infernal magic the skaven poured into those spheres when they slammed into a target they had the power to melt stone and vaporise iron. The less thought given to their effect upon flesh the better.

Still, despite the savageries of the skaven, Mandred could feel the lingering majesty of the place, the sense of legacy that seemed to exude from the very walls. He understood why the von Orns had wanted the graf to meet with his council here. It was their way of demonstrating to Mandred and his allies that Averland had been a great and prosperous land. It would be again, now that the skaven were in retreat.

The scope of that retreat had confused Mandred at first. In

other lands, any great victory had been followed by almost innumerable small skirmishes as contingents of his army were dispatched to force the skaven from every village and town. In Averland, despite the magnitude of the skaven infestation, virtually every settlement had been abandoned by the monsters after they lost Averheim.

The answer came by way of intelligence culled from the few ratmen taken prisoner. Under none-too-gentle interrogation from the dwarfs, the vermin revealed the identity of the white skaven Mandred had fought and whose ear Legbiter had cut away.

He was Vrrmik, and they referred to him by a variety of grandiose titles, the most prominent of which was Great Warlord. Vrrmik, it transpired, was the successor of Vecteek, the skaven overlord Mandred and his father had slain during the Battle of Middenheim. With the Great Warlord himself present in Averheim, it seemed clear to Mandred that the rapid abandonment of the rest of Averland could only have been accomplished under Vrrmik's orders.

The question was, why? To what end would Vrrmik concede the whole province to his enemy? Try as he might, Mandred couldn't wrap his mind around whatever treacherous strategy the skaven were trying to implement. To try to outguess the skaven would be to think like one of the monsters. No matter how vile, he could think of no man, not even the escaped murderer Beck, who was so debased as one of the skaven.

'The major strongpoint of the ratkin in Solland is Pfeildorf.' The speaker was Captain Aldinger of the Knights of the Black Rose. He was addressing the lords and generals gathered in the great hall. The map he pointed to was a great sprawling tapestry depicting the entire southern half of the Empire, a gift bestowed upon the von Orns by the dwarfs of

Zhufbar. 'They've turned the city into a distribution point for the slaves they capture when they raid into Talabecland and Wissenland.'

The explanation brought angry snarls from many in the room. Mandred was pleased to hear that anger. It meant that his forces were seeing beyond the limitations of their own people and their own lands. They were thinking in terms of the Empire as a whole, in mankind as a single...

Cries of surprise and confusion rose from the back of the hall, interrupting both Aldinger's explanation of the situation around Pfeildorf and Mandred's thoughts. He turned away from the extravagant map, trying to see the source of the disruption.

The cause was a dusty, bedraggled man in the livery of the von Oberreuths, the ruling house of Stirland. More than the man's alarming appearance and dramatic entrance, it was the words he spoke that made an impact on the assembly.

'Woerden is lost!' the messenger cried. 'The skaven have slaughtered everyone in the town!'

Mandred watched as Hulda made her esoteric preparations for the ritual. He wondered if it was a sign of weakness or desperation that he should turn to the witch, or if perhaps it was evidence of stubbornness and superstition that he hadn't consulted her before. Whatever his feelings, he knew that this was certainly his last recourse. If this didn't work, there was nothing else left to try.

The great hall in the Averburg fortress was empty now. Mandred and Hulda were the only ones inside. The great map Aldinger had referenced was laid out on the floor now, combined with a second massive tapestry depicting the northern provinces. At each corner of the map, Hulda had set a tallow candle, ringing it round with a circle of dried herbs and crushed leaves. A great wooden framework had been suspended over the map and from this a wild array of tiny stones had been tied, the loop of each cord fastened in such a way that it could slide along the wooden runners.

At the base of the map, however, was the most macabre instrument in Hulda's conjurations, the hollowed-out skull of a ratman, inverted over an open fire. A strange concoction boiled away inside that skull, sending a strange and nauseating smoke wafting through the hall. Hulda squatted beside the skull dressed only in a thick robe of wolfskin. Beside her on the floor rested the severed tail of Poxmaster Puskab Foulfur and the severed ear of Great Warlord Vrrmik.

Oh, it had been fiendishly clever, Vrrmik's plan. Mandred had to concede a certain monstrous brilliance to the verminous creature. He'd withdrawn his forces from Averland so that he could deploy them elsewhere. Not for conquest, but simply to destroy. Woerden had been almost razed to the ground, virtually its entire population massacred. Vrrmik could have conceived no better way to shatter the army that had driven him from Averheim. The disparate forces that made up Mandred's army, so close to that unity of purpose he had struggled so long to invest them with, were once again becoming fractured. Every nobleman, every peasant was worried about *his* home now, wondering when Vrrmik's vengeful horde would rise up to annihilate *his* city or town.

The skaven didn't need to bring some mighty army to conquer Mandred in the field. Vrrmik could simply stage terror raids in the lands the humans thought safely liberated and bleed away Mandred's forces piecemeal as each province scurried home to protect their own land.

There was only one chance, one way to outguess Vrrmik and beat the rat at his own game. If Mandred could predict where Vrrmik would strike next, if he could get his army there ahead of the skaven, then he would restore the confidence of his commanders and rekindle their faith in the vision of an entire Empire freed from the ratkin.

If he guessed wrong, however, nothing would keep Mandred's force united. They would scatter and, eventually, the skaven would pick off each province one at a time.

Hulda motioned for Mandred to stay where he was. She'd cautioned him earlier that any movement, any sound could prove disastrous. At best, the divination would be spoiled. At worst, her magic might unleash a denizen of the aethyr, the malignant forces all men knew as daemons.

Mandred listened as Hulda invoked the name of Ulric, her voice dropping in tone and distinction until it was little more than a bestial growl. The inhuman timbre of her voice set the hairs at the back of his neck crawling, yet worse was to come. From where he stood, he could only see the back of the witch, her wild mane of hair and the heavy wolfskin cloak. It was only when she reached to the floor beside her that he saw anything more, and what he saw made him shudder. The hand that picked up the scaly skaven tail was scarcely a hand at all. It was covered in white fur, the fingers distended into long bony talons, each digit tipped by a blackened claw.

A foul sizzling noise rose from the skull as Hulda dropped the tail into the boiling liquid. It seemed to Mandred that he could see a weird mist drift away from the skull, wafting above the map and slithering among the suspended stones. There was no mistaking, however, when one of the stones began to shudder and dance, shivering at the end of its tether as though it were a thing alive. The cord slid along the framework, the stone beneath it straining at the end of its tether at an angle.

Hulda reached for Vrrmik's ear, this time her hand little more than a lupine paw. Again, Mandred heard the sizzling sound as the ear followed the tail into the ghoulish cauldron. Once again he fancied he could see a mephitic vapour rise up and blow across the map. Another of the suspended stones shivered, its cord sliding along the wooden runners until it took up position near the first stone. Both of the tiny rocks strained at the ends of their tethers, pointing to a spot on the map below.

'Hergig,' Hulda's distorted voice growled. 'At the time of the next new moon, the skaven will attack Hergig.'

Mandred nodded. Hergig, the capital of Hochland. It made a fiendish amount of sense. Hochland was at the very centre of most of the provinces that had joined with Mandred. If Vrrmik struck there, he would exhibit in no uncertain terms that he could strike the neighbouring provinces as well.

Hergig. It would be a long, hard march from Averheim.

Altdorf, 1124

The slime-coated walls of the Catacombs glistened in the rushlight as armed soldiers stalked through the cramped dungeons far below the Courts of Justice. Inarticulate moans, the rattle of rusty chains, desperate cries for mercy or death echoed through the dank corridor but did nothing to stir whatever dregs of sympathy still lingered in the hearts of the gaolers. Already hard and brutal men, the intrusion of Gazulgrund's killers had made these men even more vicious. Though the Kaiserjaeger had doubled their guards and increased their defences, the gaolers couldn't shake the feeling that death might strike at them without warning at any time. Savagery went far to make them forget their own fears.

Kreyssig stalked along the corridor behind his soldiers and the guiding gaolers. He wanted a particular cell and a particular captive: someone he had entombed in the darkest corner of the Catacombs.

The Protector cursed the desperation that made him resort to such an extreme, but there was nothing else to be done. Von Kranzbeuhler had escaped and the Kaiserjaeger had yet to turn him up. Should the knight reach Graf Mandred and disclose Kreyssig's treachery then all of his careful plans would be for nothing.

Fortunately, the very urgency that drove him to this black pit beneath Altdorf was also working in Kreyssig's favour. His spies reported that Mandred's army was on the march again, driving towards Altdorf. They could be expected almost any day. Von Kranzbeuhler didn't have much time to get to Mandred and warn him. The Kaiserjaeger had Altdorf sealed as tight as a drum, so Kreyssig was certain the outlaw was still somewhere in the city. The loss of Ghal Maraz all those years ago had been a painful, but profitable lesson.

The gaolers didn't bother to hide their fear when they reached the cell. They hesitated before the door, none of them making a move to turn the key. Kreyssig had no patience with the trepidation of his men. Angrily he pushed past his guards and took the ring of keys from the head gaoler. Turning the key in a lock that almost seemed a solid block of rust, he pushed open the door and thrust the rush-light he carried into the cell beyond.

The light cast by the smouldering brand revealed a ragged creature chained to the slimy wall. It lifted its head as Kreyssig stepped inside. The Commander of the Kaiserjaeger

struggled to keep his composure as the thing stared at him
with the glistening clutch of spider-like eyes that pockmarked the left side of what was left of its face. The right
side was a shapeless mush of flesh, as though it were made
of wax and had been left too close to a flame. The entirety
of the creature was a mismatched patchwork of mutation.
The fingers of one hand were hard and calcified, resembling
nothing so much as the thorns on a rose. The creature's
other arm was split into two spindly limbs at the point
where its elbow had been. The thing's back was crooked, yet
at the same time its overall mass and build was that of some
misshapen giant.

Gazing upon the abominable thing, Kreyssig felt the
temptation to withdraw. Instead he held his ground and
called it by the name it had possessed when it was still
human. 'Beck,' he called to the creature. 'How would you
like a chance to get revenge?'

The mutant had been captured months before by one of
the rural nobles. The fact that it had been carrying a charm
fashioned from one of the black rocks the skaven coveted
had brought the creature to the notice of the Kaiserjaeger.
They in turn had brought the thing to Altdorf. Under the
tortures of the Dragon's Hole, the mutant had confessed
all. It said its name was Beck, that it was a knight from
Middenheim, bodyguard to Graf Mandred in fact. Beck
had been devoted to his master, serving him with absolute
selflessness, or at least that was what the mutant insisted.
There had been a falling out between master and servant
when he'd been caught murdering Mandred's lover, the
Lady Mirella. Beck's intention had been to clear the field so
that his master might pursue Baroness Carin of Nordland,
a relationship that had far more to offer the graf by way of
political alliance and territorial gain. Mandred hadn't seen

things that way, and Beck had been forced to flee for his life.

He'd been making his way back to Middenland when he'd been caught. The taint of mutation had started when he was in Averland, but it had accelerated dramatically after he left Mandred's army. Beck's belief was that the deformities that afflicted him were caused by the curse of Hulda, a witch who had ingratiated herself into the graf's confidences. Kreyssig was less sure; he'd seen for himself the strange effect the skaven stones had on things. Beck's belief in the witch's curse, however, was something the Protector could use.

Chains rattled as the mutant raised its head. The spidery eyes shifted in their orbits, fixing Kreyssig with their multitudinous gaze. 'Revenge,' the thing hissed, the word almost unintelligible as it was pushed past the creature's jutting fangs.

'Graf Mandred, your old master, is coming here,' Kreyssig informed the mutant.

Beck tried to lunge forwards, what was left of its face contorted in rage. Kreyssig noted with dismay that the iron staples set into the wall shuddered in their fastening. Just a little more force and the mutant might break free all on its own.

'Good,' Kreyssig laughed with more levity than he actually felt. 'I see that we are of one mind.' Beck settled down, sinking onto its haunches like some pensive predator. The eerie eye-cluster watched him with sinister intensity. 'I might be persuaded to give you a chance, if you can convince me I can trust you.' That, of course would be impossible, but if he could get the mutant to behave itself until it was no longer useful, Kreyssig would be content.

'Mandred,' Beck snarled, foam dripping from the mutant's jagged teeth.

Kreyssig nodded. 'Yes, you could kill him. But I think your,

our revenge needs more than that. Mandred dreams of making himself Emperor. We can snatch that dream from him the moment he reaches out to take it. He would have to live with the knowledge of what almost was.' He pointed at Beck. 'You can make it happen.'

'Kill,' the mutant growled, savouring the word as though it were the name of a lover.

'Kill the dream and damn the man,' Kreyssig said. 'What has been done to you by his witch is more horrible than any clean death. Why should you show Mandred any mercy?'

The eye-clusters lost their intense focus as Beck considered that point. The mutant lifted the bisected length of its arm, studying its abominable malformation. 'Yes,' it said. 'Worse.'

It was a genuine smile Kreyssig wore now. He'd worried about how much intelligence, how much sanity, was left in Beck after his grisly transformation and the attentions of the Kaiserjaeger's torturers. There was enough there, he decided, enough left to remember the cup of hate and want to drink its fill from that malignant chalice.

'Listen to me, Beck, and I will tell you how you can take your revenge. I'll tell you how you can kill Mandred's dream.'

True to their word, it had taken the dwarfs less than ten minutes to demolish the stone wall blocking the entrance to the palace sewers. It took them even less time to find and neutralise the pitfall the Kaiserjaeger had excavated and left as a surprise for intruders. The dwarfs were careful about resetting the trap once it had been bypassed, leaving it as a surprise for any pursuers.

Walking through the dank tunnels, Erich felt himself transported back thirteen years. He was again fleeing the Imperial palace with Baron Thornig, bearing away Ghal Maraz so that the despotic reign of Boris Goldgather might be stripped of its legitimacy. He thought too of how he'd finally escaped from Kreyssig's pursuing Kaiserjaeger through the help of the insidious ratmen.

'We'll need to leave the city,' Erich said as the dwarfs marched through the muck of the sewer. 'Maybe a boat or a barge we can hide in.'

Dharin turned to him, shaking his head. 'There's no getting out of Altdorf.' He looked over at Kurgaz, waiting for the other dwarf to nod in agreement. 'Not for you,' he added. 'Ever since the skaven attack, Kreyssig has kept the whole city under lock and key. Nothing gets in or out without his Kaiserjaeger knowing about it.' He spat into the slime around his feet. 'This city is shut tighter than Karaz-a-Karak.'

Erich glared down at the dwarf. 'Then what do we do? Go back and surrender?'

'We die fighting,' Kurgaz snapped at the knight, a fierce fire in the slayer's eyes. 'Better a clean death than whatever that grobi-fondler has in store for you.'

Dharin listened to the slayer's outburst, and then barked out a condescending laugh. 'The Smallhammers were always weak of mind,' he said. 'Always ready to fight, never ready to think.' He pointed the haft of his axe at the other gold grubbers. 'The debt between us is between us,' Dharin stated. 'Do you think I'd involve these lads if I didn't have a plan?'

Erich stepped forwards, motioning Kurgaz to wait before pouncing on Dharin and trying to smash the sneer off his face. 'What's your plan?' the knight demanded.

'You can't leave the city,' Dharin repeated. 'But you can hide. There's one place that even Kreyssig can't get at: the Great Cathedral. Your Grand Theogonist is his bitter enemy, and one who's too powerful for Kreyssig to do anything about. Take sanctuary with him and you'll be as safe as you can be in Altdorf.'

The knight considered that option. Grand Theogonist Thorgrad had been a weak man, easily bent to the demands of Emperor Boris, but from what he'd heard the new Grand Theogonist Gazulgrund was far different. He was a religious fanatic, a firebrand who refused to compromise his principles for anyone or anything. He was also the man who had conceived the Night of the Holy Knives. To entrust their safety to a fanatic and mass-murderer was a cheerless prospect, but it seemed the only option left to them.

'Do these sewers run beneath the Great Cathedral?' Erich asked.

Again, the question brought gruff laughter from Dharin and his tax collectors. 'Any time a manling wants an important building raised, he has dwarfs build it for him. When we build, we dig tunnels to ease the movement of workers and supplies. When the work is done, the manlings have us turn the tunnels into sewers. At least until they want a new building, then we have to turn them back into tunnels.' He wagged his axe at the dripping walls around them. 'Yes, human, these sewers connect with the tunnels under the cathedral. All we have to do is follow this main passage and wait for it to branch off into a tunnel walled with red limestone. That's the path that'll lead us right under the cathedral.'

Erich nodded his understanding. He looked at Kurgaz. 'It sounds like a plan,' he told the slayer. 'We can hide there until we figure out some way to get a warning to Graf Mandred.'

Kurgaz scowled. 'I don't like hiding and sneaking,' he said.

'Always ready to fight, never ready to think,' Dharin laughed. Before the slayer could lunge at him, the gold grubber was already walking off down the tunnel, waving his axe to beckon the others to follow him.

It seemed like hours before they reached the red limestone tunnel. Several times Erich had been suspicious that Dharin had become lost. He was wise enough in the ways of dwarfs, however, to avoid mentioning his suspicion aloud. He had enough to worry about without adding a dwarfish grudge to his troubles.

Finding the red limestone was a relief to Erich's mind. Soon, he consoled himself, they would be safe from the Kaiserjaeger and protected by the sanctuary of the Great Cathedral. It was just as his worries began to lessen that the dwarfs leading the way stopped dead in their tracks. By the glow of their rushlights, Erich could see what had caught their attention. The wall of the tunnel was broken, exposing a crude earthen passageway.

'Skaven,' Dharin hissed, punctuating his statement with a blob of spit.

Erich stared at the burrow-like hole. He felt a chill run down his spine at the thought that the ratmen had been here. But, of course, why shouldn't they? In preparing for their attack on Altdorf, the monsters had probably pitted the whole sewer system with tunnels and burrows. He said as much to the dwarfs.

The dwarfs, even Kurgaz, turned around and stared at him with incredulous expressions. Dharin jabbed his axe at the hole. 'That's new construction,' he said, speaking as though to a particularly dull and backward child.

'What would fresh skaven burrows be doing here?' Erich wondered, a feeling of dread building up inside him.

Kurgaz slammed one fist against the other, a murderous gleam in his eyes. 'The ratkin tried to destroy your cathedral from above. Maybe they've come back to try again from below.'

The implication sent a rush of horror through Erich.

He thought of the ghastly weapons he had seen the skaven deploy, remembered the treacherous strategies they employed on the battlefield. If they were planning something for the Great Cathedral…

'Mandred,' the knight gasped.

'Aye, manling,' Kurgaz agreed. 'They might be waiting for Mandred before working their devilry.'

'What do we do?' Erich asked. 'We have to warn somebody!'

Dharin scowled. 'Warn them about what? We don't know what the vermin might be planning. It might not even have anything to do with your cathedral.'

Kurgaz grinned. 'Then we go down there and pay the skaven a visit. Spoil their game before it gets started.' He turned his head and glared at Dharin. 'And say one word about putting fighting before thinking…'

The other dwarf shook his head and fingered his axe. 'No, Smallhammer, I was going to ask if you'd like some help. It's been too many years since I split a skaven skull. I'd rather not get out of practice.' The other gold grubbers echoed Dharin's words, all of them eager to bring battle to the perfidious enemies of their race.

Taking a hand axe from one of the gold grubbers and the rushlight out of Dharin's hand, Kurgaz led the way into the earthy gloom of the tunnel. What they would find waiting for them at the end, none of them could say. All they knew was that they would fight to the death against whatever it was.

—◄ CHAPTER XIX ►—

Talabecland, 1124

Across fields glazed with frost and through forests dripping with ice, the columns of soldiers and cavalry marched. The vast plains of Averland and the rolling hills of Stirland had given way to the immense woodlands north of the Talabec River. Unlike the thick, wild forests of Nordland, the woods in Talabecland were less a single monstrous sprawl and more scattered stretches of growth with grasslands and marshes intersecting them. It was a region that a determined army could navigate without the sinister aid of elves and ancient primal forces.

Mandred frowned at that last thought. Was his army truly beyond the reach of powers beyond mortal ken? He glanced aside to where Hulda trotted near the head of the column, her every step exhibiting a grace that made even the most veteran scout seem a clumsy buffoon. He tried not to think about the stories circulating about her in the camp, stories that he'd ignored while Ar-Ulric was alive, but which now left him ill at ease. He'd known, of course, that she was a witch. Whatever her claims about being a servant of Ulric, an oracle and voice for the White Wolf, Mandred knew her powers were witchcraft. Faced with an enemy as inhuman and vile as the skaven, however, even the prospect of using witchcraft against the fiends hadn't troubled his conscience.

What did trouble him was the idea that Hulda was more – or perhaps less – than a witch. He couldn't shake the image of her – change – during the divination ritual. He couldn't forget the lupine paw that had reached out for Vrrmik's ear or the bestial voice that howled an incantation into the darkness. If he'd stirred from where he'd watched the ritual, what might he have seen? Would he have found the beautiful features of Hulda staring down into the cauldron or would it have been the fanged muzzle of a wolf?

Even the Graf of Middenheim, growing up inside the luxury of the Middenpalaz, had heard the shuddersome stories of the *Ulricskinder*, the half-human beasts who wore their fur inside their skin except at such times as they reverted to their animalistic selves. The werewolf, the loping horror that stalked the night, raging and ravening for human prey. It made even Mandred's heart quiver to think that Hulda might be one of the Children of Ulric.

He shook his head. His fear was unworthy of him, forged from myth and superstition. He must judge her by her own deeds, not the fables told him by his mother when he was a babe in swaddling. Hulda's counsel had been a source of strength to him, her eldritch knowledge a boon to the whole army. She'd warned them of the skaven ambush in Nordland, guided them through the haunted Laurelorn. She'd exposed Beck's murderous treachery.

Mandred let his eyes linger on the witch, forcing himself to see the woman, not the beast he'd half-glimpsed during her divination. Yet, if she was the beast, why should that disturb him? The white wolf had sought only to bring good to him. The animal had led him to the camp of the Kineater, enabling him to save Arch-Lector Hartwich and Lady Mirella from the beastman before they could become its next prey. The wolf had saved his life, savaging the Kineater before it could kill him. Later it had led him to Hulda's cave, where her counsel brought him the confidence he needed when self-doubt might have sent him scurrying back to Middenheim. And, more recently, it had been the white wolf that had fought to protect the shrine of Ulric and save Ar-Ulric during the skaven attack on Mandred's camp.

No, Mandred decided. He couldn't doubt Hulda. Whatever she was – prophetess, witch or werewolf – he had to trust her. If he doubted her now then he must also doubt her vision of the next skaven attack. He'd gambled everything on the accuracy of her divination. If Vrrmik didn't make his attack on Hergig, if the vermin instead struck somewhere else, everything would come falling apart. His army would scatter, returning to defend their homes. That would be the end of his crusade against the ratmen and, he knew, must eventually see the end of the Empire. Piecemeal, the skaven would pick off each province. It was only as a united force that they had any hope of survival.

Through the steel of his gauntlets, despite the chill in the air, Mandred could feel a warmth emanating from the golden head of Ghal Maraz. The ancient warhammer was lashed before him across his saddle where it was both within quick reach and clearly visible to the men marching around him. Hartwich had underestimated the hammer's potency as a symbol. It had given the soldiers a new sense of purpose, a new feeling of pride that made them accept even the ordeal of this long march without complaint. In every

fiefdom they had crossed, peasants had appeared to bring
such food and clothing as they could spare, selflessly sac-
rificing what little they had to aid Mandred's cause. When
these humble folk, the simple clay of humanity, gazed upon
Ghal Maraz, the look of awe and wonder in their faces told
him why they did what they did.

Mandred prayed that he might prove worthy of their awe,
that within him beat the heart of the hero who could deliver
the Empire as Sigmar had done over a millennium before. He
had grown beyond the hatred, the base brute lust for revenge
that had driven him when he'd first marched his army into
Drakwald. He knew now that this crusade against the skaven
was bigger and more important than simple hatred. It was
a war that had to be fought to ensure human survival, from
the most blue-blooded nobleman and esoteric priest to the
humblest peasant. Class meant nothing when the foot of
skaven oppression was on the neck of all men.

Riding beside him, General von Boeckenfoerde, the ren-
egade Reikmarshal, struck ice from the branch of a tree
standing beside the trail. 'This is the gentlest winter I've seen
in my sixty-four years,' he remarked. 'The gods must favour
this enterprise. By rights we should be knee deep in snow
right now.'

Mandred nodded. After almost a decade of unremittingly
harsh winters, this respite was like a gift from Ulric. As god
of both winter and war, perhaps the old wolf had set aside
the one so that he might facilitate the other. But it would all
depend on how accurate Hulda's divination was. It would
only hasten the destruction of his army if they made this
long march with no enemy at the end of the trail.

'Forgive my impertinence, highness,' von Boeckenfoerde
continued, 'but what reception do you expect your dignitaries to receive in Altdorf?'

'I am not counting on the army of Reikland to come marching forth to aid us,' Mandred confessed. 'All I have heard of Protector Kreyssig makes him out to be as much of a monster as Boris Goldgather was.' He let his hand fall again to Ghal Maraz's reassuring warmth. 'No, I think a calculating villain like him will sit back and wait to see what happens.'

'Yes, I think that swine will do just that,' von Boeckenfoerde said. 'He was always as cunning as a weasel. He had to be to rise so swiftly in Boris's service.' The general arched an eyebrow as a question that had been nagging at him found its way to his tongue. 'Do you think it was wise sending Captain von Kranzbeuhler? The man is Kreyssig's mortal enemy, after all.'

'He's the only man for the job,' Mandred said. 'Kurgaz will keep him safe, and Kreyssig won't dare make a move until he knows how our campaign in Hochland fares. He'll need to know if he is in a position to dictate terms or if he'll be the one being dictated to.'

Mandred looked away, turning his eyes again to Hulda and the long road ahead of them. 'I have room in my heart right now for only one enemy,' he said. 'When that enemy has been vanquished, then I'll turn my mind to the problem of Adolf Kreyssig.'

Water dripped from the vaulted ceiling of the old dwarfish tunnel, splashing against the toppled pillars and broken statues that had once lined this branch of the Ungdrin Ankor, the great Underway between the dwarf strongholds. Breached and shattered by both the elements and invaders, the tunnels had become a haunt for noxious creatures, few more vile than the beasts the dwarfs reviled as *thaggoraki* – murderers.

Among the ratkin, there could be no monster more murderous than Great Warlord Vrrmik. The hulking white ratman sat perched atop the headless shoulders of an ancient dwarf statue, slowly wiping the blood coating his claws into his pale pelt. His motions were slow, deliberate, designed to induce the maximum amount of fear in his followers. This stretch of the tunnel was almost a sea of furry bodies, beady skaven eyes glistening in the green glow of worm-oil lamps.

Vrrmik savoured the stench of their fear. He cast his gaze down to the twitching body at his feet, the simpering emissary from Clan Skully and the Old Rat Under the Hill. The villainous Murderlord Raksheed Deathclaw had defied Vrrmik's command, turning his slinking killers against the dwarfs of Karak Kadrin instead of responding to the warmonger's demand for fresh troops. Nor was Raksheed the only one to defy Vrrmik! The hordes of Clans Grikk and Skab had refused to send more than a few hundred emaciated slaves, citing their own attacks against the dwarfs as an excuse for their infidelity. Clan Mordkin, Clan Fester, even the minor clans like Gnaw and Fylch had refused to answer Vrrmik's muster.

There was a reason of course, one that made Vrrmik angry enough that he brought the enchanted head of Skavenbite slamming down into the body at his feet, splattering the corpse's brains across the tunnel.

Treachery! Base and vile treachery of the lowest and most miserable sort! Directed against the mighty Vrrmik, He Who is Twelfth, the right-paw of the Horned Rat!

Vrrmik's nose twitched as he sniffed at the dank air of the tunnel. He had dozens of Skrittlespike troglodytes and Moulder-bred rat-wolves sniffing around too, weeding out the sick and infected from his army, sick and infected with the great plague that Clan Pestilens had unleashed against the humans!

The plaguelords had grown powerful since unleashing their creation, but so too had Vrrmik. Now it seemed they wanted to try to topple him, to seize complete dominance for themselves! They'd turned their plague against skavendom. It was easy to understand how it had been achieved. Begin in Skavenblight and the contagion would swiftly disseminate across the Under-Empire, for wasn't the old adage that all tunnels lead to Skavenblight true?

Vrrmik gnashed his fangs and dropped his hammer into the mush at his feet a second time. As annoying as the lethality of the disease among the ratmen was, an inconvenience to his demands for bigger and vaster armies, it was the foolish rumours that spread which had wrought the most havoc. The credulous flea-brains were claiming the plague was being turned back on the skaven by Man-dread's curse, that the humans were now infecting *them*! Hence the lack of enthusiasm for pressing their attacks on the man-things, for expanding their control over the surface, the sudden interest in redirecting their forces and resources against the dwarfs, the blatant defiance of Vrrmik's own orders!

Vrrmik glowered to his left where Poxmaster Puskab Foulfur came creeping into the tunnel. The plaguelord presented a ridiculous sight, hobbling along in a rolling, surging gait as he tried to adjust his balance for the tail he'd lost. The antlers projecting from his skull kept threatening to drag his whole body face first into the ground.

Still, as ridiculous as Puskab might look, at the moment he was Vrrmik's best and truest ally. It was Puskab's magic that had created the Black Plague, now it was his magic that kept the disease at bay. Like Vrrmik, the Poxmaster didn't for an instant believe the stories about Man-dread's curse

and human transmission of the plague. No, he saw the
paws of his fellow plaguelord, Vrask Bilebroth behind this
calamity. His rival was jealous of Puskab and taking extreme
measures to discredit and destroy him.

Puskab's advice was for Vrrmik to turn his army against
Skavenblight, to destroy Vrask. The Supreme Warlord of
Skavendom, however, was too cunning to allow himself to
fall into such a trap. Getting involved in the feud between
the plaguelords would only bleed his own resources. There
was always the chance it was all just a plot to weaken Clan
Mors so that Clan Pestilens could assume complete control.

No, Vrrmik had a much better idea. He'd planned to whit-
tle away Man-dread's army by threatening their warrens, but
now he didn't have that luxury. He had to force a confronta-
tion with the human, butcher him in the open field before
the eyes of all skavendom. With Man-dread's blood soaked
into his fur, Vrrmik would quell the rumours of a curse and
the imbecilic fear that had spread among the ratkin. He
would show them that the only thing they should fear was
the ire of Great Warlord Vrrmik and the crash of Skavenbite
against their skulls!

Even now, he had spies following Man-dread's army. Once
Vrrmik was certain of their course, he would pick a place
to confront them. Ground of his own choosing. Ground
that would become a killing field under Vrrmik's merciless
command.

Skavenblight, 1123

Seerlord Queekual's procession forced its way through
the teeming hordes of ratmen. The streets and tunnels of

Skavenblight were crammed to bursting with the terrified masses. In places the skaven were heaped atop one another five and six deep, uncaring that those on the bottom of the pile would be crushed or smothered. The vermin feared a different sort of death, a death that stalked their burrows and warrens like a marauding beast, slaughtering great and lowly with indiscriminate abandon.

The Black Plague was loose in Skavenblight. It was raging in the lower depths, infesting the subterranean tunnels and warrens. Outbreaks had erupted in the most squalid of the surface areas, principally the mud-caked menagerie of docks and piers that stretched out into the foggy swamps. The gangs of slaves and farm-rats who tended the stands of black corn in the marshes had been decimated by the disease, entire barges leaving the city only to be found weeks later reduced to floating death ships with nary a twitch of life among the crew.

Fear gripped the hordes of Skavenblight, an enormity of terror such as the city had never seen. The skaven knew how the plague had exterminated the man-things, the agonising death to which Clan Pestilens's creation condemned the creatures. Now that hideous weapon had been turned back and unleashed upon their own kind. Hoary old rat-men recalled the long-ago affliction of Clan Verms and the quarantine of their stronghold underneath Skavenblight. They urged the warlock-engineers of Clan Skryre to purge the afflicted regions with their warpfire projectors, to burn the disease from the city.

It was too late for that, however. The plague had spread beyond any single clan, had established itself too broadly to be isolated and destroyed. In their desperation, some of the ratmen turned to the plague priests for salvation, abandoning themselves to the diseased heresy of Pestilens in the hope that doing so would save their lives. Many, the vast majority, took the opposite view. They saw Pestilens as the enemy. They saw Nurglitch as an ambitious tyrant and Puskab as a murderous betrayer. In such a stew of panic, confusion and outrage, the skaven fell back upon the beliefs and tradition of the past. They recanted their opportunistic rush towards the power promised by the plague monks and grovelled once again before the might of the Horned Rat.

Such a flood of despair and turmoil was like a font of limitless power for the skaven ruthless enough to tap into it. Seerlord Queekual was such a skaven.

While the other Grey Lords had retreated to their surface-world dominions, joining Vrrmik in his quest to destroy the Man-dread and quell the creature's uprising, Queekual had steadfastly refused to quit Skavenblight. Let the others squander their strength chasing after an uncertain fortune. Queekual knew better. He knew the past held the key to domination. The ancient proverb that 'all tunnels lead to Skavenblight' was a simple truth and behind it was the wisdom that only from Skavenblight could a ratman control the teeming hordes of the Under-Empire.

A canopy of weasel-skin was held above Queekual's horned head by a retinue of docile acolytes. A cloud of antiseptic incense wafted about him, surrounding him in a luminous fog as the grey-cloaked adepts bore smouldering braziers before him. A small army of red-armoured storm-vermin, their fur stained snowy white, their musk glands withered by special unguents to lend them a cold emotionless quality, formed the outer cordon of the Seerlord's procession. Mixed among the stormvermin were lesser grey seers, paw-picked by Queekual for their oratorical ability. From their fangs flew a ceaseless stream of condemnation and excoriation, the accusing voice of a god most of skavendom had thought to neglect.

Behind them all, carried upon the bed of an enormous carriage with thirteen sets of iron-banded wheels, nestled within a casement crafted from the bronzed skull of a giant, was the holiest relic in all skavendom: the Black Ark, the compact between the Horned Rat and the first Seerlord. Imprinted upon a block of purest warpstone, its quality unsurpassed by the richest ores ever found, were the thirteen tyrannies, the sacred dictates by which the skaven might placate their terrible god and achieve the promise He had made to them: that one day the ratkin would inherit the whole of the world.

The scent of the Black Ark, the aethyric pulses of energy rippling from its warpstone heart, excited the senses of the ratmen, hurling the weakest into apoplectic fits and reducing even the strongest to worshipful fright. The Black Ark was the foundation of the Order of Grey Seers, the rock upon which they had built their power. It was the holy of holies to those who cowered before the malign divinity of the Horned Rat. Rarely did the grey seers bring it forth from the secret vault at the heart of the maze deep beneath the Shattered Tower, and when they did it was a portent of gravest moment.

Seerlord Queekual drank in the intoxicating scent of the Black Ark, feeling its power flow through him like a dark shadow. For all their pretensions and heretical claims, the plague priests were nothing but charlatans playing at holiness. *This* was the true manifestation of the divine, not the febrile plagues and poxes brewed by the sickening Pestilens.

Queekual cocked his ears back in bitter amusement. There was nothing miraculous about the accomplishments of Poxmaster Puskab! Had he himself not smelled with his own nose a miserable, pathetic man-thing slave-meat re-create the vaunted Black Plague? Had he not himself unleashed this concoction against the impious vermin of Clans Scruten and Gangrous?

That thought gave Queekual pause, so much so that his step faltered. The acolytes carrying his canopy actually went ahead two paces, leaving their master's horned head exposed to the hated sky. They glanced at one another, glands clenching as they expected the wrath of their vicious Seerlord, but for once he had a worry taxing at his brain more dire than even his pronounced agoraphobia.

Scruten and Gangrous! Scum who dwelt in the lowest depths of Skavenblight! How then had the plague advanced into the warrens of Clan Grikk and the wharfs of Clan Sleekit? How had it spread so quickly into the burrows of Skab and Gnaw? Certainly it was to be expected that the disease might bleed over into the squalor of vermin like Skrittlespike and Feesik, but how could it strike into the enclaves of Ferrik and even Rictus?

Somehow the plague had slipped beyond Queekual's ability to control. If he hadn't taken such pains to destroy everything in the Moschner-man's laboratory, if he could credit mere slave-meat with such cunning, he'd almost be prepared to think the plague had somehow been released directly into the tunnels! But that was impossible! He'd taken pains to execute the stormvermin who burned Moschner's lab and collapsed the roof onto the remains. Their executioners too had been obliterated in the flames of a warpfire thrower and Queekual himself had attended to the warpfire operators, ensuring that there were no survivors at any level who could even hint at the nature of his grand scheme.

Yet, however impossible, the plague had defeated his

careful protocols. A few times Queekual had even enter-
tained the loathsome thought that perhaps the spread of
the disease had been the work of Pestilens themselves or
their daemonic god.

If so, the strategy devised by their diseased brains had spun
around and nipped them in the nethers! The unleashed
plague hadn't cowed the skaven into meek subservience to
the plaguelords! Far from it!

The mewing, chittering pleas of the hordes lining the
streets of Skavenblight were a cacophony of terrified devotion, prayers to Queekual begging him to intercede with
the Horned Rat and save the doomed masses. At every step,
his armoured bodyguards were compelled to stab and beat
the desperate crowd back, and even so there were those
who slipped past the white skaven, risking their lives in an
effort to touch the Seerlord's robe in the belief that his holy
raiment might endow them with some manner of divine
protection.

Queekual wasn't pleased by such signs of devotion,
alarmed by the proximity of afflicted skaven to his person.
It was true that he'd equipped himself with the most potent
protective talismans before venturing forth into the streets,
but there was no wisdom in forsaking caution. He'd made
examples of many of the offenders, obliterating them with
spells of such horrific violence that even his acolytes cringed
and looked away. No matter how thoroughly he annihilated
the trespassers, however, there were always more to take
their place.

Faith – it was a thing little removed from fear in the
mind of a skaven. And like fear, it was something a clever
manipulator could twist to his own purposes. Queekual
gloated over the magnitude of that exploitation. With each
death, with each fresh outbreak of the plague, the very fabric

of skaven society threatened to come crashing down. The Council of Thirteen was impotent to either contain or harness the terror of their vast horde of subjects. Only the grey seers could do so, only they could entice the masses away from unrest. Only they could offer the one thing that would stifle the turmoil. Only they could offer hope.

Queekual listened to the grisly crunch of bone being pulverised beneath the Black Ark's carriage. The iron-shod wheels smashed the bodies of the ratmen thrown beneath them with merciless violence. It was a variant upon the delusion that touching the Seerlord's robe would bring divine blessing. A sacrifice offered to the Black Ark was said to bring good fortune. There might be no truth in the myth, but the horde thronging the street was taking no chances. Again and again, ratmen were pushed out from that mass, thrown beneath the wheels by their fellows. A trail of black blood, like the slime of some titanic slug, stained the path behind the Black Ark.

The devotion and despair of Skavenblight's populace had been willingly surrendered into the paws of Queekual. From them, the Seerlord would forge a weapon even mightier than the Black Plague, a weapon that would tear down the arrogance and heresy of Pestilens.

⊰ CHAPTER XX ⊱

Hochland, 1124

The rocky slopes of Hochland's Howling Hills were pitted and scarred, slashed by ravines and gorges. It seemed as if the gods had simply dumped all the leftovers from the Middle Mountains onto the plains, a deranged jumble of limestone and granite stretching across leagues in a grotesque sea of stone. Blighted, barren of tree or shrub or any green thing, the rugged stone run was a lifeless wasteland.

Or at least it had been.

From their tunnels deep below the earth, the skaven had crept and crawled up into the Howling Hills. Swarms of the vermin lurked in each ravine and defile, their bestial squeaks and snarls rumbling up from the depths like the snarl of some subterranean behemoth. The noxious fug of skaven fur and musk slithered across the rocks in a pervasive stink, emboldening the ratkin with the scent of their overwhelming numbers.

Every ratman Vrrmik could coerce, bully or threaten had

been marched into the Howling Hills. The Supreme Warlord of Skavendom wasn't satisfied with the horde, of course. It should have been ten times its size, a swarm of skaven that would have made the Horned One himself spurt the musk of fear to watch it sweep across the land.

Naturally, such a concentration of ratkin had brought severe logistical problems. Entire thrall clans had been set upon as 'tunnel pork' during the march, their flesh sustaining Vrrmik's more valuable warriors. Whole tribes of goblins had been attacked and devoured by the rapacious rodents. Hordes of scavengers had been loosed upon the farms, fields and forests of Hochland to strip the region bare of every last scrap of food. Tree bark, grass roots, beetles and fleas, no source of sustenance had been spared.

Standing upon a stone column, a natural finger of rock protruding above the stone sea, Vrrmik could gaze down into the nearest of the ravines. It was like a pool of fur and gleaming skaven eyes, the clanrats packed so tightly that he suspected some of those closest to the walls of the fissure had been crushed by the press of their comrades. Such casualties wouldn't linger long; they'd be soon devoured by those around them. Indeed, a few more food-cycles and Vrrmik would have to demote another thrall clan from 'ally' to 'support'.

The massive white skaven preened his whiskers, dismissing the possibility with a shake of his head. It wouldn't come to that. Vrrmik's spies, the best sneaks and stalkers warpstone bribes could entice away from Clan Eshin, were even now filtering back to him and reporting the nearness of Man-dread's army. He could imagine their horror when they found the land stripped bare, offering nothing to sustain them or their horses. After their long march, the humans would be hoping to rest and fatten themselves before giving battle. The depredation of the land would give them no such chance. They would have to either fight or disband. Either way, Vrrmik would claim victory.

Of course, the great warlord hadn't left anything to chance. He'd been pleased by the way Man-dread had reacted to Puskab's attack on his camp. To that end, he'd ordered the scavenger bands to forsake some of the fodder they'd encountered. In each village and hamlet the ratkin had attacked, they'd left little stacks of decapitated heads to greet Man-dread's troops. Just the thing to make the deranged fool-meat too angry to think. The trail the scavengers left behind them was obvious enough for a troll to follow – straight from the scene of each atrocity and back to the Howling Hills.

Vrrmik stroked the gore-crusted head of Skavenbite, feeling the hot sizzle of the warpstone spikes singe his fur. The Howling Hills would become an abattoir. It was ground created for slaughter such as Vrrmik envisaged. The rocky, crumbling slopes were impassable for horses, stripping the man-things of their mobility. The ravines and gorges offered shelter from their archers and the dwarf thunderers who had joined them. The only choice left to Man-dread was that of attacking the skaven directly, he couldn't wait for the ratkin to come to him. Vrrmik could simply order the more useless of his troops butchered to feed his warriors; the man-things were too stupid to be so pragmatic. They'd waste away and starve instead.

No, Man-dread would come to Vrrmik. He would march his men straight into the Howling Hills where the vast tide of the skaven would exterminate them all.

The last hope of the man-things would die beneath Vrrmik's hammer.

* * *

After marching through the ravaged countryside of Hochland, through forests of denuded trees and villages of
slaughtered men, the bleak desolation of the Howling
Hills presented a culminating horror for the army that
had marched so long and so far to save this land. Gazing up at the stone run from the plain below, the soldiers
felt oppressed in spirit and mind by the hellish sight. The
sounds and stink of the skaven told them that somewhere
in that desolation their inhuman enemy lurked, waiting for
the men to dare to trespass upon the craggy slopes of stone.

Mandred felt the mood of his army falter at the edge of
despair. All this way, across half the Empire, these men had
followed him, taking heart from the hope he offered them.
The vision of a land freed from the ratkin, the dream of a
world liberated from the tyranny of monsters – these were
the promises that had spurred these men on, made them
persevere in the face of cruellest hardship and adversity.
Now the faith that had sustained them for so long was frag-
menting, crumbling away before his very eyes. The hope of
victory was gone, vanished like a mocking illusion. To fight
the skaven in open battle would have been hard enough,
but to fight them in such terrain as this, to engage them
in the desolate stone flow with its concealing ravines and
gorges, seemed a hopeless prospect.

There was no going back. Mandred knew that. To turn
away now would see his army scatter to the wind. The only
choice he had was to fight. They had to fight here on the
ground the skaven had chosen, ground that robbed the
humans of two of their advantages over the ratkin: the
mobility of cavalry and the reach of archery. The ratmen,
with their greater speed and numbers, sheltered among the
rocks, able to manoeuvre by scent around the confusion of
boulders and ravines, held every advantage now. It was only

through such superiority that the beasts would countenance any battle. If their leader, Vrrmik believed there was any possibility the humans could win, his force would never take the field.

Only one advantage still remained to Mandred, an edge that Vrrmik could never take from him. The soldiers who marched behind his banner were men and it was the hearts of men that beat within their breasts, hearts that could be moved to selflessness, could be stirred to valour and fired with courage. However numerous Vrrmik's horde, they were skaven, they were cringing beasts driven by fear and greed, incapable of believing in anything more vital than their own skins. Terror and avarice were the forces that drove them on, but such things could only stretch so far, overcome only so much. Mandred's troops could endure more than Vrrmik's monsters. That was the one strength the skaven could never equal.

Mandred marched before his troops, eyes roving over the face of each man, matching each gaze, peering into each soul. 'The road has been long to reach this place,' he told his men. 'Never have men endured so much, come so far for such noble purpose. You have not marched here for plunder, you have not taken up sword and spear in the name of conquest, you have not left behind your homes and families simply to fill the coffers of kings and lords. No, it is nothing so base that has led you here but rather a nobility of spirit that drives you to seek a dream greater than yourselves. In your veins burns the fire of a glory mightier than gold, a splendour greater than that of kings and courts! In you I see the majesty of mankind, the foundation upon which the future will stand! You are the pillars of a thousand tomorrows; on your deeds will your children and your children's children upon their many generations look back in awe and wonder. They will whisper of your valour, of the strength in your arm and the boldness in your heart, and they will marvel that such might could be contained within mortal clay!

'Our enemy is vile, obscene in their foulness! You have seen their savagery! You have seen their cruelty! You have marched through the lands they have despoiled, heard the people they have enslaved! Hochland has been razed by these monsters, transformed into a lifeless desert by their hunger! Such will be the fate of your homelands if the vermin prevail!'

Mandred clenched his fist, shaking it at the heavens. 'The skaven will not prevail!' he told his troops. 'Here they will be broken, shattered upon our steel! They fight for domination, to sate their greed. We fight for our homes, for our families, for those we would keep safe from the horrors of Old Night. It is our cause that is just; it is our fight that is righteous!'

He watched as he saw the old determination settle once more on the faces of his men as they rallied to his words. Mandred felt his pride swell as he saw the unyielding set of one Nordlander's jaw, the defiant scowl on the face of an Averlander, the cold fury in the eyes of a mercenary Roppsman. He pointed his hand at the soldiers, waving his finger at them. 'Do not let the enemy frighten you with their numbers. However overwhelming they may seem, remember that they are but vermin. However many they are, each of them fights alone. You fight with comrades! You fight knowing the man beside you guards your back! You fight knowing that your deeds will be remembered, that if you fall your sacrifice is not in vain! You fight for the Empire and the gods themselves will praise your valour!'

Mandred raised the bulk of Ghal Maraz high, letting the glow of the warhammer shine out across his soldiers. He brought the weapon swinging down, pointing it at the Howling Hills, at the great spire of broken stone where the tattered banners of Vrrmik and Clan Mors fluttered in the breeze. 'I march to bring death to the ratkin,' he snarled. 'I march to strike terror in their craven hearts. I march to show them that they are not masters of men, but simply vermin to be crushed underfoot. Who marches with me?'

A great shout rose from Mandred's army. He could feel the ground shudder under his feet as thousands of soldiers followed their commander up onto the broken sea of stone. They knew the enemy was waiting for them, that theirs was to be the most dangerous and vital role in the battle, yet they marched boldly into the battle knowing that their leader, the valiant Graf Mandred, marched with them. Mandred asked none of them to brave danger that he shunned for himself, demanded no risk greater than his own.

Behind them, the soldiers left the archers and cavalry, the artillery and the whole of their camp. They had their own part to play in the battle, but first the infantry must spring the skaven trap.

Mandred would see that trap turned in upon itself, that it might catch the hunters instead of the prey.

Either way, the Howling Hills would soon become the greatest graveyard in the Old World. For man or ratkin was the matter that remained in question. And upon the answer rested the fate of the whole Empire.

Sylvania, 1123

From the shadows of the forest, eyes burning with hate studied the silent battlements of Vanhaldenschlosse. The

fortress was as still as the tomb. For a year there had been
no sign of life within its grim halls, yet such was the terrifying aura that clung to the name of the place that even the
boldest grave-robber had shunned it like the plague. Even
in death, the power of Vanhal held Sylvania in a grip of fear.

A withered hand clenched into a bony fist. All the world
believed Vanhal dead, slain at the Battle of Fellwald by the
skaven. Only one soul in all creation knew better, knew the
venomous intellect that even now reposed upon his skeletal
chair replenishing his arcane power.

Vanhal was so confident in that power, so arrogant in his
mastery of the black arts that he had become dismissive of
any rival. So far above any other sorcerer or warlock was
he that he allowed himself to forget that these too were
wielders of magical power. In orchestrating the humiliating
destruction of his apprentice, he had ignored the fact that
Lothar von Diehl was a necromancer in his own right.

It had taken every reserve of magic he could call upon
to stave off death when the fangs of Nekrot ripped into
his flesh, but Lothar had survived. He had dragged himself from the field of battle, hidden himself in a place
so benighted and forsaken that even the skaven couldn't
find him. There, over the long months, he had nursed the
embers of life clinging to his ravaged body into a blazing
furnace of hate.

The filthy peasant had left him for dead. Now Frederick
van Hal would rue that mistake. He would discover in his
last moments that whatever power he could command,
Lothar von Diehl was still better than him. Nobility would
always be superior to base-born scum.

Lothar pictured his hated mentor ensconced upon a
throne of skulls. In his memory, he retraced the corridors,
re-walked the stairs that climbed to Vanhal's sanctum. Every

step, every turn, was etched indelibly upon his memory.

The necromancer raised his withered claw, making sorcerous passes he had studied in the profane pages of *De Arcanis Kadon*. The tome had brought him to Vanhal, elevated him from a mere dabbler in the occult to a true practitioner of the black arts. Vanhal had expanded his own power with the eldritch knowledge of Kadon, had profited greatly by the forbidden secrets. Now that profit was at an end. Now Vanhal would become a victim of the very spells he had plundered from the shadows of Mourkain.

The grisly thing standing beside Lothar shuddered into a semblance of life as the necromancer's magic saturated its decayed flesh and corrupt bones. The Voivode of Sylvania, the merciless Count Malbork von Drak. Lothar had found the nobleman's corpse lodged under the roots of an old oak tree. Some vindictive foe had torn open the tyrant's chest and removed his black heart.

It was inconsequential. Malbork's body didn't need a heart to respond to his commands. Malbork's spirit didn't need a heart to whisper its secrets in the necromancer's ear. Through the reanimated husk of the voivode, Lothar had acquired what he needed: the weapon that would spell Vanhal's doom.

Lothar pointed to the massive lead casket resting on the ground beside him. As a living man, it had been necessary for Lothar to remove the sacred chains and holy seals with which the Verenan priesthood had protected the casket. That was as far as he would go, however. What was within the box was reputed to be so deadly that the slightest brush against it was to invite death. No, it was not for the necromancer to tempt fate. That was the duty of his undead slave.

Dutifully, as when claiming the casket from the vaults beneath Castle Drakenhof, the zombified carcass of Malbork von Drak bent down and fumbled at the catches. It took the creature some time, but at last its rotting fingers threw back the slide. A mephitic vapour vented into the air as the lid was thrown back. Inside, wrapped round with the mouldering shreds of a holy tapestry, was a wicked blade of blackened metal, not iron or steel, but some infernal ore that exuded a foul atmosphere of malice.

Even before he'd acquired *De Arcanis Kadon*, Lothar had known of this sword. His grandfather had tried to bribe a lay priest at the temple to steal it, but the thief was discovered by the inquisitors before he could make good his crime. According to his grandfather's notes, the sword was enchanted, endowed with the most murderous magic ever conceived by man. So steeped in death was this sword that it would drain the life from the very hand that wielded it.

This was the magic he would pit against Vanhal. Lothar knew all the secrets of the fortress, all the traps that lay in wait for the unwary. It would be almost as easy as murdering his father in the family castle.

A snap of his bony fingers sent Lothar's slave shambling off, the black blade clenched in its decayed fist. Malbork staggered at first, but Lothar infused him with greater energy, conjuring the very same incantation Vanhal had termed his 'Danse Macabre'. With firmer step, guided by the terrible resolve of its master, the zombie marched into the haunted halls of Vanhaldenschlosse.

The dark fog of dream and nightmare bound itself about the essence of Vanhal. Each pulsation of aethyric power brought with it new images of might and horror. He could see great vistas of desert oblivion, awesome obelisks and titanic temples lying shattered and forlorn in the drifting sand. The phantoms of a thousand yesterdays distilled into a single moment of terror, the gestalt scream of a murdered world its echoes rippling across all the tomorrows that might ever be.

Amid the panoply of death there was the silence and serenity of the eternal. Pain, suffering, the slow decay of toil, the cruel deceit of hope, the malign mockery of achievement, the ceaseless pursuit of wealth – these were abolished, exterminated to plague man no more. Nothing was left but the peace of oblivion.

Vanhal winced as shadows drifted through his soul. He felt the presence of others, others beyond that black fire which blazed within the core of his being. They were faint, fleeting shapes, faces almost half-forgotten: a man, a woman and a child. They beckoned to him with desperate severity, crying out to him. They did not beg for themselves. They begged for the man who had been Frederick van Hal.

Agony erupted through Vanhal's wizened body. He could feel the poisoned blade being thrust through the back of his throne, breaking his spine as it gouged its way sideways to skewer his heart and crack his ribs. When he opened his eyes, he could see the black tip of the blade protruding from his chest, his blood steaming upon its corrosive edge.

He knew that blade. Something inside him knew the searing pain, recalled it with cold and merciless memory. There was a cruel, terrifying irony that this blade should have endured from the age of antiquity, survived to again play such a part. Even the magic of a god was unequal to the loathsome magics that had been infused into the assassin's sword. It was the very finger of Death itself.

Vanhal could hear the spectres in his mind crying out to him, striving so hard to bear his spirit away with them. Ghostly tears fell from the woman's eyes. Almost he could put a name to her. Anya? Alyssa? She had been important to him. Once.

Invoking the last of his sorcery, the necromancer forced his cold flesh to move, to turn his head and face his killer. The assassin already lay upon the floor, the husk that had been Malbork von Drak was rapidly decaying into a pool of corruption. Vanhal could sense the ribbons of magic yet clinging to the corroding zombie, a familiar pattern that lent fresh vigour to his fading spirit. The flame of vengeance banished the beckoning wraiths, leaving only a fearsome determination. Across the evaporating ribbons of energy, Vanhal projected his hatred, following the trail of the conjured back to the conjurer, back to where his erstwhile apprentice Lothar was exulting in his murderous accomplishment, the triumph of his undead assassin over his terrifying mentor.

Lothar's jubilation collapsed as Vanhal's hatred made itself felt. The voice of the master necromancer whispered in the mind of the apprentice. 'When you die,' it said, 'your flesh belongs to me.'

Vanhal's hate dissipated, leaving Lothar curled up upon the barren earth, shuddering and weeping in the grip of his horror. The apprentice knew he had succeeded, knew he had destroyed his master's body and sent his spirit into the darkness of the beyond.

But how long would the hate of Vanhal remain in the void? That was the question that would haunt Lothar the rest of his days.

How ever many the ghost of Vanhal saw fit to allow him.

⤙ CHAPTER XXI ⤚

Hochland, 1124

Great Warlord Vrrmik chittered in delight when he saw Man-dread's troops begin climbing up onto the broken slopes of the Howling Hills. The fool-meat had divided his forces, leaving many of his soldiers on the plain below. He could see the long line of archers, the little blocks of horsemen, the squads of dwarfs scurrying about the encampment assembling their catapults, as though they might lay siege to the hills above them! The boulder-strewn river of stone would make a mockery of their pathetic efforts. What did it matter if they added a few more rocks to the natural rubble, if they crushed a few dozen hapless ratmen here and there? For that matter, how well would Man-dread's archers fare trying to pick off skaven in those brief intervals when there was neither crevice nor boulder to conceal them? Their only real chance would be to loose their arrows when the skaven rushed Man-dread's infantry, and Vrrmik knew from past experience how squeamish the man-things were about shooting into their own forces. Better for the fool-meat to have armed the bowmen with knives and brought them along as a meat-shield to act as a buffer between Vrrmik's clanrats and his more valuable fighters.

Vrrmik's tail lashed in anger as he considered the cavalry below, waiting behind the line of archers in squadrons of lancers and knights. The arrogance of such deployment infuriated him. Man-dread was so confident of routing the skaven that the cretin actually held his horses in reserve, hoping to use them to run down the ratmen when they broke and tried to flee! The pomposity! Vrrmik would butcher his way through Man-dread's infantry and then unleash his entire horde upon the dispirited knights when *they* turned to flee. Their steeds would make excellent eating after weeks of roots, tree bark and tunnel pork.

First would come the destruction of Man-dread. Vrrmik snarled at the chieftains around him, sending the vermin scurrying off to rally their clanrats. The great warlord had been very careful about calculating how many warriors to unleash against Man-dread's troops. Too few and the humans would simply march right over them. Too many and the humans might be overwhelmed. There had to be just the right amount of skaven in the first assault to hold the humans and weaken them. When it was time for the kill, when Vrrmik was certain Man-dread had been weakened enough, it would be himself and Clan Mors that would strike the final blow.

'Puskab,' Vrrmik snarled, glaring at the decayed plague priest as the noxious creature scuttled into view. 'Bring-fetch your monks. They will take the position of honour when I lead the final attack.' Puskab looked less than enthusiastic about using his remaining followers as the vanguard of Vrrmik's attack, but a display of the warmonger's fangs improved his attitude drastically. Bobbing his horned head, the plaguelord scampered off to carry out his orders.

Vrrmik laughed as he watched the plague priest slither back into the ravine and bully his way through the massed ranks of armoured stormvermin. Puskab was a useful idiot for the moment, but once this battle was finished Vrrmik would need to reassess the Poxmaster's usefulness. With the Black Plague beyond the ability of Clan Pestilens to contain or control, Vrrmik was reconsidering the advisability of associating with them. The grey seers and their leader Seerlord Queekual were enjoying a resurgence of influence and popularity in plague-ridden Skavenblight. Offering them the pelt of the Poxmaster would go far in winning their friendship.

The great warlord turned his baleful gaze back to the slope and the pathetic human force climbing up to confront his mighty horde. First things first; he would scratch these fleas out of his fur and then worry about the Pestilens-tick.

As the first swarms of clanrats rose up from the rocks and charged into Man-dread's ranks, the delicious smell of blood and slaughter struck Vrrmik's nose. It mattered little that much of the blood carried the tang of ratkin, the odour was intoxicating just the same. It excited his metabolism, made his mouth salivate with the hunger for battle. He knew the same sensations would be pulsing through the bodies of his stormvermin, goading them into a fury that would be sated only with the flesh of fallen foes in their bellies and the taste of man-thing blood on their fangs. That there were so few of the humans would goad his warriors to fight all the harder for there wouldn't be enough manflesh to go around.

Fool-meat Man-dread, who dared to think he could match

wits with Mighty Vrrmik! The great warlord was almost ashamed that the battle was so one-sided.

Not that he would have had it any other way.

The glowing head of Ghal Maraz came smashing down into the armoured head of a skaven war-chief, shattering both the steel helm the beast wore and the skull beneath. The creature crumpled into a gory heap at Mandred's feet, its rancid blood spilling across his boots. The graf stepped over its twitching carcass and brought his warhammer swinging around into the chest of the sword-rat lunging forwards to exploit the gap left by its slaughtered leader. The creature uttered a terrified squeak and was flung back into the swarming ranks of its verminous kin.

Another skaven dove in from the side, flecks of foam dripping from its fangs as it tried to spit Mandred on the end of its spear. The attack ended in an agonised squeal and a welter of black blood as the cleaving edge of Legbiter came slashing down, ripping the ratkin from shoulder to collar. Arch-Lector Hartwich wiped the skaven gore from his face and smiled at Mandred.

'Don't you trust Sigmar to look after his Wolf?' Mandred laughed at the priest.

Hartwich raked Legbiter's edge across the face of another charging skaven, sending the ratman stumbling back and pawing at the ruin where its eyes had been. 'Just putting the sword you loaned me to good effect,' he said.

'A runefang's place is in battle,' Mandred returned, smashing the legs out from under an armoured ratman. 'And I have my hands full with the gift you bestowed on me,' he added, bringing Ghal Maraz hurtling down to crush the head of the wounded ratman.

'Save your praise for Lord Sigmar,' Hartwich advised. 'I am

but his instrument.' The priest's words ended in a grunt as one of the ratmen hurled the thrashing body of its wounded kin and brought its blade slashing down into his shoulder. The mail beneath his priestly vestment thwarted the biting edge, but the impact left him staggered. Before the skaven could capitalise on its foe's impairment, it was itself spitted by a spearman, one of the peasant troops who had flocked to Mandred's banner. The creature collapsed to the ground, trying to push its entrails back into its belly. A second thrust from another spearman transfixed its throat and ended its loathsome struggles.

All around him, Mandred bore witness to the veracity of his words to his men. Noble, priest or peasant, they fought together, comrades-in-arms, each soldier watching out for his fellow. The ratkin had no such camaraderie. They attacked alone, they died alone and their wounded were trampled beneath the paws of their own kind. They were unleashed against the humans in bestial packs and like beasts they fought. It was the coordination, the mutual support of the humans that repulsed them time and again, forcing them back, breaking each successive wave.

There must come a tipping point, however. No matter how coordinated his troops, Mandred knew there would come a moment when the superior numbers of the skaven would overwhelm his men. For each ratkin they killed, six more seemed to come scurrying out from the rocks. The skaven reserves seemed limitless, while each casualty the monsters inflicted represented an irreplaceable loss. For the nonce, the formation was holding, the outer ring of shields and swords protecting an inner core of spears. Like a steel turtle, the armoured shell was protecting the soft body within, allowing the formation to creep slowly up the jagged slope. Once that shell was punctured, Mandred knew the cohesion of his command would be finished.

Desperately Mandred wanted to look back down to the plain below, wanted to see if the other half of his plan was being put into action. General von Boeckenfoerde knew his orders, knew he couldn't act too soon or it would all be for nothing. Mandred's infantry had to climb far enough into the Howling Hills to break through when the tide turned. He had to be near enough to exploit the confusion when it came, to charge straight up into the mouth of the trap. They had to assault that high point where the ratkin banners had flown, the peak where Hulda assured him that the scent of Vrrmik was at its strongest. If the great warlord escaped, there could be no victory here, all they could win was a reprieve.

Jubilant cheers sounded from the men at the centre of the formation. It was the first indication to Mandred that von Boeckenfoerde had ordered the attack. As he pulped the body of a skaven warrior, the graf could see a ball of fire hurtling overhead to his left. The mass of vermin assaulting the formation blocked his view of the missile as it came crashing down among the rocks, but the cacophony of squeaks and squeals told him of its impact and the impact of dozens like it all across the stone river.

The Howling Hills, that jumble of broken rock and jagged boulders, were like a natural fortress, a place teeming with hiding places for the skaven to lurk in ambush. To try to unleash a barrage against the entire range would have been futile, instead Mandred had conceived the plan to strike along a very narrow front – the flanks of his own advancing force. As the skaven came swarming to the attack, creeping and crawling through the ravines and gorges, they brought themselves into the killing ground. More, by the route of their advance they exposed to the men below their hiding places, providing the artillery with still more targets.

The missiles thrown by von Boeckenfoerde's catapults weren't stones. They were fireballs cobbled together from broken-up wagons, dead trees, tents, blankets, spare clothing – anything in the army's supply train that would burn. Gunpowder from the dwarfs was added to some of the missiles, bags of pungent dung to others, anything to further confuse and disorient the ratkin whether by sound or smell. As the burning missiles slammed into the stone flow, they shattered, raining down into the ravines and gorges, filling them with heavy black smoke.

All along the stone flow the raucous squeals of the ratkin became deafening. Deep down inside their ravines, the skaven didn't know the reason for the blazing debris that rained down on their heads, the distant crack and boom of gunpowder reverberating among the rocks, the noxious stench of the blinding smoke that billowed across their positions. They were unable to appreciate the magnitude of the attack. Isolated and alone, communication severed by the assault of the catapults on the plain below, the skaven were only aware of their own small piece of the battle.

Panic reigned as the besieged ratkin began to flee their hiding places, scampering back down the narrow fissures running throughout the Howling Hills. As the assaulted positions broke, they charged headlong into their own warriors further back among the hills. Like an infection, their panic spread to the other skaven, the scent of their fear impacting against the other vermin and sending them likewise into full retreat.

The tide was turning, but Mandred's infantry were still merely a tiny island in a sea of ratkin. Victory was anything but assured.

* * *

'Fool-meat! Dung-sniffing flea-fondlers!' Vrrmik brought the murderous head of Skavenbite slamming down into one of his sub-chiefs, obliterating the ratman's rib cage and sending his maimed body spinning down among the rocks. The rest of the great warlord's retinue cringed away from their enraged overlord, chittering anxiously to one another, sometimes trying to push a despised rival just a little closer to Vrrmik and his hammer.

Vrrmik licked the blood of his slaughtered minion from his muzzle and glared down at the shifting battlefield. The Howling Hills had taken on a hellish appearance, smoking as though a lava flow were running through its ravines. More and more of the burning missiles were hurtling down into the stone sea, pelting the ratkin in the ravines with flaming debris and filling the crevices with smoke. Many of the weak-livered vermin were in full rout, scampering away through the ravines, hurrying back to the tunnels that would lead them back into the underworld.

As infuriating as that was, Vrrmik found the actions of his bolder warlords and chieftains still more aggravating. Perhaps more aware of what was happening than the routed ratkin, these chiefs were leading their warriors down the slopes to attack the humans on the plain below. Vrrmik could easily imagine the moronic thirst for glory and favour that motivated these weak-minded dolts. They thought they could jockey for better position by ending the barrage and recovering the situation for the great warlord. What they were actually doing was leaving the safety of their cover and scurrying straight into the murderous archery of the man-things below! That nine of every ten of these suicidal mobs carried the banner of Clan Mors or one of its thrall clans only added to Vrrmik's fury.

Two of the swarms actually reached the plain with some

strength left in them. From the height of the hilltop, Vrrmik could see that their success had only brokered them a different kind of death. The human archers fell back as the skaven came leaping down from the rocks, drawing aside and allowing the waiting cavalry to come charging in. The resultant massacre was like watching a troll wrestle a goblin.

Vrrmik gnashed his fangs. His carefully conceived plan was coming apart all around him. The strength of Clan Mors was bleeding away between his fingers, threatening his position as He Who is Twelfth and his authority as Supreme Warlord of all Skavendom!

Drastic measures were called for if he were to snatch survival from the fangs of destruction!

Imperiously, Vrrmik pointed the dripping head of Skavenbite at Puskab Foulfur and his plague monks. 'Poxmaster!' the white skaven snarled. 'You will attack now! Kill-slay all man-things! No worry-fear. Great Vrrmik will follow you into battle!'

Suppressing a shudder, the plague priest snapped commands to his followers and the green-garbed monks began scurrying down the slope towards Man-dread's warriors. Vrrmik let them gain a good lead before ordering his own stormvermin to advance.

It wouldn't do to follow too closely. There was just a chance that Puskab might have his own ideas about exploiting the confusion of battle to remove an ally he no longer found beneficial.

The successive waves of skaven crashing against Mandred's troops finally began to falter. The vermin on the flanks and at the rear of the human wedge broke away, slinking back into the rocks. Von Boeckenfoerde's barrage had driven off their reserves and depleted the press of fresh ratkin rushing to bolster the assault. Without the hordes of ratmen at their back, the attackers finally lost heart, their ferocity collapsing into fright. First by ones and twos, then by the score, they turned tail and fled.

It was a near thing. The human battle-line had been savaged, most of the men in the outer ring sporting at least one wound. The bodies of many comrades lay strewn in the wake of Mandred's advance, littering the slope below. The tightness of the contracted formation told Mandred better than words how severe the casualties had been. Perhaps as much as a fifth of his force lay dead among the rocks. The strength of those who remained was starting to ebb.

Yet there was still much killing to be done. Seeing the skaven on the flanks and to the rear falter, Vrrmik pressed home the attack at the fore, throwing armoured, black-furred monsters at the humans. The brutal killers hacked away at Mandred's troops, pushing them back, forcing them in upon the lightly armed peasant troops at the core of the formation. Wielding Ghal Maraz, Mandred found himself becoming separated from the line, the warhammer's magic enabling him to prevail where the swords of his comrades faltered.

Only Arch-Lector Hartwich remained at Mandred's side. The two men guarded each other's back, Legbiter and Ghal Maraz taking a butcher's toll from the ratkin. The havoc wrought by the magic weapons became too much even for the black-furred monsters. They began to cringe back, whining and refusing to listen to the threats of their chieftains.

Finally, the stormvermin broke away entirely, falling back and leaving a gap between their ranks and the ground Mandred and Hartwich defended. Before the two leaders could start to withdraw back towards their own troops, the black wall of stormvermin parted, opening a path for the ghoulish creatures that came charging to the attack.

Mandred recognised the diseased stink of these creatures as much as their decayed green robes. Plague monks, the pestilential progenitors of death and disease that had wrought such havoc among the great cities of the Empire, the foul monsters that had decimated Carroburg and enslaved its populace. The plague monks rushed forwards with rabid ferocity, wielding wooden staves and rusty swords in a frenzied assault. Behind the robed monsters, Mandred saw a creature he recognised from the reports of the Teutogen Guard, the antlered plague priest that had killed Ar-Ulric.

Roaring with the fury of the vengeance that burned in his heart, Mandred brought Ghal Maraz whipping around, pulverising the first clutch of plague monks as they leapt towards him. Their pulped bodies were hurled through the air, crashing down among their comrades, tripping them up as they charged forwards.

'Now is our chance!' Hartwich urged Mandred, tugging at his shoulder, trying to pull him back towards their own troops.

The graf shrugged the priest off. Grimly, he stalked forwards and brought the blazing hammer swinging around again. Roaring in rage, he crushed the skull of one plague monk and collapsed the chest of a second. Oblivious to the fate of their kin, the rest of the diseased monsters continued their attack, a grisly green light blazing in their putrid eyes.

Mandred staggered back at the force of the attack, pressed back by the intensity of the plague monks. He could see the horned priest behind them, its talon raised in a scabrous benediction, each claw glowing with the same baleful light that burned in the eyes of its disciples. Witchcraft! Some abominable sorcery driving the other plague monks to suicidal fury. Mandred howled at the monstrous injustice. To come so close only to be cheated by such perfidious magic.

The howl seemed to echo among the rocks, answered by a still more savage cry. The ranks of stormvermin lifted their heads, sniffing at the air and chittering nervously. The plague priest turned its head, a tinge of fright playing about its eyes. Leaping out from among the rocks, hurtling above the heads of the massed ratkin, was a creature more bestial than them. A great white wolf, an animal Mandred had seen many times before, a beast he knew only too well.

The wolf landed among the plague monks, ripping at them right and left with its snapping jaws. The fright in the eyes of the plague priest grew into outright terror as it beheld the beast that had bitten its tail off. The glowing claws of its outstretched hand blazed with even greater intensity. The ensorcelled plague monks desisted in their attack on Mandred, turning instead to attack the wolf. One of their cudgels smashed against the animal's head, driving it low.

Before the monsters could fall upon the stunned wolf, Mandred was among them. Ghal Maraz crushed them like insects, spattering the hillside with the filth of their bodies. Legbiter clove through the verminous brutes that slipped away from Mandred's assault as Hartwich rushed forwards to support the nobleman's advance, refusing to abandon the graf.

'Guard her,' Mandred snarled at Hartwich as Ghal Maraz sent the carcass of the last plague monk spinning through the air. He waited only to see the Sigmarite nod before he turned towards the horned plague priest.

The glow had faded from the creature's claws. It glared malignantly at Mandred, snapping at the stormvermin around it, ordering the armoured skaven to attack and defend it from the human. The other ratkin weren't so eager to rush within reach of Ghal Maraz after seeing it in action.

Snarling in its wrath, the plague priest spun around. Its

jaws opened wide, vomiting forth a stream of corrosive vileness such as it had used against Ar-Ulric. This time the ratman loosed its magic against its own kind, burning down a dozen stormvermin and sending scores of others scampering off in terror.

Mandred was confused by this treacherous, fratricidal attack until he saw the hulking white-furred ratman standing amid the steaming carcasses of its murdered warriors. He recognised the skaven warlord whose ear he'd clipped in Averheim, recognised too the stolen Drakdrazh clutched in its paws. Some fell magic had preserved Vrrmik from the plague priest's magic, merely disorienting the monster where those around it had been killed. The horned priest was presenting Mandred with a choice: attack it and sate his vengeance or attack Vrrmik and win his battle.

The choice was a bitter one, but Mandred knew which path he must take. As he charged across the corroded bodies of the stormvermin, he could hear the plague priest chitter in amusement. It was no stretch of imagination to picture the fiend skittering away.

Great Warlord Vrrmik reeled as his world was suddenly enveloped in steaming, searing pain. The anguished squeaks of his own bodyguards filled his ears, the stink of their melting flesh filled his nose. He tried to blink away the gibbous green blaze of Puskab's magic.

Traitor-meat! No fawning excuse or flattering lie would save the Poxmaster now! Vrrmik knew the scent of the worm-eater's sorcery. He'd feed the maggot his own spleen, make him eat his own paws one by one before he allowed the mouse-livered scum to die! No hole in the Under-Empire would be deep enough, no burrow in all skavendom remote enough to hide Puskab from his wrath! He'd...

As vision returned to Vrrmik's eyes, he forgot about vengeance against Puskab. Charging through the parted ranks
of his stormvermin, trampling the steaming corpses of his
slain warriors, was Man-dread, an enormous warhammer
clenched in his hands!

Vrrmik leapt back, narrowly avoiding the downward
sweep of Man-dread's hammer. Baring his fangs, growling
his fury, he swung out with Skavenbite, investing his attack
with all the outrage and wrath Puskab's betrayal had sent
coursing through his heart.

Man-dread blocked the downward sweep of Skavenbite,
locking the haft of his own hammer against that of Vrrmik's
before the brutal enchantment locked inside the warlord's
weapon could shatter every bone in his body. They stood
there a moment, man and skaven, each struggling to push
the other back. Vrrmik's raw, brutal strength began to tell,
his warpstone-enhanced musculature overwhelming the
brawn of his human foe. The ratman squeaked in delight,
not even bothering to call in his warriors to assist him.

When Man-dread suddenly rolled away from Vrrmik, the
overlord's hammer came smashing down, pulverising the
stones and sending little slivers of rock scything into the air.
The skaven reared back, springing back to the attack with
the inhuman swiftness of his verminous breed.

Man-dread's hammer was already swinging towards
him. Skavenbite's destructive magic, dragon-slaying runes
engraved upon it by dwarf runesmiths in ages past and further magnified by bands of pure warpstone, collided with
the enchantment of Ghal Maraz's glowing head.

Vrrmik was thrown through the air as Skavenbite shattered against Ghal Maraz. Fragments of the broken hammer
slashed through the ratman's flesh and fur, digging deep
furrows in his body as they pierced his warpstone armour.

Tattered, bleeding and broken, the Great Warlord of Clan Mors, the Warmonger of Skavenblight, the Supreme Warlord of all Skavendom, lay sprawled among the rocks. He struggled to lift himself, to crawl away, but severed nerves and torn muscles refused to obey him. He could only gnash his fangs when he saw Man-dread standing above him. As he watched the human lift Ghal Maraz overhead, Vrrmik hissed only a single word, a curse he wished upon the head of the ratkin who had brought him to such an end.

'Treason!' Vrrmik snarled in the instant before Ghal Maraz came crashing down.

Mandred turned away from the twitching carcass of Great Warlord Vrrmik, casting his smouldering gaze across the ranks of skaven warriors who had just watched him reduce the head of their leader into a bloody smear. One step towards them was enough. Squeaking in terror, the ratkin fled, scurrying back into the ravines and crevices.

Slowly, Mandred made his way back to Hartwich. He noted with some confusion that the priest no longer wore his vestment over his armour. Instead the arch-lector's robe was thrown about the body he knelt beside.

The Sigmarite was visibly pale as he met Mandred's questioning gaze. Hartwich didn't speak, he simply nodded.

'No one must know,' Mandred said. 'Whatever she is, she has served all men, all gods this day.'

'You cannot keep this secret,' Hartwich said.

'Together we can try,' Mandred told him. He stared down the slope, watching as his troops drove off the last skaven assaulting their line. 'Take her down the hill. Hide her in the camp. Whatever it takes, whatever power Sigmar has given you, don't let her die. I'll see you after I have thanked my soldiers for this victory.'

Hartwich nodded again. He watched as Mandred strode down to join his troops, and then the priest took up the body lying wrapped in his robe, the body he had watched change from the white wolf into the form of Hulda the witch. As he held her close, he knew it would be simplicity itself to let her die. Mandred would never question him, he trusted the Sigmarite too much to doubt him.

It was because of that trust that Hartwich carried Hulda down the hill to where he could tend her wounds.

The ways of the gods, Hartwich realised, weren't always as simple as men or even priests would like them to be.

As he descended towards the camp, Hartwich could hear the troops cheering Mandred. They hailed him as 'Skavenslayer', liberator of the Empire. The first title he had already earned, but Hartwich knew there were things still to be done before the Empire could be truly declared liberated.

Skavenblight, 1124

A ragged pack of ratkin slunk through the streets of Skavenblight, keeping to the least frequented alleys and passages. At every turn, they were met with furtive chitters and subdued snarls. From every crack and crevice, beady eyes watched them with hateful scrutiny. Sickly scavengers scurried away at their approach, running with such indecent haste that they cast aside their miserable pickings, leaving the gutters strewn with old bones and scraps of soiled ratskin.

Puskab Foulfur scratched at the boils clustered about his antlered scalp. He hadn't dared to hope his small retinue could creep back into Skavenblight ahead of the calamitous news. Defeat in the Howling Hills, the ruination of all the skaven had achieved in the past thirty-nine birth cycles. It was all that pompous braggart Vrrmik's fault, of course. A flea-licking goon with pretensions of grandeur, imagining himself to be Vecteek's successor! The Man-dread should have made the mouse-livered trash suffer for such delusions! As though Vrrmik were even a patch on Vecteek's despotic pelt! The Supreme Tyrant of Rictus should never have allowed the armies of skavendom to be dealt such a resounding defeat!

The stink of disaster infested the scents of Puskab and his companions – the few plague monks who had escaped the Howling Hills. It wasn't a paranoid imagining, but a vile odour secreted by the glands, a vile broth that conveyed both fear and submission. How despicable that such a smell should affix itself to a Grey Lord, to the mighty Poxmaster of Pestilens! It was an indignity that he found almost impossible to endure, an imposition that had caused him many times to turn on his small entourage. Decimating their numbers, however, had done nothing to assuage the tremors in his glands. If anything, it had made the noxious fug even worse. For a time, it had been possible to blot out the smell with pestiferous incense sticks, but the supply had run out long before they reached Skavenblight.

Puskab hesitated as he heard a particularly loud snarl rise from the shadow of a partially toppled archway. His baleful glare sent the utterer scampering off with his tail tucked between his legs, but the mere occurrence of such an incident bespoke an unbelievable boldness of impudence. He was a Grey Lord! The Grand-High Poxmaster of All Skavendom! Architect of the Black Plague and Favoured Spawn of the Horned One! For a common gutter-haunter to possess the spleen to dare snap at him – whatever impropriety might exude from his glands – was outrageous beyond belief!

His claws tightening about the gnarled staff he carried, Puskab vowed to avenge these indignities. The scum of Skavenblight would learn what it meant to trifle with the plaguelords of Clan Pestilens!

Snapping commands to his retinue, Puskab hurried them through the decrepit back streets. Now, more and more, the plague monks found eyes watching them from the shadows, furtive figures scampering along the rooftops.

Rounding a corner that connected to one of the city's main runs, Puskab was startled by the sight of hundreds of bodies lying rotting in the street. The evidence of violence was everywhere, a gory litter of carnage that stained the ground and spattered the walls. A diseased stink rose from the carrion, a stink Puskab knew only too well. It was the corruption left behind by the Black Plague.

A tremor of alarm raced through the Poxmaster's glands. The plague, *his* plague, running rampant through Skavenblight? It couldn't be! Only the plaguelords had the necessary knowledge to inflict such catastrophe upon their fellow ratkin. Yet why would they? There was no sense in slaughtering the very creatures they had invested such effort towards enslaving!

'The Bilious Basilica, scurry-hurry!' Puskab growled at his entourage. The plague monks turned away from the piles of dead, the hacked remains of skaven driven mad with disease and despair. They rushed down the narrow lanes, scurrying along ancient boulevards reared by the hands of men and dwarfs long before the first skaven stirred from its hole. Decayed pillars and broken masonry choked many of the pathways, compelling the ratmen to scurry over and around the obstructions. Here and there, heaps of dead skaven lay clustered about the rubble, their pelts blistered with the sores of plague.

Sinister whispers now pursued Puskab through the confusion of avenues. He didn't need to threaten his minions to greater speed. It was all he could do to keep from falling behind. There was no denying the presence of lurking skaven on the rooftops, no questioning the skulking shapes that watched them from behind boarded windows and locked doors. Every rodent instinct in Puskab's body was alert to the threat that hovered nearby, the brooding menace that seemed to swell and grow with each passing breath.

The Bilious Basilica, the fortress-monastery of Clan Pestilens, their most prominent holding on the surface of Skavenblight, reared up before Puskab's gaze as he scurried out from the cramped morass of tottering tenements and collapsed storehouses. Once it had served as a factory of some kind, but the imposing stone structure with its tiered levels and soaring parapets had long been the domain of Clan Pestilens. The plague monks had erected a massive wall around their monastery, a fortification thrice as tall as any skaven and nearly a dozen feet thick. The Poxmaster breathed slightly easier when he saw the ragged banners of Pestilens displaying the triple pimple symbol of the Horned One flying from the battlements. He could smell the sentries prowling the walls and hear the sharp cacophony of their scratchy chant.

Instead of reassuring him, the sentries brought a renewed sense of disquiet to Puskab. There were too many guards on the walls, far more than he could ever recall seeing. There were other smells too, the pungent tang of plague fumes rising from incense burners, the necrotic decay of neglected corpses. Drawing nearer, Puskab could see the heaps of dead ratmen piled outside the walls. The evidence was as obvious as it was incredible: the feckless hordes of Skavenblight had tried to storm the basilica!

Controlling the panic rising within him, Puskab marched towards the great double-gates of the monastery. He waited a moment, the stump of his tail twitching with imapatience as he waited for the guards to admit him. When, after a moment of inaction he lifted his gaze, he found the sentries still at their posts, not so much as twitching a whisker to open the doors.

'Poxmaster Puskab Foulfur command-demands entrance to basilica-nest!' he growled with a flash of yellowed fang.

'Poxmaster Puskab can rot with the dead,' an oozing voice growled back. Puskab knew that oily inflection, the tones of his hated rival Vrask Bilebroth. Sniffing the air, it was an easy thing for him to pick out the other plaguelord's scent. Craning his antlered head back, he could see his enemy perched upon one of the upper parapets.

'I return from battle-fight,' Puskab declared, trying to keep his voice firm and superiority in his posture. 'Vrrmik-meat is dead.'

Vrask's attitude remained challenging even in the face of the important news Puskab brought with him. 'Much ska-ven-meat dead-dead,' Vrask announced, his words slashing like claws. He pointed a scabby paw at the carrion heaped about the walls. 'Black Plague,' he hissed. 'Kill-slay much-much.' He curled back his lips, exposing his sharp fangs. 'Too much-much!'

Puskab didn't like the accusation in Vrask's voice. He could imagine the delusional maggot taking it into his head that Puskab was behind the contagion. Certainly Vrask had been envious of the trust and honour accorded to the Pox-master by Vrrmik, but certainly he must understand how Vrrmik's death changed all that? Puskab was concerned only with increasing the strength of Clan Pestilens, not petty per-sonal ambitions and jealousies.

'I want-need speak-squeak with Arch-Plaguelord Nur-glitch,' Puskab said. Nurglitch would support him and punish Vrask for showing such temerity.

Vrask chuckled, a sound like the slopping of swamp water in a rusty bucket. 'Nurglitch gone-gone. Left Skavenblight. Take-want pilgrimage to Blisterdeep.'

Puskab blinked in disbelief. Nurglitch had abandoned Skavenblight, had made the arduous journey back to Blis-terdeep? Blisterdeep was the most distant of Clan Pestilens's strongholds, a jungle pit far to the south, beyond the great deserts and the vast savannah. What could compel Nur-glitch to stage such an unseemly retreat?

'Black Plague kill-take many skaven!' Vrask howled down at Puskab. 'Kill-take Skurvy and Skab, Fester and Ferrik, Gnaw and Scruten, Rictus and Mors! Kill-slay Moulderkin and Skullykin, leave none to watch-guard slave-meat! Slave-meat fight-flee in lowest tunnels, kill-steal much-much!'

What Puskab had mistaken for arrogance and supremacy in Vrask's voice was quickly becoming exposed as fright. The plaguelord slurred his words together in the terrified squeak of a lowly clanrat. It wasn't the Poxmaster's return that evoked such fear. No, Vrask was afraid of something else, something so formidable that Nurglitch had fled Ska-venblight, leaving Vrask behind holding the bag.

Puskab stared again at the heaps of dead. He cocked back his ears, listening to the chorus of squeaks and whispers in the streets he had so recently abandoned. The hordes of Skavenblight, the teeming thousands who dwelt within and beneath the mighty city! Surely they couldn't be so foolish as to think Pestilens had deliberately loosed the plague on them!

A glance at the piled dead convinced Puskab that the hordes of Skavenblight were indeed that foolish. More, he noted for the first time the crude patches and emblems adorning many of the dead, the brands marking their fur. They wore the cross-bone symbol of the Horned Rat, the same symbol employed by the grey seers to denote their archaic order.

'Queekual...' Puskab snarled as the realisation struck him. No plaguelord, not even Vrask would have been so unwise as to loose the disease among the teeming hordes of Skavenblight. Their knowledge of plague was too extensive, their appreciation of the difficulties of containing and controlling an outbreak in such conditions too acute. The Black Plague was too lethal in its effects to leave enough survivors for the plague monks to convert to the true path of the Horned One. But an outside force, an interloper who didn't understand the workings of sacred plagues, he might be so insane. Certainly it was obvious the Seerlord had been exploiting the disaster to restore the prestige of his antiquated religion.

The Poxmaster's fur bristled as his senses were thrown into a paroxysm of alarm. A sniff of the air told him that hundreds of skaven were advancing upon the basilica. A glance over his shoulder brought the image of scraggly figures creeping out from the streets, clubs and blades clenched in their emaciated paws. Puskab looked back to the parapet, desperately hoping Vrask would relent and open the gates before it was too late. His rival simply glowered down at him, displaying his fangs once more in a murderous grin.

'The Shattered Tower!' Puskab snapped at his cringing retinue. There was no sanctuary for him here, but however bold the mob might have grown they wouldn't dare to violate the sanctity of the Shattered Tower, the very heart of skavendom.

Angry whispers rose to vengeful howls as Puskab and the

plague monks fled from the walls of the basilica. Back into the winding streets they ran. From every cellar, from every rooftop, mobs of enraged skaven appeared. Doors were smashed open, shuttered windows battered to splinters as diseased ratmen rushed to intercept the fugitives. Skaven from scores of clans, chittering in a maddened discord of dialects and accents, flooded the avenues. Their cries were for blood and vengeance, shrieks that bespoke the outrage of the doomed and abandoned.

'Puskab die-die! Die-die Puskab!' the mob roared in a thousand-fold voice of thunder.

The plague monks with Puskab were forced to cut their way through knots of ratmen, slashing them down with murderous sweeps of their swords. The dying ratkin pawed at them, trying to drag their killers down with them into the gutter. Several times a plague monk would linger too long freeing himself from the grip of a skaven he had slain. Their shrill wails as the enraged mob caught them lent new speed to the feet of the survivors.

After what seemed an eternity of twists and turns, Puskab could smell the brackish water in the basin of the shapeless fountain that bordered the broad plaza at the base of the Shattered Tower. Only a few plague monks remained with him now, the others dragged down by the mob which was close behind. With sight of the fountain and the near-formless lump of bronze poised above it, Puskab knew precisely how far it would be to the steps of the Shattered Tower. Too far to outdistance the mob.

Without a second thought, Puskab brought his staff cracking against the knee of a plague monk. The stricken creature yelped and crashed to the ground, his momentum causing him to slide along the cobblestones and slam against the base of the fountain. Puskab didn't spare the betrayed wretch another glance. Slaughtering the plague monk would delay the mob for a few breaths. Long enough for the Poxmaster to reach safety.

Racing into the plaza, Puskab's heart leapt into his throat. Every street was choked with enraged ratmen. Word had spread through every quarter of the city, drawing the terrified masses together into a vengeful tempest of fangs and claws. The Poxmaster gnashed his fangs at the sight. The last of his retinue made a break for a darkened alleyway only to be brought low by a skulking gang of red-cloaked Skully murder-rats.

Drawing upon his sorcerous power, Puskab set a pestilential torrent spilling from his fangs, spattering the nearest mob with sizzling acid. The agonised victims staggered back, their pained seizures impeding the advance of those behind. The Poxmaster seized upon the space he had gained. Springing forwards, he leapt towards the great stone steps at the base of the tower.

A lone figure stood there, sombre and sinister in his charcoal robes. Seerlord Queekual's eyes glittered with arcane power as he glared down at Puskab. The prophet pointed a claw at the plaguelord. 'The Horned Rat has judged! You are guilty of heresy! You and your spawn shall be cleansed in blood!'

Puskab threw forth his paw. From each splayed claw a ribbon of noxious green light sped towards the Seerlord. 'Eat-gnaw heresy!' he spat.

Queekual flinched as the green light crackled about him. His paw clenched tight about the mummified talisman hanging about his neck. For an instant, the green light started to collapse towards him. The next moment, Puskab's spell was shattered in a spray of bile and worms.

The Seerlord's staff blazed with fire as he brought it

swinging around. From the horned head, a bolt of malignant energy leapt. There was a flash of leprous yellow miasma as the bolt shredded through the protective barrier Puskab tried to invoke. Then Queekual's magic slammed into the Poxmaster, tearing the staff from his claws and hurling him through the air.

Puskab landed in a heap, his head ringing from its impact against the unyielding stone. He found himself staring up at the top of the Shattered Tower, the steeple where he had won his duel with Wormlord Blight and claimed his position on the Council. For an instant only did the memory flicker, then it was blotted out by the dozens of savage skaven faces that crept into view and glared down at him.

'Fear your tormentor no more!' Seerlord Queekual shouted from the steps. 'The beneficence of the Horned Rat has delivered the Poxmaster unto your paws! Cleanse your warrens of his plague with his blood!'

Queekual lingered over the scene, savouring the shrieks rising from Puskab Foulfur's tortured carcass as the panicked mob tore the fallen Poxmaster limb from limb.

—< CHAPTER XXII >—

Altdorf, 1124

For the better part of an hour, Kreyssig could hear the jubilant crowds cheering Graf Mandred as the Middenheimer made his entry into Altdorf. The details of the Battle of the Howling Hills might not be known to the peasants; even the accomplishments of his army during its march through Averland and Stirland were probably unknown to these people. Yet something, some force made them respond to this man, cheering his procession as it rode past the Königplatz and headed towards the rebuilt bridges.

Kreyssig fumed at the sound of those cheering mobs. He'd sent agitators to poison the commoners against Mandred, engaged them to spread the most obscene rumours about the Middenheimer. Given their newfound adoration of the Sigmarite faith, Kreyssig's spies had told the peasants that Mandred intended to abolish the Temple and establish an Ulrican priesthood in its stead. He'd told the peasants that Mandred intended to conscript every fifth man to be sent to

Middenheim and rebuild the City of the White Wolf. He'd even gone so far as to spread Beck's stories that Mandred cavorted with witches and took counsel from followers of the Ruinous Powers.

All of that, and still the people cheered. Sitting astride his horse outside the gates of the Imperial palace, it was an ordeal for Kreyssig to keep calm and wait. It would be beneath the dignity of his position as Protector of the Empire to ride out to meet Mandred. No, since Kreyssig was the Emperor's surrogate, it was Mandred who must ride to meet him.

'The people seem to be pleased with their new Emperor,' Duke Vidor observed. As one of the most important nobles in Altdorf, not to mention Reikmarshal, Kreyssig had felt obligated to include Vidor among his own retinue. There was still no love lost between the two men, as Vidor lost no opportunity to remind him. 'Peasants can sense noble blood. They know who is a legitimate lord and who is simply a poseur.'

'He isn't Emperor yet,' Kreyssig hissed through clenched teeth.

Duke Vidor feigned a look of profound surprise. 'Really? I thought he had the hammer! I thought he had the blessing of the gods! I thought he just purged half the Empire of ratmen!'

Kreyssig leaned around in his saddle and glowered at Vidor. 'Apparently he is simply returning Ghal Maraz to where it belongs,' he told the duke. 'As for the rest, gods are even more fickle than people about who they give their favours to.'

Vidor shook his head. 'The peasants don't seem to think so,' he said, waving his hand as the sound of cheers drew nearer.

Kreyssig did his best to look regal and composed as Mandred's procession came into view, rounding the street and marching past the Courts of Justice. The attempt faltered when he saw the hero riding a great white stallion adorned in a crimson caparison. Mandred wore a suit of glistening plate armour that seemed to fairly blaze in the sun. His helm was the open-faced visage of a snarling wolf, the nobleman's own face framed by the steel jaws. At his side, he wore Legbiter, the runefang of Middenland, but resting across his left shoulder was the magnificence of Ghal Maraz itself. The warhammer of Sigmar really did seem to exude its own brilliance, a shine that had nothing to do with the sun overhead.

All of this, Kreyssig took in at a glance, trying to get the measure of his enemy. But it wasn't Mandred's appearance that told him what sort of man the Empire had made into a hero. It was the long line of foot soldiers who flanked either side of the procession. They seemed to have been carefully selected in their arrangement, a Middenlander marching beside an Averlander with a Stirlander and a Nordlander following behind. Every land, every province Mandred's army had fought in was represented, a visible manifestation of the unity and solidarity that had allowed him to rout the ratkin from the territories they had conquered.

There was more, however, a display that had muffled every rumour and story Kreyssig's agents had spread, an exhibition that had subdued even the fiercest of peasant malcontents. Each of the marching soldiers held a pole in his hands and stretched across the frame atop each pole was the pelt of a skaven. Every soldier marching into Altdorf bore with him a talisman of Mandred's conquests, a token of the enemy that they had fought and destroyed.

In a city that had suffered an attack by the filthy monsters, no one was about to jeer at a man who had killed so many skaven.

Kreyssig forced a smile onto his face and spurred his horse away from his retinue as he moved to meet Mandred. 'Your highness, I welcome you to Altdorf.'

Mandred stared back at Kreyssig, no warmth in his gaze. 'I thank you for your welcome, Protector, for the welcome of all Altdorf's people. But I fear I must delay my expression of gratitude.' He patted the jewelled haft of Ghal Maraz. 'First I would return Sigmar's Hammer and honour him for his part in my victories.'

Inwardly, Kreyssig bristled at this insulting breach of tradition and respect. 'Of course, your highness. It is only right that you should do honour to Lord Sigmar.' He wheeled his horse about, turning in the direction of the Great Cathedral.

'If you would follow me, highness,' Kreyssig said. He could afford to choke on his pride a little longer. After all, if Mandred wanted to speed himself to his own death, why should he stand in the fool's way?

'Hurry-scurry! Quick-quick!' As he shrieked at his underlings, Sythar Doom gnashed his fangs in frustrated fury. He dearly wanted to kill a few of the incompetent wretches, but there were too few of them to kill out of hand.

There were maybe a hundred skaven in the cave, scrambling about the apparatus, rolling sealed cylinders of powdered warpstone to the periphery of the contraption. Masked ratmen took charge of the cylinders from there, slipping them into copper casings arrayed across the ovoid surface of the machine.

It was a design of Sythar's own creation, appropriated from a moderately competent warlock-engineer named Zaprik just before he suffered an extremely fatal accident with a set of whisker-pluckers. If it functioned as the plans promised it would, the resultant explosion would make a hold-full of warpcaster ammunition seem like a firecracker.

Sythar shivered at that image and immediately regretted making such a connection. He could still smell the salt-water in his fur after all these years. The prestige he'd lost after the fiasco at Dietershafen had cost Clan Skryre much of its power. Many of their allies had deserted them; some warlock-engineers had even gone rogue. Worst of all, there was the plague, marauding through skavendom with the same rapacity with which it had decimated the lands of men. Skryre had been especially hard hit, nearly eight of every ten of the clan catching the disease. Sythar had been forced to employ the most extreme measures to ensure the ratmen he associated with were free of contagion.

Dimly, Sythar noted the sounds of some commotion among his workers. If one of them had started to exhibit the marks of plague he'd have to kill the whole pack and fetch new workers! Such inconvenience was intolerable!

Clan Pestilens and their brave new ideas! Puskab Foulfur, the rat who would bring the world of men to its knees! Well, the traitor-meat had neglected to mention that his wondrous creation was going to do the same to skavendom!

The warlord forced himself to grow calm. Puskab and Pestilens were problems that would wait for another day. Today he needed to concentrate on an entirely different sort of revenge. His warpstone heart nurtured a special hatred for the man-nest of Altdorf. He bared his fangs as he cocked his head to one side and stared up at the ceiling. Overhead was the Great Cathedral, that miserable little temple that had defied his efforts to destroy it during his attack on the city, indeed, that had seen his defeat unfold at its very doors.

Well, it wouldn't stand much longer, and when it vanished

in a warpstone cloud, it would take with it another enemy Sythar Doom longed to destroy – Man-dread, the foul king-thing who had treacherously bypassed Sythar's carefully prepared ambush and attacked Dietershafen without warning, the filthy little human who had the audacity to turn the Far-Claw against its own inventor.

Yes, it was a shame Sythar could only kill Man-dread once, but at least he could do so in such a manner that all humans – all skaven – would cower before the might of Clan Skryre!

Sythar Doom's whiskers twitched as an unexpected smell reached his nose. He turned around, causing the scaffolding he was on to shift and wobble. His tail lashed from side to side as he stared at one of the tunnels leading into his secret grotto.

Why were there dwarfs here? And why were they attacking his workers? And why, above all, were those spineless vermin running away?

Sparks flew from the warlord's fangs as he drew the pistol from his belt and aimed at one of the ratmen fleeing before the dwarfs. As he pulled the trigger, a crackling band of green lightning sizzled into the fleeing skaven, dropping him to the ground as a smouldering husk.

'Fight-fight or die-die!' Sythar roared at his minions. Some of those closest to the dwarfs were still intent on running away, but the others started grabbing up tools and weapons, whatever was near at hand. Their posture remained timid, however, and Sythar didn't like the fear in their scent. He glared across at the mouth of the tunnel. Unless there were more enemies hiding somewhere, all he could see were seven dwarfs and a lone human. Sparks flew from his metal jaws as he gnashed his fangs in frustration. 'There's only eight of them!' he shrieked, holding up one of his paws with all five fingers displayed. Given the quality of the minions he'd been forced to take, Sythar realised very few of them would notice the numerical discrepancy.

The first pack of skaven were rushing over to confront the dwarfs when they ran smack into a bare-chested, orange-furred dwarf. Instead of retreating before the pack of skaven, the dwarf charged into them, hacking them apart with his hand axe. The crazed fury of that single dwarf's assault broke that first mob of skaven, sending the survivors scampering off towards the tunnels.

Sythar lashed his tail in frustration. He wondered how many more of his underlings he'd have to shoot before they understood they weren't allowed to run away.

The sanctuary of the Great Cathedral was filled with a vast throng of people, a mixture of the elite of Altdorf and Reikland and the Sigmarite clergy. Such was the excitement and awe caused by Mandred's entry into the city and his return of Ghal Maraz to the cathedral that for once no distinction had been made between noble and commoner, wealthy merchant and humble monk. All had been welcomed into the sanctuary to observe the restoration of Sigmar's Hammer to his people.

Kreyssig had kept close to Mandred during his ride to the temple. It could only be beneficial for him to be seen with the popular hero, after all. The inconvenience of Ghal Maraz turning up in Mandred's possession had been neatly blamed on the late Emperor Boris, though the exact details had been left nebulous. Kreyssig would work them out with the people who knew the truth, find some mutually satisfactory compromise. Even idealists like Hartwich would have their price. Preservation of the Empire, stability of the state, that sort of thing would pull at the arch-lector's heartstrings.

As soon as the procession entered the temple, Kreyssig slipped away. He lingered at the back near the door, his bodyguard of Kaiserknecht ensuring he had a clear view down the central aisle. He didn't want to be too close to Mandred now, but he most certainly wanted to see everything that was about to happen.

At the end of the aisle stood the altar where Ghal Maraz would be reconsecrated. Standing behind the altar with his censer bearers and attendants, as well as Arch-Lector von Reisarch, stood Grand Theogonist Gazulgrund. Kreyssig smiled when he found he had such a clear view of the hated priest. Yes, he certainly wasn't going to miss anything.

Mandred's procession continued their unhurried march towards the altar, Ghal Maraz held across the graf's chest. Beside him walked Arch-Lector Hartwich and a scarred knight his spies told him was Grand Master Vitholf of the Knights of the White Wolf. Between priest and knight walked a stunningly beautiful woman in a fur cloak. Kreyssig's spies had been unable to learn much about her, but Beck had told him all he needed to know. That was Hulda, the wolf-witch. That Mandred would have the graciousness to bring the witch here with him was almost too good to believe. Once the bloom fell off the rose, Altdorf would see for themselves that their mighty hero consorted with witches and the Ruinous Powers.

Kreyssig looked away for a moment as a bee buzzed around his head. It took him most of a minute to shoo the annoyance away. When he looked back, his smile was almost diabolical in its vicious amusement. Mandred's procession had nearly reached the spot where the Kaiserjaeger had posted Beck. The mutant was disguised as a mendicant monk, his entire body concealed beneath a heavy hood and thick robe. He'd been standing there for most of the morning awaiting his old master. A few yards more and the procession would be near enough to Beck that everyone in the sanctuary would believe Kreyssig's claims that Mandred had given the mutant a signal to attack Gazulgrund.

Before Mandred's group could close those last few yards, however, Hulda left her place in the procession, darting ahead of the graf. Her attitude was tense and alert, her head shifting from side to side as she seemed to sniff the air.

'Beware!' she shouted to Mandred. 'There is treachery here!'

Too many things happened then for Kreyssig to put them in their proper order. The area around the altar quickly became a mass of clergy as warrior priests and templar knights rushed to protect the Grand Theogonist. Beck sprang into the aisle, throwing back his hood and glaring at the wolf-witch with his clutch of spidery eyes. Hartwich and Vitholf seized Mandred and tried to pull him back.

Beck's claw hand licked out, cracking against the face of the witch who'd sniffed him out. The blow sent her flying into the pews, delivered with such inhuman force that her momentum smashed down the spectators she landed among. The mutant risked one look at the altar, but decided that there was no way it could reach Gazulgrund through the cordon of his protectors.

Instead it stepped towards Mandred. 'If I can't kill the dream,' Beck growled. 'Then I'll kill the man.' The mutant punctuated its words by drawing the sword it had hidden beneath its robes, holding it in one of its bifurcated hands.

Mandred tore free from the hold Vitholf and Hartwich had on him. Brandishing the brutal mass of Ghal Maraz, he strode towards the monster that had once been his bodyguard.

'You've killed enough dreams, Beck,' Mandred growled

back, the venom of hatred dripping from every word. 'Now it's time for you to die.'

Erich gaped in awe at the immense machine the skaven had assembled deep beneath the streets of Altdorf. It was shaped like a gigantic metal pumpkin. Ribs of copper stretched down its sides while spurs of what looked to be ceramic projected from its top in a sort of crest. Ugly black stones, glowing with a greenish light, were embedded amid clusters of gears and pistons arrayed about the machine's base. What something of such size and complexity could be intended for, the knight couldn't begin to guess. If Dharin and the other gold grubbers were right, they were directly beneath the Great Cathedral. The knight wasn't terribly familiar with dwarfs, but he had always heard their skill at navigating underground, even in total darkness, was almost preternatural.

He might not know what the machine was for, but he agreed with the dwarfs that whatever it was, its purpose boded ill for the city above. Arming himself with a hand axe Dharin gave him, Erich charged out of the tunnel with the dwarfs, falling upon the skaven before they were even aware that they were under attack. The pungent stink of oil and pitch and noxious unguents explained the ease of their ambush. Their noses filled with the stench of the chemicals and compounds they were working with, the ratmen were disoriented. As the dwarfs dove into them, as Erich lashed out with his borrowed axe at a piebald skaven wearing an oily apron across its body, the knight found the creatures erratic and confused. Their speed remained incredible, but their coordination was muddled. It was easy to slip around scratching paw or snapping muzzle to slash at the creature's body.

The impetus of the initial attack quickly petered out as many of the ratmen turned tail and started to run. Kurgaz, the fury of the slayer upon him, rushed headlong after the vermin. Erich started to go after him, but his attention was drawn to a ghastly-looking ratman standing on a wooden scaffold overlooking the immense machine. The creature's eyes were like crimson lamps, its jaws a mass of metal that sparked and crackled with electricity. The monster was snarling at the skaven below, emphasising the importance of its commands by drawing a strange weapon from its belt and loosing a bolt of lightning into one of the fleeing ratkin.

More ratmen came boiling out from around the side of the machine. Unlike the first monsters the dwarfs and their companion had set upon, these creatures were armed, exhibiting a riotous array of hammers, spanners and blades in their paws. Kurgaz didn't hesitate an instant, but flung himself straight into the monsters, laying about him with the hand axe with such savagery that he was soon coated in the foul black blood of his victims.

From the scaffold above, the metal-fanged ratman continued to shriek and snarl orders at its fellows. Again the creature fired a bolt of green lightning from the bulky weapon in its paws, but in its rage, the monster didn't think to fire at one of its enemies. Instead it loosed destruction upon another of its cowardly kin.

The murderous discipline did its work. Scores of skaven came charging around the side of the machine. Even Kurgaz would have been quickly overwhelmed, but his methodical slaughter of the wounded ratkin left behind by the first rat pack delayed him long enough for Erich, Dharin and the other dwarfs to join him. Together they formed a solid line, defying the vermin as they came lunging forwards. Appreciating that other lives depended on him, Kurgaz held his own death wish in check, guarding the flank of the small formation. Erich caught up a rusty sword one of the dead skaven had been using. With his height and the reach of the sword, he stayed behind the dwarfs, chopping down at the ratkin when they tried to climb over their own comrades to reach the dwarfs and hacking away at any of the vermin who managed to slip past the axes in front of him.

The slaughter was abominable. Many times the ratkin tried to break and run, but whenever they did, the metal-fanged monster on the scaffold drove them back to the attack with a bolt of lightning.

'We'll never break them with their leader shooting them down every time they try to run!' Erich shouted.

'That's good, manling!' Kurgaz growled. 'Means we don't have to chase after them!'

Erich couldn't share the dwarf's view. They'd killed maybe thirty skaven already and there seemed no diminution in the numbers attacking them. Meanwhile their own losses were all too noticeable. Two of the gold grubbers had been dragged down by the ratmen, one with a spear in his belly and the other when a seemingly dead skaven erupted into life and hamstrung him with a knife. As he pitched forwards, the crippled dwarf had been stabbed by at least half a dozen of the monsters.

If they kept trading blow for blow with the skaven, the superior numbers of the vermin would prevail. That might have been fine for the dwarfs, a testament to their stubbornness and courage that they had stood their ground and defied so many. For Erich, there could be no victory in such a gesture. If they were killed, the skaven machine, whatever it was, would be left to wreak its havoc upon the city above. After what he'd seen in Averheim, the most grisly possibility that occurred to him was that the thing was some kind of bomb. The thought sent ice running down his spine, the image of the Great Cathedral being obliterated in an explosion was too hideous to contemplate.

Erich made his decision. The next time the dwarfs drove the skaven back and their cringing resolve faltered, the knight rushed through the ranks of the gold grubbers. The sudden attack only drove the ratmen into further dismay. He heard the metal-fanged monster shrieking and snarling, then he uttered his own shout of alarm as one of the ratman's lightning bolts crackled against the ground beside him. The near miss actually proved a blessing, scattering the skaven ahead of him, making them scramble out of his way lest they be hit by another near miss from their chieftain.

The knight screamed the war-cry of the Reiksknecht as he flung himself at the base of the scaffold. He had seen the way the platform shuddered and shifted every time the rat-chief stomped across it. Now he slashed at the ramshackle construction, splintering wooden planks and severing ropes with every thrust.

The chief-rat shrieked again, but this time there was a note of fright in its tone. With its perch bucking and shifting beneath it, the murderous brute was calling to its minions to save it. Even if they were of a mind to help, the chance was denied them. Rushing ahead in the confusion were Kurgaz and the other dwarfs. They drove into the flank of the startled skaven, reminding them that they had other enemies besides Erich. The dwarfs fanned out in a semicircle, working to keep the skaven at bay while Erich demolished the scaffold.

A few more cuts and the structure came crashing down. So abrupt was its fall that even Erich was taken by surprise. The knight found himself smashed flat beneath a mass of rotten beams and splintered planks. He tried to move, but all he succeeded in doing was bringing more of the weight pressing down on him. He was pinned, trapped in the debris.

Through the cloud of dust and dirt thrown up by the collapse, Erich could see a pair of lights burning behind the murk. Beneath the lights he could see the glow of electricity crackling along metal fangs. The lights were the ghastly eyes of the skaven warlord. They turned towards the knight and stared directly at him. Erich felt his blood curdle when he heard the monster's savage hiss. With its crimson optics, the ratman could see the trapped human quite clearly. Nothing pleased a skaven more than helpless prey.

The weight on top of him became even greater as the skaven leapt down from wherever he'd landed when the scaffold came down. Erich suspected the nimble creature had simply ridden the wreckage as it fell, letting the platform absorb most of the impact. Certainly the skaven gave no evidence that he was injured. He hopped down onto the wreckage directly above Erich, leaning forwards so that the rubble pushed down on him with the ratman's full weight added to it.

'Fool-meat!' the skaven snarled, foam sizzling as it evaporated against the monster's electrified fangs. 'Think-dream you can oppose-fight the mighty Sythar Doom, Great Warplord of all Skavendom!' Sythar raked the claws of his foot across Erich's face, slashing open his cheek and nearly piercing his eye. 'All man-things learn-listen! All man-things shiver-tremble!' Uttering a chittering laugh, Sythar shook one of his paws at the huge machine. 'Sythar Doom fetch-take revenge on man-things! God-house will die-burn! The Man-dread will die-burn! All-all die-burn!'

Erich felt his heart freeze as Sythar boasted of his intentions. The machine was some kind of bomb, and the monster intended to use it to blow up the Great Cathedral.

Not only that, but it was cunning enough to wait to wreak its revenge. Somehow it had learned that Graf Mandred was coming to Altdorf, that he would return Ghal Maraz to the cathedral. The skaven was waiting for that auspicious moment to detonate the bomb, inflicting in a single instant a blow that would annihilate the entire leadership of the Empire and the man many were already cheering as the new Emperor.

The knight struggled to free himself, putting every scrap of his strength into a supreme effort to break loose and hurl himself upon the gloating Sythar. The ratman chittered as he saw the futile struggle. Viciously, he raked his foot across Erich's forehead, one of the claws digging a hole in the side of his nose.

'All-all die-burn!' Sythar Doom laughed.

'Then let's start with you, ratkin!' From out of the dust, Kurgaz's brawny frame lunged at Sythar. The dwarf's massive arms coiled about the ratman, bowling him over in a savage tackle. Skaven and dwarf rolled through the debris, their bodies smashing through planks and rotten beams, their momentum carrying them to the edge of the rubble.

Sythar broke away from Kurgaz, fiendishly pounding his paw against a huge sliver of wood lodged in the dwarf's bicep. The blow drove the sliver still deeper, wrenching a snarl of pain from the slayer. Before Sythar could scamper away, however, Kurgaz lunged at him again, catching the warplord's tail. Savagely he tugged at the tail, jerking Sythar off his feet and slamming him to the ground. Even as he started to rise, Kurgaz was on top of him, smashing him down into the dirt.

'We'll start with the dying part,' Kurgaz growled at the monster. 'I'll see what I can do about burning what's left later.'

Sythar growled back at the dwarf, worming his body out from under the slayer, twisting his head about so that he could sink his electrified fangs into Kurgaz's forearm. The dwarf's body snapped back, twitching and flailing as the electricity crackled through his body. The sickly smell of burning flesh permeated the air, the grease in the slayer's spiked crest of hair caught fire, blood streamed from nose and eyes, ears and mouth. Never, even in Kreyssig's dungeons, had Erich seen such utter and total agony inflicted upon a living creature.

Somehow, through the anguish sizzling through him, Kurgaz managed to hold onto his hatred. With Sythar's jaws still clamped in his forearm, delivering their lethal charge, the slayer reached with his other hand to the sliver of wood in his bicep. 'Grimnir!' the dwarf roared as he ripped the piece of wood from his flesh. Reversing his grip on it, he slammed his fist into the skaven's chest, impaling the monster.

Sythar's jaws tightened, the fangs digging down to the bones in Kurgaz's arm. The ratman's claws raked at his attacker, but it was a spastic, unfocused effort. Already the vitality of Sythar Doom was draining out of him. The sliver of wood had impaled the warlord's black heart. The warpstone-powered heart of Sythar Doom.

The dwarf only had a moment to understand that his enemy was dead before the vindictive trap built into Sythar Doom's mechanical heart activated. It exploded with the force of a blasting charge, reducing both the ratman and his killer to ribbons of bloodied meat. The force of the explosion sent dirt and rock raining down from the ceiling, making the walls tremble. Erich thought the entire cavern must collapse in upon itself.

The knight wasn't the only one. Squealing in terror, more

at the thought of being buried alive than any sadness at their leader's death, the surviving skaven fled the cavern. Erich could hear the squeaks fading down the tunnel as they vanished in the dark.

The prospect of being abandoned even by such monstrous enemies, left to rot alone in the subterranean blackness, spurred Erich to greater effort. Again, all of his strength wasn't enough to dislodge the rubble.

'You seem to be in a spot of trouble, manling.' When he heard the words and turned his head to see Dharin and his surviving gold grubbers climbing down the wreckage, Erich felt such a wave of relief that tears streamed from his eyes.

Dharin misunderstood those tears. 'Don't cry for Small-hammer, manling,' the dwarf said as he shook his head. 'It was a fine death he found. The sort of death that every slayer longs to find.'

Erich felt a profound sense of shame when he heard those words, guilty that the tears hadn't been for Kurgaz, a hero who had not only saved Erich's life, but those of Graf Mandred and all who would be with him in the Great Cathedral.

'Come,' Dharin said, lifting one of the beams imprisoning Erich. 'Let's get you out of there.'

The crowd within the sanctuary, those closest to where the mutant had suddenly emerged to challenge Graf Mandred, tried to scatter, to flee the hideous monstrosity and the violence that was certain to unfold soon. Those further back in the pews strained forwards, trying to see the reason for the commotion, blocking the retreat of those who only wanted to get away. In that bedlam of shouts and screams, the two enemies glared at one another in silence.

Mandred thought of Lady Mirella, cut down by this monster. He thought of Burggraefin Sofia, murdered in her sick bed by this creature. He thought too of Princess Erna and how close she had come to sharing their fate. Beck, the man he had trusted, the warrior he had considered friend and confidant, was nothing more than a cowardly assassin.

The mutant had its thoughts too. Memories of how it had swallowed its pride, debased its honour to serve Mandred. It had forsaken its own dreams, its own hopes in order to serve the von Zelts. It had believed there could be no greater purpose than to make Middenheim strong. Strong leader, strong land. All it had done was in service to the Middenpalaz. In the end, its reward had been betrayal, the ruination of its name and its very humanity.

The mutant spun around as Hulda came rushing out from the crowd where Beck had thrown her. Her face was almost feral in its ferocity, her eyes burning like those of a beast. The people standing near her had the impression of strange ticks and twitches going on just under her skin. Those nearest almost swore they saw long fangs glistening in her mouth.

Hartwich rushed forwards, a look of horror on the priest's face. 'Hulda! No!' he cried. Better than anyone, Hartwich knew what would happen if she lost control here of all places. He knew how the Sigmarites would react if they saw her other self. They might have accepted the Lady of Sigmar, but they would feel only terror at the Daughter of Ulric.

In his rush towards the witch, the arch-lector came too near Beck. The mutant's claw lashed out, severing the fingers of Hartwich's outstretched hand. The maimed priest was sent sprawling by the blow, crashing in a tangle against the pews. Hulda rushed over to him, her concern for him forcing the lupine rage into abeyance.

Mandred blocked Vitholf and his other retainers from rushing Beck. 'The monster is mine,' he declared in a voice like steel cutting ice. 'If it kills me, then it's yours.'

Beck's mouth stretched into a jagged smile. 'If I kill you, nothing else matters,' he snarled, springing at Mandred. The mutant's claw flashed down, slicing across the graf's shoulder, ringing as it nearly crumpled the steel pauldron. As it landed on its feet, Beck's sword licked out, slicing at Mandred's face.

The graf blocked the sword with the jewelled haft of Ghal Maraz and then brought the peen of the warhammer cracking against Beck's bifurcated arm. The blow snapped one of the mutant's wrists, sending the sword flying from its broken hand. Before he could bring the massive head of the hammer swinging around, Beck sprang to one side in a display of alarming agility.

The mutant drove in on Mandred, thinking to charge him while the momentum of his strike held him off balance. Beck didn't consider that his foe had honed his fighting instincts for four years battling skaven, creatures far quicker and more agile than any man... or a thing that had once been a man. Mandred turned his missed strike into a spin, turning his body with the hammer in a motion that was almost reflexive to him. When the mutant rushed at him, the head of Ghal Maraz struck it. Golden light blazed from the ancient relic, the divine ire of Sigmar made manifest.

The sound of Beck's arm shattering boomed through the cathedral. The mutant was flung down the aisle, tumbling and rolling as though it had been launched from a ballista. It landed in a broken huddle, mewing painfully as it tried to regain its feet. It turned its misshapen face towards the enraged man storming down the aisle towards it. 'Everything was for you, all of it for you,' Beck snarled.

Mandred brought Ghal Maraz cracking down, smashing one of the mutant's legs and hurling the creature further down the aisle. Those watching from the pews couldn't decide which was more terrible, the monstrousness of the mutant's face or the fury that held Mandred's visage.

Again, Beck struggled to rise. 'Sofia threatened you,' it growled. 'She was sick. Plague-ridden. You would have caught it if you...'

Ghal Maraz struck the mutant's bifurcated arm, crushing it into a pulpy mess. Once more Beck was hurled down the aisle.

Coughing blood, the mutant rose once more. 'You let your affection for Mirella blind you to what marriage to Carin would bring to...'

This time Mandred didn't swing the warhammer, he merely drove it into Beck's chest. The crack of splintered ribs accompanied Beck as the mutant was tossed back.

Defiance, the pride of hate, made Beck rise again, its spidery eye-cluster glaring balefully at the advancing Mandred. 'Erna threatened your alliance with Kreyssig,' the mutant spat. 'She would have set you against the man who promised to make you Emperor.'

Mandred drove the head of Ghal Maraz into Beck once more, breaking more of the mutant's ribs and flinging it through the great doors of the cathedral. Beck landed in a bloody heap on the steps, those same steps where Gazulgrund had rallied the people of Altdorf against the skaven hordes. As there had been on that day years ago, a vast crowd filled the plaza, the teeming multitudes of the city who couldn't fit inside the sanctuary. They gasped in shock as the mutant came tumbling down the steps, then an awed hush fell over them as Mandred came striding out of the cathedral, Ghal Maraz glowing with golden light.

Beck didn't try to stand, even hatred could only command so much from its broken body. From the steps he sneered at his old master. 'Graf Gunther charged me to protect his son, even from himself! All I have done, I have done for Middenheim!'

Mandred stood over the mutant and raised Ghal Maraz up high. 'One more thing then, you may do for Middenheim,' he told the creature. Ghal Maraz came smashing down, obliterating Beck's head in one brutal strike.

⌐ EPILOGUE ⌐

Altdorf, 1124

The observium high atop the Great Cathedral of Sigmar was a marvel of architecture, a miracle spun from steel and glass. Transparent walls looked out over the sprawl of Altdorf, offering a vista of the Imperial palace and the Courts of Justice, the River Reik and the Königplatz across the river. The glass ceiling above the grand hall opened out upon the stars. The room had been constructed by the dwarfs, taxing even their near-magical engineering abilities, a gift to the Temple of Sigmar in honour of the First Emperor, the man their High King had honoured with the revered title 'dwarf-friend'.

Like many before him, when Arch-Lector Hartwich stepped out into the observium he felt as if he was walking among the clouds. A strange vertigo threatened him, making his steps uncertain and unsteady. He leaned against one of the tables where the temple astrologers normally worked, studying the heavens and interpreting the positions of stars and comets within the dogma of their faith. The tables were vacant now, the astrologers all dismissed, granted a holiday to celebrate the coronation of Emperor Mandred. The benches where the blind augurs commonly sat in meditation were likewise empty, they too dismissed from their divinations to pay respect to the new Emperor.

One man alone waited for Hartwich in the observium. Grand Theogonist Gazulgrund sat in silent contemplation of the stars when the arch-lector entered. At the sound of his visitor's arrival, he slowly lowered his head and turned towards the other priest.

'You came,' the Grand Theogonist declared.

'You summoned me, holiness,' Hartwich corrected him. Though he tried, he couldn't quite keep the disgust from his voice or the contempt from his face. One of the things he'd desperately tried to believe was that the Night of Holy Knives had been some atrocity concocted by Kreyssig. His return to Altdorf had shown him otherwise. The massacre had been carried out by Sigmarite witch hunters on the orders of the Grand Theogonist.

Gazulgrund saw the loathing in Hartwich's eyes, heard the scorn in his tone. 'My ascension to this post was a mistake,' he said, his voice low and humble. 'It was the will of a tyrant that put me here, not the will of Lord Sigmar. I have tried to make the best of that accident, tried to conduct myself in a manner that would not disgrace our god and our Temple.'

Hartwich pushed away from the table, took a few faltering steps towards Gazulgrund. 'Many have died for Sigmar,' he said. 'Our faith has been watered with the blood of martyrs, but never did I think those martyrs would die by the hand of their own holy father.'

Gazulgrund nodded. He reached to his neck and removed the jade talisman on its golden chain. Reverently, he ran his fingers over the sculpted griffon. 'I am a weak man. Through my weakness, a tyrant gained power over me. Through me he thought to gain power over Sigmar's Temple. I did what I had to do to cut away that weakness.'

'Thousands of innocents are dead,' Hartwich said, his words cutting into Gazulgrund like a knife. 'You have murdered the families of your own priesthood. For what? Some mad vision of purity?'

The Grand Theogonist set the talisman down on one of the benches. 'I did the only thing I could to stop Kreyssig,' he said. 'I was too weak to see any other way.' Slowly he tugged the golden ring from his left hand, the jade ring from his right and set them too upon the floor.

An uneasy feeling grew in Hartwich's breast as he watched Gazulgrund strip away the badges of his holy office. 'You are still Grand Theogonist. Whether by the hand of a tyrant or no, Sigmar works and speaks through you.' He thought of his words to Lady Mirella in the Temple of Ulric when Mandred wept over the body of his father. 'The gods may build great things from tragedy.'

Gazulgrund's eyes were damp with tears as he listened to Hartwich explain how pain was the medium through which heroes were born. 'Your words gladden my heart,' he said. 'But I can have no part of them. For every villainy there must be a reckoning. There is a price to be paid for every cruelty. Sigmar will build great things, but He will need strong servants to act as his hands, wise leaders to speak his words. I am neither. I was a frightened, weak creature who did the only thing he could do to keep a monster out of the temple. I became a bigger monster.'

Hartwich rushed forwards when he saw Gazulgrund take up the immense hammer Thorgrim, the weapon he had used to rally the peasants of Altdorf during the skaven attack. The Grand Theogonist waved him back. 'The tyrant will be no more. Emperor Mandred is a good man, a great man. He will not allow the disease of Kreyssig to linger. You must show the same kind of strength. The Temple needs a good and great man to lead it. A man who is strong enough to remove the monster from his house.'

'There is always penance,' Hartwich said. 'Redemption. Salvation.'

Gazulgrund sighed. 'There is too much blood on my hands. When I am alone, I can hear the voice of my daughter and the voices of all the others I had killed. They are waiting for me at the Gates of Morr. Redemption isn't something for me to seek, but for them to allow.'

Turning towards the closest window, Gazulgrund brought Thorgrim smashing against it, shattering the centuries-old glass and crumpling one of the steel frames. Wind whipped through the hole, plucking at the priest's raiment. He threw the warhammer to the floor and again raised his hand to ward off Hartwich. 'Let me atone for my sins,' he said. He smiled, a cold and forsaken expression. 'If Sigmar forgives me, His mercy will bear me aloft.'

The next moment, Gazulgrund was through the window. Hartwich rushed to the edge of the gap and stared down. The Grand Theogonist had plummeted hundreds of feet before impaling himself on one of the spires below. He could see Gazulgrund moving, writhing like a bug on the end of a pin. Faintly, the priest's voice drifted up to the observium, groaning out a prayer of apology to Sigmar and those he had killed.

It took three days before a ladder tall enough to reach Gazulgrund could be built and raised. In all that time, it seemed to the people below that the impaled man's voice never faltered; his prayers never fell silent. When they pulled him down, he was dead, but even then many claimed the sound of his prayers lingered on, a ghostly warning that would rise when a northern wind blew across the spires of the Great Cathedral.

The bricked-up framework that had once housed Emperor Boris's extravagant *Kaiseraugen* flanked the former council chamber. The great table of Drakwald wood had been removed, the carved chairs of the council taken away. The raised dais remained, rising on marble blocks from the tile floor, but no mighty throne reposed upon it. Instead there was only a simple stool of horsehide, a bit of furniture that had travelled from Middenheim across the whole of the Empire as Mandred hounded the ratkin from land after land and city after city. It was a relic of his campaign to cleanse the Empire of evil and it was as a symbol of that fight that he had ordered it brought here and set upon the dais. He could think of no more majestic seat from which to watch the final battle.

Emperor Mandred Skavenslayer settled himself on the chair, the Imperial crown upon his brow, the purple robes draped about his shoulders. Across his lap rested Ghal Maraz, behind him Grand Master Vitholf held the Standard of Middenheim while the reinstated Reikmarshal von Boeckenfoerde held the Griffon-Rampant of the Imperial Throne. Between them, its stink subdued by a saturation of perfumes and unguents, was the stretched hide of Great Warlord Vrrmik carried by Captain Aldinger of the Knights of the Black Rose.

All the panoply of Empire surrounded the dais. Mandred's closest allies were gathered about him, Baroness Carin of Nordland, Arch-Lector Hartwich, even the witch Hulda.

Before him, on bended knee, was Adolf Kreyssig, the

Protector of the Empire. The commander of the now dis-
banded Kaiserjaeger tried his best to present a confident
and imperious presence, but he couldn't quite hide the
sweat beading his brow or the tremor in his limbs. He'd
been abandoned by all of his friends and allies after his
connection to the mutant Beck had been exposed. Only his
manservant Fuerst remained with him, bearing his regalia
as he was summoned before the new Emperor.

Emperor Mandred didn't give the murderous villain
the dignity of courtly language or politic dialogue. When
Kreyssig entered the hall, when he knelt before the dais,
Mandred only glared down at the killer. 'It would give me
no greater pleasure than to have you taken from this place
and beheaded,' Mandred told Kreyssig. 'I would set your
head on a spike as a warning to all despots.'

A thin smile crawled onto Kreyssig's face. He'd been afraid
of his standing, afraid that Mandred's popularity as the
Skavenslayer would trump his own popularity as the Hero
of Altdorf. Because the new Emperor expressed himself
the way he did, Kreyssig felt his fear lessen. Even Mandred
appreciated the support Kreyssig enjoyed among the peasants. 'Kill me, and you will have an uprising on your hands,'
he warned.

Mandred returned Kreyssig's smile, but it was as cold as a
daemon's grin. 'I am going to give the people of the Empire
too much to do for them to worry about the echoes of
old tyrannies. I am going to rebuild this land and make it
greater than it has ever been. There will be no place in my
Empire for a monster like you.'

Kreyssig rose to his feet, pointed his finger at Mandred.
'Yet even you do not dare to execute me,' he snarled.

'That is because he is leaving that honour to me.' The
words were spoken by the knight who came marching into

the hall, resplendent in his shining suit of plate, the tabard of the Emperor's Champion draped across his chest. At Erich von Kranzbeuhler's side was the formidable runefang Legbiter. At his other side walked the graceful figure of Princess Erna Thornig. When she lifted her eyes to stare at Kreyssig, she at first looked away. It took her a moment to gaze again at her husband, but when she did, all the fear was gone; the set of her jaw was as firm as that of the knight who stood beside her.

Kreyssig laughed. 'A whore and her lover!' he sneered. 'Truly the Imperial crown has fallen far that such a mongrel should be made Emperor's Champion! The lie of noble blood proves itself once again. Deeds make nobility, not breeding!'

'Deeds make monsters too,' Erich challenged. 'The Emperor has given me the honour of trying your crimes through combat, Hound of Boris! To me he has bestowed the right of avenging the good men you murdered. Grand Master von Schomberg, Prince Sigdan,' he glanced aside at Erna. 'Baron Thornig, your own father-in-law. All the thousands of others who have suffered by your cruelty and tyranny. Their blood calls out for justice!'

'And they choose an adulterer to wield their blade?' Kreyssig sneered. He turned his back on Erich and Erna, staring instead at Emperor Mandred. 'Am I to understand that if I kill this swine I will be granted my life and my liberty?'

'It is trial by combat,' Mandred said. 'The gods themselves will decide. Even an Emperor can't deny divine judgement.'

Again, Kreyssig laughed. 'Then I will be leaving your court, Dog of Middenheim!' he hissed. Snapping his fingers, he motioned Fuerst forwards. Timidly, his retainer handed Kreyssig the sword he carried among the Protector's other regalia. It was another of the runefangs, one of Legbiter's sister blades forged in the days of Sigmar for his twelve chieftains. The name of the sword was Beast Slayer, the sword traditionally held by the Elector of Drakwald. With the murder of the last count of that realm, the blade had been passed down to Kreyssig.

'You see, whoremonger?' Kreyssig snarled at Erich. 'We are matched, blade for blade!' He whipped Beast Slayer from its scabbard, making a grand flourish with it. The muscles in his arm, the arm that had been healed and strengthened by the witchcraft of Baroness von den Linden made the heavy blade feel as light as a feather in his hand. 'But mine is the greater skill! We've crossed blades once before. I would have killed you then but for the meddling of the skaven. This time, no vermin will preserve you.'

Erich glared back at the tyrant. Handing Legbiter's scabbard to Erna, he advanced towards the gloating Kreyssig. 'Your wife is anxious to be a widow,' he hissed as he leapt to the attack.

With contemptuous ease, Kreyssig warded away Erich's strike. He laughed as he saw the knight reel from the impact of his parry. He hadn't expected the superhuman vitality behind that swing. Kreyssig laughed again as he saw the righteous confidence drain out of Erich's eyes. Now the fool understood how things really stood. No divine judgement, no innocent blood crying out for justice. Only skill and strength, qualities that were on Kreyssig's side.

As he brought Beast Slayer up for a slashing strike at Erich's shoulder, Kreyssig reeled back, swatting his left hand at the bee that had suddenly flown before his face. The buzzing annoyance harassed him again as he blocked Erich's riposte, forcing him back.

Kreyssig drove in at his foe, slashing for the knight's head, rolling Beast Slayer around Legbiter's intercepting steel and hacking at Erich with a vengeful return for his midsection that he could answer only by retreating back and hastily bringing his blade crosswise against his own hip. Swiftly, Kreyssig brought his sword up, and then Beast Slayer came slashing down once more, this time towards the knight's leg. Again Erich was forced back. Kreyssig ducked beneath Legbiter as the runefang came flashing at his head.

Viciously, Kreyssig whipped his blade at the overextended knight's belly. With an awkward twist of his body, Erich pulled himself back, the enchanted edge of Beast Slayer raking across his armour, knifing through it as though it were made of cheese and leaving a deep gash in the steel plate. Again, he retreated before Kreyssig's assault, narrowly intercepting another strike at his head.

Kreyssig smiled. Each step he forced Erich back drove the knight closer to the bricked-up window. Once his foe's back was to the wall, the mobility that had preserved him thus far would be lost. He saw the mounting panic in Erich's face, knew that the knight also appreciated his predicament and how swiftly it would plunge him into disaster.

Erich caught the downward sweep of Kreyssig's sword, fending off Beast Slayer with a rolling twist that spun his enemy's body around. Snarling his fury, he pressed the attack, slashing at the villain's knees. Kreyssig jumped the scything sweep of Legbiter, the toes of his boots just clearing the runefang's keen edge. The savage chop he directed at the knight's skull was fended off only by Erich's sudden shift to the left, Beast Slayer's edge coming so near that the wind of its passing tousled the man's hair.

Erich lunged at Kreyssig, thrusting Legbiter at him in a long drive. His adversary blocked the runefang, but found his shoulder seized by the knight's other hand. Using the momentum of his attack, Erich threw his weight behind the clutching fingers. Kreyssig became a fulcrum, propelling Erich forwards while spinning the villain back. In an instant, their positions were reversed. Now it was the former Commander of the Kaiserjaeger who had his back to the wall.

Snarling in outrage, Kreyssig slashed at his foe. Rage replaced caution and no longer did he try to conserve his strength and wear down his enemy. Instead he threw the full might of his sorcerously strengthened arm behind the attack. Beast Slayer crashed against Legbiter once more, but this time Erich's parry was swatted aside with a humiliating ease. The knight staggered back, reeling from the power behind Kreyssig's renewed assault.

Abruptly, a sharp pain flashed up Kreyssig's sword arm. Risking a glance, taking his eyes from his enemy for the briefest instant, he gazed upon impossibility. The harassing bee had thrust itself between the links of mail at his elbow, stabbing its stinger deep into his flesh. The deliberateness and intelligence of the attack sent horror rushing through his mind. Baroness von den Linden, the witch he had murdered in Boris's apiary – in what shape might her curse be visited upon him?

Erich's renewed attack drove Kreyssig back. The superhuman strength of his arm was deserting him, boiling away as the bee's venom infected his veins. Beast Slayer became a ponderous weight in his hand. He could almost feel his arm withering inside his armour, shrivelling back into the withered limb Baroness von den Linden's magic had healed.

When the finish came, when Legbiter's edge came cleaving down into his skull, Kreyssig couldn't even raise his sword. He had been called the Hound of Boris by his enemies and like a dog he died upon the floor of the Imperial Palace.

Erich stared down at the dead despot. Leaving Legbiter

buried in Kreyssig's skull, he embraced Erna as she came rushing to him. 'Now we have each killed a monster,' he whispered to her as he held her close to him.

Behind them, on the dais, Emperor Mandred rose to his feet and brought his hands together in applause, an applause that was soon echoed by the rest of his court.

ABOUT THE AUTHOR

C L Werner's Black Library credits include the Space Marine Battles novel *The Siege of Castellax*, *Mathias Thulmann: Witch Hunter*, *Runefang*, the Brunner the Bounty Hunter trilogy, the Thanquol and Boneripper series and *Time of Legends: The Black Plague*. Currently living in the American south-west, he continues to write stories of mayhem and madness set in the worlds of Warhammer and Warhammer 40,000. He claims that he was a diseased servant of the Horned Rat long before his first story was ever published.

WARHAMMER
IRON COMPANY • GRIMBLADES • WARRIOR PRIEST
THE EMPIRE
DARIUS HINKS • NICK KYME • CHRIS WRAIGHT

An extract from Warrior Priest
by Darius Hinks

Sparks flew as weapons collided and in the brief flashes
of light, Ratboy saw Wolff fighting desperately against a
creature so big it had to stoop beneath the chapterhouse's
vaulted ceiling. The light was gone too fast for him to be
sure of the monster's shape, but he was left with a vague impression of massive, coiled muscle and long, curved horns.

Ratboy tried to draw breath, but retched instead, powerless
to call for help. As he felt around in the dark for his knife,
he heard Wolff muttering something nearby. Then, as the
priest uttered a final, fierce syllable, glittering light flooded
the chamber and the creature looming over them was revealed in all its monstrous glory. It was obviously the same
species as the bodies outside, but even more grotesquely
oversized. As holy light poured from Wolff's hammer, shim-
mering and flashing off the whitewashed walls, the creature
bellowed and swung an axe at the priest's head. The weapon
was almost as big as the priest himself, and as he leapt out of

the way it smashed into the wall, cutting into the stone with such force that the whole building shook, sending masonry tumbling from the ceiling. The priest's warhammer slipped from his grip as he landed, clattering across the flagstones and disappearing from view.

The room plunged into darkness once more.

The grunting and smashing sounds continued until Ratboy heard Wolff cry out with pain. As the monster moved back and forth, brief bursts of light crept in from the outside, and in one such flash he suddenly saw the beast lifting Wolff from the ground, about to smash him against the wall, swinging him as easily as a straw doll.

Ratboy tried desperately to rise, but he was still unable to breathe and fell to his knees again, whimpering pathetically as he crawled towards the two combatants.

There was a final, deafening *bang* and then silence filled the chapterhouse.

Order the novel or download the eBook
from *blacklibrary.com*
Also available from

and all good bookstores